CODE OF THE KING

A Deadly Search for Ancient Wisdom

The Award-Winning
BOOK 1

Of the New Supernatural Thriller Trilogy

MASTER OF THE EDGE

Jeri Castronova

Cover: Egyptian Wish Formula: Long Life, Prosperity, Good Health.

Cover design:
Rosemerrie Christie
Jeri Castronova

Additional copies of this book can be ordered directly from the publisher at Booklocker.com, or from your favorite online or neighborhood bookstore.

Acknowledgements

I am blessed with an abundance of friends who are writers as well as supporters. They all have my eternal gratitude for their encouragement and advice over the years.

Kris Neri, literary guru, whose guidance and simple questions contained many answers to serendipitous discoveries of the past and present that brought deeper understanding of the story.

Rosemerrie Christie, spiritual advisor in so many ways, for lending an ear to my manic musings, and offering suggestions of multidimensional journeys both personally and plot-wise that served to open new perceptions into unknown realms.

Elizabeth Kaites, for her enthusiastic support and inspirational tweaks.

Susan Lanning, who was the first to see a very rough draft and to my great delight took the manuscript under her wing and guided me through many dark, bumpy chapters into daylight.

Kate Robinson, for her copy editing expertise.

Marian Powell, for her astute insights into the characters.

Chris Hoy, who had the fortitude to read two drafts, and provided comments with his usual witticism and unequaled skill.

Leslie Hoy, for her endless computer knowledge.

Jerry Simmons, for his publishing expertise that served to lead me in the right direction.

And all the Suspicious Characters and Prescott Writers for their vigorous critiques.

The most beautiful thing we can experience is the mysterious.

It is the source of all true art and all science.

Albert Einstein

Prologue
Jerusalem. Friday, 9:10 PM

A blast of hot air sent him reeling. Instinctively, his eyes closed. The heat entered his nose, burning his lungs. He shielded his face with one hand. With the other he felt the back of his head where a sharp pain began. Where did that staccato whirring come from? Was it the wind, or the anger of the spirit ancestors?

He looked down into the dark cavern that hid its secrets in the mists of hoary time, feeling its web of seduction surround him.

Another searing sting on his right temple drove his head sideways. He felt oozing warmth. Blood. The whirring grew louder. Now he knew. He should not have disturbed their resting place.

The Pool of Siloam beckoned with secrets that lay at the deepest level, beneath the primitive stones. He had searched a lifetime for this moment. An epochal portent of glory that inevitably came with discovery of an ancient site.

He turned to the direction of the attack. In a flash it came at him again and hit square in the forehead. He sank to the ground.

This couldn't be happening. Not to him, the most renowned archeologist of the Herodian era. He tried to call out, but his voice failed. His hand reached out, but no one took it. Bitter bile leapt into his throat, fury spilling out of every pore.

Where were they? Enraged that his constant followers, who basked in his giant shadow over the years, had vanished, he cursed their desertion and reveled in the perverted notion they would no longer feel the warmth of his sun.

Except one. A livid pang of remorse swept over him as he saw her face one last time.

His consciousness jerked from his body. He rolled uncontrollably toward the gaping maw. Scorching heat greased his way. The long descent into the Cave of the Matriarchs was the last journey he would ever take.

Chapter 1
Santa Barbara, California. Friday, 1:15 PM

"It's like telling people not to have sex."

Dr. Sydney Grace, Professor of Egyptology, stood to one side of a large screen showing a color image of a beautiful Mayan relief. Keeping one eye on the notebook monitor perched on the center lectern, she pointed the red laser at specific details on the screen, clicking through various photos of high-quality antiquities. Dim lighting in the huge lecture hall brought the representations up close and personal, mimicking the nearby Cineplex.

Several students in the University of California class who had been surreptitiously text messaging under their desks abruptly sat up. A sure-fire method to get their attention—works every time, she mused.

"Collectors want gorgeous objects. They don't care if it's *hot*. They care even less about provenance."

She clicked on a photo with thousands of holes sunk into a large expanse of earth, the remains of rubble left by looters. The next slide showed a large limestone statue minus the head. In the next image U.S. Customs officers smiled as they opened the serene female head and posed for the cameras.

After all the global trafficking lectures of disappearing antiquities and landscapes pulverized by grave robbers, her blood still bubbled and her fury rose at the contemptible acts of desecration.

"In the Yucatan," she clicked on a typical rural village, "a teenaged boy actually approached me, lowered his back pack, and took out a small piece of stone. It didn't take an archeologist to recognize Mayan glyphs." She lowered her voice to imitate the seller. *"You want it? There's a lot more where that came from"*

A girl in the front row snickered at Sydney's imitation, and then looked around when she realized no one else laughed.

Sydney flashed back to the scariest day she had ever known. A day when a straw hat nearly cost her life.

A member of the university group sent to study an archeological site near Chichen Itza, she asked the boy where he got the stone. He pointed to a run-down shack at the edge of the village. Most of the group was busy at the site, a new area near the cenote, sacred well, where ancient objects had recently been discovered. Returning to the small hotel for her broad-rimmed hat brought her face to face with the boy. When they reached the hut, he kept walking.

"Donde, where?" she asked.

"I show you."

Wary to go further with a stranger in a strange land, she stopped, turned around. The unpaved village street lay empty except for a donkey munching hay and a dog lying nearby. Her curiosity aroused, she decided to follow him a short distance into the jungle.

"How far?" she asked.

"Close. Come. I found it myself."

There must be twenty shades of green in here. Only a few steps from the hut, a canopy of lush tropical fronds of all sizes cast speckled shadows across the well-worn path. Dense vegetation seemed to jockey for space and cast out long arms of branches onto the ground, grabbing onto anything they could entwine.

She looked behind at the path and could not see the village. Wanting to go back, yet interested in his find, she followed as he turned off the path, moving through ominous strands of unknown flora. Just when the hanging branches from the sky fell like bars in a cage, she felt the jungle surround her with an overbearing atmosphere. He stopped at several holes in the middle of a small clearing strewn with pottery shards, rubble, shovel and pails.

"Found it myself!" he said proudly. "Me, Ricardo!" He reached into a hole and pulled out an intact pot with Mayan glyphs and figures painted in black. Before she could take it from hi, they heard voices.

"Quick! Hide!" He bent down, ran through the jungle in the opposite direction from the voices with Sydney close behind. They knelt at a spot with thick undergrowth.

"Looters," he whispered.

She rose slightly. Three men, armed with assault rifles. Getting closer. "They don't know we're here," she whispered.

This is their territory—it all belongs to them."

Their voices grew louder as they rushed through the opaque forest.

"I've got to get a photo." Her camera out, flash off, she held it over her head and clicked, then again.

They heard sudden silence. Then angry voices shouting in their direction.

"Run," Ricardo whispered, as he took off.

Sydney's hunched position did not lend itself to speed. Ricardo didn't look back. She heard them running behind her.

Suddenly above, the deafening thump of rotor blades appeared from nowhere. We're goners, she thought.

Ricardo knelt, looking up.

"Is it a police chopper?" she asked.

He shook his head. "Looter chopper—to pick them up."

They watched their pursuers turn, running in the direction of the chopper. Two looters stopped, raised their rifles, and sprayed the area, rounds bouncing off a big rock beside Sydney. She dove for the ground, her heart in her throat. Then they turned, disappearing into the jungle.

She clicked on a jungle scene of three armed camouflage-garbed men and briefly told the story of her dangerous encounter with black market thieves.

"Did you get out of there alive, Dr. Grace?" asked a voice, bringing laughter to the room.

The next shot showed a young man next to a dilapidated hut smiling at his Mayan shards.

"Ricardo never found the path we took in, but somehow he found the way out of the jungle."

She clicked on more devastation. A Mayan limestone monument known as a stela was stripped of its carved front by a chain saw, leaving the rest of the mangled stone in the ground.

"It was too heavy to carry out intact. Maybe my little artifact thief chipped off a piece. No one in our group bought anything from him. I saw to that," she said vehemently. "But he'd have no problem selling what he found. Tourists snagged anything Ricardo showed them, and then made a profit off dealers in the states, who sell to museums."

The class sat in silence. "Unfortunately, the Metropolitan in New York, the British Museum, Berlin Museum, Israel Museum, and others, all deal in looted and faked artifacts."

"In the Yucatan, Belize, and Guatemala, looters are obliterating sites of the Mayan civilization. If it weren't for the two dozen sites actively excavated by archeologists, *all* the jade, gold, silver, wall carvings, and statues would be gone. *More damage has been done by looters in the past twenty-five years than the previous ten centuries.*"

Sydney looked at the rows of students in the lecture hall, which led upward into the dark unknown at the top of the stairs. At this point in her lecture, she usually paused, both to give her students time to assimilate the information, and to allow herself to calm down. This was not one of her favorite topics, but one she felt passionate about. Of the fifty students, most looked stunned into silence.

As she steadied herself on the lectern and nearby chair, she felt a tingle in her knees, climbing up her body, causing...what? The sound of the whirring fan in the laptop filled her ears until it roared into the room. She was aware of an acrid smell emanating from the interior of the computer. This was not her usual calming down technique.

A sudden inner squall began in her heart and forced its way up to the place where words are formed. Forget it, she thought. Concentrate!

The sound of the fan whirred itself back into the soft background until Sydney heard a whisper arise from the formless motion. *"Go to the lake of salt."*

In a state of shock, she looked at her students. Had they heard the voice? But her students weren't there. Nor was the screen, the computer, or the lectern. The room had vanished! She stood by herself in a lecture hall that seconds before had been filled with students at long tables in dim light watching a screen of antiquities images.

She stood in the center of a bright blue light that filled the room. Somehow the whispered words became her senses, such that her shock merged into awareness of a greater part of her being.

"Find the Code."

A sense of warmth accompanied the voice—a heady sensation that streamed through her blood like a bubbling rivulet after the first spring rain. The steady thump of her heart reverberated with the words in an inexplicable beat of familiarity. Her eyes searched the light, seeking the source of the voice.

"Who said that?" she managed to mutter.

The room slowly emerged out of the haze. Several students in the front row stared at her, then each other, their expressions as one: the prof has definitely lost it. The students looked up quietly from their laptops.

She touched the lectern with her palm maintaining her balance. A couple of students shifted uneasily in their seats. Sydney took a sip from her water bottle and looked at her notes, reviving her memory. Clearing her throat, she continued, forcing her attention back to the room.

She shifted gears in her lecture, trying to bring her mind back to reality. "The...um, as we've just seen," she clicked the remote to a photo of the desert, "many things are hidden in the sands." She turned slowly to the screen, suddenly realizing the truth in that statement.

"We now turn to ancient Egypt." She went to the board. "There were legends, old even to the Egyptians, about the god Thoth." She wrote his name, underlining the first *h*. "Silent *h*, long *o*. He would appear in person to the pharaoh during annual rituals." Her heart stopped thumping; she took a deep breath and relaxed. "The statue of the god was said to actually come alive in the temple and guide the king in all matters—military campaigns, agricultural advancements for better crops, harnessing the Nile, construction projects."

"Was the king just hearing a voice, or did the statue actually stand up and speak?" a deep voice asked from the back of the room.

She took a drink from her water bottle. "Sounds unbelievable, doesn't it? The ancient writings say the god stood up and walked with the pharaoh." She clicked on an image of the god. "No one else was in the temple at the time, so we only have the word of the king. This was one way Thoth disseminated his wisdom—first through the pharaoh, then the priests, then to the people."

"Maybe it was just a propaganda ploy of the kings," said a burly youth close to the front of the hall.

Sydney turned back to the board. "If it were, it was an excellent ploy, since this hierarchy lasted for thousands of years. Even the earliest Egyptians searched the sands looking for antiquities they believed to have miraculous powers." Still confused by the bizarre experience, she was filled with a sense of awe at the overriding sensation that still lingered.

Stick to the lesson, she told herself, as she turned back to the class. "There are other stories from the Middle Kingdom about legendary golden statues that were used by the ancient Egyptians for healing the male-female schism." She paused. What was it she needed to say?

Her eyes cleared. *They're looking at me with confused expressions.* Can I blame them? She clicked on a gold coffin from the tomb of Tutankhamun. "Coffins, not one but several, inside the outer sarcophagus. Tomb walls lined with solid gold hieroglyphs. Great quantities of gold were used over thousands of years."

Uncertain of what just happened, she knew she heard a voice inside her head—very clear—that directed her to go to a lake of salt to find a code. The class seemed unusually quiet.

"Their wealth of gold was attributed to magic given to the Shemsu by Thoth. It was said they could mysteriously transform base metals into gold. But, as sometimes happens, the power was misused. To ensure it would never again fall into the wrong hands, the priests buried the golden objects somewhere in the desert."

"Shem who, Dr. Grace?" asked the student in the front row.

Where did that come from? She had no idea what she just said, sat down in the chair by the lectern, and clicked off the laptop. Was she possessed? Sweet Malarkey! Or did a ghost come into the room? She did not believe in supernatural events or anything she could not see, examine, or explain in rational, scientific terms.

She glanced at the student in the front row. His eyes looked other-worldly and seemed to take in more than he would ever admit.

The bell sounded the end of class. She was the first one out the door.

Chapter 2

"I tell you, Jess, it was the craziest thing that ever happened to me." Sydney picked at her Caesar salad. "As if I were going to jump out of my skin."

Sydney sat at a table with a starched white tablecloth, a vase of white daisies next to the stainless salt and pepper shakers, her usual Friday lunch with Dr. Jessica Pearce, Chair of the Ancient Religions Department. Despite its popularity with students, many faculty members frequented the café for its nouvelle Asian food and proximity to the University of California-Santa Barbara campus.

"Have you been under stress? More fatigued?" Jess bit into her sushi.

Sydney looked at her friend's grey hair piled on top of her head, kept in place with a wide tortoise shell comb. Jess was approaching retirement. Not looking forward to slowing down, she enjoyed the intellectual stimulation of teaching and was still passionate about the subjects she taught. After instructing in Ivy League colleges, small private institutions and large universities, Jess chose the West Coast for its weather, casual lifestyle, and open learning environment, which suited her personality.

Sydney sipped her peach-oolong iced tea, ignoring the clatter of dishes and chatter. "No more than usual, but the weird part is, it didn't interfere with the lecture. I just kept going. In fact, I seemed *more* energized and intense about the subject matter. Has that ever happened to you?"

Jess popped a ginger quail egg into her mouth and shook her head. "Never. I have no idea what it was. You're too young to be going through menopause. And too old for puberty."

She gazed at the young woman, smiling at the blue LA Dodgers baseball cap that Sydney wore pulled down over her dark hair. "In our four years of working and socializing together, I've never seen you lose control over a situation, Syd. Come to think of it, I've never noticed a chink in your rational scientist armor, except over Carter."

Naturally Jess would disapprove of her relationship with Carter. Jess was the mother Sydney had lost so many years ago, the woman of wisdom to whom she could express personal and professional issues about which male peers had no clue. It was Jess who helped find the Mediterranean house close to campus when Sydney moved to Santa Barbara from Pennsylvania. And Jess to whom she confided during the dark days with Carter.

Sydney let the fork fall listlessly into her half-eaten salad. She picked up the glass of tea, played with the straw, and looked around the café, hoping none of her students were there. She sat the glass down, and stroked the petals of the white daisies.

"What did the voice say again?"

Sydney waited for the waitress to refill her glass and leave before she answered. "Go to the lake of salt. Find the Code."

"Lake of salt," mused Jess. "Salton Sea, down in Southern California?

"Could be, or the ocean, or the Great Salt Lake in Utah. I don't know."

"What kind of voice was it? Male or female?"

"I couldn't tell." Sydney thought for a moment, trying to remember. "Maybe male. It seemed ... kind. If a disembodied voice can be kind or anything else. This is crazy. I better not tell anyone in the psych department. They'd say I was hallucinating."

Jess reached out and touched her arm. "Well, you're okay now, so I wouldn't be too concerned about it. If it happens again, then we can start to worry. These things happen. Who can explain them?"

Sydney smiled at her, grateful to have such a loving friend and mentor. They paid the check and walked back toward campus.

"Syd, there's something I want to show you before we go on spring break. It just arrived in the department and may be something you're interested in."

They wound their way across the expansive grassy knolls of the campus through the outdoor arched corridors toward Jess's department.

Jess's corner office signified her academic tenure. The smell of old books wafted over Sydney as she shifted a pile of new research volumes from one of two padded chairs. Among the stacks was a copy of Sydney's own book on the Pyramid Texts. What she called "ground-breaking," others had labeled "controversial and shocking."

Jess unlocked a grey metal cabinet and brought out a wooden crate nearly three feet high filled with packing material and newspaper. She lifted a Styrofoam container out of the crate and set it on a table. Opening the Styrofoam, she carefully raised a small object and unwrapped it from the brown paper.

She held up a statue of a female figure about twelve inches in height, naked, with a strange headdress Sydney had never seen—two plumes straight up, and two gracefully slanted on either side. The statue's arms were bent so her hands curled around her breasts. Jess handed Sydney the statue.

"It's beautiful. Where is it from?"

"It was found in Lebanon. My friend at the Hebrew University can vouch for the authenticity of the statue. He said it was found by a Bedouin who brought it to him. Says he's going up there to look over the ground. It's a ruined spot now, but that area was once well-populated." Jess shifted manila folders off the other chair and sat down, adjusting her glasses.

"What are you going to do with it?" Sydney turned the white alabaster statue over in her hands. The back was gracefully curved and smooth to the touch. A vague recollection overcame her. She tried to bring it forward, without any luck.

"The University wants to display it in the Ancient Religions Museum on campus."

"A Bedouin?"

"I know what you're thinking, and my colleague says it's authentic."

"I believe you believe him." *A Bedouin who just might be part of the large-scale looting going on all over the Middle East.*

Jess smiled broadly. "It's definitely a goddess figurine. She who is worshipped for her life-giving body. And it's not just a fertility figure, as male archeologists would call it. She's calling attention to her breasts, the symbols of her power in every way—sexual, political, and spiritual. The means of survival for the people."

"Carter's over there now, in Jerusalem. I'll tell him next time I talk to him." Sydney's attention was drawn to the black onyx eyes. She felt her focus slipping silently away, the glassy-eyed reflection penetrating her soul as the arms inexplicably reached out. Her fingers felt a quiver in the legs of the figurine, her own legs matching the tingle. The room suddenly was shrouded in a fog. She gazed into the eyes and the black eyes stared back. As the mist cleared, she found herself standing in a cave. The rough stone walls were lit by an unseen light. The scent of damp earth, decayed roots, and the remains of numerous organisms filled her nostrils. Cool air gently stroked her skin. The splash of running water was the only sound. Until, out of a large flat stone in the middle of the cave, a voice emanated, speaking of birth and death.

The statue slipped from her hands and fell to the floor.

Chapter 3
Friday, 4:25 PM

Unnerved by the day's events, first in the classroom, then with the statue, the sight of her house brought a welcome relief as Sydney approached the front door.

The flowered red brick walk that led to the porch had an irresistible appeal that always seemed to soften the jagged edges of her days. Small compared to other residences on the block, the house suited Sydney and her two cats, who relished in the landscaped backyard with its plush grass, azalea bushes and jacaranda tree that sprouted beautiful lavender blooms every spring and left a carpet of violet on the lawn.

The phone rang as she stepped into the blue and buff tiled foyer. Nearly stumbling over Van Gogh, a bright orange tabby, she raced across the hallway into the living room, her mind still searching for a scientific explanation of the day's experiences. "I don't believe in mystical stuff," she told Jess, watching her pick up the unscathed statue, grateful it landed on the Turkish carpet. "I'm a scientist."

She reached the phone. "Hello."

"Sydney, it's Carter, we're …"

"Carter! It's great to hear your voice." It was always good to hear his voice, she thought. But why they ever decided on a long-distance relationship, she still had no clue. They never work. Or so her peers at Penn reminded her after Carter left for his teaching position at Stanford. Summer vacations and holidays became the highlights of their time together.

She threw her mauve leather attaché and black Sak purse onto the blue leather sofa and sank into the matching recliner.

"Something's happened, Syd." He paused. "Bill Jarvis was found dead at the bottom of the cave. His neck was broken and he had several gashes in his head."

"What? Oh, no, that's terrible." She felt tears well up and heard her voice crack. "What happened?"

"Looks like he lost his balance or something, we just don't know at this point."

"Bill dead, I can't believe it." She felt like she had been kicked in the solar plexus and gasped for breath.

"I know it's a shock. It's after one in the morning here and we're all exhausted, but I wanted to call you." His deep voice sounded sympathetic and calming. "Are you okay?"

She reached for the tissue box next to the phone. "No, I'm not okay." She wiped tears from her eyes. "When did it happen?"

"Not too long ago. We all came back from dinner and one of the students went down to the cave and saw him lying there. We called the police and they've started an investigation. If only someone had stayed around. But he wanted to catch up on his notes." He paused, allowing her time.

She blew her nose. "He was as agile as a billy goat on his digs."

"That he was."

The weird events of the day combined with the news of Bill's death left Sydney with the unfamiliar sensation of not trusting herself or her emotions. Van Gogh jumped up on the recliner and settled himself on her lap. Or was it Carter she did not trust?

When she did not respond, he said, "Syd, I'd like you to come over here. I need your support *and* your expertise."

"I understand the support, but you're in Israel—land of archeologists galore. Why do you need an Egyptologist?"

He hesitated, and then blurted out, "I can't say anything more over the phone."

In all the time she had known Carter, he had never sounded so urgent, or mysterious. "Can you give me a clue?"

"Just that it's right up your side of the street."

"That narrows it down to a stadium." She lowered her voice saying, "Doesn't it, Van Gogh?" She kissed his mangled ear and scratched his neck, remembering the day he showed up at her door with blood on his fur and a half-chewed ear.

"What?"

"Just talking to the cat." She picked up another tissue. "We all loved Bill." And wiped her nose. "I can't believe he's gone."

Isis jumped up on the sofa and joined Van Gogh, fitting themselves like pieces of a jigsaw puzzle onto Sydney's lap. Part-Siamese and part-domestic, Isis laid down the house rules when Van Gogh entered her domain. Over the years they had made a sort of peace, a restrained tolerance of each other.

"Spring break is just starting." Sydney took a deep breath. "I'll come."

"Great!" She heard the relief in Carter's voice. "Let me know when and I'll pick you up in Tel Aviv."

She slowly laid the receiver back, her head filling with dozens of questions. Dr. William Jarvis dead. The world-renowned archeologist, among the first to dig at the ancient ruins of Herodian, the fortress built by Herod the Great. *How do I tell Jess?*

She remembered her first meeting in Bill's office. She was a fourth year student planning to enter graduate school. Bill's reputation as a first-class Egyptologist was the main reason she requested him as her advisor. They talked long after her next semester's schedule was set, and he drove her home. She warmed to him immediately and signed up for all his classes to learn as much from him as she could.

The purring cats brought a smile to her face. She shook her head. "He's gone," she said to them. Isis' blue eyes looked up at her; then Isis got up, touched noses and licked Sydney's. "You understand, don't you?" Sydney kissed her on the head. Isis responded with a throaty murmur.

Carter and his brother, Alexander, had been in Jerusalem for several months with the University of Pennsylvania team. They had been banned from the Temple Mount and other Arab-controlled locations. She wondered how the archeologists were able to get approval to excavate *anywhere* in these terrorist days. The Israelis eventually approved a site next to the Siloam Pool near the Old City of Jerusalem.

She lifted the cats off her lap and walked to the kitchen. Bigger than she needed, it was loaded with counter space, cupboards and new stainless appliances. She was not much on cooking, but had promised herself one day she would cook a meal for Jess. *How can I tell her?* The cats trotted behind and jumped onto the counters. They watched as she opened two cans of kitty tuna and placed the bowls on the floor.

She remembered Bill's kindness, his genuine interest in her career goals. And in her. Flattered by his attention, she did not discourage his advances. The first time they made love, she realized the joys of bedding an older man. No fumbling, foul language or the shameful apologies of a quick ending. They laughed and talked and played, taking time to enjoy each other.

It was only afterwards that she felt guilty. She didn't tell him at first, but she finally admitted that he reminded her of her father, a history professor at an eastern university. Bill reluctantly agreed to end their relationship. As her dissertation advisor, he encouraged her to expand her research into a book. It took several years of intense labor, but she completed it. If not for him, she wouldn't have applied to the University of California at Santa Barbara for her first teaching position in Ancient Egyptian History. Nor would she have met Jessica.

While the cats ate at their monogrammed blue and pink bowls, she made an internet reservation with El Al for the next day's flight and arranged for the neighbors to watch the cats. Then she packed a bag and left a message on Carter's cell.

How do I tell her? They were so close, worked together for many years, what can I say? Jess had been friends with Bill since their graduate school days and during their first assistant professorships at Yale. She picked up the phone, replaced it, and picked it up again.

"Jess ..." Sydney said after Jess answered, her throat constricted.

"Syd? What's wrong?"

She sighed, unable to bring herself to break the bad news. "It's Bill. I just heard from Carter ..."

Jess said softly, "He's dead, isn't he?"

"I'm sorry, Jess."

"Oh, my God, I don't believe it. I just talked to him on the phone day before yesterday."

"Carter said he must've tripped and fell into the cave. It was late and no one else was around."

Sydney could sense Jess struggling to keep her voice steady, without much success. "He said they uncovered several interesting things," her voice cracked, "he wanted me to take a look at."

"I'm sorry, Jess, I know it's a shock." Sydney's tears rolled down her cheek. After a moment's silence, she said, "we both loved him. He told me he was glad when I decided to come out here and work with you."

"Me too, you're the daughter I never had."

Sydney teared up even more. "You're my mother now, the one I've known longer than my own."

"We'll make it through this, Syd."

She wiped away the tears. "Carter wants me to come over to Jerusalem. I'm taking the flight tomorrow morning." She was concerned about Jess after she left.

Jess stopped sniffling. "Tomorrow morning? There's nothing you can do over there." She paused. "He calls and you run."

"No, it's not like that." Sydney wondered if that's exactly why she was going.

"Or maybe you're running away from the voice and the weird experiences," she sniffled.

Am I? Sydney thought. "I don't know." And I don't care.

She wanted to get to Tel Aviv immediately to find out what was going on. The plane couldn't leave soon enough.

Chapter 4
Tel Aviv. Sunday, 3:50 PM

The masses of arriving passengers at Ben Gurion Airport moved as one through customs, baggage claim, and immigration. Sydney stumbled through the process. What a flight. She still tasted the bitterness of grief and fear, a mounting sense of unease about this trip and the man who lay dead. Why this sense of foreboding? Why this tension in her gut?

She forced herself back into the present and was cheered by the sun shining brightly through raindrops falling softly into a pool in the center of the concourse. Though security was even tighter than just after 9-11, travelers took it all in stride as they had for centuries in this, the Holy Land.

She walked toward the exit. All her attention was suddenly drawn to Carter smiling as she walked through the gate toward him. His cowboy frame moved easily in tan Columbia pants and dark blue denim shirt. Even with two days' stubble and deep circles under his eyes, he still looked hot. He took her in his arms and bent slightly to kiss her. A warm, slow kiss that filled her with promise and whispered volumes of more to come.

Carter's embrace seemed the beginning of a new chapter that spoke of twin stars in the galaxy of seasons. "You're beautiful as always. How I've missed you." His deep chestnut eyes sparkled, but his voice was strained. Sydney caught it and wondered if it was grief or something else?

Jess was wrong—she wasn't running away from anything—she was *running to* him. Melting into his arms, her eyes misted with both the loss of Bill and the familiar sense of Carter. "I can't believe Bill's gone."

"Are you holding up okay? You two were so close." Carter seemed to examine her for assurance.

She sighed and lowered the bag from her shoulder. "Now that I'm here with you, I'll be able to get through it," she lied. She knew she would get through Bill's death in time, but was there enough time in the universe to heal the pain of her's and Carter's past? She refused to even consider that at the moment and noticed the fleeting pang of fear that crossed his face.

He shifted into another gear. "The Israelis are investigating Bill's death. They don't think it was an accident," he said softly.

She stopped suddenly. "What? They think he was killed? But who … why?"

"There's something else I didn't want to tell you over the phone." He was practically whispering, and very intense. "His laptop is missing. We can't find it anywhere. It's filled with everything—his notes, artifacts uncovered, maps of the new tunnels."

"Carter, you're scaring me. This is worse than I thought. The knot in my stomach just got tighter." She slowly stepped back, keeping one of his arms around her.

"I know what you mean. It's giving all of us the jitters." He gave her a brief squeeze, and then continued guiding her forward.

The chatter of Japanese, German, Hebrew, Arabic and English combined in a cacophony that reverberated through the airport. Sydney allowed herself to be distracted by it, and the bright flowing garb of the international assembly. Some were met by loved ones, others by strangers holding placards with various names. Black-veiled women whose hems brushed the floor herded their children through the throng. Taxi drivers hawked their services and motioned to the waiting vehicles. Carter took her wheeled bag and led her to the exit. Sydney stepped through the door and inhaled the desert air. She was aware of the inner glow that rekindled whenever Carter was near. She felt a sense of safety around him, even when trudging into unknown territory, and flashed back to their Yucatan dig, where she first met Carter and his older brother, Alexander. The University of Pennsylvania had sent a team of students to study the ancient Mayan civilization under the tutelage of the esteemed Dr. Bill Jarvis. She took an immediate liking for Alexander, the more bookish of the two, and spent many hours with him pouring over translations of the Mayan hieroglyphs. She admired his proclivity and ease with which he interpreted the glyphs. He thought highly of her abilities to see similarities of the Mayan writing with Greek. She wanted to spend the season just working on translations, but Professor Jarvis had other plans.

Carter led Sydney to his rented Subaru and loaded her luggage into the trunk. He pulled out of the airport lot into traffic, bypassing the city, and headed onto the road to Jerusalem.

Sydney marveled at modern Tel Aviv. Its residents and tourists enjoyed a variety of activities along the stretches of Mediterranean beaches, visited museums, art galleries, world class restaurants, music festivals, outdoor cafes, and wandered open-air markets.

She reached into her black Travel Smith jacket with dozens of zippered pockets inside and out. After the third zip she found her dark glasses. As she took in the sights of the city, she felt Carter's gaze.

He smiled at her. "Those dancing blue eyes and athletic body never seem to change."

A twinge of remorse passed through her, a longing for something more than he was able, or willing, to give. Was he saying that for himself or for her? She needed more stability—consistency, but this was not the time.

He glanced in the rear view mirror, frowning. "Strange."

"What? What's strange?" She turned around.

"That same dark green Saab followed me here and it's still behind me."

She saw the car. "You're being tailed? Who is it? Do you know?"

"Not really. Could be Israeli intelligence. Maybe Muslim clerics."

"Why would either one be following us?" She turned to face front.

Carter sped up, weaving in and out of traffic. She turned back to see the Saab doing the same. She held onto the roof handle as her heart pounded.

"Neither wants us to get too close to anything important." His hands were tight on the wheel.

"Is the cave that important to them?" She wanted to keep talking to keep the panic out of her voice.

He moved to the right lane between two trucks. "Bill was with the Israeli archeologists who recently discovered the *real* Pool of Siloam." His words quickened each time he changed lanes. "It's southeast of the Byzantine pool, which was thought to be the Pool of Siloam since the fourth century CE. This new pool dates to the first century BC and is much bigger."

She glanced back at the truck, which blocked them from the Saab. Her voice caught in her throat. "That's an amazing discovery. I didn't know he was working with the Israelis."

Her hands braced the dash, as he braked within inches of the truck ahead.

"Sorry." He looked over his shoulder. "Bill knew everyone, so when he asked if he could dig in the unexcavated sides of the steps, they obliged." The truck sped up. "Since it's so close to Temple Mount, he had a hunch one of the tunnels might be near." His words accelerated as if they were connected to his gas pedal. "And he was right! He found a tunnel *under* the Pool of Siloam. Just a small, narrow one that leads back to the City of David. There's a lot of silt and mud, but it's definitely a tunnel. And it's close to the Cave of the Matriarchs."

Her breath escaped at the stunning discovery just as she glanced back. "Wow! Is it part of the water tunnel that leads into the Old City?"

"Looks like it could be." He rode the tail of the truck, willing it to keep the same speed. "It may be an offshoot of the tunnel leading out of the Byzantine Pool. Alex thinks it may be something else but doesn't know what. And he thinks that's what Bill was really after, something having to do with the Cave."

She knew Alex would be searching for inscriptions. "The pool water is from the Gihon Spring, isn't it?"

"Flows from the spring in the Kidron Valley. Very old spring used by the Phoenician-Canaanites. Bill was passionate about Canaanites in pre-Hebrew Palestine."

Sydney tried to recall her Bible history about the pool to keep her mind off the tail, clinging to the roof handle. "Didn't Jesus do something at the pool?"

"Cured the blind man," Carter said quickly. "He spit on the ground, mixed it up into a paste and put it on the blind man's eyes then told him to go and wash it off in the Pool of Siloam. The man came back able to see."

26

The truck slowed to exit. Carter slammed on his brakes. Her hand automatically went to the dash. "What scripture calls a miracle I call in my book the ability of an advanced initiate to manipulate nature." She watched the truck depart the highway. "The Egyptian priesthood learned these healing techniques."

He glanced in the mirror, sped up and glided into the fast lane.

Still hanging onto the roof handle, she asked, "Do you think we lost them?"

"I don't see the Saab."

She blew a huge breath of relief, loosened her grip and rubbed her white knuckles. She leaned over on Carter's shoulder. His arm went around her. Carter's presence alleviated her fear, just like their first real encounter in the Yucatan. The local Indians randomly interfered with archeologists, who they felt disturbed their ancestors' graves. Even after paying and gifting them, relations remained tense. Bill warned the students to take extra precautions.

She was unnerved by Bill's warning and thought she saw natives behind every tree, waiting to pounce on her when she turned her back. When Carter tapped her on the shoulder, she jumped a foot off the ground.

"Don't do that!" she shouted at him.

He put his hands in front of his chest, backed off a step and grinned at her. "Okay—I didn't mean anything. Just wanted to tell you the prof assigned us to work together."

Her first response was negative. "I'm working with Alexander on the translations." They worked well together, their minds clicked in unison at difficult glyphs, and she had no intention of …

He was wearing khaki cargo shorts, dark knit polo shirt and a black Greek fisherman's hat that framed the dark unruly strands stuffed under it. His easy manner and open expression spoke of an inner confidence that would propel him into all kinds of adventures. They hadn't had much contact but something told her she might like this assignment.

She heard herself say, "Okay—where do we start?" She immediately felt the eyes of natives dissolve behind the trees.

Later she spoke to Alexander about the change of plans Bill made for her. His knowing expression told her he knew it was just a matter of time until she discovered his brother.

She glanced over her shoulder. "What could be *under* the pool that would interest Bill? Besides more tunnels."

"That's what I didn't want to tell you over the phone."

"You mean it's not about Bill's laptop being stolen? There's more?"

He nodded.

"I can't take much more!"

"I know you must be tired," his voice softened, "but there is more. We were clearing the tunnel with two of the student volunteers. Bill and I hacked into a side chamber. Our foreman, Tovar, yelled and pointed. We ran to where he pointed." He paused with a teasing grin. "

"Well?"

He turned to her, took a deep breath. "The wall was filled with hieroglyphs!"

Her mind went into overdrive. "What? Hieroglyphs? In Jerusalem? Couldn't be. It must be Phoenician writing." She shook her head vehemently.

Carter was clearly enjoying himself. "I saw them! They're hieroglyphs all right, maybe even grid glyphs—up one way, down the other. They're confusing" He glanced in the rear view mirror.

"Many of the grid hieroglyphs can't be translated. Most Egyptologists can't do it, or don't believe it can be done." Her mind still reeled.

"Alex could only get so far. We're just waiting for an expert translator." He gazed at her. "Know anyone?"

"Wow! Hieroglyphs in Jerusalem." Her breath caught in her throat. The past few days had been filled with one surprise after another, one too many shocks.

Carter relaxed his hands on the wheel. "We're pretty frustrated how slow it's going. We've only got four students digging out the tunnels. More will come over next season."

She wanted to know more, felt a surge of warmth and vitality at the prospect of undiscovered hieroglyphs in this unlikely place.

A golden gleam came into view, reflected off the Dome of the Rock mosque, the most famous landmark in Jerusalem.

"The Dome looks brighter than I remember it." Sydney squinted into the sun.

"It *is* brighter. It's been re-gilded. Several years ago King Hussein of Jordan spent ten million dollars to put a new gold paint job on the Dome so the world would know of his magnanimity."

Seeing the city never got old. It was always the place where Sydney learned something new, despite her skepticism of traditional religions.

The streets of Old City and New City were filled with young and old visiting the sacred places, shopping in the outdoor bazaars, carrying bags from the markets and malls, and enjoying a sunny day.

She had been here in her student days to explore the vast Hebrew culture, Essenic Dead Sea locations, and the landscape's geological configurations at Phoenician-

Canaanite sites. She was drawn to Israel and its many potential discoveries but eventually settled on Egypt as her prime focus for graduate studies.

"We're almost there." Carter bypassed the Old City and turned onto Ha-Shiloah Road, not far from the city wall.

As they approached the site, Carter pulled into a parking space, slid down in his seat and exhaled deeply. Sydney's cool demeanor turned quickly to alarm as she watched a dark haired man dressed in brown work pants, light green short sleeved shirt and dirty white cap with a soccer emblem came running toward them, shouting.

Carter opened his door and turned to him. "Tovar, what's wrong?"

"Alexander's been kidnapped!"

Chapter 5

Sydney and Carter bounded from the car. He grabbed the foreman on both shoulders, and shouted, "When? ... How?"

"Right after you left for the airport. Levin saw him get into a van with a man pointing a gun at him." Tovar held a cigarette in one hand, an envelope in the other. "He left this."

Carter ripped it open. Sydney stepped closer to read the note, shaking in Carter's hand. *"Translate the hieroglyphs and nothing will happen to Alexander. Deliver to the Sheraton addressed to Herod. You will be contacted.* What do we do?"

Carter's eyes darted around the grounds, hoping to see his brother sitting at the folding table under the tarp, cigarette dangling from his lips as usual, both hands on the keyboard. Then he simply stared. She followed his gaze to the small covered area next to some rough stone steps which led to the pool.

Two large tents were set up as work and study areas on the corners of the U-shaped steps. Covering most of the pool was at least ten feet of debris along with two millennia's growth of trees, shrubs and weeds. Yellow police tape cordoned off the entire area, announcing a crime scene as well as an archeological site.

She took his hand. "Call the police?"

"No. I don't want them brought in until absolutely necessary. Tovar, how did it happen? Where was he working at the time?"

Tovar removed his cap and wiped his wrinkled, grimy face. "In the tent studying the notes Dr. Jarvis entered into the computer yesterday. We still can't find his laptop, but it doesn't matter, really. It's networked so it's all in the computer."

"And in the hands of whoever has the laptop. Alex said last night he thought Bill had found more hieroglyphs but didn't say where they were," Carter said. "Could be more on the wall we discovered in the cave."

Tovar took a drag on his Turkish cigarette, looked down at a large area next to the stone steps where a young man in khaki dungarees and splotchy painter's cap shoveled overgrown brush and debris into a pile. "The note was left in the tent. Levin didn't get a good look at the man. They were too far away."

Carter read the note again and shook his head. "If anything happens to Alex ..."

Sydney drew him close, holding him for several minutes until his breathing deepened. She tried to calm herself from her mounting fear, holding onto Carter for support.

He shouldered her blue backpack. "Come on," he took her hand, "I want to introduce you to someone."

He led her toward the most extraordinary anomaly she ever saw at an excavation. The first thing she noticed was his immaculate appearance, the grey fitted suit with narrow cream stripes, light blue shirt with dark blue and Naples yellow fleur-de-lis tie. Black shoes without a speck of dust on them. He was in his mid-forties, dark slicked back hair and dark mustache. And the piece-de-resistance—white cotton gloves! The broad-brimmed tan canvas hat kept the sun from his face. He was leaning over the four-foot square pit next to the steps that had been dug down several feet and held a student sifting the dirt.

"Gently there—even small bits can tell us something," said the man in the suit.

Sydney whispered to Carter, "Who is this—Hercule Poirot?"

Ignoring her, he approached the anomaly and introduced her to Dr. Roland Winkowski, the new team leader.

Carter handed him the note. As Winkowski read it, his indignation became palpable. "This is terrible! We've got to call the police."

Carter shook his head. "First Bill, now Alexander. No police, Roland. We'll handle it the way the note says."

Winkowski reread the note. "Who is this Herod? And what does he want with Alexander? Maybe there's a connection to Bill's death." He patted Carter on the shoulder. "I have a friend in intelligence, Yuval Goldman. He's very discreet."

"Okay, call him. I'll show Syd the wall."

Sydney looked around the site as they walked. Not a very large area as excavations go, it had several piles of loose rubble, pieces of rock fill, and slabs of white stone in all sizes and shapes, probably from the steps of the pool. The day was bright and sunny. She was glad she wore the breathable beige linen pants and light blue cotton blouse. She took off her knit jacket and slung it over her shoulder.

Sydney flashed back on the Yucatan dig. She and Carter had climbed to the top of the Chichen Itza pyramid and talked of everything but their studies.

One of Carter's appeals was his natural affability that allowed for easy interaction with people of all cultures, especially the women. Alexander was older but Carter was the natural leader, the outgoing one who acted first and talked later. Their anthropologist parents honeymooned in Greece and named their first son for the Macedonian conqueror. Their second son was named for the discoverer of the tomb of King Tutankhamun, Howard Carter.

A male student hoisted a basket of dirt from the four foot square hole in the ground. He dumped it onto a screen that lay atop a large tin tub. Sydney watched as another student carefully brushed and sifted the earth, hoping for any small gift that would reward her for the day's difficult work.

"I'm not sure what kind of team leader Roland will be," Carter said in a low voice. "As you can see, he doesn't like to get dirty, so all he does is watch what everyone else does. It'll keep the students on their toes. At the end of the day the students wash and label everything that's found. But without Alex at the computer documenting the day's activities, we're going to lose time and information."

Sydney turned to watch Winkowski brush off his gloves, then take out a white handkerchief to wipe his high gloss leather shoes. "Why is an archeologist, who doesn't like to get dirty, on a dig?"

"He was Bill's protégée. Bill said Roland has a nose that sniffs out artifacts. He's done it several times on this dig, finding a few coins in the muck the rest of us missed."

One of the students came up to Carter. Her blond ponytail bounced beneath the Penn baseball cap. Her jeans were caked with mud. "Carter," she said sweetly, "all we've found is more mud. Can we stop now?"

"No," he said curtly. "There may be more coins in that mess. Keep digging and sifting."

She wiped her forehead and left a smear.

Sydney stifled a smile. "I'm Sydney Grace."

"Sorry, this is Gena," Carter said distractedly. "Dr. Grace is here to translate the hieroglyphs. I'm going to talk to you all in a few minutes."

They turned and continued toward the pool. "They don't know about Alex. This is going to spook them even more. They were really shook up about Bill."

Sydney watched Gena slowly turn and walk back to her mud, not looking in the least shook up. "What was that about coins?" Best to keep him talking. "Roland found one in the mud. Dated to the late Hasmonean period, right before Herod the Great took over the throne. Bill thought that was the second phase of the pool, when it was used at the time of Jesus." The panic in his eyes lessened. "Whether it was in use at the time of King Hezekiah in 700 BC is still unknown. That's why we're sifting. If we find any Iron Age pottery or coins then we'll know we're in the right spot."

Good, thought Sydney. Supervising the dig would help keep his mind off his brother.

"Ten feet of dirt and muck covers the rest of the pool. We won't be able to finish until the new students get here in the fall. The heat will shut us down in a couple of months."

Sydney looked down at the ragged steps, the remains of a very large pool which overlooked the Kidron Valley. "How did they find it?"

"Like most discoveries, they stumbled on it. City workers were repairing a sewer pipe that runs from the valley west of the City of David over to the Kidron Valley on the east. The heavy equipment slammed into the steps. They had to stop work so the archeologists could come in. The Orthodox Church owns the surrounding land. They gave us permission to dig next to the pool, as long as we didn't chop up the steps."

She gazed out over the valley. "It must have been a lovely spot in those days."

"This pool was one of the most important to the ancient Jerusalemites. There are three sets of five steps leading down to the bottom level. The people could either stand or sit on the landings to soak. Only this end has been uncovered so far. We estimate the pool was 225 feet—bigger than the Byzantine pool."

Only three feet from the corner steps, Sydney saw the shaft which led to the tunnel. A wooden ladder leaned at an angle from the surface. Two male students labored to bring up buckets of debris from the chamber ten feet below. They greeted Carter, who introduced Sydney, and stopped to gather the empty baskets.

"This was where Bill fell." Carter said solemnly. "It was late, and the student noticed the ladder was gone. He looked around the grounds, couldn't find it. So went to get another one. When he got down there, he saw Bill's body. The ladder beside him."

Sydney gazed into the shaft, puzzled. "He's climbed longer ladders. It just doesn't make sense."

Following Carter down the ladder, she stepped off into a limestone cave approximately twenty feet square lit by halogen lamps set around the perimeter. She shivered involuntarily, her ugly claustrophobia monster opening an eye.

She recalled the day at the Yucatan site when they went into the huge pyramid at ground level to climb up inside and view the red jaguar painted on the wall by the Mayan artists. She had walked into the narrow space behind the other students. It was close and dark and musty. She stopped in her tracks. Carter, right behind, bumped into her.

"I've changed my mind. I don't want to see the red jaguar."

"It's okay, Syd, the stairs are perfectly safe," Carter said, holding her.

"Let me out! Everyone back up. Please, Carter, back up!" She was starting to panic and didn't want to lose it in front of her peers.

The three students behind Carter all moved quickly as Sydney roughly pushed him through the entrance, and she dashed for the side of the pyramid, gasping for air.

"Sydney, are you all right?"

"I'm okay now. It was too crowded in there." She wiped her forehead. They sat in the shade of the pyramid until the others came out.

She brushed the memory aside. That was then, this is now. I'm fine.

Carter stood in the center of the cavern. His voice echoed off the walls. "We can tell from the chisel marks this cave is manmade. That small opening in the back leads to a tunnel. Bill thought it connects with Hezekiah's water tunnel. It's taken several weeks to clear the cave to get this far."

Sydney ran her hands along the rough stone wall. She estimated the cave stretched upward to fifteen feet.

She took Carter's hand, wanting to comfort him and needing him close at the same time. He took her in his arms. "I'm so grateful you came," he said.

Sydney felt his need for her, how vulnerable he was with Alexander's life in the balance. She kissed him tenderly, wishing for a better time.

"I'd like nothing better than to go back to the hotel right now," his voice husky.

She caught her breath. "You and me both."

He held her tightly for several long moments.

She was aware of dripping water farther down the tunnel. The air was moist and dank, musty with centuries of oblivion, stagnant and oppressive. He bent down to get the lamp. Her anxiety rose at the thought of exploring the further reaches, much less working down here. She turned around, grateful she could still see light from the stairs to the top.

He shone the light into the fetid darkness onto the walls. "You know, up to now it was known as the 'so-called' Cave of the Matriarchs. No one knew when or why it was named, but now we do. We made a startling discovery several days ago. We found a statue of a female figure about a foot high, naked except for a feather headdress, and holding something round."

She looked at him, trying to find a connection, remembering the strange sensation when she held the figurine in Jess's office. "A statue? Before I left Santa Barbara, Jess showed me a goddess statue from Lebanon. They sound very similar. I definitely want to see yours."

"I figured you would." He smiled at her.

Another step and the light caught the writing on the wall. Hieroglyphs! They looked severely faded to a dull shade of gray from the black paint that must have been used originally. Some were smudged, showing the scribe did not, or could not, take the time to clean up his work.

She felt as out of place as the hieroglyphs were. Egyptian writings in the seat of Judea. They covered several feet in length and maybe three feet in height. She ran her hand across the characters, and the chill that ran up her spine was as cold as the writings. A greater incongruity could exist nowhere else.

They appeared to be painted in a hurry, lacking the scribes' usual precision with individual figures. The ancient scribes were as meticulous with their writing as the carvers with their sculptures, the jewelers with their exquisite lapis and gold necklaces, and the tomb engineers with their burial chambers.

"Can you read them?" Carter asked breathlessly.

"Looks like New Kingdom or before... something about Osiris... directions to another wall..." She read right to left and saw something interesting. "Carter, these seem to be clues to hunting something valuable."

"You mean like a treasure hunt?"

"Yes, but I don't see anything that says what the treasure is. I'll have to go through it all. Maybe the final translation will tell us what it is and where the other wall is located."

Something caught her eye farther down the wall at the corner. An X surrounded by a square. On a hunch she looked at the top corner. There it was again. The same X, the same square. She couldn't believe her eyes. This was getting exciting.

Carter perked up and followed her to the other end of the wall. She adjusted the beam of light, looked up at the corner, then down at the bottom corner. Another X and square on both corners.

"This is unbelievable! It was written in a hurry. By someone who was trying to communicate a secret." Her mind raced and her heart pounded with the anticipation of discovery. She knew she was on to something valuable, but what? She had to find out what the hieroglyphs said. In her zeal, she forgot about Alexander, Herod and the note. These glyphs were hot! Her passion for Egypt was definitely aroused.

Carter grasped her excitement. "What does it mean?"

The words tumbled out. "If it means what I think it does, we've found another KV5!"

Chapter 6

On the other side of the New City of Jerusalem, Herod sat at an outside table in front of the Billy Rose Art Garden Café. He nonchalantly sipped a cup of strong Turkish coffee. He was resplendent in a tailored charcoal suit with monogrammed violet shirt and tie, a diamond and ruby studded gold dragon ring on his right index finger.

He watched a young couple follow a boy of about eight as he romped with his younger sister. They came out of the Shrine of the Book Museum and strolled slowly through the gardens, apparently pondering the jigsaw puzzles called the Dead Sea Scrolls.

He recalled that the plans for the garden were presented and subsequently rejected by ultra-Orthodox Jews because of the modernity of the collection donated by the New York entrepreneur Billy Rose. Too offensive, they had said. The Prime Minister overruled them and now sculptures by Rodin, Picasso, Maillot, and the curvaceous shapes of Henry Moore were represented.

Herod remembered the first time he saw the Isaiah Scroll. The Old Testament book, the only one found fully intact, was carefully unrolled and studied. The centerpiece of the museum, it proved a magnificent display. The only book that could be read in its entirety validated its biblical counterpart and gave credence to the other Scrolls.

He appreciated it for its antiquity and the fact it survived over two millennia. He didn't care about its relevance to the Old Testament. He cared nothing for the Essenes, the Jewish sect believed to have written the Scrolls. He cared less about anything else connected to the Jewish religion, ancient or modern. Their belief in a God who deemed them 'chosen' was certain to be their downfall.

He admired it for its history. The greatest of all the prophets, Isaiah, was the adviser to King Hezekiah, and foretold the destruction of Jerusalem by the Babylonians. Isaiah also foretold the coming of a king to Israel who would claim victory over the Jewish oppressors and bring peace to the land. When a 'teacher of righteousness' appeared centuries later, the large populace of Jews and Gentiles who followed his teachings accepted him as the Messiah and forged a new religion. How ironic the Jewish priests rejected him.

King Hezekiah. The same one who built the tunnel the archeologists were excavating. The tunnel filled with hieroglyphs that shouldn't be there. He looked around the museum garden and saw children running after each other, parents sitting on benches watching them and talking, waiters smiling at tourists, hoping for a bigger tip, and tourists at tables studying books on the Scrolls. They all enjoyed a day of recreation. His day of recreation would come soon.

A smile crept across his face. He would first visit the Hinnom Valley to buy his favorite drug. How ironic! The Hinnom Valley, so close to the sacred place of David's Tomb, now a haven for drug dealers. Another instance of stupidity on the part of the Jewish authorities. Or were they aware and skimming off the top?

He rubbed his arm through the soft suit fabric and closed his eyes to enjoy the temporary cessation of his irritating skin disease. The red patches covered with white scales brought constant itching. Like his namesake two thousand years ago who also suffered from psoriasis, the high salt content of the Dead Sea brought welcomed relief.

He knew the reason Herod the Great built the fortress of Masada near the Dead Sea was not for military reasons, but to be near the soothing saline water. Even in those days people with rheumatism, arthritis and skin diseases would journey to the great lake to smear themselves with the thick, black mud that brimmed with therapeutic organic elements, then soak in the water.

He remembered his ride out to the Dead Sea, early that morning before the heat and the tourists. He didn't go to the spa entrance where the changing rooms, shops and restaurants were, but rather to an easily accessible place away from the road that had no facilities. His black Mercedes was well stocked with gallons of fresh water, bath towels, and chilled Perrier.

He had stripped off all his clothes and walked to the shore. To others she was Dead; to him she was the Love Sea. Looking around to make sure no one was near, he saw nothing from that spot, not even on the road.

Salt clumps scattered the top of the water as they broke off from bigger clumps along the shore and under the water. She beckoned him. Hearing her song in his head, he was careful to enter her slowly, letting her lead him, feeling the buoyancy lift him into her arms. Her salty water kept him on his back, his arms outstretched, and his legs floating easily. She always seduced him the same way, taking him into her saline breast, willing away his power, holding him completely under her control.

He kept his eyes shut, not wanting her to splash into them. Not wanting her to see his vulnerability, his need. Even if she did, he knew she was forgiving. She always forgave. No matter what he did or was about to do. She was the only one who truly knew him. She was true, innocent. She purified him, sucking out the toxins, soothing his scaly skin. Sanctifying him for his holy mission.

He liked being alone with her. Soon the hordes of tourists would arrive, coming from all over the world, despoiling her. She allowed him to think, to organize, to get straight in his mind exactly what to do.

He had taken his time and floated easily in the salty water. When he had the next planned steps clearly in his mind, he gently climbed out of the water, washed off the salt with jugs of fresh water, toweled his fresh skin and dressed, then poured the chilled Perrier into a champagne flute just as the tour buses clamored down the road toward the spa.

He opened his eyes now to gaze on Rodin's strange marble, a copy of *Fugit Amor,* Fleeting Love. Its transient theme punctuated his own dark cavities, stinging him through identification with the man, lying on his back, reaching out to hold the woman who was slipping away, trying to escape.

Moore's undulating sculptures reminded him of water. He gazed at the massive rounded bodies and felt himself becoming a part of them, moving from one curvaceous piece to the next, feeling their artistic essence. The dark recesses and cavities within Moore's art spoke to his deepest longings, for he felt the same holes in himself, devoid of the divine spark held within each piece.

He felt the thump of their hearts beating within the cold bronze as huge molecules dancing in the air, as breezes reach innermost buds on the lowliest ferns of the thickest forest. So he felt himself reaching the inner core of the artist through the spatial thickness of the bronze, and he became both artist and creation.

It struck an echo in the deep emptiness of his soul that longed for the grandeur of their erotic longing, their fervent stride into the desires of flesh.

He sat in a Zen-like trance, swaying gently from side to side, oblivious to anything or anyone around him. Lost in the throes of pure creation, or was he found? He let the sculptures carry him to their essence, the curving stone metamorphosed into dim water, moving sensuously. The intertwined pieces of water sculpture were, he knew, in the throes of sexual union, the artist's true intent.

He became both participant and observer, lover and loved, male and female, the sculpted bronze and the sculpted water, flowing over himself in the abandoned ecstasy of whitewater down a narrow gorge, roaring its thunder as it crashed into boulders on its way to the canyon, spilling into the pool below.

He became the formless sound in the sculpted shapes of liquid bronze.

He rose and walked slowly to his car. Now he would relish his time with the American translator.

Chapter 7

Sydney had both hands on the wall, reading the hieroglyphs right to left, mumbling as she pointed out various symbols, nodding, then shaking her head. Carter turned to see the two students watching her. He motioned them up the ladder with their loaded baskets.

Before he could ask anything about this amazing find, they heard Tovar shouting.

Carter dashed up the ladder, yelling over his shoulder, "You stay here. I'll see what it is."

She unzipped her bag, rummaging through the contents, hoping she brought everything she would need. Using her flexible steel measure with sticky backing, she measured the wall: five feet long and three feet high, adding all four sides, for a total of sixteen, probably a sacred number in Egyptian measurement, which she would check later. The Egyptians were symbolists in all things, including sacred numerology. They did nothing by chance. Everything, especially in tombs and temples, meant something, represented the many gods and goddesses interacting with the royal families, as well as historical cosmology from the ancient past.

Sydney returned to the right side of the wall, moving one of the floor lamps closer. She lifted the laptop out of her bag and sat on the floor trying to balance it on her lap and read the glyphs. It didn't work. She found a rock to boost one end of the lamp so it tilted toward the top of the wall. It wasn't perfect but it shed some light.

The laptop was something else. She sat down and crossed her legs with the computer in her lap, a modern day scribe, but from there couldn't see the figures on the top. She tried standing, which enabled her to see the writing, but could not hold the laptop and enter the figures at the same time. Her anxiety mounted to the same level as her excitement. She needed both hands on the keyboard. She glanced back at the light streaming through the entrance, reassuring herself.

She decided to wait until Carter came back and she could send him for a table. In the meantime, she would read as many of the hieroglyphs as she could remember, then sit down on the floor and enter them.

The software allowed her to read the text by transliterating the hieroglyphs into letters and signs and then translating them into English. So much faster than the old way of copying the glyphs and translating on the spot or later.

It was eerily quiet in the cave after the commotion. Where was Carter? She felt a prickle at the back of her neck. She looked around. Nothing. Just her and her personal monster. She turned back to the wall.

Suddenly a shadow appeared in front of her and moved slowly across the wall from her left. A figure projected itself onto the hieroglyphs. Was it her imagination or did the lamp move by itself? *There was someone behind her.*

Momentarily mesmerized by the shadow creeping along the wall, she watched as it loomed in the light, freezing her to the spot. She heard a noise and quickly turned around, just as the dark predator on the wall moved beside her.

She jumped up. As the laptop fell to the ground, she saw a hooded figure. A long black coat swirled behind him like a shadow that followed thunder across a darkened landscape that heralds an oncoming storm.

A hand reached out and covered her mouth. The other hand on her neck, pulled her toward him until she was tight against his body. Paralyzed with fear, she felt his strength and knew he could snap her neck in an instant. She got a whiff of something sweet, similar to a spice of the desert. He pressed his mouth to her ear.

"Give it up, Dr. Grace." A raspy voice, soft yet threatening. "If you die decoding the wall, will it be worth it?"

A chill wrapped around her as she tried to push the hand away, but couldn't budge it.

"Next time I won't be so gentle."

He threw her backward. The last thing she remembered was hitting the wall hard and tumbling to the floor.

Chapter 8

Sydney felt like she was falling into a dream. Or was it a dream? What else could it have been?

The artists carved the name of the Pharaoh, Menkheperra, into the temple wall. The official cartouche indicated the ruler over everything touched by the sun. They were meticulous as usual, and completed the rest of the text in gleaming gold paint.

She felt disoriented, unsure whether she was alive or dead, awake or asleep. She couldn't remember who she was, even her name. Or how she got to this temple. This temple? What was she doing in a temple?

She turned to the nearest artist and asked, "What is this place?"

His dark eyes held steadily to the wall. He kept to his work, carefully dipping the soft brush into a ceramic cup of liquid gold, oblivious to her question. She asked again. He turned and spoke to another artist. He didn't speak English, or Egyptian Arabic, or any language she recognized. Then she noticed their clothes. Or lack of clothes. They wore only white cotton kilts and sandals. Their heads were bald. The only adornment was the woven colored bands encircling their foreheads and trailing down their backs.

The artists stood in a large circular chamber surrounded by huge pillars painted in bright colors. She noticed an elegant man at the center of the chamber who radiated a powerful essence that seemed to be directed at each artist. His one-piece, gleaming, white linen garment covered one shoulder and was belted at the waist, ending at the knees. A single-strand gold diadem encircled his bald head, a crystal set squarely at the third eye.

He looked at her and smiled. "He can't see or hear you."

Curious, she thought, that the artist can't see or hear her, but this man can. "Who are you?"

"I am a priest of Ptah, god of artists, and the great overseer of this temple project."

"Is this Egypt?"

"No. We are in the land of our enemies. We have won all our battles and will return to our black land with much treasure. I will show you where we are." He glided toward her.

Sydney felt herself lifted out of the temple into the sky over a beautiful blue lake that glistened in the sun. Close by the lake was a vast army of men, horses, chariots, tents, wagons and piles of weapons. The earthy stench merged with the smoke of sizzling chunks of meat on the campfires, bread baking in clay ovens, and barley beer flowing into double-armed ceramic pitchers.

They floated together across the huge expanse. "Our soldiers swim in the water to revive their health. These rocky outcrops provide us fresh water and food."

Sydney realized she was looking down on a scene right out of the movies—any moment the director would yell "Action." The archers would pull their bows and the chariots roll. An entertaining movie—just like her classroom—but they had it wrong.

She felt a hand on her cheek and looked over at the priest.

"Believe it," he said, turning toward the direction from which they had come and pointing to the base of the cliff.

Sydney followed his gaze, and thought her eyes played tricks. This could not be happening! Not even in a dream! She watched as a stone block the size of a truck rose slowly off the ground. No ropes, no pulleys, no hundreds of slaves pulling it up a ramp. It floated by itself at least a thousand feet up to a level spot where two men, dressed in the same garb as the priest beside her, stood at each side of the plateau.

They seemed to be controlling the course of the stone so it floated between them, moving gently toward the back of the flat ground. Sydney followed and realized they were actually building the temple! Was this a manifestation of the legendary Egyptian magic?

A surge of warmth filled her body as the dream dissolved in front of her, the gentle priest fading from her vision. Suddenly she felt herself slipping into unconsciousness, disoriented again, and tumbling back to earth—falling forward into time.

Chapter 9

Sydney heard Carter's voice from far away. She struggled to open her eyes.

He knelt over her and gently moved her hair and wiped the side of her head with a small damp towel. "God, Syd, what happened? Did you fall?"

She tried to remember something about an artist and a cartouche. And a brilliant blue lake. And tender eyes. But like a dream, the tailings kept slipping away.

She felt the hard floor beneath her, the wall near her head. Carter was kneeling beside her. She looked up at one of the students as if seeing him for the first time. Then she saw the blood on the cloth. Her head ached.

"Someone came in and attacked me." She tried to sit up. "There was a shadow on the wall." Or did she just dream that?

Carter and the student moved her up so she could lean against the wall.

She felt woozy, touched her head, and closed her eyes. "He told me to quit working on the wall. Now I remember." She opened her eyes and looked at Carter. "He said I might die if I continue and will it be worth it. That's what I said to you in the car!"

"Let's get you to a hospital and then we'll talk about it." Carter motioned for the student to lift her.

"I'll get the sling," the other student yelled as he dashed up the ladder.

They managed to get her into the canvas and hauled her up through the shaft, as Carter climbed the ladder holding

51

onto Sydney and the sling. She imagined herself a whale being hauled from the sea, and hoped they didn't drop her.

They struggled to pull her to the top where she was set easily onto the ground, then lifted up and carried to the car. Carter held the door while the students lowered her into the passenger seat and clicked the belt. He ran around to the driver's side, slammed the door, turned the key, and quickly drove off. He swerved into the line of traffic, darting into the fast lane, and narrowly avoided hitting a car making a left turn.

Sydney bounced on the seat, trying to keep the cloth tight against her head. Even with the belt buckled, she steadied herself on the dash with her other hand. "I don't need to go to the hospital." She lowered the towel to look at it. "Almost stopped bleeding anyhow. Nothing they can do." She was pressed against the seat as he sped up.

"It's not far. I think I remember where it is," he said, turning toward Mount Scopus.

She was sore and dizzy, no reason for a hospital. After her older brother, Ryan, nearly died from an accidental overdose of insulin administered by a well-meaning nurse, she vowed never to get sick enough to be admitted to any hospital. Especially a foreign one.

Her protests fell on deaf ears. Carter motioned for her not to speak and kept saying, "You'll be all right ... we're almost there."

The Hadassah Hospital was off Derech Churchill Drive. Carter parked near an ambulance in the lot and ran to the emergency room for a wheelchair. As he wheeled Sydney inside, she saw EMS personnel hovering over a gurney, heard the beeps and rings of cardio-pulmonary equipment and computers, and glanced up at the colorful stained glass windows.

The powerful scent of antiseptic greeted them, along with a middle-aged nurse with wire-rimmed glasses on a gold chain, who rose from her desk and showed them to a private room.

The nurse took the hand that held the bloodied cloth away from Sydney's head and in an urgent voice asked the orderly to summon a doctor. They lifted her out of the wheelchair and she stepped up to the treatment table. When the young oriental doctor came in, Carter stood to one side with the nurse as she pulled the curtain and began the paperwork.

The doctor gently examined the wound. Another nurse came in. "Ow." Sydney did not like doctors poking around.

"Sorry," the doctor replied. "You're lucky." He smiled at her. "If you call a mild concussion lucky. But you won't need stitches. We'll get you cleaned up and you'll be on your way." He nodded to the nurse, who swabbed the wound, then applied a bandage.

"Be right back," Carter said, slipping through the curtain.

"You may need one of these," the nurse held a small medication cup containing a blue pill. "For pain."

"Will it make me drowsy?" Sydney asked. The nurse assured her it wouldn't. After the three medical personnel left the room, she hesitated, and then took the pill.

Carter came back into the room. "I'm sorry, Syd." He took her hand, stroking it as if to punctuate his apology. "Does it hurt?"

"Yes, and I'm sore all over." She began to wonder if she made the right decision to come to Jerusalem.

Before he could respond, the nurse came back with the paperwork, which Sydney signed, and then they helped her to the wheelchair. Sydney touched her bandaged head, glad she didn't have to walk, and looked up at the beautiful stained-glass windows as she rolled along to the exit.

"They were created by Marc Chagall," the nurse said proudly, as if they were her own, "the Russian-Jewish artist. Twelve windows for the twelve tribes of Israel, each represented by a symbol and the tribes' social role." The nurse pointed. "Several windows were damaged in the 1967 War. Chagall repaired them himself and left one bullet in that green pane as a testimony to the fighting."

Sydney could not see the hole.

Carter opened the car door and Sydney got in. As he drove out of the hospital lot, he fished a small round metal object from his pocket.

"I found this transmitter under the carpet in the car. No telling how long it's been there." He turned into traffic.

She gazed at it. "Who would put it there? And why *your* car?"

He shrugged, rolling up his blue denim sleeves as he juggled the wheel. "It doesn't make much sense."

"I don't get it. Why threaten me if they already have Alexander and they *want* me to translate the wall?"

He looked at her sympathetically, shaking his head. "One of the students fell off his ladder."

"Is he okay?"

"Yes, but I started thinking it could've been a setup."

"To draw you away, leaving me alone." She shuddered, which brought the pain back to her head.

"Did you see him? Anything at all?"

"Not much." She thought back to the horrible experience. "A hood covered his head and face. His voice was low and raspy. He lifted me up by the neck with *one hand*."

"Let's consider some hypothetical possibilities." He stopped at a red light. "What if there's someone else? Someone who *doesn't want* you to translate the wall? Someone who wanted Bill out of the way? Someone who doesn't want us digging at the pool?"

"Okay." She lowered her window for air, which also brought in the traffic noise. "You've got the orthodox Jews and the orthodox Muslims who aren't happy with people digging up their backyards. But will they kill to stop them?"

Carter shrugged. "Maybe they already have. Their whole religion could be revolutionized if we find proof of the validity of the Cave of the Matriarchs and goddess figurines in the land of the patriarchs."

She recalled the strange sensation when she held the figurine in Jess's office. Since she arrived, things had only gotten stranger. "Who *wants* the wall translated?"

"We do, and someone else who thinks there's something of value involved. A treasure? An artifact? A burial chamber? An Egyptian mummy?"

"So, Herod *wants* the wall decoded, and this attacker *doesn't?*"

"Looks that way. And we're right in the middle."

"Carter, we *have* to save Alexander. I've got to get back to the wall."

"I know. I hate to think where he might be or what's happening to him." He approached the site.

"Someone must be pretty desperate to do away with Bill, kidnap Alexander, and assault me." She thought of Alexander's wife. "Are you going to call Lydia and tell her?"

"Not yet. I don't want her to worry and there's nothing she can do in Pennsylvania anyhow."

"Let's see. What groups do we have? Al Qaida ...Palestine Authority ...Hamas ...Fatah ...Hezbollah. What possible interest could any of them have in the hieroglyphs?" He drove up to the site and parked the car. "The Palestinians are interested in *anything* the Israelis do." He ran around and opened her door. "And the Palestinians are watched closely by the Israelis when it comes to artifacts."

They walked toward the tents. Dr. Winkowski came toward them. "My dear, how are you after that ghastly attack? All right, I hope?" He took her hands in his white-gloves and looked at her bandaged head. "Come into the tent and sit down. I just made tea."

"I'm fine, Doctor" she lied, as she entered the tent and sat on a camp chair. She felt woozy, unsure of her ability to translate the glyphs.

To Sydney's surprise, the long table in the center reflected Winkowski's penchant for order. A single laptop rested at one end with a white porcelain cup set squarely on a coaster. Carter looked around. "Where is everything?"

"I tidied up. Sit! It's all out there." He pointed to the back flap.

Sydney went to the flap with Carter behind. Another table held books, magazines, laptops, shoeboxes filled with pottery pieces, stacks of canvas, twine, tape, propane lamps, picks, brushes, screens of all sizes, and remains of half-eaten sandwiches that looked as ancient as the pottery. They returned and sat at a small table.

Winkowski poured steaming tea from a flowered ceramic pot. He handed the cups to Sydney and Carter and passed a platter of baked goodies. Then poured himself one and set the pot back on the small table. Sydney helped herself and bit into a tasty fig muffin.

"I got hold of Yuval Goldman of Israeli Intelligence. He's coming over today and wants to talk to you." He sipped his tea. "He'll also be taking over the investigation of Bill's death. He says there's a Rabbi in the Jewish Quarter who might be able to help us find Alexander."

"How could a Rabbi know anything about a kidnapping?" Carter sighed, sipping his tea.

"He knows there are Muslims who don't want any digging going on anywhere near the Temple Mount. We're in the City of David, close to the Mount. They'll try to sabotage us any way they can. He's willing to talk to his contacts in the Muslim community."

"Okay, Roland, when he gets here, we'll go see the Rabbi."

They finished their tea. Sydney felt better, but her head was sore. She and Carter left the tent, walked to the pool, and climbed down the ladder.

Tovar was inspecting the cave, a cigarette dangling from his lips. "I set up some lights for you, Dr. Grace, and a table and bench." He saw her bandaged head. "Oh my God. Are you all right?"

"Yes, just a little tender all over." She looked around. The cave was well lit. Tovar had placed her laptop on the table, with lights near it.

Tovar knelt by the hieroglyphs, his brown pants worn to tan at the knees and seat. "These writings near the floor are hard to see. In fact, I think they might go *below* the floor. Look at this."

She saw a hieroglyph disappear beneath the floor. "You're right. Can you chip away some of the floor?"

"We can do that," Carter said. "I'll get one of the students. We don't want to leave you alone in here." He climbed the ladder while Tovar adjusted the wires and lamps.

She settled onto the bench and began the process of entering the writings. She must have dropped the laptop when she was attacked, but couldn't remember if she was sitting or standing.

The ancient Egyptians wrote almost exclusively for royalty, the wealthy and religious, as well as the military. Of course, scribes recorded everything. In some cases with some hieroglyphs, a specific writing could be attributed to a specific scribe.

The hieroglyphs were always associated with art. The scenes and texts were created as one, complementing each other. This was one of the problems with artifacts plundered from their sites. They were robbed of their associations with sculptures and other scenes that belonged together. They could not be understood unless seen and considered as a whole.

The ancient and modern robbers not only stole sacred and common objects, they also erased the historical context of the finds. Whenever Sydney thought of this, her blood boiled at the outrage, so she tried not to think of it.

The wall told the story of an Egyptian army led by a warrior-king who came to consolidate prior conquests and expand his territories. She considered the possible Egyptian armies that had been in the area over the centuries of dynastic dominion.

Just then Carter called down, "Syd, Yuval Goldman just arrived. He's going to take us to see the Rabbi in the Old City."

She saved the translations, popped the disk out and slipped it into her pocket. As she climbed the ladder, she paused midway to clear the dizziness, and then reached the top, deeply relieved to be out of the cave. And wondered if the weird experiences back in Santa Barbara were omens.

Chapter 10

Entering the Dung Gate into the Old City with her three companions was a walk into the past. Sydney never tired of the centuries-old streets and watching merchants haggle the way their ancestors did thousands of years ago. She inhaled the history around her. You didn't *see* the Old City. You *experienced* it. With all your senses and all your preconceptions of religion and culture. Except that she had no organized religious beliefs with which to experience the city.

There were times she felt more akin to the ancient Egyptians, who did not have a concept of *faith*. They believed in dualities, which provided balance and completion. Judeo-Christianity was never big on balance.

She, Carter, Winkowski, and Yuval Goldman of Israeli Intelligence were swallowed into the swarms of tourists, locals, pilgrims, and soldiers as they slowly made their way into the Old City. These streets were familiar with the floods of humanity from all parts of the globe visiting this most sacred of cities.

She knew religion lived every day on the streets, the churches, the synagogues, the temples, the shops, the vegetable stalls, and the park benches. Here the past came alive despite the encroaching present. The bible took on a reality of its own within the hearts and minds of each individual, regardless of religion.

Small groups of soldiers, young women and men, Uzis slung over one shoulder, laughed and talked to each other, while they kept their eyes on the most revered spot in the city—the Wailing Wall. Sydney remembered herself at their age, or younger, when she and her brother were taught about guns—how to shoot a pistol and the proper handling of a rifle—by their father.

Groups of pilgrims prepared to enter the segregated open plaza, now a permanent place of worship. The huge stone blocks were part of the retaining wall of the Temple Mount where the first and second temples were built.

She hung onto Carter, feeling the strength in his arm as they made their way through the crowded narrow streets.

Liberating the Wall during the Six-day War became a defining event in the history of the Jews. Residents went to pray, and tourists made a point to visit the spot and write their requests on little scraps of paper to jam into cracks between the stones.

The Hassidic Jews, young boys to old men wore the same black clothes and black hat contrasted by the long white fringes of their prayer shawls peeking through their coats. Their side locks of hair danced at their temples, punctuating their debates.

Crucifixes hung from the waists and necks of Catholic priests and nuns as they hurried, despite the length of their gowns, to vespers in the Christian Quarter. Sauntering slowly through the square in deep conversation, two Franciscan friars in traditional brown cassocks ignored the noise around them.

As they walked, Yuval Goldman questioned Sydney on the circumstances surrounding the attack, trying to coax out every bit of information she could remember. He took her arm in his to guide her through the throng with minimal jostling, Carter on the other side. Feeling more vulnerable in public, she was glad for the protection. Winkowski walked ahead, smiling at the sellers by their carts of souvenirs, shaking his head when they offered their wares.

Graceful Arab women in bright colors walked purposefully through the marketplace balancing baskets of produce on their heads. Laughing children wove in and out through the international bodies of awed somberness into the nearest sweet shops.

Not far from the Western Wall, among many other shops in the Jewish Quarter, they climbed the slick stone steps, walking toward a middle-aged man with a dark beard and black suit who sat in a white plastic patio chair with large cushions. Despite the bustle of tourists and residents, he calmly read a prayer book. Winkowski turned around. He watched as Yuval Goldman approached the seated man.

"Yuval, my son. Good to see you." Rabbi Benjamin Sternberg lowered his prayer book and stood to embrace Goldman. "My foster father," he said, introducing Sydney, Carter, and Winkowski.

The rabbi introduced his son, Ruben, who had just finished selling tourists a large menorah of polished brass and inlaid blue stones. The couple seemed pleased with their purchase and smiled at Sydney as they walked toward a fruit stand.

"Come in the back," the rabbi motioned. "We can talk there."

Weaving through tables laden with religious objects, ancient pottery and modern wall art, Sydney noticed the shop was larger than it appeared from the front. Colorful Arabian rugs lay on the floor and hung from the walls.

The rabbi pulled a hanging rug aside to reveal the entrance into a large storage room filled with more merchandise. As he motioned them to sit on the cushioned teak chairs before an aged silvery-grey harvested teak table, a teenager with an indecisive light brown beard brought a large tray holding two copper teapots, small ceramic cups, and a sugar bowl.

"My youngest son, Joseph, works in the family business. After his studies. He's about to enter his service in the army." Joseph smiled at the group, set the tray down, and quietly left the room.

"I heard about your brother, and the attack on you, Dr. Grace." The rabbi looked at her bandaged head. He picked up one of the pots and poured tea into the black cups. "Bad business. You have my sympathies, but I can't promise anything. No telling at this point who is responsible."

"We got a note." Carter unsnapped a pocket of his pants and pulled out the note left by the kidnapper. He unfolded it and handed it to the rabbi.

"Hieroglyphs? You found hieroglyphs?" Surprised at the contents of the note, he looked at all of them. "What else have you found?"

"You know they have the full cooperation of the Antiquities Association of Israel, Benjamin," Goldman said. "But someone doesn't want them digging at the pool. Bill Jarvis was found dead, Alexander just kidnapped, and now Sydney nearly killed. Do you have any idea who this Herod is? Can you help them?"

The rabbi looked down at the note while he considered the question. He stirred a spoonful of sugar into the brew and slowly sipped from his cup. "If you leave it in my hands, I'll do what I can. That's all I can say."

Frustrated, his guests rose to leave.

When the room was clear, Rabbi Sternberg scribbled a short note and called his son, Joseph.

"Take this to The Fox," he said. "Hurry! And get a reply!"

Chapter 11

After Sydney, Carter, and Winkowski left the shop, Yuval Goldman returned and sat down at the rabbi's table. "Do you think The Fox can help?" he asked.

The rabbi tilted his head at an angle and shrugged his shoulders. "Could be. This is a new one, these hieroglyphs. Never heard of Egyptian writing found in any part of Israel. I suppose it's possible, considering the pharaohs were up here in those days, even to the north. I'll ask again: did they find anything else? Statues, weapons, gold?"

"No, I don't think so. And frankly I hope they don't. With so many of our artifacts being looted, I'd hate to think they were part of the problem."

Pensively, the rabbi stroked his bushy black beard and leaned his cane against the table. He settled his ample yet firm frame into his cushioned chair. "You were a good friend of William Jarvis, the one found dead. How well do you know the others?"

"Not too well." He paused to consider everyone at the site. "But enough to believe Bill would not bring people over here he couldn't trust to have integrity in their work. It's hard to deal with the fact he's dead."

"How's the investigation going? Have you uncovered any evidence that he was pushed?"

Goldman shook his head. "Nothing. He was used to climbing over ruins and down into caverns. He'd done it for many years and wasn't prone to taking risks at great heights or depths. It could've been an accident but I don't see how."

"I have faith you'll solve the mystery. What about the hieroglyphs? Where were they found in relation to the tunnel?

"Not too far from the entrance to the cave. The pool itself is not far from the wall. Alexander thought the pool ran closer to the wall when the writings were painted, that there was a steady flow in those days. Of course, the weather was probably more temperate in this area." Goldman poured himself another cup of tea. "Tovar told us Bill arrived at the site early every morning to review the previous day's finds and plan the day ahead. He had the whole pool area mapped and diagrammed in his laptop. Tovar said he always had it with him."

"You mean the underground tunnel system was in his laptop? Maybe there were printouts somewhere?"

"It was shared software, so Carter has it on his computer. We've checked his tent and our officers walked the grounds but nothing was found that could tell us anything else. His quarters were also searched. He stayed with Tovar and his family many times. Tovar's wife told us nothing was out of the ordinary that morning. Bill ate breakfast with the family and then they left together. At the pool, Tovar went off to supervise the students and Bill went to his tent. The last time Tovar saw him was later in the afternoon. One of the students found Bill at the bottom of the cave after they came back from dinner. His laptop was missing."

They sat sipping tea until Joseph summoned his father to speak to a customer. Benjamin leaned on his cane and went into the shop. Goldman rose and followed him, nodding as he left. He walked into the narrow street of the Jewish Quarter, turning toward the Old City Police Department near the Jaffa Gate. He thought about his time as a young police officer and his promotion to detective several years ago.

With the help of The Fox, he was able to crack a well-organized ring of artifacts thieves, one of whom worked for the Israel Museum. Thereafter, the museum installed a high-tech security system and hired new employees to maintain the computers.

Just this year he was asked by the Chief himself to take on the new task of overseeing the entire Israeli Stolen Artifacts Program. As Intelligence Director, he would maintain the integrity of each archeological site. His staff would patrol the borders and deserts for looters of ancient objects. Since his superiors knew the looters proliferated each day in their quest for new sites and new buyers, they promised more staff, but had yet to deliver.

Goldman remembered his first contact with an ancient artifact, one he discovered himself. As a teenager he loved walking around the caves overlooking the Dead Sea in the En Gedi area.

One day he was hiking along the bottom of a canyon, watching the hawks flying overhead, the wild goats scampering across the canyon walls, and the scorpions flitting over the sandy rocks. Something sticking out of the sand caught his eye—a burnt umber curved piece of clay. He knelt down and brushed away the sand, and gasped at what he saw. Two gladiators in silhouette. Gently, he pulled at the object and brought it out of its grave. About a foot high, the pottery jar had two handles on either side. Not an ordinary jar, it was painted with a beautiful scene of gladiators in combat with an oval of delicate black swirls surrounding them.

He carefully carried it back to his foster father, Rabbi Benjamin Sternberg, who had cared for the boy since his parents were killed in a car accident. "It looks Roman,

Yuval." His father examined the jar. "You've made quite a discovery."

"Can I keep it?"

"No, my boy. It must go to the Museum to be put on display. You can tell them where you found it and how it was sticking out of the sand. That way, they can add it to the Roman exhibit."

"I'll go back to that same spot and look around. Maybe there are more pots buried, and maybe even gold!"

"You may have discovered a Roman burial site. They were out there in those days, and at Masada."

"I'll bet I could get a lot of money for it if I sold it to a tourist."

"Yes, you probably could." Goldman remembered his father gazing into his eyes and holding his hands. "But you'd be selling your own history and your own culture. This is part of our past—Rome was here in Judea and kept us enslaved. We want to keep what's ours *here* where it belongs."

Now as he walked through the Old City, Goldman remembered the words of his foster father and knew he would *never* sell his history or his people's heritage. He would do everything in his power to ensure no one else did either.

Chapter 12

Chink...Chink...Chink...Chink...

Sydney watched as Levin's sledge hammer slammed steadily into the stone floor, ever widening the hole that followed the hieroglyphs on the wall. And each blow reverberated in her head with the same intensity of a morning after the night before but without the celebration.

She had to constantly adjust the light, the chair, the laptop, and wipe sweat dripping off her forehead onto the keyboard. It didn't make the situation any better that she kept glancing back at the entrance, assuring herself she was still close to fresh air and daylight.

Trying to ignore it all, she focused on entering the glyphs into the software, clicking on each one, clicking on the color, then the translation code as she went along. Egyptian text claimed the left side of the screen, while the English translation appeared on the right.

She was on the second row, on the right working to the left. The Egyptians wrote right to left mainly, but they also wrote left to right. So the owl which represented the letter *m* faced right when the text began on the right. Specific glyphs determined which way to read the text based on which way they faced.

Luckily this was standard text. So far it chronicled an Egyptian invasion of the Syrian-Palestinian land. No cartouche naming the pharaoh appeared anywhere on the wall. That was the first thing she had done—checked for a date, a battle, the name of a king or some means of identifying the text. She had found none.

If this had been a tomb, the hieroglyphs would have been written with exquisite detail, both in paint and relief. Sacred contexts in Egyptian tombs and temples meant they were built to last forever. But the texts on this wall were not sacred, nor were they meant to last forever. They seemed to be mere lists of goods, materials, weapons, pottery, grain, beer, and slaves.

Sydney kept asking herself why they wrote all this in a conquered land rather than taking the information back to Egypt to glorify the pharaoh. Alexander was kidnapped for this? An unimportant wall of lists? And which was worse—the pounding of Levin's hammer or the pounding in her head?

As he kept hammering the sledge hammer, loosening the floor, widening the gap, Tovar came in. "Stop!" he shouted. "Look what you're doing!"

Sydney and Levin both stopped and looked at the hole. He had been thumping the floor, moving back as the hole widened, and the loosened floor of stone, grit and sand had fallen into the hole.

Tovar shined a light on the descending wall. He took a final drag from his cigarette, dropped it on the ground and stepped on it. "Dr. Grace, look at this."

She moved over to the wall, careful not to get too close to the edge. The writing continued down at least six feet to what looked like a floor. What she saw took her breath away. Deep blue, bright yellow, brilliant crimson hieroglyphs like she'd never seen before outside a textbook! Hieroglyphs so beautiful and pristine she couldn't believe her eyes.

Oblivious to the danger, her excitement drew her closer to the edge. "Oh my God! Tovar, look at it! Look at the writing! Those colors! They could have been done yesterday!"

"They must have been in this dark, airless room a very long time, Dr. Grace, to be in that condition. I've never seen anything like it."

The three of them stood gaping into the hole in awe.

Sydney started to lie on her belly to get closer.

"Don't get too close." Tovar warned. "This floor was added later. See how thin it is?" He picked up a small slab and crumbled it in his hands. "Must've been a rush job to cover the bottom wall."

He was right. After the top sand and grit were brushed away, the materials of the floor were apparent. Stone and plaster.

A stable enough surface at the time, but not one to last forever. Sydney trusted Tovar to know what he was talking about. He had been supervising excavations around the Temple Mount and the rest of Israel for twenty years. He had been at the Qumran site several years ago for the discovery of the Qumran ostracon, a slab of stone that lent validity to the Dead Sea community of Essenes who wrote the Dead Sea scrolls. Sydney relied on him to know what he was talking about.

"I can't believe this—that a wall of such beauty, such exquisite colors could be found outside Egypt! I've known of similar walls in tombs, but this is not a tomb." She raised herself, standing back from the edge. "The big question is *why here* and why under this pool? I want to get a closer look at it. This is a major find that needs to be contained in this room until I can get to the translations."

Tovar placed his hand on her arm. "Dr. Grace, this is a valuable piece, very valuable. There are people who would pay a lot of money for this wall. I know. I've seen how they cut up whole carvings and reliefs and get them out of the country without anyone knowing. It's big business now. I know you're excited about this, but there's an underground network that handles only authentic artifacts. They go to big collectors, millionaires who pay top prices and they don't have any problems finding people to do it for them."

She knew he was right. Wealthy collectors were the reasons countries with an ancient past were losing their heritage. The National Museum of Iraq was still in the process of reclaiming pieces stolen during the Iraqi War. Egypt, Peru, Iran, Afghanistan, Turkey, and others had all lost pieces of their tombs, temples, gravesites, mummies, pottery, and gold treasures to plunderers. In many cases, it was the only way the robbers could feed their families. The poor had no interest in their history. They sold what they dug up for whatever they could get. Even so, her excitement mounted.

Tovar turned to the workman, "Levin, you must not say anything to anyone, do you understand? You must keep quiet about this."

"I promise." Levin touched his heart. "Not even my family. I won't tell anyone."

Sydney realized he could promise anything, but later he might sell out his secret, and all of them. He had to be paid off.

She needed to get down there and start the translations. Then suddenly, a sense of dread crept over her like a python that sees its prey basking under the blue sky, unaware it is about to be squeezed to death.

At that moment her cell phone rang. She jumped, and flipped open the phone. It was Carter.

She didn't want to say anything over the phone but wanted him to hear her urgency.

"Carter, I've run into a snag on the wall." Her throat constricted as the python crawled closer. "Can you get down here as soon as you can?" A big find, maybe the biggest of her career. She couldn't panic now.

"OK," he said anxiously, "I'll be there in a minute."

She closed the phone and felt the snake at her feet. She knew logically there was no python near her, no reptile of any kind. That it was her fear creeping closer, waiting to squeeze the confidence out of her and constrict her thinking. Sucking out the joy of discovery and overwhelming her with fear.

Sydney studied the wall. It seemed to run at a strange angle. She noticed something else. The animal figures faced left. That meant the writing started at the bottom. She would have to go down to the floor and start there.

She felt the python of her fear and claustrophobia winding itself around her legs. She knew it would be impossible to work down there. Her heart began pounding and she felt smothered. The python wrapped itself closer, climbing up her thighs, feeding off her cold sweat. It surrounded her, crushing her lungs, stopping her breath. She gasped and felt herself totally in its grip. Tears filled her eyes. She closed them in the hope of closing out the snake.

When she began swaying, Tovar grabbed her and sat her on the chair. "Dr. Grace, are you okay? What happened?" He took a cigarette out of the pack in his shirt pocket, placed it in his mouth without lighting it.

She knew he saw nothing. No python crushing her, no outer evidence of her inner turmoil. She took a few breaths and tried to stop swaying. Why did this have to happen now? The biggest discovery of her career. And Alexander. She *had* to save him.

"Tovar," she said with a gasp, breaking into a sweat. "I know it's silly. I know it's irrational. But I can't go down there. I can't do the translations!"

Could she *will* the reptile away? It was totally wrapped around her, slowly squeezing.

"Why, Dr. Grace? You could do these top ones okay. Why can't you do the colored wall?"

Sydney gasped and leaned back in the chair, trying to catch her breath, trying to break free of the python. "Tovar, I'm terrified of enclosed spaces!"

Chapter 13

Sydney sat on a faded tan canvas-backed chair in Bill's tent surrounded by Tovar and Carter. The 'python of panic,' as she called it, slowly slunk away as soon as she started climbing the stairs out of the cave. Now able to breathe fresh air and see the sky, her head cleared and the oppressiveness of the underground disappeared. She drank the pomegranate juice Tovar handed her and ate a small round pita bread smeared with tahini and black olives.

Carter pulled up a chair and sat next to her, gently stroking her back. "I'm sorry I wasn't there with you, Syd. We'll have to figure out how to get to the colored wall without you going down to the bottom. Maybe I can enter the glyphs and you can translate later."

Sydney slowly shook her head. "No, I don't think that would work. It would take too long for one thing and another thing—you might enter the wrong phrases inadvertently. Sometimes the Egyptians wrote the glyphs in imaginary squares so they were grouped harmoniously. They were so aesthetically-minded, they didn't want any unsightly gaps in the writing. And for better spacing they would transpose the order. This makes it difficult for us because we're used to a linear alphabet."

Carter and Tovar stared at her with blank expressions. "How anyone can make sense of hieroglyphic writing I'll never know," Tovar said. "I have enough trouble with ancient Hebrew."

In her studies of the ancient glyphs, Sydney knew the scribes also abbreviated words, transposing them for some sign combinations, particularly bird glyphs which were used with tall thin signs or small squat ones. Early inscriptions were vertical, later ones were horizontal.

"Okay, I'll get the camera," Carter said. His cell phone rang. He fished it out of his pocket. "Hello." As he listened, he looked at Sydney, nodded into the phone and said, "I understand." Closing the phone, he said, "That was Herod. He swears Alexander will be released after I deliver the translation to him at the Sheraton tonight at ten." He sighed heavily. "I don't trust this guy. How do we know he'll keep his word?"

"We don't," Sydney said, taking his hand. "I've omitted the part about something valuable being hidden somewhere in Israel. Grid hieroglyphs might be on the colored wall, and will take me longer to translate."

They looked up as Winkowski entered the tent, brushing himself off. "Why would they?"

"They could be read vertically *and* horizontally, like a crossword puzzle—the double-read kind, as Carter calls them. They were only used in very ancient times to connect with the 'divine star beings' in their ceremonies. I only discovered this when I was researching my book. It's part of the Pyramid Texts, very old and very mysterious."

"Didn't you write in your book that the Pyramid Texts were found in early tombs but were thought to have been written much earlier?" Carter asked.

"You've done your homework." Sydney smiled at him. "As far back as 2345 BC, in the writings on the walls of the burial chamber of Unas, out at Saqqara, the king asked the ferryman of the gods to ferry him in the boat in which the gods are carried. There he would be reunited with his father Ra-Atum and sail with him across the sky into the realm of Orion. In their mythology the king was taken across the water, which they believed separated earth and sky. To the Egyptians the Lord of the Underworld, Osiris, was connected to Orion."

"Orion in the sky? That Orion?" Tovar asked, as he began unwrapping a tarp.

Winkowski brushed off a canvas camp chair and sat down. Sydney watched him slowly peel off his white gloves one finger at a time. Carter also watched the display that could have aroused envy in a stripper.

"In Greek mythology Orion was a giant hunter killed by the goddess Artemis. The Egyptians knew about the Orion constellation because it was on the equator east of the zodiac sign of Taurus," Sydney said, as Winkowski flexed his naked fingers, stretched the gloves back into shape and neatly tucked them into his pocket. She wondered if he rinsed them out every night.

Carter rose from his chair. "You wrote in your book that you think archeologists have misinterpreted Egyptian beliefs."

"I think there was more to the interpretations. They were not only death rites, but birth, death and resurrection rituals experienced in an initiation process, not by the dead, but by the living. They went through what we call a multi-dimensional experience—actual shamanic ceremonies connecting them to the spirit world."

He stood behind her, his hands on the corners of the chair, leaning over so his chin rested on the top of her head. As she turned, his head moved in the same direction. "You make a good case," he said through clenched teeth, then stood, "since shamans in all cultures use magic for healing the sick."

"The Pyramid Texts describe these rites. Bill Jarvis thought I was way off mainstream Egyptian thought—which

I was. He believed they were the funerary guides and spells that enabled the king to overcome hostile forces in the Underworld so he could join his father, the sun god Ra, and other 'divine beings.'"

"How does the treasure part relate to the Texts?" asked Carter.

"The top wall mentions 'divine beings' and a connection to something on the lower wall. Maybe it's a clue to this valuable object."

"A clue to the treasure? Where is it?" Winkowski asked.

"As Sherlock Holmes would say—the game's afoot, Watson!"

Chapter 14
9:45 PM

"How well do you trust your students?" Sydney asked, as she printed out the translations in time for delivery to Herod.

Carter sat next to her at the table near the upper wall. "Bill brought in the students and Roland Winkowski, and has known Tovar for years, even stayed at his home. I trust them as much as Bill did." He kissed her and rose from the chair.

She was suddenly very worried. "Be careful, Carter."

"I will. Let's hope this gets us Alexander back safely."

And let's hope this Herod is nothing like his namesake, Herod the Great, she thought, a paranoid megalomaniac who murdered his own wife and sons, as well as anyone else who stood in his way.

She watched him climb the stairs. The Sheraton was not far. He could deliver the translation and be back in no time. Unless something unexpected came up. What if Herod kidnapped Carter? No, she shook it off. She had to keep a clear head.

A feeling of dread came over her, but to her surprise, this time it wasn't the python. She was coming to terms with Bill's death, but was acutely aware of the bleakness at not knowing the status of Alexander. And what if something happened to Carter? She couldn't bear to think about that possibility, especially since she had seen something in him she hadn't seen before. What was it? He seemed different somehow. She could sense it more than define anything specific.

The experiences of the last few days left her uneasy, out of sorts. The voice in the classroom, the statue taking her to a cave with a talking stone, the dream of the wise man in white showing her the Egyptian camp. Not normal events. Not even abnormal. They were more paranormal, way out of her scope of understanding. She felt out of control, a very unfamiliar feeling.

She had always been the master of her ship. One of the main lessons she and her brother, Ryan, learned from their father after her mother died. As an adolescent, she grew to womanhood without a mother figure until Jess came along.

She wanted to immediately email Jess everything that had happened, especially Carter. But there was nothing tangible she could say. And Jess would only reply that she was projecting her own desires onto Carter. As usual. Maybe Jess was right. Was she prepared to hang around until Carter grew up?

Chapter 15

Alexander stepped from the back doors of the van as soon as they opened. He had bounced around the hard seat in the darkened rear of the vehicle for what seemed like hours, his apprehension increasing with every mile. The gunman, who forced him from the Siloam Pool site, took his cell and watch, told him nothing, and did all the talking with his weapon.

Darkness had fallen on what looked like a large compound that reminded Alexander of a Mediterranean estate. He knew they were out of Jerusalem—he could smell the sea. That meant Tel Aviv, Haifa, or somewhere else along the coast.

The gunman, who wore the common Israeli garb of short sleeve shirt and slacks, ushered him into a large room that, judging from the masses of bookshelves, computers, and papers strewn on a large table that ran the length of the space, was the library. Dim lighting cast a peculiar glow on old books, manuscripts, and luxurious furniture that had seen better days. The musty odor reminded him of his parent's library, a comforting place of calm and reflection.

Alexander knew it would do no good to ask where he was or why he was taken. The gunman merely pointed with his pistol as a means of giving directions. Carter must have returned with Sydney from the airport by now. Did they find the ransom note his captor left in the tent? Their excavations had found nothing of value at the pool site, except maybe the hieroglyphs.

When his captor left, Alexander turned to the door, tried it, and was not surprised it had been locked. He tried all the windows, and they, too, were locked. He considered breaking one to make his escape and noticed alarm stamps at the bottom of each window. So much for escape. Terror consumed him, as he sank into a corner of the lumpy couch that exuded decades of dust, and awaited his fate.

Chapter 16

Sydney sat on a mat and peered down into the hole. She lowered a light on a long cord, trying to get a fix on the length and depth of the wall.

Tovar stepped off the last rung of the ladder. "Dr. Grace," he said wearily, "we're leaving some guards tonight. They'll be patrolling the grounds."

"Okay, I'll be here for a while. Knowing there's protection will help me breathe easier."

"My wife expects me home for dinner." He brushed at his trousers, which only served to rub the dirt in even more. "Are you sure you won't come? She'd love to have you."

"No," she smiled at his attempt to spruce up. "I'll eat later, when Carter gets back."

"I'll come back to see how you're doing." He climbed the steps to the top.

Sydney gently swung the light across the brilliantly colored wall. Something stood out. Something familiar. But what?

A sedge plant and a bee. Symbols of Upper and Lower Egypt. Carefully rendered feathers in the hieroglyph of a goose, the sun god Ra by its side. She adjusted the light as she stretched out on her belly, leaning her head into the hole. The glyphs seemed to be a rhyme—some kind of verse, totally out of place in this type wall writing. She reached out and took hold of the table leg and stretched further over the gaping hole. Trying to read the first line of the verse, her excitement rose, causing her hand to slip off the leg. Before she could right herself, she tumbled into the chamber.

She hit the floor hard, kicking up dust that seemed to hang in the air. Mouth open, gasping for breath, she lay on her back fearing the worst. Was anything broken? The light swung back and forth on its cord, casting an eerie glow over the colored wall, the middle section at once flooded with light, then dark, moving shadows casting the brilliance of its design and purpose in a kaleidoscopic haze to her blurry eyes, following the course of the moving light as it guided her vision.

The cave was huge, high-domed and rugged with stalagmites as large as temple columns. Then she saw it—a cartouche in the middle of the wall. She had seen it recently, but where? The throne name, Menkheperra, of the Pharaoh, Thutmose III. This was no tomb—his tomb was in the Valley of the Kings.

She raised herself and crawled to the wall, bait held by the light, feeling herself in the throes of a peak experience only dreamed of by archeologists.

At first glance, the wall held grid hieroglyphs—written in the form of the ancient of ancients—read either from right to left or vice versa. But the writing wasn't that old. What an anomaly! It seemed to be written at the same time as the wall above, the one referred to in the middle of the upper wall.

But something else stood out. Carefully scanning the glyphs, Sydney noticed something odd—they were *not* facing *either* right or left. They were facing *both* right and left. The hieroglyphs seemed to run together in a way that made no sense. She had never seen anything like this and felt totally out of her element. She had no idea what to do, or how to proceed.

And yet, somehow it all seemed … familiar.

She had literally fallen into the biggest find of her life. Her senses became heightened with a fear that could easily overwhelm her. Sometimes her fear of panic was greater than the panic itself. Nothing seemed broken. But she was trapped. Alone. And scared to death.

She felt the cool air on her skin and a damp musty smell accumulated by eons of underground water mixed with decayed roots, bat droppings and hard limestone. There was only a distant sound—water's gentle lapping. But she realized the sound was *above*. The stream was now over her. This must be part of the ancient tunnel system Carter talked about—King Hezekiah's water system. But he wasn't the king of this code's era—the writing was seven hundred years *older.*

She looked around. The wall was part of a rough-hewn chamber that extended back into a tunnel. Shining the light in a slow circle into the darkness, the damp walls sparkled in the light. The soft dirt on the floor kicked up wisps of powdered white smoke and the ceiling seemed to recede into the far distance, giving the eerie sensation that the sky itself capped the chamber.

She wanted desperately to go farther into the tunnel, but feared the dark, the enclosed space, and the unknown. Then she suddenly felt something. The familiar tingle that enveloped her in the classroom and the feeling she was not alone. Had Tovar searched the cave?

Her reasoning told her this was the perfect situation for the python. But something else refuted that belief. She gazed at the beam of light and saw the little girl desperately trying to get out of the closet, screaming at her brother to let her out before the giant reptile swallowed her.

Hours later, spent, traumatized and nearly suffocated, she tumbled out as the door was opened by her father. The emergency rescue team rushed her to the hospital. She still remembered the concerned faces when she opened her eyes.

Even her brother, who had forgotten about her and gone off to play.

The adult knew logically the fear was unfounded, but to her dismay, it would appear at inopportune times and overwhelm her analytical mind with panic. Over the years she tried to explain it away, rationalize that it didn't really exist. It never worked.

Until now. The vibrating in her body seemed to protect her from the fear. She became even more perplexed because she could not explain it, and she had an overriding need to understand everything.

The unseen, unknown beckoned. She moved slowly into the tunnel, following the dim beam of her flashlight. Suddenly she was in a cave, the womb of the tunnel, a living breathing part of the iconic mass that could devour her utterly and leave her powerless to find her way back

For the first time in her life she was at one with something alive, a part of herself she had sensed many times but felt too inadequate to fully experience, like a child who rings the front doorbell of a haunted house, and then runs before the door is opened.

What was happening? The analytical scientist wanted a logical explanation. But the last few days had been unexplainable. She felt like a blank canvas that was suddenly being painted by a master artist.

The past had fled, her reason for coming to Jerusalem forgotten. Nothing mattered but her mergence with the cave, the necessity to understand it, to know the secret of the earth itself, the reason for its being a stream, a cave, a tunnel. There was inexplicably no python, no panic.

Suddenly, as if she stood in a beam of pure light, she knew the history of the tunnel, how it had formed with limestone that absorbed rainfall into solid rock, which created small holes over the centuries, like Swiss cheese, that stored water in its pores.

Out of the light she saw an image on the rough cave wall. A blue river flowed across the land beside which early people settled. Flashes of new generations appeared, each building more permanent structures as populations increased.

The images quickly moved as Sydney felt how they worshipped *her*. She was the object of their adoration, revered by the people because she was the creator, the one who birthed through her waters and brought forth life through her essence. She felt the love flow through her into the water and into the people as they created great civilizations. Their statues showed women plump with life, some in the throes of birthing.

She was the Mother Goddess, the one to whom they came for wisdom, guidance, healthy babies, protection from enemies, and water for their crops. She brought them abundance for thousands of years. Her tunnel extended for miles, the birth canal that carried the water across the plains from the North to the South, East to West, even to the great sea.

She saw the battles and wars of the invaders who came to conquer this land of plenty. Some died, some left, and many stayed. The last were the Hebrews who brought their authoritative god that urged them to conquer nature rather than live in balance with it. She knew her time had come and that she must stay underground, keeping her secrets, her wisdom hidden. These new invaders disrespected the land, destroyed so much of it that it never replenished itself, and relegated her sacred feminine rituals to the realm of mythology.

She was grateful even for that, for in mythology lay the truth of the earth, the symbolic relationship of humans and spirit. She knew there would be a time in the future when her stories would re-emerge and be told again, the stories behind the mythology that lived in the recesses of the human heart and could only be rediscovered if the human heart opened to the new vision.

The light shone on a large flat stone in the center of the cave. When Sydney sat down on it, warmth flooded her entire being. It seemed to cushion her, and warmly molded itself to her. The stone radiated its essence and she felt it speak directly to her. It was somehow communicating, reinforcing what she had just experienced, strengthening her belief that this was real, not imagination.

This felt familiar, like a dream. And she had lived it in her awake life—when she stood in Jessica's office and held the alabaster statue that looked up at her and stretched out its arms. When she saw the cave and talked to the stone. It seemed so long ago, but it was only yesterday.

The stone communicated an amazing story. In the beginning the god, Thoth, taught humans how to build great cities with temples and pyramids. These huge monuments were built all over the world with tools the god gave them.

Thoth left the memory of the planet within the consciousness of three life forms: animal, vegetable, and mineral. He chose the whale, the tree, and the stone. These three, and their descendents, would maintain the earth record within them for all time. The human guardians became the Followers of Horus—the Shemsu Hor.

She heard the now-familiar voice—the one in the classroom—echoing off the cavern walls. "This is the heart center of the Cave of the Matriarchs. It has held the vision of the cave from the beginning to the end of time. It will always be here, beating as a heart, pumping the lifeforce from itself into the furthest reaches of the tunnels, circulated by the stream. Your beating heart is now merged into the heart of the Earth Goddess."

She sat stunned into silence. The voice was so distinct, speaking directly to her as it had in the classroom. The light still moved slowly, casting weird shadows that seemed to bounce off the voice.

"Who are you?" She managed to murmur, wanting to assure herself she was not imagining the voice more than she really wanted to know who it was.

"I am Thoth."

She looked around, expecting to see him, who the Greeks called Hermes, but saw nothing. Nor could she summon her voice.

What do you say to a god?

Sydney had heard of such things, and thought them shamanic rituals, magical multi-dimensional happenings, not real. Now she knew what the ancients experienced in their ceremonies of birth, death, and rebirth. The oral traditions of the old knowledge, the gnosis, bringing balance between human and spirit, male and female, light and dark. Not simply a thought process. Rather an experience within the very soul of each participant, who then *knew* connection with the essence of life. Becoming one with something greater than oneself, one became a god. Or goddess.

She sat quietly on the heartstone and clicked off the light that plunged her into absolute darkness. She knew this was what death felt like. The end of the cycle when nothing material mattered anymore, when the best thing to do was step off the precipice and let the angels take you. The two heartbeats became one. She felt her heart would always beat in rhythm with the heart of the stone.

She sat in the tunnel, drenched in tears, and knew she had just been born.

Chapter 17

How could this be? She was a scientist who did not believe in such things. She was an academician, a researcher of statistical methods who did not believe in anything that could not be tested, measured and analyzed with theoretical approaches and experimental processes.

These things happened to crackpots, people who believed in UFOs and fairies, ghosts and crop circles.

But it was so real. She clicked on the light. How could she explain it logically, make sense of it? She felt the tears on her face. They were real. The voice of Thoth, the stone beneath her. They, too, were real. Or were they? Yes, she decided, her ears heard him and the stone definitely molded itself around her. And the most overpowering thing was the sense of oneness with the god and the Earth Mother. She wondered why this revelation was given to her.

She knew in her bones that it had really happened. She heard the words and the words were meant for her. The question was *why?* Since the day she got the phone call from Carter, and before, these strange things happened with no logical explanation.

"Hurry up. We don't have much time."

"Get the ladder down. Bring the chisels and sledge hammer."

Sydney heard voices, switched off the light, and crept to the mouth of the chamber. She heard the sound of chain saws revving up and the pounding of sledge hammer on chisel. She turned toward the loud noises. What's that? She thought.

Peering out from behind the tunnel into the chamber which housed the colored wall, she couldn't believe her eyes. A stocky man in his forties in rumpled khakis and plaid shirt squinted in the bright lights pointed at the wall. He adjusted his Greek fisherman's hat so the bill rested on his goggles. When he pulled up the painter's mask, Sydney saw his frazzled salt and pepper mustache. Slung from his shoulders was a leather tool case. He laid a flat tape measure on the wall and began marking off sections with a red grease pencil.

A rope ladder was lowered into the chamber. A young dark-haired man threw down grey blankets, yellow nylon rope, duct tape, and assorted metal clamps.

Two muscular white-clad figures wore goggles and painter's masks to protect from the flying shards of slashed stone. Cutting carefully, one figure held a chain saw that sliced into the wall, spewing fine powder that covered their hair and clothes, settling onto the uncut glyphs, turning them into faded shadows of their true colors.

After the saw cut through the wall, the other figure jammed a crowbar into the top of the colored wall, and with great force, pulled the hieroglyphs away from the wall, each section a three-foot square, four-inch thick slab of ancient history.

Looters! Sydney thought. They're stealing the wall!

In a frenzied moment of outrage that overcame her natural caution, she unleashed her fury at the three men. "What the Hell are you doing? You're destroying a precious piece of Egyptian history that's over three thousand years old!"

All three turned around as one. "Dmitri!" The chain saw thief shouted.

The stocky man who was marking the sections stepped toward Sydney. "Relax, Dr. Grace," he said calmly. "We're not harming the wall."

"How do you know my name?"

"Get back to work," he growled to the two workers.

"Guards! Guards! Where are you?" she shouted.

"They can't hear you." His tone was threatening.

"You killed them?"

"No, I didn't kill them. But I might kill you. Give me your cell." He snarled as he pulled out a pistol.

She pulled out her phone and handed it to him, but said quietly, "They're destroying valuable hieroglyphs."

He took her arm and led her up the rope ladder into the hole through which she fell. "The wall will be put back together as it was. The colors cleaned to their original brilliant shades." His voice sounded gruff but he took pains to help the young man raise the first section of the colored wall, and showed him how to wrap it securely in the blankets.

The panel was numbered, tied with nylon rope and hoisted out of its thirty-five-hundred-year-old bed. It was heaved again from the second level to the surface. He motioned her up the stairs into the moonless night.

Sydney looked around for the guards. The site was deserted except for the thieves below and two above. Her mind raced. What could she do? If only Carter were there. If she only had a weapon. The leader watched her closely, seeming to read her mind, ready to grab her if she bolted. They both knew she was alone. Not good odds against six buff thieves.

The panel was lifted onto a cart by another white-clad figure that rolled it to the ramp of a truck. Once into the truck, it was lifted to a waiting wooden crate with its side open. The crate was filled with Styrofoam, the panel padded again with blankets, the wooden side hammered to the crate, and the panel number marked on the side.

The sound of the chain saw cutting through the wall, the chisel hammering into the back to actually peel the panels away continued. They hoisted the panels and loaded them into the crates. How could they strip the wall so fast? How many times have they done this, she thought? They looked like experts. And very organized.

The leader walked her toward the truck. She saw the wooden crates that held the panels and was grateful they at least took precautions to pack carefully.

The leader told the white clad figure to watch her while he went back down. "Hurry up," he shouted at the men down in the hole. "We're leaving in five minutes!"

The driver led her to the metal ramp, handcuffing one of her hands. She resisted getting into the back of the truck. He forcefully pulled her to the wooden crates and shifted one until she saw a vertical metal grip on the inside of the truck. He clamped the cuff on the grip.

"No!" she shouted. "You can't leave me in here! There's no air! I can't …"

He slapped her across the face, as she staggered back against the side of the truck and fell to the floor.

"You're lucky we don't kill you," he growled. His face was worn and wrinkled, with stubble of beard that would have brought blood if it had touched her. A cigarette hung from his lips and the ashes scattered on her legs as she fell. He turned, jumped off the ramp, and pressed the lever next to the tail light, which lowered the ramp.

She had to do something! Thinking fast, she pulled off an earring and tossed it out, hoping the driver didn't see it, and desperately hoping Carter would.

He slammed the heavy doors. Sydney heard the bolt slide into place holding them securely.

Grey gloom surrounded her. The truck started to move. She lay where she fell as the truck bumped out of the area. Her right arm hung above her, at the lowest end of the grip. She reached for the cuff with her left hand, tugged and pulled, but that only served to tighten it. Furious, she kicked the wooden crate.

Across the street sat a car. In an advanced state of stupefaction, the driver watched this blatant display of illegal activity, unable to comprehend what he just saw with his own eyes or the speed at which it happened. He quickly pressed his dial.

The Fox would not be pleased with this new development.

Chapter 18

Still handcuffed in the blackened rear of the truck as it bumped along the rutted road, Sydney wondered if Carter had delivered the envelope, whether he was on his way back to the pool. Would he be able to find her, or would she ever see him again?

Was she part of the thieves' original plan, which seemed to be well organized and executed? The leader had known her name. As they drove, she tried to keep track of city sounds and distances, but she had no idea of mileage in an unfamiliar city. Her arm was bent at the elbow, which helped the circulation, but they'd left her in such an awkward position, her arm kept bumping against the side of the truck.

She took a deep breath, stood up, and shifted her hand at the grip. She stepped closer to the back doors trying to peer through the small slit between them. In the darkness outside, she saw headlights behind the truck. She continued deep breathing, and tried to focus on the cave, and the words of Thoth. It didn't help. The monotonous hum of the tires amplified her anxiety.

She reached into her pocket and pulled out a small medal—St. Jude, the patron saint of hopeless causes. When her father gave it to her many years ago, he said it didn't matter if she was not religious. But it would remind her of him, and whenever she got in a tough spot, she'd remember nothing is hopeless, only difficult. The medal returned to its pocket.

She felt around the floor and found a packing blanket. She pulled, but it was caught under a crate. Yanking hard, the crate shifted slightly, freeing the blanket. She adjusted it under her and on the side of the truck to lean against, easing her discomfort.

What had the stone said? She couldn't quite remember. Something about Thoth teaching humans how to build huge monuments all over the world. And guardians who became the Shemsu Hor. *She smiled at herself. Here I am, a prominent university professor, handcuffed, locked up in a truck, and talking to a stone!*

Her eyes fluttered shut as the truck rolled repetitiously along. Looters. She was being kidnapped by looters. Her head tilted back against the blanket...

Back in the classroom, she was giving her favorite lecture on stolen antiquities.

"This is part of the Lydian Hoard from around 600 BC in the area of west central Anatolia in Turkey. They were buried in a royal tomb during the reign of King Croesus of Lydia."

She clicked on more photographs of found objects including carved marble sphinxes and fragments of tomb paintings that had been ripped off the walls. "These objects were buried for 2600 years. They were found in 1966 by grave robbers. Any guesses where they wound up?"

"A museum?" Two voices proclaimed loudly from opposite ends of the classroom.

"Correct!" Sydney acknowledged both students. "Within three years, the biggest rogue museum, The Metropolitan in New York, had acquired *every object* from that tomb, all 360 pieces. Most archeologists and museum curators knew they were looted artifacts, and even the *Director* of the museum stated he believed 'the stuff was illegally dug up.' He bought the stuff anyway.

"The Turks in the meantime arrested the thieves, who all gave statements and were subsequently convicted." She clicked on the remains of some of the tomb walls. "The Met didn't display the artifacts right away, probably too racked with guilt. They were packed away to the basement and not displayed until 1984. And labeled as *'East Greek Treasures'!* Even though it was obvious they weren't Greek but Anatolian.

"The Turks knew where they were from and wanted their treasures back. They brought a civil suit against the museum, who stated the statute of limitations ran out while the artifacts were in storage for nearly twenty years. So the lawyers came up with a brilliant idea. *They brought in the looters themselves!* They gave eyewitness accounts how they used explosives to gain entrance to the tomb and handed the objects up to those on the surface. They actually recognized some of these same objects displayed in the Met's glossy catalog.

"The museum's acquisition policy was turned back upon itself by Turkey's American lawyers. Too bad the museum curators weren't convicted along with the looters," Sydney said sardonically.

"This story does have a happy ending. The Metropolitan Museum returned the artifacts in 1993 in an out-of-court settlement. The pieces now reside in the Museum of Anatolian Civilizations in Ankara."

"So if the Turks hadn't pursued their treasure for those six years, they never would have gotten their stuff back?" A student looked up from her monitor.

"That's right," Sydney clicked on another photograph of the treasure. "They considered the two million dollars in legal fees money well spent. They sent a big message to the worldwide illegal artifacts racket. But in this case it took the looters themselves to win their case."

The truck lurched and threw her sideways against the panel. She had no idea where they were taking her.

Chapter 19

Approaching the pool site, Carter saw it lit up by floodlights, the cool dampness around the lamps casting hazy haloes through four millennia.

Tovar saw Carter as he bounded up the steps. "She's gone! I can't find her anywhere," he shouted. "And so's the wall! It's gone too!"

Carter grabbed him by the shoulders. "Sydney's gone? Are you sure?"

"I've looked all over—the cave, the tunnels, around the grounds, even down at the colored wall. She said she was going to start on it," he said breathlessly, shaking his head. "She's nowhere! And the wall! You've got to come and see this."

They ran to the steps and started down. Carter saw that someone had gotten a ladder to the bottom of the colored wall. They climbed down.

"They stole it! They stole the wall!" Tovar touched the rough naked wall. "Look. Here are some leavings. Done by a chain saw. I know it was. Seen ravaged walls before, just like this. It's all my fault. I shouldn't have left her." He hung his head, long dark hair falling in his face.

"How could they do it so fast?" Carter paced the chamber anxiously, trying to find something that would tell them where Sydney had gone. At the Sheraton, he had delivered the envelope addressed to Herod and was told to wait, which he did. For two hours. Now he knew why. Sydney was left alone, easy prey for the thieves.

"They're swift, Carter. If they're the same ones who stole the wall painting in one of Herod the Great's palaces in the Old City, they know what they want and are very meticulous. They don't destroy anything unnecessarily. Like here, they took the colored wall, but left the one upstairs alone. This was the most valuable one."

"If Sydney was down here, then they took her too," Carter said slowly, reality sinking in. "Let's look around, see if we can find something, anything that she may have left to give us a clue." He walked into the tunnel, flashing the light on the ground.

"I looked around the ground topside." Tovar pulled something out of his pocket. "I found this." He handed it to Carter.

It was an earring, gold filigree on three prongs with dark blue and aqua glass beads. "I gave her this." Carter looked closely at it, holding it up by the pierced end. "When we graduated. She liked these Middle Eastern beaded ones. Said they looked Egyptian." He remembered their last romantic dinner when he gave her the earrings, just before he left for his new position in the Department of Archeology at Stanford University in Palo Alto, California. He asked her to come with him, they could get married, and she could apply to teach.

She told him she wanted to say yes, but she needed to stay at the University of Pennsylvania to complete her book, which was based on her dissertation. Proud of her ground-breaking research, he encouraged her efforts and agreed they should wait for marriage. But waiting was difficult for him. It always had been. His mother tried to instill patience in her younger son who never seemed to understand why he could not be instantly gratified. Her eldest carried the hopes of his father in hard work and dedication when he followed the family profession into anthropology.

Carter found himself forced into a situation of waiting for Sydney to finish her book, move to Santa Barbara and begin an academic career. He began resenting the delay, expressing it in withdrawal from her, and started an affair with one of his students. When Sydney found out, she broke off their relationship and refused to speak to him. After several more flings with students, he decided Sydney meant more to him than any of the students. When he asked her to take him back, she refused, saying he had betrayed her and why should she ever trust him again?

When they finally got together last Christmas, he felt they made a good start, even if she refused his advances for intimacy. That definitely challenged his patience, but it made him realize how much he loved her.

Carter held the earring tenderly. He heard Tovar from far away.

"I nearly stepped on it." Tovar headed for the ladder. "If I hadn't got the light right on it, I would have missed it."

They climbed to the upper wall and checked the area. Tovar pointed to the floor. "This must've been the spot they stacked the panels. See the deep indentations? Then they hoisted them to the surface. They needed a truck to carry the load. It would leave tire tracks." He dashed to the surface.

Carter came up the steps. "Herod got the translation. If he's true to his word, we should hear from Alexander soon." *I hope.* "I'm calling Yuval Goldman." He pulled out his phone.

Tovar pointed at the markings. "Tire tracks *and* shoe prints! They must've been in a real hurry not to brush them away."

"Alexander *and* Sydney kidnapped." Carter pressed his speed dial. "They could both be killed!"

Chapter 20

Sydney shifted positions on the cold, hard floor while she tried to get the circulation back into her arm and labored to creak one eye open. The truck stopped. She heard one of the cab doors slam, then the other. The bolt slid out of its slot. The heavy doors creaked open. She stood next to the crates, blinking in the floodlights. The driver lowered the ramp and jumped into the truck. He unlocked the cuff and she rubbed her reddened wrist. He helped her onto the ramp.

Dmitri walked over to a waiting man garbed in a long black silk robe with embroidered golden dragons on each side. "We got it all, *including* the translator." He said to the robed man, who nodded.

Sydney looked out at a long arcaded Italianate villa with a portico extending to each end of the building. The curved drive at which the truck sat was lit up by floodlights and well landscaped. The cold night had turned to dawn.

The robed man bowed ceremoniously. "Welcome to my humble abode, Dr. Grace." He was tall, with dark eyes, wavy steel grey hair, grey mustache, and olive skin. His voice matched his hair, smooth and cultivated, with nothing out of place. He took her hand in both of his. "I'm so sorry to have inconvenienced you and subjected you to this long ride. But it was unavoidable."

"You stole a priceless piece of Egyptian history," she said with a scowl, stepping unsteadily off the slope. "This wall should be in a museum."

"And so it shall." He helped her off the ramp, and kissed her hand. "One of the *best* museums in the world." He put his arm around her waist and led her toward the massive carved front doors. She tried to turn away from him, but could not dislodge his arm. The walkway was made of cut stones worn smooth by what must have been many years of high volume foot traffic. They entered through the ten-foot oak doors, replicas Sydney thought, of the Baptistery doors in Florence.

The reception hall had the same stone floor with twin gold-flecked black marble pillars on each side of the entranceway. A century-old chandelier blazed from the center of the ceiling.

She looked up at the chandelier. "Where is this place?"

"Ah, please excuse my lapse in etiquette." He turned back to the front door with a sweeping gesture. "This is Haifa, an ancient Crusader-run fortress town that has changed hands countless times through the centuries. And we are on Mount Carmel." He smiled and turned to lead her into the estate.

A medieval wooden pew stood against one wall. Two marble busts of Roman generals sat on a long mahogany table on the other wall. Sydney recognized one as Pompey the Great.

On the other side of the reception hall was a large room filled with centuries of antiques. He led her into the room and motioned her toward a sea green embroidered silk Louis XIV settee. As she sat down, Sydney felt like she was in an eighteenth century Byzantine palace. A fire crackled in the arched walk-in royal blue and gold mosaic fireplace, flanked by a pair of Empire torcheres. A large round table in the middle of the room held an etched silver vase out of which spilled orchids and foliage of all shapes and colors.

"I am a collector," he said, lifting a decanter off a silver tray on the antique French bar. Pouring a yellow-green clear liquid into cut-crystal, he offered her the glass.

She eyed it suspiciously.

"It's Akko-tea, Haifa's best," the robed man said. "Oh, I forgot something." He took back the glass.

She watched him closely.

He walked back to the bar, set the glass down, and reached for a large crystal bowl that held several dark green leafy sprigs. He cut off two leafs, placed one in his glass and one in hers, then returned to her with the drink.

She took the glass, held it to her nose to sniff it, realized the leaf was mint, and then set it onto a side table of inlaid wood carved in the shape of a bull. She looked at the bull and quickly raised the glass. It was an exquisite piece of furniture, something she instinctively knew was very old and very expensive. She felt extreme contempt for this man, but could not damage such a piece of art, even though she had serious misgivings about its acquisition. There was nothing to set the glass on. She held it carefully in her hand.

"Why am I here?" she asked. "You won't be able to get a ransom from anyone at the dig. They have very little money, and it all goes into the site."

He laughed with a high squeaky chirping sound that ended in a guttural cough. "Ransom? Does it look like I need money? Could I even *get* anything for you?" He finished his Akko tea and sat opposite her on a Chippendale sofa of ivory damask weave that looked like it just came off the jacquard loom.

She eyed the sculpture on a green marble pedestal.

"Nineteenth century Italian Carrara marble. Apollo and Daphne." He moved close to her and took her free hand in his. "Beautiful, isn't it? Many of the furnishings are Louis XV and XVI. The tapestry is seventeenth century Flemish."

Dmitri appeared in the doorway, coughing to announce his presence. "We're ready to unload."

"Thank you, Dmitri, I'll be right there." He squeezed her hand, leaned in to kiss her and Sydney turned her head. He frowned at her, and then smiled. "Excuse me, Dr. Grace, I won't be long."

Alone in the room, she took a sip of the tea. It had a pleasant taste, not too sweet, not too bitter. With the hint of mint it was quite refreshing, and she needed a quick fix. She rose to look at a painting that caught her attention. It couldn't be, she thought! It must be a copy. She had liked it since childhood and knew the original hung in the Hermitage Museum in St. Petersburg.

Called 'Portrait of Saskia Dressed as Flora,' it showed Rembrandt's wife, his favorite model besides himself, as the Roman goddess of flowers. This painting showed her with a variety of flowers on her head and draped in a soft textured fabric. The artist liked dressing her in all kinds of shimmering silks and brocades to display her as many characters. His mastery of texture, light and color was evident in this masterpiece. Sydney could swear it was the original but how could it be?

She looked around the room for more paintings and saw a small framed sketch, a self-portrait of the artist in a fur hat. There was no signature on the sketch, but she knew it had to be a Rembrandt.

Sydney went back to the settee and finished her tea. She saw the early strains of a pink sunrise as it flooded the floor to ceiling windows and wondered what the man in the dragon robe had planned for her.

Chapter 21
Monday, 8:15 AM

Victoria Lucelli relaxed at an all-weather picnic table with four chairs attached. The blacktop playground of the Lucelli School was big enough for soccer and basketball, a prime benefit in the crowded Old City of Jerusalem. The younger children had an area on the other side of the school with swings, slides, monkey bars, and sand pits.

An umbrella stuck in the middle of the table kept the morning sun out of her eyes. She tried to stay in the shade and shifted her seat. She wore light blue cotton pants and matching flowered top, just in case she wanted to join her students' games. Despite her short, prematurely-grey hair and weathered face, her body kept up with the volleyball games and her students loved beating the headmistress of their school.

The Lucelli School was well respected in the Jewish and Catholic communities for its broad based educational curricula as well as its focus on religious principles of both faiths. The faculty was chosen by Victoria's husband, Robert, for their training and experience, as well as personal religious values.

Across from Victoria sat Ferah, her counterpart from the Palestinian school that visited one day a month. The new program was an interfaith experiment, which provided the beginning high school students with face-to-face dialogues, rather than shouting matches and rock throwing so prevalent among the youth of the divided country.

Victoria was proud of this outreach program, now in its second year. She was also pleased by the special appearances of Dr. William Jarvis who, when he was in Jerusalem, would visit the school and talk to her students about his work and the importance of archeological research. A shadow hung over the school at the news of their friend's untimely death.

They watched the students from both schools play a co-ed game of soccer. "Children are the same no matter where you go. They all know how to play and they all want to win," Victoria said to Ferah.

Ferah smiled. Her long dark hair was tied back with a colorful scarf. "And if they don't win, they know it's just a game and they'll have another chance to win tomorrow. Then they all go off together laughing and teasing each other. The rules are so simple. Too bad they don't carry over to adulthood."

Victoria nodded. "They get on me when I call them children. They're *teens.*"

They watched as two 14-year-olds—Zaki, Ferah's son, and Ellie, a Jewish girl—laughed and chased each other around the schoolyard, then stopped to catch their breath. They walked toward the sloped area and sat down on a small patch of grass.

Ferah straightened her long yellow and blue flowered skirt to accommodate her notebook computer on her lap. "Your experiment is a success so far, Vicki. Maybe next year we can come once a week, if the Muslim clerics don't shut us down or restrict the funding."

Victoria stood up, reaching for the whistle dangling from a chain around her neck. "You've done a remarkable job of maneuvering through the minefields of your male colleagues' displeasure, Ferah. I hope they eventually see the benefit to the students and Palestinians in general."

She blew the whistle. The children turned from their games and ran laughing to line up in three straight lines before the two teachers. They quieted down and walked into the building.

Back in the classroom the thirty students sat on the floor of a large carpeted area in a circle with Victoria and Ferah sitting together near the chalkboard.

When they were settled and quiet, Victoria asked, "Who remembers what we talked about last time?"

Zaki raised his hand. Victoria nodded at him. He stood up proudly and spoke in a clear voice. "The Koran is the holy book of Islam. It contains the words of Allah which were spoken directly to Muhammad by the angel Gabriel. Muhammad was able to recite exactly what the angel told him. Muslims today can recite the Koran just like the Prophet."

"Why do we recite these words out loud?" Ferah asked.

"When we say the words we are worshipping Allah. *Tajwid* is our direct contact with Allah."

"Very good, Zaki, you may sit down," she told her son. "Who can tell me something about Muhammad?"

Ellie raised her hand. "Muhammad was born in Mecca in 570 AD. He gradually received revelations during his lifetime that explained the meaning of life. He could recite everything he was told. His disciples wrote down some of his verses after he died." The girl sat down.

"That's very good, Ellie," Ferah said. "Your assignment for next month," she said to the class, "is to pair up with someone in the other school and create a project that shows cooperation between our two cultures."

Ellie and Zaki looked at each other and smiled.

"As you know," Victoria said, "The Bible Lands Museum here in Jerusalem sponsors this class which brings

Arab, Jewish, and Catholic students together to trace the history of our lands and discover our roots through the journey of our common patriarch, Abraham, from the land of Ur to Canaan. The Museum has provided several ancient artifacts so we can see the roots of our history."

Ferah lifted a box from the desk, and held up a small gold coin. "This is a coin from the time of Darius, the Persian King, who ruled in the sixth century BC. He was the first king to coin money. It's called a 'Maric' and weighs one hundred thirty grains, about one-third of an ounce."

Victoria heard the door open behind her. The school administrator slowly approached her. "Sorry to interrupt, Dr. Lucelli," she said in a low voice, "but this came marked *Urgent*," and handed her an envelope.

Victoria turned to Ferah, "I'll take this outside. Carry on the class." She followed the administrator to the hallway, walked slowly in the other direction.

She read the note. It was not signed. She hurried to her office and picked up the phone.

Chapter 22

Her desperation rising as quickly as the sun, Sydney looked around the opulent room for a phone and saw none. There must be a way to get out of here, she thought. I've got to call Carter. She rose from the settee, peeked out to the reception hall, and crept toward the outer wooden doors.

Pulling open one of the heavy doors, she saw an armed guard on the stone steps. He glared, shifting the rifle to his other arm. She quickly stepped back and closed the door. As she turned around, a petite middle-aged blond woman in a white satin dressing gown floated toward her.

"Good morning, Dr. Grace. Welcome to our home. We're so glad to have you," the woman gushed.

Sydney stared down at her, unable to speak anything at this anomalous apparition.

"Please come to the dining room for breakfast." Her hostess led the way past the artifact room out to the large inner courtyard.

Sydney followed her into the Romanesque cloister, which was surrounded on four sides by white marble glowing gold from the rising sun, and stone columns entwined with pink clematis. The covered walkways behind the stately, somber buildings held large terra cotta pots filled with miniature orange trees.

"My husband gets so involved in his business; he forgets he has people waiting for him." The three-inch silver heels on her diamond-studded slippers served to bring the top of her head even with Sydney's shoulder. Impeccable makeup and coif accented her demure appearance—the perfect hostess to her husband's unexpected guest. Sydney wondered if she had occasion to welcome another guest—was Alexander here?

Her hostess turned to the right and went to the corner of the building. A guard stood at the end of the walkway, an orange glow behind him heralding the start of day. As they approached the dining room, the aromas of freshly baked bread and brewed coffee wafted into the courtyard.

Sydney hesitated in the doorway, surveying the room for possibilities of escape. Quickly turning to check behind her, the guard appeared and motioned her into the room. Her inclusion into the family gathering was now assured.

A long table covered by a white damask tablecloth with six place settings took up the center of the room. Beneath the table lay a pale blue Oriental rug. A gold gilt Italian Empire figural carved console and mirror with pietra dura verde Carrara marble top held domed silver serving dishes. Platters of fish, cheeses and breads were scattered along the console. A turn of the twentieth century Venetian glass chandelier with twelve lights and gold with enamel trimmed glass flowers hung from the ornate ceiling.

"Help yourself, Dr. Grace. Pierre is an excellent chef. We got him from L'Escoffier in Paris." Her hostess approached the buffet and handed a gold-rimmed ivory plate to Sydney. "He's learned to upgrade the gastronomic desert of our Holy Land food to make it more palatable to our taste. He creates many new dishes from the produce and herbs we grow in our gardens. We still eat many dishes with our fingers or using bread as a scoop. He's discovered how to make pitta iraquit for us, a large, pancake-thin version of pita bread."

Sydney limply held the plate as she considered the bizarreness of the situation. *Prisoner or houseguest?* Either way, escape seemed impossible. She had no choice but to remain in the hands of this unlikely couple.

Under the domed silver serving dishes Sydney found a variety of Middle Eastern baked goods, grilled vegetables, and fruits. Enticed by the smell of the food, she was unsure if she could down anything, but ladled fruit salad and yogurt onto her plate.

"I have to watch what I eat because of a ghastly ulcer that acts up at the most inopportune times," Mrs. Collector said as she sipped her date and mango juice cocktail.

Sydney nodded and took a seat at the table, her anxiety mounting at the number of guards visible in the home of this woman who seemed the epitome of hospitality.

"The talented Dr. Grace, I presume?" said a male voice behind her.

Sydney turned toward the voice, which belonged to a young man who looked like he stepped from the pages of Gentlemen's Quarterly. Tight black leather pants, bright green shirt, black leather jacket with silver studs, black boots. Industrial strength gel appeared to keep the spikes in his blond hair sharply pointed.

"Dr. Grace, this is my son, Marco." Mrs. Collector turned her cheek to receive a kiss from her son.

"Hello, Marco," Sydney said. *Curiouser and curiouser.*

He walked around the table, took Sydney's hand and kissed it provocatively. "Hello again, Dr. Grace. I didn't know archeologists were so beautiful."

"We're not." Sydney pulled her hand away. *First kidnapped, and then hit on by a father and his horny son. What next?*

"I changed my name to Marco, you know, Marco Andretti? Girls like it better than Eleazor," he said as he filled his plate.

"I can imagine," Sydney said, stifling a snicker.

"Please have some more coffee." Mrs. Collector passed the silver coffee pot.

"Thank you, Mrs....?" Sydney hoped to get a family name. She poured coffee into her hand painted bone china teacup.

"Everyone calls me Lily. Like the flower. Lilies are my favorite flowers. We have them in the garden. I'll show you later if you like."

Her husband came into the room. "Show her what?" he asked abruptly. Sydney noticed he now wore a red silk oriental robe embroidered with black dragons piped in silver.

"Good morning, dear. Do come and sit down," Lily said solicitously. "I was just telling Dr. Grace about the flower garden."

"That can wait. We have business to attend to." He turned to Sydney. "Come, Dr. Grace. You may be interested in what I'm about to show you."

Sydney set her teacup into the delicate saucer. "Thank you, Lily," she said unsurely, as if she had been cast into a giant game of chess in which she was the pawn, "for your hospitality."

As Sydney followed her captor out the door, Marco shouted, "After you see mother's flowers, I'll take you around the city in my new Porsche Boxster."

"No you won't," The Collector shouted at his son. To Sydney, he said, "I suppose I do spoil the boy. He's our only child now. Our daughter was killed several years ago in an accident. Nearly killed Lily too. She still hasn't recovered. So Marco gets our attention, such as it is."

Sydney noted sadness in his tone, unusual she thought, but filed it near the front burner of her mind.

They walked out to the main peristyle garden where Sydney admired the surrounding colonnade and beautiful grounds. "Was this once a monastery?" she asked, not really caring what it was, but finding out the lay of the land might offer an idea for escape.

"One of the first of the Carmelites. They couldn't keep it up and it was abandoned for many years. We bought this whole side of the mountain, renovated the monastery into an Italian villa, built on much of what you see. I added the Corinthian columns, the most ornate of the Greek orders with their carved acanthus leaves. We also modernized the interior, knocking out walls to expand space for the collection. Our living quarters are over here. The collection is on that side. We're going through the garden."

A rose marble bench by a bronze fountain with two standing intertwined dolphins spouting water in two directions was the centerpieces of the garden. He motioned her to sit beside him. "I read your book on Egyptian mysteries and artifacts and believe you're the best translator for the job." He rubbed his arm, and then raised the fabric to scratch the scaly skin. "I was impressed with your interpretation of the Pyramid Texts and the true nature of their meaning. I have faith you'll do a good job translating the hieroglyphs."

He's read my book? He stole the wall and kidnapped me. Did he have me attacked so I wouldn't translate the wall for anyone but him? Did he also kidnap Alexander?

He took a handful of bird seed from a bag next to the bench and threw it onto the pink flagstone to the small, waiting song birds. "Your book was a ground-breaking piece of new information to present findings that the pyramids and Sphinx go back at least ten thousand years." He pulled a small tube from his pocket and squeezed out a glob.

She watched him smear the white stuff onto his scaly arms. "I was not the first to present that material." A guard slowly circled the perimeter of the garden. "You're too modest, Dr. Grace. It was a convincing argument based on the precession of equinoxes. It's a puzzle to me why other archeologists are not studying the pyramids in relation to astrological maps."

"It's not a puzzle to me. Egyptologists are taught to toe the six-thousand year party line. They think nothing came before that time. My book was barely published before my colleagues' wrath began. They would have to redefine their whole professional belief system to acknowledge my work. They would never do it." She felt a twinge of regret.

After graduation Carter received an offer from Stanford University in Palo Alto, California. Sydney planned to stay at the University of Pennsylvania to finish her book. Dr. Bill Jarvis offered her various teaching assignments and consultations with graduate students, "to keep you here as long as I can." He tried to rekindle their romance, but for her the fire was out.

She continued research into the Pyramid Texts, the so-called funerary writings of the ancient Egyptians. To Bill's horror, she went beyond the bounds of traditional archeological research into the hidden wisdom of ancient Egypt, enigmatic lore woven through many indigenous tales of 'teachers from the stars,' and the sacred feminine in early Mediterranean cultures.

"If you publish this fringe female stuff, you'll be an outcast in the traditional Egyptology community. Your book just won't be accepted, Syd. You can't do it," he had pleaded over and over.

"I know what I'm doing. 'Gnostic Egyptology' is going full speed ahead." She was determined to stand her ground regardless of the outcome in her professional ranks.

She reached a new high when the first printing of "Stellar Wisdom in the Pyramid Texts: Initiation in Ancient Egypt," was published by the University of Pennsylvania Press.

The Collector threw another handful of seeds to the small, chirping birds. "I know as much archeology and anthropology as the experts, without the restrictions they're under. I've seen ruins in our land predating their six thousand years. Jericho, for instance."

"I suppose I know why you brought me here," she said, watching the birds, her anxiety mounting despite his glowing review of her book, "but I can't guarantee the translation."

He rose from the bench, his full height imposing as he stood before her, his face intractable. "I am not one to mince words, Dr. Grace. Unless you translate the hieroglyphs to my *complete satisfaction,* I'll kill Alexander."

Chapter 23

Carter sat at the folding table Bill Jarvis had used for a desk. Alone in the tent, he reread the note from Herod. Winkowski had gone to the New City for supplies and Tovar accompanied an investigator inside the tunnel, looking for anything helpful to the police the looters might have left. Carter contacted Goldman for an update on the kidnapping, and was told they were waiting for results from the lab on the tire and shoe imprints.

Tovar shouted across from the pool, "Carter, come and look at this."

Carter left the tent, climbed the steps, and followed Tovar down to the colored wall, where the investigator stood.

Tovar pointed to the ground leading to the tunnel. "It looks like one of the thieves came in at least this far. And so did Dr. Grace."

Carter followed Tovar's light. "I don't see anything."

Tovar shone the beam onto the scuffed dirt. "After a while, I can recognize *all* the prints of the people I work with. Many years of digs and a lot of time with nothing to do except study the ground. This one's new." He walked slowly into the tunnel. "These here prints are Dr. Grace's. She went in this far. Most of the prints are up above, and only three sets of prints, besides Dr. Grace's, are down here."

"But there was no ladder. How'd she get down here?" Carter asked.

"The area's pretty well scuffed over, but I'd say she jumped, or fell," the investigator said.

"No, she wouldn't have jumped. She must've fallen and tried to hide from the thieves."

"Looks like she got back this far." Tovar shone his light on the flat stone. "I'd recognize the prints if I saw them again. We'll keep digging at the colored wall. Who knows? There may be more hieroglyphs around the area."

He had urged Carter to stay at his home so Tovar's wife could be with him, but Carter insisted on coming to the pool. He wanted to be there in case Sydney or Alexander showed up or if Herod called.

Scanning his memory of the Sheraton, he quickly speed-dialed Goldman. "Tovar," he shouted as he climbed the steps, "I'll be gone for a while." He got to the surface and raced to his car.

Chapter 24

"You're Herod? You kidnapped Alexander?" Sydney stood up as she faced him, outrage overcoming fear.

"Sit down, Dr. Grace," he said emphatically. "You will hear what I want you to hear when I want you to hear it."

She resumed her seat, eyes darting around the edges of the estate. Where could he be?

Herod walked toward the front of the villa, motioning her to follow. When he opened the tall wooden doors, he turned to her. She saw it was a portcullised entry, a grating of iron hung over the doors for fortification.

"This is a modern and ancient city, as is all Israel," Herod said matter-of-factly.

First he threatens me, she thought, now he lectures me.

The guard turned and greeted him with his Uzi, moving to one side as Herod and his companion walked to a stone parapet at the edge of the building. They climbed the steps to the rampart used by the crusaders to defend the port. The rampart patio had been festively decorated into an outdoor pavilion covered with a yellow and white striped tent whose sides were drawn back to let in the blue Mediterranean on one side and Mount Carmel on the other.

"My wife is having a group for lunch and card games." He gazed up at the mountain.

Sydney looked out at the glistening Mediterranean with a mounting sense of unease at the crusader fort she was in, the threats against Alexander's life, and the perfectly acceptable gathering of his socialite wife. She watched him warily, as she would the occupants of a reptile cage hidden under their sawdust.

Beyond Haifa Bay lay the harbor of Acre. Sailboats skimmed over the water. The harbor buzzed with docked power boats and people strolling the lovely paths near the bay.

"This bay has been fought over for four thousand years," he began, sounding like a tour guide. "The Egyptians wrote about the importance of this harbor they called Akko. It was naturally well-protected and had a well watered inland for many crops. Strategically placed on the coast road linking Egypt to Phoenicia, now Lebanon, in the north." He motioned to the guard who carried a cooler chest up the stairs to the parapet patio, set it down, and returned to his post.

What is he doing? She thought. I've got to get out of here.

"There are crusader vaults under the Turkish Bathhouse and Refectory and a twelfth century subterranean city that tourists visit today. Also secret tunnels the Crusaders built that lead to the harbor. We've found some marble Crusader tombstones down there and are still looking for more finds."

Sydney took the initiative and sat down at one of the filigreed white iron tables with cushioned chairs and colorful umbrellas, wondering what all this had to do with her. "What's that gold dome?" She figured the longer she could keep him talking, the more she could learn what he was up to.

"That's the Baha'i Shrine, the center of the faith, where the believers come from all over the world on their pilgrimages. Over there to the right, set in three hundred acres, is Technion, the center for Israel's scientific innovations. Two-thirds of our university research in technology, engineering, science, medicine, architecture and town planning is done here," he said proudly.

"I never heard of it."

"Most people outside of Israel don't know about it, but you'd be surprised at what goes on in those buildings. Eleazor—Marco—will start his university studies there in the fall. That is, if he can keep his hands off the girls."

Sydney surreptitiously surveyed the grounds for a means of escape, as a slightly disarming smile crossed her face. This had to be the most terrifying situation she had ever found herself in.

As if he read her mind, Herod raised the lid of the cooler chest. At the same time two Dobermans loped over to the patio. Taking out two large T-bone steaks from the cooler, Herod tossed one over the low stone arches that separated the raised patio from the area below. Then he threw the other steak. The dogs took off down the steps toward the black iron security fence. The lead dog seized the chunk that landed short of the fence. The other steak lodged in the fence.

The fence immediately crackled and popped with sparks of electricity and the dog came to a dead stop. The raw meat was flash cooked in an instant. Sydney watched in horror as the chunk of meat sizzled into a charcoal mass in the fence and fell onto the pavement. The dog turned on the lead dog for the remaining meal, but Herod already had another steak in his hand, throwing it to the deprived dog. After they finished their meal, the dogs returned to their patrol duty.

"Here in Haifa and across the bay at Akko," Herod continued, pride etched on his face for the performance of his security system, which was in fine working order, "Jews and Arabs live together, an ethnic mix prizing peace more than discord. That's why I chose this place and this mountain. This mountain is where Elijah fought the priests of Baal and won. His cave is over there," he said pointing.

Sydney followed his gaze to the cave, trying to calm herself, and looked back at the fence with the black mass on the ground. "Quite impressive."

"Follow me," he said as he walked back to the carved wooden doors, his long silk robe skimming the ground behind him. He led her to the left side of the villa opposite the living quarters and dining room, through a walkway toward the mountain. The green terraced garden spread out from the villa with broad walks, tall cypresses, stone benches and marble statues. Lily's flower gardens bloomed with her namesakes in all colors.

An arched stone entrance held a door featuring a stained glass transom. They stepped into an alcove bathed in colored light from the stained glass. Sydney stopped in mid-stride. The alcove merged into a huge cave with a domed ceiling which rose to at least fifteen feet. In the dim lighting she could see large wood and glass display cabinets containing a variety of objects. She shivered in the cold.

The circular way in which the cave was configured enabled the main exhibit to be located at the hub of the wheel, with the spokes of other exhibits radiating out from it. She saw a rectangular glass enclosure at the hub which held a huge sarcophagus with the lid propped to one side. Was it empty? She wondered, or did it hold something?

Herod motioned her toward the hub. Slowly she walked toward it while he watched, amused. She caught a glint of gold. Something blue, a golden crook, a gnarled hand holding the flail. She could not believe she was looking into the face of a golden pharaoh, the death mask of one dead at least thirty-five hundred years.

"It can't be," she murmured.

"But it is," Herod said casually.

"Then, who is it in the Cairo Museum?"

"A duplicate."

"How did you ...?" she couldn't finish the sentence.

"They took it gladly, along with one of the inner gold coffins."

"Where was he found?"

He shrugged. "Near the tomb itself. Luckily he had been moved before the major looters struck."

"Rameses the Great." She murmured, hardly breathing.

Close by the glass case stood a marble column with a colossal head of Rameses resting on it, a plaque stating it was from the Ramesseum, the mortuary temple of the Nineteenth Dynasty king, which lay not far from the tomb.

"Would you like to see the mummy?" he asked.

"Yes," she stammered, "of course I would."

Herod pushed a button on the floor with his foot. Sydney heard a hum and the unmistakable gurgle of pressure transmitted when a quantity of liquid is forced through a tube. She saw the hydraulic sensors lift the glass cover on four steel rods located at each corner. When it was several feet above the coffin, it stopped.

He reached down to the gold mask and lifted it off. "Here," he said to Sydney. "Hold this."

She took it gently out of his hands, cradling it in both arms. When she looked down into the coffin expecting to see the mummy, she was astonished to see *another* gold mask with more predominant features that showed the king as a young man.

"How he wanted to appear for his eternal journey," she whispered. "Young, vibrant, potent. He must have driven the women crazy."

"Yes, he was a handsome devil."

Herod lifted off the second mask to reveal the mummy of the so-called greatest builder in Egypt since the construction of the Great Pyramid. He had the well-known hawk nose. His eyes remained slightly opened to see the sights of eternity. His mouth was open to reveal the loss of some teeth. The tuft of red hair on the mummy in the Cairo Museum, said to be Rameses, was not on this mummy. This one had a smooth, well-formed round head, but not a trace of hair. No doubt he had his choice of many wigs as well as gold headdresses throughout his lifetime.

"I only show my most prized possession to those who will appreciate him. To most people a mummy is a mummy." He paused. "A book can tell a lot about the author. Not only the information presented, but the core beliefs and secret longings. You could not hide in your book, Dr. Grace. It gave you away. You seek hidden meanings in the hieroglyphs you read, the artifacts you find, and the mysterious people of the ancient world. Your book fairly screams, 'What are we missing? What can you tell us we don't know? Where do we look for the answers?'"

He had touched a chord, but she refused to acknowledge his insight.

"We are alike, you and I." His voice was low, beckoning, seducing her with his prizes. "We both seek truth. To hold in our hands the beauty of ages, as you do now. The finest artistic creations ever produced by men."

She held the bulky gold mask, which was getting heavy. She ran her fingers over the face, feeling the smooth nose and lips, the ridges of the beard, the hulking cobra at the forehead. She gently touched the cheek and felt it curve toward the chin. Was it her imagination, or did it feel soft? Yes, and warm? As warm as a living being? The inlaid black and white glass eyes seemed to look into her eyes, into her soul.

She recognized the eyes of her father, the one who had brought her to the Nile on the day she became a woman. Sydney felt like herself and someone else simultaneously. As she gazed into the eyes, she became the daughter of Rameses. She nearly dropped the mask.

Herod watched her juggle it. "Careful," he said, "it might not break but it *will* bend, even after all these years."

She steadied herself and held it lightly now, a thing alive with its own beauty, its own being. The eyes stared up at her as a child stares at its mother in recognition for the first time.

He replaced the inner mask on its setting, positioned over the face, so it did not directly contact the body. He took the second mask from Sydney. She released it as she would a child—with regret, a great deal of sadness, and at the same time, acquiescence.

Chapter 25

The manager's office occupied a corner of the administrative wing on the second floor of the Sheraton. After Goldman flashed his Israeli Intelligence ID at the assistant, requesting to see her superior, she hurried past him.

Carter and Goldman were ushered into a large office with views of the city before which sat a round desk. The dark-suited manager rose from his high-backed black leather chair and offered his guests the two chairs in front of him.

"As my desk officer told you gentlemen, no Herod was checked in last night," the manager shrugged.

Carter leaned forward in his chair. "I delivered an envelope here last night addressed to Herod. He assured me he would be here."

"Who did you deliver it to?" The manager looked from Carter to Goldman.

"He said to leave it at the desk where he would pick it up later."

The manager picked up the phone and pressed a button. "Who was on last night?" He waited for the reply. "Put her on." He put his hand over the phone. "Was it a young woman?"

Carter nodded. "Yes."

The manager dropped his hand. "Who picked up the envelope addressed to Herod last night?" He listened, picked up a pen and wrote on a small hotel pad, then nodded quickly and hung up the phone.

"Fifteen minutes before you arrived she received a call that a Mr. Herod would be checking in and an envelope would arrive for him. She was to accept it and deliver to him when he arrived."

Carter and Goldman both leaned forward.

The manager spread both hands on his desk as if to push himself up out of the chair. "He never arrived. A limo driver picked up the envelope."

"But she told me to wait!" Carter's voice matched his frustration at the snooty face before him.

"Apparently Mr. Herod told her to tell you to wait."

Goldman turned to Carter. "Do you remember seeing a limo driver in the lobby?"

Carter rose impatiently. "I was there for two hours! People were in and out. I suppose a limo driver could have come in. I was watching everyone." He was angry at himself for not returning to the Sheraton earlier.

Goldman turned to the manager. "What time did the limo driver pick up the envelope?"

"Ten o'clock."

Carter sat down. "Did Herod give her an address or phone number when he made the reservation?"

"Of course. We always require our guests' addresses and phone numbers." The manager tore off the top sheet of the pad and handed it to Carter.

Carter grabbed it out of his hand, stood and walked toward the door, excitedly pulling out his cell phone, Goldman right behind him, an appreciative wave at the manager.

Carter dashed down the stairs as he punched in the number. When he got to the lobby he pressed *Talk*. After one ring it was picked up. The female voice said, "Jerusalem Police Department."

Chapter 26

Ferah sat at the kitchen table sipping coffee and talking quietly to her husband, Moishe, a dark-haired, light-skinned Palestinian with a well-trimmed mustache. His dark eyes sparkled with affection for the woman opposite him. Their son, Zaki, was in his room getting ready for school. Their house in Bethlehem was small but comfortable and they enjoyed living in the Palestinian city, even with the dangers that plagued the residents daily. They lived on the outskirts of the city, which kept them reasonably safe in the twelve years they had been there.

"You're taking too much of a chance," Moishe said. "You don't know that much about them. How can you trust them?"

"I know they believe as we do, and that's good enough for me. It's just instinct."

"You and your instinct may get us killed one day. I don't like it."

Zaki came in the room. "Mom, I'm meeting Ellie at the Bible Lands Museum to work on our project. Can you drive me?"

Ferah looked at her son. He had the light brown skin of her husband with curly black hair, and the shapely nose and mouth of the men on her side. He would be tall like his father. She remembered Moishe looking the same at that age. "Yes, Zaki, what's your paper going to be?"

"We've decided on the Temple Mount and how Abraham nearly sacrificed his son on the rock, the same rock Mohammed stood on when he went to heaven. Also, because it was a power place then, and a power place now. Maybe we can get into the Dome of the Rock and do research."

"You be careful, Son, do you hear me?" Moishe said firmly. "That's not the safest place to be these days, even for Muslims. *And stay off buses!*"

"We will, Dad," said Zaki, on his way toward the door.

"Wait a minute," Ferah turned around. "What do you mean, 'power place?'"

He shrugged. "There's a buzz that comes off the Mount. Haven't you felt it?"

Ferah looked at Moishe. "What kind of buzz? Something the Supreme Muslim Waqf is doing up there with buzz saws or drills?"

He shook his head impatiently. "No, not that kind of buzz. It's from the ground. Ellie feels it too, but none of the other kids do."

"*Feels* it? You mean she hears it."

"No. It's not a sound. We feel it in our skin. It's a power place." He was out the door quickly.

She glanced out the window, watching him lift his new Ten-Speed Special into her car. She shook her head. "I learn something new from him every day. But I still worry. He goes all over the city with that bike you got him."

"A boy's got to have wheels. He's getting big now, and we have to let him have some freedom."

"I suppose. I'm just glad his school is close enough to ride to. I don't want him around those kids who just hang out on the streets all day and don't go to school. All they talk about is fighting the Israelis. Why don't they do something constructive?"

"It's those ultra-zealot Muslim clerics that keep them stirred up," Moishe said. "I tell Zaki every day not to listen to them. He's a pretty savvy kid. He knows how extreme they are. I'm glad we can keep him in that private school, even if it is expensive." He kissed her goodbye. "See you at dinner."

She finished her coffee, thinking about herself at Zaki's age. She lived in East Jerusalem in a hybrid family. Her Jewish father and Palestinian mother had gone against both their families and cultures to make a life for themselves and their children. Ferah grew up walking in both cultures, knowing the animosity and resentment of the Palestinians and the need for re-establishing the new nation so ingrained in the Israeli soul. She could so easily see both sides of the issues and made it her life's work to bring them together.

Zaki stuck his head in the door. "Are you coming?"

"Just as soon as I check my e-mails." Ferah sat down at the computer on the small desk in the kitchen. There was one interesting message.

'Possible x at high noon. Come at 2.'

Chapter 27

The glass case lowered itself back onto the floor over the impressive sarcophagus that held the mummy. Sydney saw Herod insert a key into the base of the glass near the floor. She hadn't seen him do that before. Watching her, he stepped on the button, pulled out the key, stepped on it again. "It won't matter if you memorize the order. It's changed every day. So the only one who knows the reset sequence is me. And I never write it down," he said with bravado. The alarm beams flashed brightly over and around the glass case.

He walked toward another large glass display case. "You may also be interested in this, Dr. Grace." His tone changed abruptly into matter-of-fact casual. She averted her eyes from the case, trying to figure out his intent.

"It was one of my first acquisitions. You look for answers, as do I. You ask in your book, what are we missing? This answered many questions over the centuries archeologists couldn't answer." Now he sounded vulnerable, seeking her approval.

Sydney followed him to the case. Her mouth dropped open when she saw the black basalt stela inside the case. She would have recognized it anywhere. "The Rosetta Stone! It's a pretty good fake. Looks just like the real one in the British Museum."

"This *is* the *real one*," he said arrogantly. "The *fake* is in the British Museum."

She eyed him. "I don't believe you. How could *you* have the real Rosetta Stone?"

"See for yourself," he said with a sniff. Stepping on a floor button and turning a key, the alarm beams were deactivated and the glass began to rise on the four steel rods just as the other case. It rose higher than the other glass and he stepped to the front of the stela.

Sydney walked over to it and knelt down, touching the granite and carefully inspecting the stone. She tried to remember where it was found and by whom, recalling that Napoleon had mounted an expedition to Egypt to colonize the Nile Valley under the guise of 'cultural exchange and intellectual scholarship.' The group of talented scientists and artists were brought together by Napoleon to 'study all of Egypt, spread enlightened ideas, and furnish information to the occupying authority.' In other words, 'find, select, conserve, interpret and transport' whatever ancient items could be taken back to France.

It was no coincidence that Gaspard Monge, a chemist and mathematician who accompanied the French army in Italy, was part of the commission who decided which art collections and museum pieces were to be claimed by the French Republic under terms of the peace treaties. It was Monge's efficiency which determined the placement of the world's most famous painting, the Mona Lisa. Tourists, and the French people, visiting the Louvre today had Monge and the commission to thank for their appropriation of specific war booty.

When it came to the Rosetta Stone, the French were not so lucky. Found by a soldier in the Nile Delta in a pile of boulders used as ballast by ships docking at a nearby port, the scholars and scientists recognized it as 'some inscriptions which may offer much interest.'

When the British fleet led by Admiral Horatio Nelson defeated the French army, Napoleon abandoned his men and fled Egypt in a fast ship. In the surrender, the French were allowed to keep some of their Egyptian collections, but not the Stone. King George III ordered it housed in the British Museum in London, where it has remained to this day.

Or so the official story went.

"The key to the Egyptian language," Sydney said with reverence as she sat looking at the Stone.

"I knew if anyone could appreciate this amazing find, it would be you," he said proudly.

"The royal decree that went out to all of Egypt in 196 BC told of the Pharaoh's succession to the throne. The priests left their instructions right on the Stone." She began to read the hieroglyphs. "They shall write the decree on a stela of hard stone in the script of the words of god, *the formal hieroglyphs,* the script of documents, *demotic,* and the script of the Ionians, *Greek,* and set it up in the first-rank temples, second-rank temples and third-rank temples, in the vicinity of the divine image of the Pharaoh living forever."

With a sweeping motion, Herod drew a soft damp cloth from his pocket, knelt and wiped the Stone. The cloth immediately turned black! Sydney examined the cloth, and then looked closely at the Stone, which had become *grey.*

Herod smiled at her dismay. "It's not black basalt as the experts believe. The French coated it with a layer of black ink to make rubbings which they sent out to scholars. I've only discovered in the past year, quite by accident of course, the black washes off. The true color of the stone is grey."

"Grey basalt?'

"Grey *granite.* Quite common in Egypt, as you know," he said, beaming at his extraordinary discovery. He closed the case.

"*This* was the most important thing Napoleon did in Egypt. Not his military campaign, which was a dismal failure," Herod said, "but finding the dictionary, the words to the ancient language that opened up the world of the Egyptians. For this alone, I can forgive him everything else in his ridiculous life. He brought about an intellectual revival that began new interest and discoveries in Egypt."

"Yes, along with the revival of tomb-robbers who filled the mansions of the wealthy, and added to the galleries and museums all over the world."

"Think about it, Dr. Grace. If the French, the Italians, then the British and others didn't go searching for lost cities and buried treasure, these ancient artifacts might never have been found. Surely it's better for scientists, scholars and art dealers to study and display them, to place these objects in museums and galleries, where they're safe from the plunderers who come in and destroy them. There was no repository in Egypt to hold the objects. The Cairo Museum wasn't around in those days."

"It is now," Sydney said passionately. "And that's where this Stone belongs. In its rightful place."

"Blame the Egyptians!" Herod barked. "Unfortunately, they didn't care about their history, or didn't even know about it, and took for granted the vast monuments all over their country. While the natives burned their temple walls black from cooking fires, and chopped off temple carvings for ballast, and carted off relief stones for their office buildings, the Europeans did them a favor by coming into their country and valuing what they found. They had a *right* to take it out."

"Maybe they did save some of the objects, maybe not," she conceded.

"The natives chopped through tombs, carvings and mummies to get to the gold—not caring what they destroyed—then sold it to the highest bidder. How much ancient gold has been melted down to raise money for today's armies? And that includes the well-known Nazi loot."

Sydney could not stop herself from agreeing with much of what he said. It was his arrogance and hypocritical rants about art and culture that showed wealthy egotism at its worst and massive denial at its best. It was obvious he felt he had a *right of ownership* to the objects in this room. That there was a price for everything and everything had a price, even her. She shuddered to think what that price was.

"And as long as they could," he continued, "they took as much as they could carry out. When Champollion discovered the language of the hieroglyphs, he did it with the help of as *many* hieroglyphic texts as he could get his hands on. Where do you think they came from?" He paused, raising himself to his full height, which allowed him to tower over her.

She moved one foot slowly backward, leaning her body, as unobtrusively as she could, away from him.

"They came from plundered tombs is where they came from! Paris auction rooms where he deciphered the texts as quickly as he could before they were auctioned off. The little bastard was so obsessed with decipherment that he didn't really care *where* these texts came from or who found them. What's important is that he cracked the code. It could have been another hundred years before someone else came up with the hieroglyphic translations if this Stone hadn't been found."

"What do you mean *this* Stone? If it's the real one, how did you get it out of the British Museum?"

"I *didn't* get it out of the British Museum," he said smugly. "I got it out of France. Out of the *Louvre itself.*"

Chapter 28

Carter left the tent when he heard Winkowski's truck pull up to the site. Tovar and Levin helped them unload the truck, and then Carter and Winkowski went back into the tent and sat at the table. Carter pulled the sheets of paper out of the envelope, the one Sydney kept with the copy of the hieroglyphic translation he'd given to Herod.

Winkowski studied it, shaking his head. "Jarvis was killed for this? Lists of onion baskets and beer kegs? It doesn't make sense."

"That's what Sydney said, but she also mentioned the four corners with their squares and crosses, saying they point to something valuable, but didn't say what it was." Carter looked for the four corners in the text, but could not find it.

"What did she mean? Anything in the text show something of value? It doesn't look like it." Winkowski looked dapper today, in a cream colored suit with a light peach and umber print vest over his ample girth, and medium-toned peach shirt. He wore the ubiquitous white cotton gloves and canvas sun-hat. "What made her think there's something else in this list?"

"Not in the list," Carter said. "On the wall. Come on, I'll show you."

They climbed down the ladder to the wall, Winkowski carefully picking his way to the ground. He studied all the corners with squares and crosses. "These glyphs are pretty faded. Did she use a magnifier?"

"I don't think so; she really didn't have much time."

"I've seen those squares on other walls. Doesn't mean a thing. She's on the wrong track," Winkowski said as he turned.

"But, Roland, look closely at the squares. They're not placed in alignment with each other like they should be. They're off, not by millimeters, but by *inches.* Something the ancient artists would never do. They were too precise in their writing to make a mistake like that."

Winkowski turned and looked again. "You're right. These are misaligned. Why do you suppose that is? Was that what Sydney meant?"

"That and the fact that the squares seem to be pointing to something within the text itself, somewhere in the middle. She didn't have time to get to that. We had to get the translation to Herod."

"You didn't see him by any chance?"

"No, I gave the envelope to the desk clerk, who told me to wait. I sat there for nearly two hours. It was a setup to keep me from getting back so the thieves could make off with the wall, *and Sydney.*" He paused, pumping a fist into his hand. "I haven't heard from Alexander at all. I hope they're both all right."

Winkowski shrugged. "Just shows we can't trust Herod. He probably wants her to translate the colored wall."

Carter turned to face Winkowski, stunned by his heartless reaction.

Winkowski realized his gaffe. "That sounded cruel, not the way I meant it, Carter." He put his hand on Carter's shoulder. "I'm sure we'll get them back."

Carter pulled his cell phone from his pocket. "I'm calling Yuval Goldman to see if he has anything. He got some good tire prints—may match those at the Herodian theft."

Winkowski nodded and sat down at the table. "The Old City is like a small town. News travels fast. Especially news about archeological finds. Herod probably has spies all over."

"That may be how he found out so fast." Carter pressed his speed-dial.

"Everyone's accounted for. Bill knew Tovar many years. And he brought the students over himself."

"Still, Roland, I'm sure of it—there's a mole at the dig, and not the furry kind."

Chapter 29

"Is it ready?" Herod asked his phone. He listened for the answer then clicked it shut and walked over to Sydney, who was still seated at the Rosetta Stone. "Time to put her back to bed," he said, as he took out the key. She averted her eyes as he began the security process.

The floor button and the key were pressed, inserted, re-pressed, and withdrawn until the glass was back in place and the alarm beams were turned on.

Sydney's curiosity soared to its peak, she had to know. "You say you got the Stone out of the Louvre? But it was never *in* the Louvre. The British took it away from the French in Egypt and sailed with it to London."

Herod's smile reflected a secret only he knew. "Because of my deep regard for you and the book you so brilliantly wrote on new theories of ancient Egypt, I will tell you the truth, Dr. Grace. The Stone *was* in France. Just one time. In 1973 the Brits let them have it for a temporary exhibition."

"The Stone was in the Louvre after all?" she asked incredulously.

"The only time they *ever* let it out of Britain. Very few people knew it was being loaned out. After the exhibition, while it was transported from the Louvre to the ship that would return it to London, the truck was, shall we say, diverted. Just for a few moments, while the motorcycle police *behind* the truck were distracted, and another truck took its place. It was a beautiful job," he beamed, "executed perfectly. No one got hurt and no one was the wiser."

"You mean the Rosetta Stone was *high-jacked* from the Louvre truck in plain sight of the French police?" Sydney was astounded. It sounded like a Quentin Tarantino heist movie.

"Not only in plain sight, but the two motorcycle cops in front were paid off with a hefty sum that guaranteed them income for life, no lump sums to give them away. The drivers of the real truck were paid off the same way. They're all still getting paid and living on an island somewhere." He chuckled in a high pitched tone. "My father thought of everything."

"Your father?"

"He was the mastermind. It was his plan all the way. He knew them all beforehand, the French cops and drivers. Trusted them with the job. They worked with pinpoint timing. They had all done it before, you see. Cool characters! No records on any of them. No one to trace. And no one saw them! It was beautiful!" He turned to the case, satisfied that it was secure.

Sydney shook her head. "What did he plan to do with it? He couldn't sell it. Everyone knew the Stone was in the British Museum."

"He never planned to sell it. That wasn't why he did it. He was the kind of man who had to have originals, one-of-a-kind priceless pieces. Very possessive of everything he had. And he had to have ancient treasures."

"It must have cost him a bundle to do all that."

Herod began walking her toward the door. "More than that, it cost him his life. One of his associates got a little too ambitious and my father caught him. But too late. He killed my father, but never got away with his crime. I saw to that."

Sydney shivered, not wanting to know more.

"He was a strange man. He'd sit for hours, staring at the Stone or the gold masks, all by himself in his trophy room, not letting anyone else in. I was young at the time, and would knock on the door wanting to see what he was doing, but when he'd finally open the door there would be nothing of real value to be seen, and he would say he was doing paperwork. Just the usual Monet paintings and Greek marble statues were in the room. It was only after he died that I found the key, and that he had written down the combination. Then I saw his real treasures."

They reached the door and he unlocked it. "It was similar to my security here. Only they could be moved hydraulically behind the bookshelves and kept out of sight whenever he let anyone into the room. My mother said she had seen his treasures only once. He wanted her to see them. After that, she never asked about them again, or anything else he did. That was probably why he showed her."

"What kind of work did he do?"

"He was an art dealer. Knew everyone, went everywhere. Knew the value of everything. Except his family," he said bitterly, with a far-away expression. "My projects went into cabinets. Or in my mother's room."

He spoke softly, holding the door handle, gazing out the half-open door. "My painted pottery was quite good, according to my teachers. But nothing impressed him. Except ancient gold, jewelry, mummies. Originals. Pages of *The Inferno* written by Dante himself. Line pencil sketches by Leonardo." His voice reflected sadness, even acceptance. "I eventually gave up and started collecting others' creations."

Unsure that he even remembered her presence, in his current state, Sydney kept a safe distance from him. He stood, unmoving, at the door.

"Sort of like Marco," he murmured. "Am I becoming my father?" He turned around and realized she heard him. "This way," he said, regaining his composure.

They walked toward the front doors. The carved figures seemed to emerge from the oak, struggling to free themselves. She followed him into the reception hall, down the walkway to the garden into an area where another door led to a cave into the mountain. As she walked into the alcove, she saw the cave was smaller than the other, and had a domed ceiling with lights strung across the top girders. Along the side she saw the men who kidnapped her.

Behind them in all its glory hung the colored wall. In the same order and state she remembered, they had assembled it onto a mesh panel that fronted the cave wall. Standing spotlights were positioned to illuminate each panel.

"You can start over here, Dr. Grace. It's all set up for you," Herod said.

A table with a laptop and printer was in front of the wall. A swivel chair and floor lamp sat beside the table. The panels had been cleaned quite carefully, she noticed.

Dmitri was clearly amused. "You see, Dr. Grace. I told you the colors would be as brilliant as the day they were painted. Well, maybe the day after."

They finished wiping the panels and cleaning the plaster from the floor that had fallen from the mesh screen, picked up the buckets of plaster and water, the cleaning supplies and rags and headed for the door. The plaster had hardened and set behind the individual panels so the whole thing looked like it was originally painted on the cave wall.

"A stolen wall with original hieroglyphs," she said, her anger rising. "I can't condone your crime." But I have to admit, she thought, the colors look even more vivid than in the cavern.

Dmitri beamed with pride, taking her anger as a compliment. By their grins, the others did the same, and must have echoed the pride of the original Egyptian tomb painters, who like them, probably received little acclaim for their work beyond their own satisfaction for a job completed in the highest execution of function and beauty.

Sydney sat down at the computer, a sense of awe surrounding her at the task ahead. The first to read this writing since it was so carefully carved and painted, she felt like the chosen one. The wall beckoned, as it had in the cave, the thirty-five hundred-year-old hieroglyphs waiting to reveal their secrets.

Chapter 30

Zaki lifted his Ten Speed from the trunk of his mother's car and headed for the entrance to the Bible Lands Museum. He waved as she drove off.

Ellie rode toward him. "I lied to my mom," she said as she slowed her bike.

"So did I," Zaki said.

"I couldn't tell her we were going to the Temple Mount. I'm a Jew. I'm not supposed to go up there."

"Neither am I and I'm *not* a Jew." He jumped on his bicycle. "Let's go."

Riding through the Jaffa Gate, they slowed down as they zigzagged through traffic, into the narrow streets. Zaki rode to the Muslim entrance onto the Mount where they locked their bicycles and walked up the steps.

The Temple Mount was the site of Solomon's temple, built over the rock on which Abraham nearly sacrificed his son, and housed the Ark of the Covenant of the ancient Hebrews. The temple witnessed many battles and the Ark was hidden during one of the wars of King Hezekiah.

The Babylonians destroyed the temple in the sixth century BC. Rebuilt by Herod the Great, who leveled and reinforced the Temple Mount platform, the second temple was later destroyed by the Romans.

The Dome of the Rock Mosque and its gold dome were built in the sixth century CE as an architectural marvel to proclaim the superiority of Islam. The Muslims believed Mohammed left earth on his night journey from that same rock.

Walking toward the Mosque on the other side of the building opposite the entrance, Zaki approached one of the Muslim guards. Ellie couldn't hear what he said, but the guard motioned them forward. They walked behind the screens that protected the dig site as a bulldozer worked next to a pit at least thirty feet in diameter and twelve feet deep, scooping out dirt and loading it onto a waiting truck.

Zaki approached a man wearing dress slacks and short-sleeved white shirt who looked like he was supervising the others. "We're doing a school project on the first Palestinian presence here. Can you help us?" Zaki asked.

The supervisor looked him over, and then looked at Ellie. "What school you at?" he asked suspiciously.

"The Bethlehem-Palestinian school. We only have a couple of days to do our report. We won't be any trouble. Have you found anything?" Zaki's dark eyes drilled into the supervisor, willing his request be granted.

Uvi Jando, the supervisor, was taken aback by the brashness of this kid, not only the topic of their project, but that he would come right to the source. He stroked his broad black beard, remembering when he and his brothers were just as reckless. He would never have gotten this job at such a young age if he hadn't been fearless.

The Waqf, the Supreme Muslim Religious Council, administered the whole Temple Mount and had made it clear to the Israelis it was *they* who now commanded *all* the digging in and around the mosque. No Israeli ever set foot on the Mount for fear of stepping on the spot where the Holy of Holies rested in the original temple. This was fine with the Muslims. Anything to keep the Jews away.

Uvi and his men were told to dig beside the Mosque, to recover whatever Hebrew items they could, as well as

Palestinian objects. He knew the Waqf was obsessed with finding 'only Islamic artifacts' to strengthen their claims to this sacred site. The problem, he thought, was that no Islamic artifacts had been found, at least anything earlier than the Dome of the Rock itself.

Besides the dirt taken out, he knew many objects had been found. All Jewish. On the ground next to him lay pillar fragments waiting to be taken out in trucks to an unknown site. There were also stacks of tiles lined up near the pillars, which he knew were more modern, but still of value to the Waqf leadership.

He knew the most valuable pieces were already on the international antiquities market. The most prized piece was found in the rubble of a room off the tunnel. A gold menorah dated to the ninth century BC. With a gilded gold stand next to it, probably belonging to the first temple period. They may have even been part of the holy objects in Solomon's Temple. Wouldn't the Jews love to know?

He couldn't take any chances with these kids. "Get out of here!" he barked.

The kid took out his notebook. "What's in the hole over there? Did you dig up anything by Mohammed's rock?"

"No! Stay out of the way!" Uvi turned to one of his men.

"Then do you mind if we go through the dirt pile before you dump it into the valley? Just to look for some bits of pottery we can use in our report."

Uvi turned around. The kid was right behind him. The beginning of a smile crept across Uvi's face. Persistent, he thought. Just like me. *Anything* to get rid of them. He whispered to one of his men, who scampered into the pit near the sacred rock. A worker held a large basket, which he set down, pulled out an intact clay oil lamp and a small carved stone figure of a female with outstretched arms.

The man ran back up and handed the two objects to Uvi.

"Here," he yelled to the kid, "take these and go."

The kid took them and shouted as he ran off the Temple Mount, "Thanks, mister, thanks a lot."

Chapter 31

The good god, Lord of the two lands, King of Upper and Lower Egypt, Men-kheper-Re, son of Re, Thutmose, given life eternally.

Sydney read it a second time to be certain she wasn't imagining the scene before her. A third time and she knew this was exactly what these hieroglyphs said. She didn't have to enter the text into the software. She knew these lines and recognized the cartouches of the king, centered in the wall.

These were the five 'great names' assumed by a king when he ascended the throne. The two principal names being the 'prenomen' and the 'nomen,' distinguished by their presence in the cartouches, or royal rings. In Egyptian, cartouche meant 'that which encircles.'

Thutmose III! His throne name, Menkheperra, was a commonly encountered name on many objects from ancient Egypt. It was found on temple decorations and statues, and carved on scarabs long after the death of the king. That was because his name was believed to bring good fortune. Even the ancient Egyptians who lived long after him were superstitious to the point of wearing a good luck symbol.

So he did pass through the Old City of Salem in the fifteenth century BC, Sydney thought. He may even have camped there during his military campaign on his way north. Thutmose III was the great empire builder of the New Kingdom and spent much of his reign on campaigns.

Alone in the cave, she looked around excitedly, her heart pounding in anticipation. She had heard the lock click into place when Herod and the others left. Light beamed onto the floor through a small window.

She realized this wall was a continuation of the other wall, and may also refer to something valuable. That was why there was no cartouche on the upper wall. Still puzzled by the glyphs immediately surrounding the cartouches in the center, she began reading at the farthest end on the right.

Ra in Heaven gave me his force and strength of the Two Lands,
Who fashioned me as a falcon of gold
I am his son, who built great cities and conquered many,
The image of birth from the god Thoth
Who brought the Code in the beginning as a guide for the end
It is written on the wall of the tomb of King Unas...

Sydney stopped reading. A Code? The voice in the classroom. What did it say? *Find the Code.*

The Pyramid Texts in the tomb of King Unas were a Code of some kind? She knew they were older than the walls on which they were found, and were copies of more ancient texts. They were thought to be funerary incantations for the dead Pharaoh, but she knew they were written for the living. She didn't remember anything like a Code in the Texts.

Which are used by the priests to see ahead in time.

They were able to be used psychically? She had never considered this when she was writing her book. But she never had weird experiences either—a voice talking to her in class about a Code, statues leading her to caves, stones talking about ancient people. Impossible! Yet they happened. *I know they happened. I just can't explain it.*

There were five priests associated with the Unas' tomb, all known as prophets. Whether this meant they could foresee future events was unknown. This put a whole new spin on the Texts and what they were used for. If they were some sort of Code, they definitely couldn't just be for the dead Pharaoh.

Sydney was stunned by this unexpected discovery. Amid a mounting sense of excitement, she returned to the center. *Was this the Code?* They did not look like grid glyphs. They were totally different from anything she had ever seen, and she was considered an expert in hieroglyphs. But there was no starting point! In most writings, the cartouche began the text. Here, the cartouche lay in the middle. If she started translating from the middle, the whole thing might not make sense, considering the back-and-forward-facing way the glyphs were carved.

Her frustration mounted along with her excitement. A physical tingle at the back of her neck, the feeling of familiarity at the edges of her reason. There was something about the glyphs she should understand—something she'd seen before, known before, or dreamed.

Chapter 32

Sydney stared at the elongated cartouche that held the name of the pharaoh, feeling herself slipping into lost time. Her vision dimmed, reframing itself into something far away from today, yet closer than tomorrow.

She floated above the huge temple of Karnak, not the ruins of today, but the original magnificent complex teeming with priests, priestesses, builders, engineers, artists and craftsmen. The colored columns in the Hypostyle Hall, the grand courts filled with obelisks and statues, and towering walls of paintings were unmatched anywhere in the world. Each ruler increased his or her own glory by adding to the pantheon of gods and goddesses.

Drawn to an enclosure within the complex, Sydney marveled at the highly decorated walls of Nile scenes—ducks riding the waves, pink lotuses along the shore, a fisherman standing on a cut log raft holding a long pole aimed at a big silver fish under the water.

Sydney counted about a dozen teenage boys sitting in a circle on reed mats. They were naked but for white cotton loincloths tied with leather thongs. The white-linen clad teacher walked slowly around the room. She noticed his bald head glistened, not from sweat, but from the oil that covered his body. Lines marked his face with years of authority and wisdom. The teacher stopped by each student, offering encouraging words on their work.

Sydney hovered over the room like a bird surveying the ground for food. She realized she understood what the teacher said to each student. A thrilling moment—hearing the spoken language of an ancient tongue—flowing yet guttural, melodic and simple.

Curious, she swooped down to two boys who held reeds with sharpened tips. They dipped the reeds in black vegetable ink and filled their faded umber papyrus sheets with hieroglyphs. Sydney read the glyphs at the top of one slate—NSL. Probably pronounced Nhasul, his name. She sensed an eerie familiarity with this boy. On the other slate, the boy had written MTM—Metem.

She watched as Metem reached over and pinched Nhasul on the upper right arm. Sydney flinched. She felt a squeeze on her right arm that propelled her up, out of the room. How could she feel that?

Returning to the room, she was shocked by the glyphs on the slates. The boys were writing in a pattern, beginning at the center, flowing down and around, up and back until the glyphs created a perfect spiral. Amazing! Nothing like it had been found in any tomb or temple by modern archeologists— ever. There was only one place she had seen glyphs written like this—on the colored wall.

Nhasul slowly raised his head, scanning the room as if searching for something. He seemed to focus in her direction, and then looked squarely into her eyes. How can he see me? She gazed back at him, and in a breath she knew not only how to read the spiral glyphs—she could also write them.

The teacher collected each papyrus slate and dismissed the class. The boys hastily departed the room. With a sense of trepidation, Sydney followed them. Running along the shore of the river, Nhasul stumbled and fell against a large rock. He cried out in pain, holding his left leg. Sydney saw blood ooze from his ankle.

Metem rushed to his friend, yelling and pointing. A large crocodile glided across the water toward them. Sydney dashed to help, as Nhasul hobbled up, grabbing his friend's arm.

What could she do? Helpless to carry the boy, she turned to the croc, which was closing fast, its giant jaws opening, teeth sharp for the kill. She stood knee-deep in the water, hurling every ancient curse she could think of at the oncoming beast.

Screaming in terror at each other to flee certain death, the boys scrambled across the sand through the brushes onto the high bank of the shore.

Uncertain what she would do if it reached her, Sydney held her breath as the croc suddenly snapped its jaws shut a few feet in front of her and, in fury turned from its course, and dove under the water.

The teacher ran to the frantic boys, who pointed and yelled at the croc, as it disappeared in the river. As he was lifted and carried to safety, the boy looked up at Sydney.

In awe, she suddenly understood the true purpose of her return to the past—she had saved the life of the boy she once was. She knew he would become the trusted advisor to the pharaoh, whose long reign would depend on the coded military messages contained within the spiral glyphs.

As she rubbed her painful left ankle, Sydney gazed down at Nhasul with an overwhelming sense of wonder and love at this vision of her forgotten self.

With her leg still aching, she felt herself being swept up in time once more, back to the wall of hieroglyphs in Herod's cave.

Chapter 33

As they headed north to Nablus in their Suzuki Aerio, Ferah and Moishe agreed on the plan of the day. If she could in some small way halt the ravaging of ancient artifacts from her homeland, she would not hesitate to take advantage of her double heritage.

"I don't understand why Israelis today are less interested in uncovering history and more concerned with modern conveniences," she said. "After the founding of the country the nation was idealistic, looking to the past to guide the future. The bible became a textbook for archeological excavations. But over the years, people have become immune to their history and young Jews don't care about their biblical background."

Moishe didn't answer. He kept his eyes on the road.

She turned to him. "I know, I know. You've heard it all before. 'Young people want to build a future rather than dig up a past,'" she quoted him.

"That's right," he said emphatically, pulling up to the whitewashed house of Khalid, the most prominent grave robber in Palestine. A wire fence surrounded the home in front and back, keeping in chickens, goats, and rabbits, which scratched and grazed the pockmarked ground. Grass competed with weeds in the expanse of yard leading to the front door.

Since the Intifada began and the closures preventing Palestinians from working in Israel were instituted, Khalid could find no work as a lawyer. He found himself reverting to his childhood love of digging in the earth, and never failed to discover a coin or other small objects wherever he happened to scoop up dirt.

Over the years, his ability to attract figurines, coins, pottery, and other artifacts had become so fine-tuned he could now read the secrets of the landscapes by shape, color and texture of the soil and plants, and then expertly guess what lay beneath the earth.

Khalid sat on his front patio surrounded by three thousand years of history. He greeted his visitors and offered them tea with flatbread and hummus.

"I'm more interested in providing for my family than proving history of the ancient Palestinians," Khalid explained to his guests after they settled onto their molded plastic chairs. "We know more than the archeologists, anyway. We've been here longer and know this country. We Samaritans have seen the Canaanites, Hebrews, Babylonians, Persians, Greeks, Romans, Byzantines and the British come in and out of our land. Why shouldn't we dig up what they left? It's ours!" He handed Ferah a pot about four inches high, with a small neck.

"You may have a point, Khalid," Ferah said. "This ceramic pot is beautiful." She touched the cool smooth surface and marveled at its mint condition.

"Turn it over," he said.

Ferah turned it upside down. "It's remarkable," she exclaimed, setting it down on her opened palm. "The round base has white markings on it, very similar to knife cuts made on a poppy pod."

"That's exactly what those markings are. It shows how the white opium base oozed out so it could be harvested," Khalid said.

"You mean that was an opium pot?" Moishe asked.

"Surprised?" Khalid asked.

"I've heard there was a Bronze Age drug trade along the Mediterranean, but this is the first proof I've ever seen that it really existed." She sniffed the neck of the pot. "Not much of an odor. Organic substances break down quickly, so I guess we can't know for sure what was inside."

"I've found many of these little pots," Khalid said. "They've been analyzed with a procedure called gas chromatography and traces of opium were found."

"We know the Egyptians did many surgical techniques. They either inhaled the smoke from the poppy as it was lit, or they ate it," Ferah said.

"Ugh, it must've tasted horrible," Moishe said.

"If you were in pain, you'd eat it and be grateful for it," she said with a laugh. "Where did you find it, Khalid?"

"Over by Sebastiya, the official ancient site where the archeologists dig. I was walking south of Sebastiya, looking for likely spots. On a hunch I dug down a few feet and found several of these pots and some jars. Look at this." He handed her a carved alabaster chalice.

"This is really lovely, Khalid. Look at the beautiful carvings of birds, Moishe. Exquisite birds in flight. Is it from the same location?"

"You're my friends, so I tell you. I found this place, but can only go there at night. Too many curious villagers close by." He rose to throw food pellets to the rabbits, which were quickly gobbled up by the goats.

Ferah held up the chalice to see the light through it. "Could be Babylonian or earlier." Much earlier, she thought.

"That's what I think," Khalid said. "Both of them together are worth a lot."

The scent of roasted meat wafted from the windows of Khalid's modest home. His wife was preparing freshly slaughtered goat baked with okra and tomatoes. Their guests would partake of the ritual of sharing a homemade meal from an animal reared in the yard. Khalid went into the kitchen and came out a few minutes later.

"Who else knows about this place?" Moishe popped a pita square dipped in olive hummus into his mouth. "Is it safe for us to go there?"

Khalid shrugged. "Maybe I can take you, but it's best to wait until sundown. Let the villagers all go home."

"If it won't take long." Ferah glanced at Moishe. "We have an engagement tonight."

"After our meal, I can't take you to the exact location, but the general area. Let us go in and eat together."

After receiving Khalid's e-mail earlier, Ferah knew he had found something special. The ceramic pot and alabaster chalice were not Babylonian. They were much older. But she would first have to buy them from him and get professional confirmation. She was also prepared to share food with the family, which she and Moishe had done on several occasions. It was part of the ritual of visiting a Palestinian home and doing business.

Ferah hoped to locate this new dig of Khalid's. He had become one of many West Bank Palestinians who looted the clues to what remained of the history of ancient Israel and ancient Palestine. By selling it off, some said he was saving history. She was not so sure.

The meal ended with cardamom-laced coffee and plates of pomegranates, figs, dates, and melons. The two couples sat at the table finishing the fruit, while Khalid lit a fragrant Egyptian cigarette and blew smoke rings into the warm Nablus air.

Three young children ran around the room and were hustled outside by their mother. They're just like us, thought

Ferah, as she sipped her coffee, or like us if we had no means of supporting ourselves except digging in the earth.

Khalid escorted Ferah and Moishe to his Nissan, opening the back door. They drove past herds of goats, olive groves and rundown whitewashed homes. He warned them not to look out of the windows. He did not want his Palestinian neighbors knowing where he went, or that he had visitors he was showing around.

Past the villages of barren landscape, Khalid told them it was safe to look. Ferah saw myriads of recently dug holes, many of which were looted ancient tombs.

Khalid stopped the car and they stepped out. "These tombs belonged to Jewish and Samaritan families who used the same burial cases for generations. Sebastiya is up there a few miles. You see how close this spot is. But these were plundered by the Ottomans."

The dark gold soil was dotted with black holes, and broken pottery covered the ground.

They returned to the car and he drove to another spot, where they walked around more holes, each one with a story to tell.

"I've gone through all these, and even dug deeper in each hole, but found only pottery. Look," Khalid said, pointing to a stand of fruit trees. "After three thousand years of people dumping garbage and burying bones, the earth is rich with nitrates. These trees, growing in the natural fertilizer, have the sweetest fruits and vegetables." He picked apricots and sour plums and passed them to Ferah and Moishe.

Ferah bit into one. "This is the best apricot I've ever tasted."

They all climbed back into the car. A mile further, Khalid suddenly swerved off the main highway and pulled the car onto a dirt embankment. He followed it for several miles. Ferah could see no signs of life in any direction. The sun was dropping into the horizon.

Khalid stopped the car and led them to a hole. "This is another spot that's been dug to pieces, literally," he said. He kicked the earth and Ferah saw piles of broken bones and teeth mixed with the powdery soil. Based on prior discoveries and today's beautiful finds, she was convinced this was something special, something that would merit further digging, not by Khalid, but by professionals.

"I found a human jawbone in this hole, more bones over there," Khalid said, "and dug several holes over there." He pointed to sparse vegetation. "The alabaster chalice I found several miles from here"

Ferah stooped down to brush away the dirt from the bones. *Whose ancestors were they?*

"I cover up everything when I leave. This is a remote spot, but the diggers are everywhere and I haven't finished here yet." Khalid started toward the car.

Ferah had heard that the archeologists who were digging at Sebastiya claimed it was the site of First Temple tombs. What if this was a similar site? What if Khalid had stumbled onto a mass grave of Jewish priests dating back to Solomon's Temple?

They returned to Khalid's home and paid him for the ceramic opium pot and alabaster chalice—two hundred dollars. Ferah knew they would fetch five times that amount at a Christies' auction.

This was an important find, one the archeologists would want to know about so they could organize an official dig to categorize the finds. Again, she was at an impasse. If she reported the location to the Antiquities Association of Israel, she, Moishe, and Khalid could all be arrested.

She knew, according to the law, she was a criminal. No antiquities could be taken from the Green Line of the West Bank into Israel. She faced fines and prison time every time she brought something back.

Many sleepless nights were spent with Moishe deliberating this dilemma. "You walk a fine line between the Jewish history artifacts and the Palestinians for the Protection of Temple Mount," he had said many times. "Even if you see both sides, they hate each other and neither side will give an inch."

"I trust The Fox to know which artifacts are authentic and which are fake. And my contacts can help The Fox cut down on the illegal trade."

She was willing to risk arrest due to her growing knowledge that Khalid's new site meant something of greater importance than the artifacts themselves. A gravesite of priests from the Age of Solomon was a momentous discovery. There could be more bones and artifacts at deeper depths than Khalid's excavations. As she considered her current plight, Ferah realized she was faced with a dilemma.

There was something she feared more than arrest that she would never tell Khalid. When the Israelis gave back Sinai, the AAI also returned to Egypt everything excavated there. Even at the time, she thought this was madness on the part of the AAI because it set a precedent, one that could decimate much of Israel's history.

If the time ever came when the Israelis gave back Palestinian territories, based on the Sinai precedent, the AAI would be forced to give back *all* the antiquities found in the West Bank.

This she could never allow.

Chapter 34

Sydney opened her eyes trying to remember what just happened. Silence filled the cave. The computer hummed on the table, the lamps shone on the wall, and her dread of Herod returned.

She rubbed her ankle. It throbbed, but how could it? She hadn't moved from the chair since she was forced to sit. Her eyes settled on the wall, the hieroglyphs stimulating her memory of Karnak, the boys, and the reason for the aching ankle.

A trick of my imagination, she thought, but so real. The language! She had heard the spoken language—more guttural than she would have thought, yet flowing and melodic. And the writing—not grid hieroglyphs at all, but spirals! Totally unknown in all the mysterious and beautiful Egyptian signs and inscriptions.

The boys had given her the key to the wall. This was a spiral Code spelled out in simple glyphs that created a pattern. She began reading out loud as she entered the Code into the computer.

One comes who sprinkles liquid gold across the land
At a time of complete darkness of Ra
Near the road of the king
Where desert flowers bloom in a garden

Not part of the Pyramid Texts, it definitely was a Code. But what did it mean?

Sothis calls forth again the Shemsu Hor
Following beams from the eye of Ra
Across the ancient lake of salt

Awakening nine faces of the stone
Her translation lacked the beauty and symmetry of the Egyptian, but made the point of the original.
Lighting up the Temple of the Code
Double seals protect the lock
And open but to double keys
A portal to the cosmic sea.
That's it, she thought. I've cracked the ancient Code! Now I know how Champollion must have felt! Barely able to contain herself, Sydney inhaled deeply and sat back in her chair. These lines read like an encrypted message. She could not tell Herod about this. She'd have to make up something. Words that resembled the glyphs. And it couldn't be too obvious.

This must be the treasure written about on the other wall. The directions to the Lake of Salt could not be clearer. The Dead Sea existed even in those days. But where at the Dead Sea? The Egyptians considered whatever was down there quite valuable. What could it be? And what was a stone with nine faces?

That part did not sound like the Egyptian religious beliefs of the Pyramid Texts. They were carved on many of the tombs which had a birth-death-resurrection component to them. The God of the Underworld, Osiris, died, was brought back to life by the Goddess, Isis, and lived again to father Horus. This son became the sun god, Horus of the Horizon, always represented as a falcon whose wings surrounded the pharaoh in protection. Thutmose proclaimed himself Horus, a god-Pharaoh.

Herod stepped through the door. "I see there are cartouches on the wall."

"Yes," Sydney said, startled. "The throne name and the common name."

"Whose name?" he asked breathlessly.

"Would you care to guess, or try reading the hieroglyphs yourself?" she asked, and then realized this was not the time to be flippant.

"*Whose name is on the wall?*" His voice reflected the tone of a wolf drooling over its prey.

A chill went up her back. "Thutmose III." She pointed to the first cartouche. "His prenomen, Menkheperra," and pointing to the inner glyphs between the cartouches, "son of Re," and to the second cartouche, "Thutmose."

"What is this?" he asked pointing to the glyphs following the second cartouche.

"Given life eternally."

She watched him as he stared at the glyphs, realizing the significance of the wall, that this was the first time anyone had been in its presence since it was painted. He probably knew how his father felt—a feeling of power which fueled his addiction.

"It is beautiful, isn't it? They speak to us from a great distance. These words were never meant to be seen or read." Except that this wall was meant to be found, and written to be read, she thought, unconsciously rubbing her ankle.

"What else does it say?"

She had rehearsed what and how much to tell him, giving him enough to tweak his curiosity for now, letting him revel in the danger of his possession. "It's a command by the king to leave a list of defeated places in the conquered land itself. The booty of the victory is proclaimed in all the land. We know from the historical records that he conquered Megiddo, but I haven't gotten that far in this text. Later, he may have camped down at Urushalem, another important city for the king to possess—one of the trade routes between

Egypt and Lebanon." And possibly the road of the king, she thought.

He turned to leave. "Continue on. I'll be back later."

She breathed a sigh of relief. No guard stood in the cave. She got up and tried the door. No surprise it was locked. She went back to the computer and wrote down the four stanzas of the Code. Staring at the printed sheet, she realized the intersected lines of objective and effect—the words in her classroom—she had been sent to find the Code. Now what?

She knew Herod would never let her go, or Alexander either. She'd seen too much. And he'd told her too much—personal information—that could be used against him. She had to act fast. Was Alexander being held somewhere on the grounds? Could she find him?

Unplugging the lamp, she lifted the stand, grabbed a small rag the workmen left behind, wrapped it on the top, and headed for the window. Too high to reach without standing on something, she pulled the chair over to it. She smashed the window as noiselessly as possible, hoisted herself up and carefully pulled out the remaining glass.

No one in sight. She wriggled through the small opening, looked around for the dogs, and dropped to the ground.

Chapter 35

The ubiquitous Turkish cigarette hung from Tovar's lips as he stood on the top of Phasael's Tower looking out over the Old City. "Word on the street is that the colored wall is out of Jerusalem. Taken by the same gang who got the Herodian wall."

"What gang is that?" Roland Winkowski asked, leaning forward on the thick embankment that surrounded the fortress, the white gloves protecting his hands.

"Herod's Hoods!" Tovar spat. "The bastard knows exactly where the goods are before they've been found."

"How does he do it? He's not a part of any organized crime group that I know of. He must have other sources."

"Carter thinks there's a mole at the dig and so do I." He stamped out his cigarette and lit another one. Tovar looked down on the tourists walking the ramparts of the Old City. The crenellated walls had the same outline as in Crusader times. Suleiman the Magnificent later added to it and extended the walls around the city, two-and-a-half miles separated by eight gates, of which seven still stood.

Winkowski stepped back and glared at Tovar. "There's only Alexander and Carter, you and me, and the students. Bill brought all of us over. Unless it's Yuval Goldman."

Tovar leaned with his back against the wall, jabbing the cigarette at his colleague. *"You* brought him in. How well do you know him?"

Winkowski slapped his hands together, dust flying off the gloves. "Well enough. It's the eyes and ears all over the Old City I don't trust. Bill gone, Alexander missing, Carter and Sydney—who knows where they are. You and I, we can't do this by ourselves. We need to bring in some fresh blood—trustworthy and honest." He walked to the other side of Tovar, shielding his eyes from the sun with his hat.

"Who? I don't know any available students."

"What about the Palestinian Gypsies?"

Tovar frowned, rubbing the nicotine from his fingers. "Not too many left these days. Most are gone from the city, except a few hundred in East Jerusalem."

"You're a Bedouin, Tovar. You could hire them. They know all the back alleys of the antiquities trade."

"I'm also Jewish. I walk in both worlds, but mainly my own." Tovar spat over the thousand-year-old wall onto the Byzantine city wall below.

"We've *got* to take action and you're our only hope." Winkowski walked to the end of the Tower built by Herod the Great, who named it after his brother, Phasael.

Tovar scowled. "The Gypsies may know the back alleys, but they didn't build them. They're craftsmen and coppersmiths, not the thieves Arabs call them. The Gypsies sing and dance, train their animals for their entertainment, just like gypsies everywhere."

"That may be so, but they're still Gypsies, and they can get access to information you and I can't."

"I won't jeopardize their freedom or anything else for you," Tovar snarled as he walked away, leaving Winkowski alone on the Tower.

Chapter 36

Alexander sat at the long wooden table that took up most of the center of the library. Rainbow colors from the stained glass over the windows painted the Persian carpet under the table various hues. The smell of old books and manuscripts permeated his nostrils. He loved the odor and knew he could spend many hours discovering treasures in every ancient book within the room.

He felt less like a captive than a researcher in this vast repository of precious manuscripts. He had met his true captor when a tall grey-haired man in a black silk dragon robe entered the room and introduced himself as 'the collector." Apologizing for Alexander's inconvenience at being taken in such an indecorous way, it was necessary for the safety of his brother. When he heard the implicit threat, Alexander decided compliance was his best course of action.

The collector wanted his manuscripts numbered and catalogued in a system already programmed on the computer. After demonstrating his specific technique, he left. Alone, Alexander began working his way through the manuscripts, which covered mainly the Middle Ages and Renaissance periods. He marveled at the exquisite illustrations, original texts and maps, and the manner in which they were strewn haphazardly around the table and floor. Although this man took him hostage, the collector seemed refined, a connoisseur of precious things, and could not be evil.

He thought of his wife back in Pennsylvania, and his two young children. Would he ever see them again? Would

Carter figure out how to find him? Carter always displayed resourcefulness, even as a child. He could get in and out of risky situations, enticing every kid in the neighborhood. Their tree house became the base of operations. But many adventures he refused to join—too risky.

Alexander had an innate desire to please his parents, and he became good at it. Mainly because he was a natural scholar. Unlike his brother, who despised studying, Alexander took to books like he took to breathing.

Suddenly, he heard dogs barking outside, people shouting and running. He got up to look out the window. Two Dobermans ran by snarling at something he could not see. A guard ran after them, rifle pointed where the dogs led.

Whatever they were in pursuit of, their prey probably didn't have much of a chance.

Chapter 37

Sydney ran along side the garden shrubs and trees, staying hunched over as she scanned for guards and dogs. The only exit would be through the reception hall, past the armed guard at the front, and trying to evade the dogs. Near impossible, she thought. Then she heard it—shouts and barking from the back garden area. Someone must have discovered her absence.

She hoped the luncheon party had not ended. She might have a chance if she could steal a car. Passing the large Corinthian columns in the peristyle garden, she crouched down behind the dolphin fountain to get her bearings. The area was clear except for the songbirds waiting for a handout.

She dashed into the main hall, slipped into the ornate room where she had drunk the Akko-tea, and bumped into the marble pedestal on which sat the Apollo and Daphne sculpture. It teetered and nearly fell to the parquet floor. She quickly caught it and placed it gingerly back in its place. Her heart thudded loudly, cold moisture settled on her body. Even with rubber-soled shoes she tried to muffle her steps.

She peered around the corner to the front doors. Sounds came from outside, voices laughing, in the throes of farewell. This was her chance.

Turning the large handle of the wooden door, she looked out the slit, and froze. His back to her, the armed guard stood not three steps away. He seemed to watch Lily walking her luncheon guests to their cars which were parked along the winding drive. The perfect hostess, Lily took her time with each lady, fawning solicitously as each headed to her car. Sydney knew she had to get out—steal a car if necessary. She silently closed the door.

"Find her! She's here somewhere," Herod's voice roared.

Sydney crouched behind the Louis XIV silk settee. The large front door swung open as the guard ran in. Then loud footsteps from the opposite direction.

"Not in here, you idiot, out there!" Herod shouted. "Search the grounds in back. Check everything!" He went through the front door.

Sydney peered over the settee and crept to the reception hall. The front door swung wide open. Then her heart sank. The dogs were out front. Herod knelt to fit their leashes.

She tore back to the large antique-filled room and looked around—no windows, no other doors. Two walls were covered with heavy drapes. On a hunch she dashed to the wall facing the drive, pulled back the drape, ripping part of it off the rings. A set of windows! She tried them. Locked. With what looked like specially-keyed locks.

She heard the dogs barking outside and quickly ran out of the room, down the long walkway toward the dining room. The dogs sounded like they were in the reception hall and then the antique room. They would be coming her way next.

She fled in the direction of the dining room. No guard. She quickly opened the door, found the room empty, ran to the end of the long serving table, now clear of silver serving sets, and crouched down. She heard the dogs at the other end of the walkway going in the direction of the gardens, collection buildings and the cave of the colored hieroglyphs.

Panicked, she rose, ran back to the reception hall and out the opened door. She was too scared of the dogs to worry about the guards. One walked the tented rampart, another the fence. Lily escorted her guests to their cars. Some vehicles had already started down the drive.

"Nothing to be concerned about," she said to several flustered guests. "My husband must be testing his alarms again." She glanced nervously over her shoulder, saw Sydney break for the car in front.

One lady hugged Lily and slid into the driver's seat, nodding at her hostess' attempt at strained sociability.

Fueled by adrenalin and fear, Sydney sprang to the lead car and knocked on the window. The startled lady had her hand on the key, ready to start the engine. She lowered the window.

"Can I get a lift?" Sydney practically had the door open before the driver could say a word. "I'd even be glad to drive." She forcefully pushed the woman over to the passenger seat and got behind the wheel, slamming the door.

"What are you doing?" demanded the woman, trying to shove Sydney out of the car and slapping her. "This is my car!"

"Don't worry." Sydney's hands were shaking and sweaty. She wiped them on her pants, flipped the key, put the car in gear, and roughly pressed the woman back into the passenger seat. "You'll get you car back as soon as I'm out of here." She stepped on the gas and looked in the rearview mirror.

Herod and the dogs came running out the entry door. She saw Lily point at the car as it moved away. Herod knelt down, unloosed the leashes and let the dogs go.

The car roared down the winding drive toward the entry gates with the dogs right behind. The other cars had just gotten through and the double irons were closing fast.

Sydney jammed her foot to the floor and raced toward the gates.

Chapter 38

The squeal of tires and roar of the hijacked car brought the guard quickly out of the gate house. He stood in front of the swinging gates with a drawn rifle pointed right at Sydney. She didn't want to, but she would have to run him down. She had to make the double gates before they closed. The woman next to her screamed and slunk down in her seat.

At the last moment the guard fired into the car and jumped out of the way at the same time, rolling to the side. The windshield split in a spider web of cracks as it took the point blank round. Her passenger clutched the seat, eyes wide with fear and screamed that she didn't want to die. The car squeezed through as the gates closed onto the rear fenders, pulling off the bumper.

Sydney made a hard right and raced down the curving hill without the slightest idea of the city's layout. She broke out of prison, that was all she cared about. At least for the moment. She looked over at the woman crouched in the passenger seat, too scared to look at her or say anything.

"Where's the nearest big hotel?" Sydney shouted at her.

The woman had tears in her eyes. "I ... I don't know," she murmured.

"It's all right." Sydney tried to level her voice. "I'm not going to harm you." She knew how the woman felt—desperate, kidnapped, her car stolen, in the hands of a madwoman who might kill her.

She screeched to a stop at a red light and looked around. The city became a stranger. Full of unknown streets, sinister buildings, hostile people looking at her, ready to call the police, or worse, Herod.

The light changed. She glanced up. The sun glistened off a gilded roof. The gold dome. Something familiar she saw from the tented pavilion of Herod's fortress. She headed for it, not knowing why, but he said pilgrims came from around the world. More than a pilgrim, she was an escapee seeking sanctuary.

The car lurched into the driveway of the Baha'i Shrine. She pulled into a parking spot and slid to a stop. Her passenger bounced into the dash and back to the seat.

"Do you have a cell phone?" Sydney asked, quickly scanning the grounds.

The woman looked at her blankly.

"I really need a phone," Sydney tried to calm her voice. "Do you have one?"

The woman nodded, then shook her head, obviously trying to give her captor the right answer. Sydney saw something out of the corner of her eye, and looked out the back window.

A silver Porsche pulled into the drive.

Not believing her eyes, she saw Marco at the wheel. She had to get away, and fast. "You'll be all right." She patted the woman's shoulder and exited the car.

Running past the beautifully manicured gardens and landscaped terraces into the shrine, she quickly looked around for someplace to hide. Rich Oriental carpets muffled the sounds of voices inside the European architectural marvel of Italian-cut stone. The dome rose 128 feet and was the burial place of the Baha'u'llah, founder of the faith.

Marco had parked his car and ran after her. She slipped into one of the groups of tourists who followed their tour guide and looked up at the dome. The guide led them across the plush carpets to the filigree veil that divided visitors from the inner shrine.

Marco walked around the perimeter of the shrine, eyeing each cluster of people. Sydney sidled into the center of the group of middle-aged tourists and hunched down. The tour guide led them out another door. They walked through more lush gardens of colorful flowers, pink and grey stone staircases, carved urns overflowing with red geraniums, emerald green grass, tall trees, down the circular terraces to the bottom of the gardens ending at the German Colony.

Sydney's desperation overcame her fear of ensnarement, as she glanced through her human shields to see Marco dashing from one group to another.

A tour bus sat at the curb of a street lined with three-story stone houses and red-tiled roofs. German names were carved into some of the lintels. The tourists read the street names and restaurants as they boarded the bus, Sydney still in their midst. She did not see Marco anywhere and hoped he was still in the dome.

The tourists noticed this strange new member and when they spoke to her, she was sure they were telling her in German to get off the bus. She nodded and quickly made her way to the back seat. The door closed and the bus drove off.

Chapter 39

"I heard from Sydney! And she's okay." As he drove north toward the Sea of Galilee, Carter dialed Yuval Goldman in his office at Police Intelligence. Carter heard the squeak of a chair that made him think Yuval sat up quickly.

"What? How do you know?"

"Sydney just called. She escaped from Herod's estate in Haifa and found a tour bus going to Yardenet. I'm on my way there now." Carter heard another squeak. Yuval must have leaned back in his chair.

"That's great news," Yuval said. "She took a big chance. They could have killed her."

"She said they followed the bus." He breezed past slow-moving cars, marveling at the green Jordan River Valley set against a cerulean sky.

"Haifa," Yuval mused. "She may be able to lead us to his place. This could be the break we need. It's the same gang that's behind the Herodian palace theft."

"How do you know?"

"Just got the lab report on the tire tracks. They match. When you pick her up, she can tell us where the estate is located. Did she see Alexander?"

"No, but he's probably being held there. I've got to make sure she's safe, and then she can tell us where Alexander is being held." He swerved to avoid a slow-moving car along Highway 90 and shouted a rude remark to the driver.

"You're probably breaking speed records to get up there, but be careful."

"It's a straight run, shouldn't be a problem." Carter passed more cars, grateful for the clear day. "Anything new on Bill?"

"We're on it, but with no leads, there's not much to go on. There was something in his computer about the Waqf, the Supreme Muslim Authority on the Temple Mount."

"I saw it too. He mentioned to us he thought they were carting off more than their official line. That's what the rabbi said when you took us to see him," Carter said.

"Yes, our contact is the same—The Fox. We know what they're doing on the Mount, but our hands are tied to stop them."

Carter heard Yuval shuffling papers. "Is this Fox part of your Intelligence Division?"

"Can't say. But The Fox can get into places I can't. That's the value of working with someone whose contacts are not the usual ones. Gotta go."

"Wait! Sydney said she thought someone was tailing the bus. Can you send a car up to help out, just in case?"

"No can do. You can pick her up yourself."

"They're dangerous! I don't want to take any chances on her getting grabbed again," Carter pled.

"Sorry. Handle it yourself," Yuval said and hung up.

Carter clicked off in frustration. His guilt over Sydney's kidnapping hadn't lessened in the least. Even hearing her voice and knowing she was alive only increased his guilt that he left her in harm's way.

He recalled their time in the Yucatan. It was not the best place to fall in love, but somehow they had. He knew at all times where she was, what she was doing, and tried to be near her. Unfortunately, Bill made Alexander his assistant, and big brother kept everyone on task. Measuring out each grid and meticulously sifting dirt, brushing and scraping became tedious and boring unless he was near her. They would simply gaze at each other and the dirt was transformed into sparkling diamonds reflected in the other's eyes.

He was glad Alexander was kept busy with many of the tasks that inevitably came up during a dig: mediating disputes about who did what and where they would do it, solving personal and academic problems, and assuaging the heightened sensitivities of students working together twenty-four hours a day in jungle heat with minimum provisions. The following year, Alexander married one of the students on the dig.

He and Sydney became inseparable when they returned for the winter semester. But when they talked about marriage, he knew he went hot and cold—wanting her, but not ready for the responsibility of a long-term commitment. *Am I ready now?*

Seeing her again fired his heart. Still sexy and magnetic. *But is she ready for me?*

Chapter 40

She did it! Sydney had escaped Herod's ostentatious prison with her life *and* the Code intact. Translating it was easy. Decoding the verses would take longer.

She looked out the window of the bus and thought of Alexander, still being held prisoner. If she hadn't taken a chance and escaped, if she had stayed to translate the whole wall, she might have been able to find him, *if* he were being held somewhere on the grounds. Her concern took a new turn. What if Herod took out his rage on Alexander?

Maybe she should have stayed and translated the whole wall, while trying to locate Alexander. She sank back in the seat, overcome with guilt and fear at what Herod would do next.

The bus rolled east along the slopes that skirted the Jezreel Plain that stretched for one hundred miles, the pivotal valley in Christian prophecy which stated the armies of nations would gather for the next world war: Armageddon.

She knew the ruins of Megiddo, the plateau overlooking the Plain, was the ancient city conquered by the Egyptian king, Thutmose III, one of his strategic positions on the main branch of the international trade highway. Dated to over ten thousand years ago, Megiddo was found to have twenty layers of occupation. It would be a very interesting place to visit again, she thought, in light of the translations coming off the wall. But only after this nightmare was over.

Whizzing by all the biblical landmarks reminded Sydney of the vast history within this small country. One professor in her undergraduate days told the class, "Plant a spade anywhere in Israel and you're sure to find something old."

She dug in her shirt pocket and unfolded the sheet that held the Code. Some of the verses were so obscure as to cause her doubt that she could decode them. Or that she had even translated them correctly. She believed these glyphs told of an initiation ritual that connected the ancestral world of heaven with the physical world of earth within each initiate. That the living united the spiritual and the physical within oneself, a shamanic process which brought about the enfoldment of full creative powers.

While she wrote her book on the Pyramid Texts, she had to continually move beyond the stilted, rigid, belief system of mainstream archeology. No Egyptologist dared consider the possibility of a mystical aspect to Egyptian religion, or the importance placed on astrology.

Archeologists tended to project their modern patriarchal religious beliefs onto the ancient writings, severely minimizing the true nature of Egyptian wisdom. Their interpretations limited their findings and compromised the value of what could be learned about the Egyptians.

Through the window she saw the marker that identified the wedding festival where Jesus turned water into wine. Gnostic knowledge of his life told of his experiences in Egypt and Tibet, where he studied the ancient wisdom for many years, until the time he was ready for initiation into the Mysteries.

Learning the secrets of nature and the wise use of the power that came with that knowledge enabled an initiate to manipulate the molecular structure of solids and liquids. Changing water in an instant to ice, or steam, or wine could be performed easily. Or calming a storm on a turbulent sea, healing the sick, or even walking on water. All shaman-priests knew the secrets of controlling nature.

They came to the crossing of the Golani Junction, an important site in the Jewish War of Independence. The monument marking this event was dwarfed by the yellow arches of a McDonald's.

The Pyramid Texts told marvelous tales of the soul's travel into the skies where it communed with the gods and received inner illumination. The similarities with shamanic journeys of Native Americans, Eskimos, Indians and other cultures pointed to a universal state of mystical experience undertaken by the shaman, philosopher, mystic and initiate. Her book presented the case that these travels were taken not by the dead, but by the living.

This is how I must approach the Code, she thought. Not with my current thought processes, or any religious beliefs, or with my colleagues' narrow views of ancient Egypt. Rather, from the perspective of a shaman. *I must think like an Egyptian.*

Glancing out the rear window, she noticed several cars. None tried to pass the bus. Were they being cautious? Or were they Herod's men? She sat back down, wiping her forehead. She peered out again.

Then she saw it and froze—Marco's silver Porsche Boxter.

Chapter 41

Victoria Lucelli sat at her desk monitoring the AAI website on her computer. It made no mention of the latest looting of the Egyptian colored wall. She had heard about the theft not long after it was stolen, presumably by the same gang that made off with the Herodian wall in the palace. News traveled fast in the Old City, especially news about ancient artifacts lost to archeological study. She gazed at her friends.

Ferah sat by a window looking out over the school. Earlier, when she picked up Zaki at the museum, he showed her the two objects he was given on his excursion to the Temple Mount. She had Moishe come for her son, while she called Victoria and Rabbi Benjamin Sternberg. Ferah had expressed growing excitement at Khalid's discoveries, and now tangible proof of the Palestinians digging at the Dome of the Rock. She unwrapped the four antiquities and placed them on the desk.

Benjamin held the alabaster chalice up to the window. The light shone through the cup, revealing thin strands of dark red woven through cream colored stone. He turned it over in his hands, gently touching the stone with his fingers. "How delicate it is, and how thinly made. Only about six inches, I'd say. Probably a religious object, but for what?"

"Maybe a container for precious oils or unguents, or wine," Victoria said, picking up the ceramic pot.

"Yes, possibly. It must have been made in Egypt. I've never seen the dark red strands in any alabaster piece. The carvings of the little birds are exquisite." He held it up to the light again.

"As is this little ceramic opium pot," Victoria said, answering a knock at the door.

"Khalid mentioned he's found many of those." Ferah folded the newspapers the antiquities were wrapped in and stacked them on the floor.

"Did he say where?" Victoria asked, motioning her assistant into the room.

Victoria smiled at her aide who handed her a letter. She signed the sheet, and returned it to her assistant, who left the room.

"Not exactly." Ferah said after the door closed. "This one was found at the spot south of Sebastiya where he took us."

The rabbi set the alabaster chalice on the desk and picked up the opium pot. "When I see a beautiful historical piece like this, I *know* we're on the right track. These two pieces could be out of the country by now, if Ferah hadn't gone out to Khalid's."

Ferah nodded. "If we don't somehow get to that spot near Nablus, Khalid will and the tombs will be vandalized in no time. He may have an idea about the rest of the contents, based on these two pieces, but I don't think he's aware the site might be tombs of priests from the time of King Solomon."

"Are you so sure it *is* the gravesite of the priests, and that he doesn't suspect?" Victoria asked, glancing at the door.

"I'm sure that Khalid will keep digging there because he knows he's on to something. He can smell a site a mile off. When he finds more bones, he's going to suspect it might be a mass grave of Jewish priests. If we don't get out there soon, these antiquities will be lost. We have to turn it over to The Fox."

"Too dangerous. You don't even know the right spot," Benjamin fondled the chalice. "Besides, if The Fox's men went anywhere near the area, they'd be recognized as outsiders by Khalid or other tomb robbers."

Victoria sighed and leaned back in her swivel chair, staring across her desk to the display cabinet on the other side of her office. Behind the glass sat many objects from the Holy Land she had collected over her ten years in Jerusalem. A history teacher by interest and ancient religions scholar in her spare time, she took a year's sabbatical from her American school and never went back.

Dr. William Jarvis came to Jerusalem once a year on his archeological excavations and Victoria became his most enthusiastic student. He introduced her to a Catholic teacher named Robert Lucelli, who she married two months later. They became ardent protectors of biblical remains and artifacts.

Her most prized possession was a tall red ceramic storage pot with two handles and thin-necked top that was probably used for wine. It was given to her by a very grateful parent whose son had finally learned to read at the late age of eight years, due to Victoria's diligent efforts at keeping an attention deficit child focused on tasks that improved his self-esteem as well as his reading ability.

Victoria leaned forward to pick up the oil jar. "Hmm...nothing out of the ordinary. These show up all over Jerusalem. They were used by the Canaanites and the Hebrews. Now this," she said, picking up the figurine, "is quite extraordinary." She turned it over. "Carved from grey granite, finely executed." Her fingers glazed the surface.

"Beautiful face, slightly extended belly. Would be considered a cult figure in any museum."

She touched the outstretched arms. "Look how the hands are facing out. Reminds me of female Hindu deities who extend blessings in this same pose. And statues of the Virgin Mary are also posed in the same way, in answer to prayers for abundance, good crops, and fertility."

"Could it be a Hebrew figurine?" asked Benjamin.

Victoria placed the statue on her desk, tilting her head to consider it. "Well, the Hebrews came into the promised land with Egyptian religious objects, many of them female deities. They eventually got rid of them as too offensive to their male god. But women being women, many kept small female figurines in their homes, sometimes surreptitiously. This could have been one of them."

Ferah rose, her fists clenched. "I *knew* they were digging up artifacts at the Temple Mount. Zaki said the workman had a whole *basketful* of objects. They must have quite a lot if they can afford to give two of them to a schoolboy."

Benjamin placed his hands on his cane, and rested his chin on his hands. "The Antiquities Association of Israel has tried to get the government to stop the bulldozing, but politics being what they are, nothing's been done. The politicians won't interfere with the Muslim religious sites. And the government lets them dump in the Kidron Valley, which is blocking off the stream, causing that bulge in the southern wall of the Temple Mount."

Victoria rose and walked around her office, turning to Ferah. "Did you tell the Waqf your group knows about them mixing garbage with the rubble from the digging to disguise what they take out and then load into the trucks and dumping it?"

"They know. And they won't let us inspect the dirt they're hauling out." Ferah paced between the windows and the door. "I think it's time for the Palestinians for the Protection of Temple Mount to take action," she grinned. "The Muslim clerics in the Waqf, the Supreme Muslim Council, must be in shock with all these goddess figurines popping up."

Victoria nodded. "The legends may be telling the truth—the Cave of the Matriarchs is *under* the Temple Mount."

Chapter 42

Speedboats dashed across the surface of the Sea of Galilee as the bus entered the popular resort town of Tiberias. Ferries carried tourists to the other side for a visit to the kibbutz renowned for its fish restaurants and good beaches. The sun sparkled on the water and tourists took advantage of the beautiful day.

Sydney knew they would be turning south. She glanced out the back window. Two cars were right behind them—the silver Porsche and a white Saab. She was trapped again, as surely as she had been in the truck, handcuffed. What could she do? Get off the bus and make a run for it, or stay on the bus and keep in the midst of tourists? The bus was best. She tried to stay calm, and started breathing again. *Carter, please be there.*

In an attempt to calm herself, she recalled some tourist facts about this area. The Sea of Galilee was not a sea at all, but a fresh water lake that was below sea level and the main source of water for the country. Was it the lake mentioned in the Code? Another possibility. It was larger when Thutmose was in the area, and not that far from Megiddo. He could have built a temple on one of the hills overlooking the lake.

This area was rich in bible lore. The disciples who were fishermen cast out their nets in this lake, abundant with fish in those days. Several important sites overlooked the lake where Jesus did much of his preaching, including multiplication of loaves and fishes, and the Sermon on the Mount. The site where he was baptized by John was not far from the lake.

The sound of German chatter filled the bus, escalating as they neared their next stop, Yardenet. Sydney was grateful to one of the women who let her use her cell phone. She got through to Carter that she was all right and to pick her up as quickly as he could. She knew Herod would have his herds of thieves, spies, and kidnappers out. Being with this group of German tourists was her best cover.

They reached the southern end of the lake which emptied into the Jordan River. The bus pulled along a picturesque stretch. The tour guide was at the front of the bus. He picked up the microphone. "There were so many Christian pilgrims who wanted to be baptized in the place thought to be where John baptized Jesus that the Kinneret kibbutz built this area they called Yardenet," he said in German, then English.

It was a beautiful location with huge eucalyptus trees drooping on both sides of the quiet water. A large stone terraced sitting area with a flat plaza was on one side for gathering before and after the baptism. Adjacent to the dressing rooms were the gift shop and cafeteria.

One last glance. The silver Porsche. No sign of the white Saab.

Sydney quickly got off the bus, staying close to a cluster of women who walked toward the dressing room near the water. They laughed as she hurriedly took a white robe from the reception desk, the American anxious to be baptized. She threw the robe on over her clothes, covering her head. As they emerged from the dressing room, she saw Marco, followed by a guard, running toward them.

The line of women, with Sydney hunched down among them, walked toward the Jordan River. It was a peaceful area, with the water gently rolling into the baptism site. Two Greek Orthodox priests in embroidered vestments, gold-trimmed white robes, and large ceremonial head gear, were performing their sacred duties, purifying each person by leaning them backwards into the water.

Sydney was in the middle of the group that began their descent of the steps. Marco ran after them, rudely grabbing each woman to face him.

"What are you doing?" asked one of the women, as she jerked her arm away from him.

"Sorry," he mumbled, reaching for the next woman's arm.

Sydney covered her face and looked back at the commotion. She was nearly to the priest and kept her head down.

"Let go of me," yelled one woman.

Sydney gripped the railing as she walked down the slick stone steps to the river, the robe billowing around her in the waist-high water. She was ready to bolt out of the water if he got any closer, but saw him slip on the stairs and fall. He held onto the railing and stepped down, only to fall again. He grabbed onto the robe of the woman ahead, who turned at this effrontery and forcefully pushed him away. He fell into the water.

Sydney reached the priests who told her to plug her nose with one hand and hold onto her wrist with the other. They baptized her, as one priest said, "In the name of the Father, Son and Holy Spirit. Your sins are washed away." Then she was dunked backwards into the water.

As they brought her up, she gasped for breath. Both priests officiously steadied her and, with a dignified look sent her on her way. Peeking through the wet strands of hair that covered her face, she held onto the railing and climbed the steps behind them toward the terrace.

She turned to see Marco emerge from the water holding onto a large woman who was grasping the rail and hitting him in the head. Another woman joined in the pummeling, while the others walked around him.

Sydney reached the terrace and turned to see Marco being dragged by the priests off the woman. He was gasping for breath, shouting at the women, and struggling with the priests. Trying to calm what they thought was a fear of purification, they told him he was about to participate in a holy rite. That he would be sanctified as a follower of the Lord.

One priest told him to hold his nose, which he refused to do. As they tipped him over backwards, the priest held his nose, Marco shoving it away as his face went underwater. Suddenly there was kicking and thrashing, a churning of white water. The priests seemed startled by this supplicant who grabbed onto their arms, knocking them off balance. They toppled into the water.

Three purified participants in the sacred rite of baptism splashed and struggled against each other trying to come up for air. In their panic, they grabbed onto one another, unable to get their footing on the slick river bottom, falling back into the water.

The men in line dashed in to help. Caught in their wet gowns, they toppled over, knocked off balance by the struggling priests. The holy ritual turned into a splashing, yelling mass of men in billowing white robes all trying not to drown in the shallow water. As soon as one got his footing he was dragged down by another who grabbed him for balance.

The priests were holding onto each other and the railing, with others grabbing their white vestments, rising slowly out of the water. The high holy hats were rescued, the water poured out, and the priests duly doffed their head gear, trying to assume a state of pious devotion to their task.

Sydney walked through the terrace where the women sat in their newly purified states watching the solemn sacrament in horror and amusement. She turned toward the parking lot and saw Carter running toward her.

She lifted the wet robe and ran to him. "Oh, Carter, I'm so glad to see you. Let's get out of here!"

He put his arm around her, quickly walking to his car. She glanced back to see the priests struggle to their feet, trying to regain their composure and continue their religious duties. The men steadied each other as they slid back in line and the ceremony concluded without further incident.

Marco's head emerged from the water at the foot of the stairs. He slowly crawled up the steps, tried to stand up and grasp the railing, watching them run to the parking lot

After they got into the car, Carter raced out of Yardenet onto the 90 South. Sydney settled into her seat, soaking wet, but free of Herod and his son. She hoped her captor was dunked into a new awareness of compassion, but doubted it.

Some baptisms just don't take.

Chapter 43

Ferah emerged from her meeting with the Palestinians for the Preservation of Temple Mount with a scowl on her face and a pain in her heart. She read the plaque that marked the spot of Station III. Beyond that was Station IV, and on the next corner Station V. The meeting had been held in the back of a souvenir shop in the Muslim Quarter on busy El-Wad Road, one of the Old City's most important streets.

The Damascus gate led to the street where the Stations of the Cross were located and onto the ascent to the Place of the Cross so revered by Christians. El-Wad Road then continued on to the Western Wall.

Most of the members had not agreed with her assessment of the excavations going on at the Dome of the Rock Mosque by the Waqf-supported diggers. The few who did agree with her could not decide how to stop the digging and suspected looting, or even how to approach the Waqf, The Supreme Muslim Religious Council.

An elderly lady wearing a green and yellow headscarf that matched her skirt sat at the other end of the table from Ferah. "They were put in control of the entire Temple Mount compound to maintain the grounds. How can we affect anything that goes on up there?"

"We've got to *try* to talk to them," Ferah said, exasperated at the timidity of her fellow members. "They may be in control, but as interested Palestinians, we can at least meet with the Waqf leaders to tell them our concerns. Most importantly, the bulldozers and trucks up there are causing vibrations in the substructure that have weakened the eastern wall. A large bulge has formed now in the southern wall, along with more cracks. That could cause a collapse and bring on a domino effect on the rest of the platform."

A young man in his early thirties shifted impatiently in his seat. "They know about the bulge, and about the vibrations. They just deny the work is causing any damage."

"And their denial is putting the whole Temple Mount at risk for crumbling walls and weakened platform," Ferah said heatedly. "Another earthquake like the one we had a couple of years ago, along with all the rain, and there could be a major problem."

"I agree with Ferah." A middle-aged man in a business suit looked up from his notebook computer. "Just because they're the Supreme Muslim Religious Council, they think they can tell the rest of us how to manage the most sacred spot in all Jerusalem. Everyone knows they've been involved in unsupervised, illegal digging the past several years."

Finally, Ferah thought. Another voice of reason besides my own. She stood in front of the ten seated members. "The Waqf's only interest is keeping the Israelis off the Temple Mount and away from anything they find near the Rock so they can erase any trace of a historical Jewish presence there. Those large stones they trucked out from the dig had carvings that were clear enough to date them to the Second Temple built by Herod the Great. Those stones are probably out of Israel by now, sold to the highest bidder."

"What do you mean, 'sold to the highest bidder?'" a member asked.

Ferah reached down to her tote. "The Israelis have their own committee for preserving antiquities on Temple Mount. They know what's going on and they said not only is the Waqf digging up artifacts from Solomon's Temple, they are putting the objects onto the international antiquities market, which we all know is illegal."

"Can they prove it?" a member asked.

Ferah placed her tote on the table, reached in and lifted two wrapped objects.

"*We* can prove it." She unwrapped the two pieces Zaki had been given and held them up dramatically. "These two artifacts were given to my son by the dig supervisor today."

The members leaned forward.

"Remarkable," said the lady in the head-scarf. "Could be Canaanite."

"Exactly," Ferah said, handing the oil lamp to the young man. "There are photographs of the large carved stones, and aerial photos of the pit they've dug. The archeologists know they mix garbage with the dug-out material loaded onto the trucks to make it more difficult to sort through in the Kidron Valley."

A young woman with long dark hair wearing tight white pants and a black sequined t-shirt, held the figurine. "The Waqf's goal is to make the Temple Mount a Muslim holy site so that non-Muslims can't enter at all. As appealing as it might sound, it wouldn't be realistic to keep the Jews and Christians off it, considering they both have history there."

Ferah pulled herself up to her full height, feeling emboldened by these few positive responses, ignoring the others. "At any time, if the Antiquities Association of Israel convinces the government the Waqf is doing this, the Israelis can come in and claim the whole Temple Mount as an ancient site and bring in the archeologists to start a supervised excavation under the Dome of the Rock. And the Waqf couldn't do a thing about it. But others could, and they wouldn't hesitate starting a bloody battle over it. We've got to go talk to them."

The businessman said, "I'll go with you. Anyone else want to go with us?"

"I'll go too," the young woman said.

"All right. We'll meet at the Waqf office tomorrow at noon." Ferah was less than hopeful of the results. But stranger things had happened in this land of religious zealots.

Chapter 44

Drooped in the passenger seat, Sydney attempted to lift the wet robe over her head. "It was the worst day I ever had." She pulled the robe up to her thighs, shifting to get it past her hips, up to her arms. "If it hadn't been for the luncheon party, I would never have gotten out of there. I was so desperate I actually wrecked that woman's car!"

Carter reached over to help pull the robe to her shoulders, keeping one hand on the wheel, glancing between her and the road. "You're okay now. That's all that matters. You did what you had to do to escape." He breathed a big sigh.

The robe came over her head in a soppy mess. She squeezed it onto the floor, which pooled at her feet, and tried to dry her hair with it, which, by a quick glance in the mirror on the reverse side of the visor, made it worse. Her hair dripped down her blouse and her clothes were soaked.

"I feel like a drowned cat. Look like one too." She threw the robe onto the back seat. Carter kept looking in the rearview mirror. "He has a silver Porsche?"

"Yes," she said anxiously. "Do you see it?"

He shook his head. "We had a big head start, and he looked pretty bad, trying to climb up those wet steps."

Sydney told Carter her harrowing night ride with the thieves and the horrific meeting with Herod, his wife and son.

"He almost got to me. If those women hadn't been so assertive, I wouldn't have gotten out of there." She smiled at the thought of Marco dunked by the priests. "He sure made a shambles of their baptism ceremony."

"Why don't you take off those wet clothes? There's a blanket in the back."

Considering what she had been through since the horrendous experience last night, escaping death, prison, and now capture, wet clothing seemed a minor inconvenience. But they were a major discomfort. As she twisted around to reach in the back seat, the wet garb stuck to her skin.

"I'll wait till we get back to the city," she decided, retrieving the blanket and draping it around her shoulders. "Any news on Alexander? I felt terrible leaving him there, but I had no choice."

"You didn't see him at all?"

"I saw a lot of Herod's estate. It's huge, right on the slopes of Mt. Carmel overlooking the Mediterranean. And the art! Rembrandts, Monets. And artifacts! You wouldn't believe what he has. The mummy of Rameses II. The gold funerary mask, similar to the one in Cairo."

Carter gaped at her. "Are you sure?"

"I'd know his mummy anywhere. And the Rosetta Stone!"

"It's in the British Museum."

"He has the *original*. I'll tell you the whole story later." She reached in her pocket and held up a piece of soppy paper. "Here's the good news—I translated the Code!"

"You got it? That's great!"

She shifted in her seat where a puddle had formed. "I had to speed-think a translation for Herod. I think he bought it."

"Anything about a treasure?"

"Hard to say. I've never seen anything like it in all the hieroglyphs I've studied. It refers to the Pyramid Texts, but it doesn't *sound* like any of the Texts I know. In fact, it doesn't even seem Egyptian!"

Carter looked at her. "It's in hieroglyphs on an Egyptian wall and it's not Egyptian?"

"I know it sounds crazy, but it didn't *look* Egyptian either." She remembered the strange sensation of sitting before the wall, unable to translate any of it due to the way the hieroglyphs seemed to face in all directions. Just when she determined these glyphs were untranslatable, she suddenly knew how to read them. She had spaced out, or something. Was it another one of her weird experiences—the classroom voice and the statue in Jess's office?

Carter swerved to avoid hitting a truck. "What did it look like?"

Sydney gazed at the turnoff to the Jordan River border checkpoint into Jordan, trying to call up the spaced-out experience, but could only recall the three glyphs for NSL, then absently rubbed her ankle.

"The hieroglyphs were in a *spiral*, something I've never seen before, or heard of."

Carter slowed at the intersection of high traffic. "Neither have I."

She noticed a skeptical tone in his voice. "I know it sounds crazy, but once I figured out what it was, I was able to translate it. Now comes the deciphering."

"Well, what does it sound like?"

"Like a cryptic poem, so far. We know the Pyramid Texts predated the time of Khufu. He only copied the old texts." She shifted her feet away from the floor puddle. "What I find very interesting is that no Egyptologist who ever studied the pyramid has questioned *why* the funeral texts were not on the wall of the King's Chamber in the pyramid. Since they all consider it Khufu's tomb. But it was never built to be a tomb."

"You make a good case in your book about that, but you'll never convince mainstream archeologists."

"I don't care if they're convinced or not. They would probably discount these spiral glyphs too. Most Egyptologists can't fathom history going back more than six thousand years. It disrupts their belief system about archeology too much and they'd have to change the way they look at ancient civilizations. They'd actually have to face the truth about some of their finds and how old they really are. The whole Judeo-Christian religious belief system would have to be revised," she said heatedly.

Carter winced. Being a mainstream archeologist, she knew he sat square in the middle of Sydney and his colleagues.

"I'm beginning to think you're right about the age of some of the artifacts we've found. When the carbon dating on one of our finds came back at over eight thousand years," he said, "Bill Jarvis declared it a mistake, and changed the dating to four thousand."

"Bill had a tendency to ignore what didn't fit into his scientific information base. That was one area where we always disagreed." She paused. "And why he wouldn't write a forward to my book."

"He *was* pigheaded about certain things, but I don't want to talk against him now that he's gone."

"I miss him already, and wish he were here to help me with this. We've got something that fairly screams its age as much more than six thousand years. He wouldn't have liked that." She turned and glanced out the back window to assure herself they were not being followed. "There's more on the wall that I didn't finish, but I couldn't stick around Herod's place. What a choice—the discovery of a lifetime or my life."

He reached over and took her hand. "There *is* no choice—your life is more important than anything. You can finish the translations anytime. They're on my laptop!"

"You photographed them? But when?" Elated that she had another crack at them, maybe more spiral glyphs would show up.

"Right after Levin hacked through the floor."

"Good thinking. Now I can see if there's more to the Code, or if I missed anything."

"Inshallah!" Carter smiled at her. "It's what the Arabs say for every situation, no matter how big or insignificant. 'God willing.'"

"God has nothing to do with it. I've always put my faith in this little guy." She reached in her pocket and pulled out her medal. "Dad gave it to me years ago. Even though I don't believe in holy objects, he said it still might be good to have, just in case" She began to wonder about this, based on her recent experiences.

He looked at it. "St. Jude ..."

"The patron saint of hopeless causes," she completed the inscription. She didn't mention the other good luck charm she wore around her neck. Ironically, a gift from Bill—the Eye of Horus—a symbol of strength.

"I never knew you carried this."

"I kept touching it all the time I was in the truck with the thieves. I wasn't sure what they were going to do with me, but I kept remembering Dad's words and knew I'd be okay no matter what happened." She had tears in her eyes, an enigma to her independent logical self who believed only in scientific means, not religious or spiritual phenomena.

He squeezed her hand. She tucked the medal back in her pocket, laid her head against the seat, and closed her eyes. She felt safe again with Carter by her side and the threat of Herod far away. Was it only a day and a half since she arrived in Tel Aviv? So much had happened. She wanted to go to sleep and slip into oblivion, away from looters, billionaires and kidnappers.

Through a blurry haze she recalled details of research in her book about the Pyramid Texts and ancient Egyptian initiations. Part of the process included encrypted verses that came from the master teachers. Through various trials, the initiate would be required to decode these messages, all of them related in some way to facing one's fears and psychological demons. The method for confronting these unbalanced character traits was encoded within the communication from the teacher. The initiate had to decode the message by using every inner resource—physical, mental, emotional, and spiritual.

Sydney remembered that part of the decoding process happened in a window of time when the initiate could more fully understand the reasons for the unhealthy behavior. What we call *addictions* the Egyptians called *missing the mark*. Decoding their message gave them strength to face the imbalances that kept them in lock-step to their emotional past. They graduated to another level of their training when they could *hit the mark*.

When she wrote this in her book it was purely an intellectual exercise. After all, we know so much more than any other civilization that ever lived. But from the weird experiences of the past few days, she began to question her belief in the infallibility of her superior intellect. Something she had never questioned before. Maybe the true understanding of the ancient ways was not the mind. Rather it was the heart. And this was the reason for initiation. Now it had become very personal.

Is the Code of the King my initiation?

Chapter 45

Carter turned onto Hillel Ben Sira. He made another right into the King David Hotel. "I thought you'd be safer here."

Sydney threw off the blanket and scrambled out of the car. "I don't really care. As long as I'm far from Herod."

They looked around at cars pulling in after them. It didn't appear that anyone had followed them from Yardenet. Carter led her to the entrance.

Sydney caught a glimpse of herself in the glass entrance, and then saw the doorman. He's probably never seen a more bedraggled guest approaching his premier hotel in sopping wet clothes, she thought. Eyes wide, the doorman scanned her and glanced over at the security officer who stood with chin up and arms folded at the other side of the entrance.

She watched the reflection of the officer, who frowned, but did not move. The doorman seemed to quickly appraise the situation. He's probably seen royalty, politicians and rock stars stroll through these doors, she thought, and turned away many gawkers who longed for a glance at one of the hotel guests.

He nodded to Sydney as she swept through the swinging door into the elegant lobby. The pink stone walls, green windows and grandiose display of colonial architecture and wooden furnishings of the impressive 1930s hotel, reflected the splendor of an earlier era. Sydney took it all in as several guests looked up from their newspapers to take her in. She realized she was leaving a wet trail behind her, but kept walking.

They stopped at the reception desk to check in. Then boarded the richly ornamental elevator.

Carter said, "I have a surprise. I didn't want to tell you earlier because you needed the rest, but we were given tickets for the big benefit tonight at the Sheraton ballroom."

"Benefit?"

"To raise money for the Antiquities Association of Israel."

"I'm in no mood for a party. All I want is a hot bath. Besides I have nothing to wear."

"Don't worry about that. I've made arrangements with the manager. He'll have hair and makeup people waiting for you. And gowns. You can pick out what you want." The elevator door opened to their floor. "You deserve a break. You've got the Code and you know where Herod lives. I've already called Yuval Goldman. But he's agreed not to go in until Alexander's safe. So there's nothing else we can do now."

They walked to the room and Carter unlocked the door. As she stepped into the room, Sydney saw a variety of ancient architectural designs and decorative elements including Egyptian, Phoenician and Greek, with some Islamic art added for interest.

Carter took her in his arms. "I'm sorry I left you alone at the wall." He kissed her tenderly. "I'm glad you're back safe and sound."

They sat at the foot of the bed. "It must've been terrifying, Syd. I worried about you. If anything had happened to you, I don't know what I'd have done." He stroked her hair and kissed her on the right eye, then on the left...

"I know. I kept thinking of you and that I might never see you again." She began peeling off the wet clothes. He undressed and lifted her onto the bed.

The breathless kiss she had awaited for a long while brought waves of passion that promised endless delights. Lost like children at play, they reveled in each other, rolling across the bed as if it were an enduring landscape in eternity. For the first time since arriving in Israel, Sydney realized she was giggling...

"Are you laughing at me?" Carter whispered in her ear, his tongue darting in and out.

"No...Yes...Just that it feels so good to be next to you. And remembering how we used to laugh."

"Mmm, yes, we used to do a lot of things."

She rolled him over and lay on top, kissing him on the neck, breathing in his musky scent. She rubbed against him, as his hands squeezed her back, her hips.

Their ripening love carried them into the furthest reaches of intense physical senses until nothing existed but entwined bodies in lustful unity.

Afterwards, they lay in the golden moment of afterglow, the sensual riches surrounding them in sated splendor. "I could stay here forever," he said, wrapping himself around her.

She nestled close to him, feeling safe in his arms, and wanting to feel this way every day. "Me too. Longer than forever. A lifetime." She closed her eyes and made a wish.

In the oversized bathroom with marble counters and brass swan fixtures, Sydney toweled off and watched Carter dry his hair. Draping the towel around his neck, he stroked a finger down her arm and kissed the back of her neck. A cell rang in the other room. He threw the towel in the tub and turned toward the ring.

Locating the phone under his clothes, he answered it. "Okay, be right there." He clicked it off. "Roland wants me to come to the site right away to see something. I'll be back to get dressed for the ball. Will you be all right?"

Sydney hesitated. She had wanted to talk to Carter, ask him about the subtle change she saw, but there was so much happening in such a short span of time no opportunity presented itself. And she definitely did not want to interrupt their lovemaking in any way. He was gentler than she had remembered, and took his time.

Maybe she would tell Jess that Carter was different somehow. Or maybe not. There was no time to analyze it at the moment. If he had changed, she didn't want to risk even drawing his attention to it, or he might revert. Acceptance is sometimes a gift.

She tied her hotel robe as she moved to the window. From the fourth floor she felt relatively safe—no one knew she was there, but the feeling of unease remained. "Go ahead. I'll call down and tell them I'm coming."

After Carter left, she remembered a printout on Bill's desk that would help with the translations. She called Roland to ask if it was still there. He checked the desk and affirmed it was. She asked him to give it to Carter when he arrived.

"I didn't expect him today. I thought he'd be with you all day." Winkowski sounded puzzled.

"Didn't you just call him to come to the site?" The sense of unease suddenly grew.

"No, Sydney, I never called him."

Chapter 46
9:15 PM

Wrapped in the plush white robe with the *King David* logo crest on the pocket, Sydney held the phone while she paced and surveyed the grounds from the balcony. Taxis drove up to the entrance to discharge their passengers. Colored lighting shone on the hotel, lighting up the distinguished exterior façade. It had been more than enough time for Carter to reach the site, but Roland said he never showed up. "Where could he be? He didn't come back here and I've left a message on his cell."

"I'm sure he'll turn up. I called Yuval Goldman, just in case. Got stuck in traffic, maybe."

"Oh, I don't think so," she said impatiently. "What if they kidnapped him?" She felt her heart racing. Butterflies danced in her stomach.

"We don't know that. Yuval's on his way to question the hotel staff. Maybe the doorman saw where he went."

"I already called the reception desk. They saw him leave." She sat on the side of the bed, smoothing out the wrinkled sheet. "I can't just sit around. I've got to do something!"

"You *can* do something. You can go to the benefit," Roland's voice brightened. "There's nothing else we can do. And he might show up."

"I can't go anywhere. You go ahead. I don't feel I could go. I've got to stay here in case Carter calls. Or maybe Herod will call."

"Carter's staying at the Sheraton. His clothes are there so he probably went to his room to change."

She rose from the bed. "He told me he'd be right back, but maybe he did go to the Sheraton."

"I know you don't want to go, but we all have our phones with us in case he calls. Can you be ready in an hour? I'll pick you up."

"I guess so." She called the Sheraton and left a message for his room, then hung up and dialed the hotel manager's office. "I'm going to the charity ball tonight at the Sheraton and need a gown, hair and makeup done in an hour. Can you accommodate me?"

"Of course, Dr. Grace. Come right down."

The Sheraton Ballroom was filled with people seated at round tables of eight. On a stage at the front of the room, the white-jacketed band played a number from the big band era to a crowded dance floor.

Roland, decked out in a tuxedo with a red rose in the lapel, escorted Sydney into the ballroom. "Even though I had to drag you kicking and screaming, you look sensational. That gown was made for you."

His words reassured her. She'd selected the gown from three the ladies had shown her. She liked the way the deep orange umber on the bottom swirled from the floor as it lightened in color to a pale coral at the beaded V-neck top.

While they fitted the dress and assembled matching shoes and evening clutch, the makeup artist went to work and the hairdresser came in. Her hair was arranged in a romantic, elegant upsweep with extensions at the top of the crown. Colored, beaded double combs kept it all in place. The front layers were sideswept across her forehead. They had even found a hiding place in the gown for the disc. She was determined to keep the Code on her at all times.

Unaccustomed to the heels, she held onto Roland for support, adjusted the gown, tucked the clutch under her arm, raised her head and took a deep breath. She scrutinized the ball gowns, cocktail dresses, palazzo and tailored pants, feeling less conspicuous as she merged into the fray.

Roland led Sydney to a table in the back of the room. "Dr. Sydney Grace," Roland said, "may I present Victoria and Robert Lucelli, and Lana Sternberg. You know Rabbi Benjamin Sternberg."

Victoria introduced the other couple, "Ferah and Moishe Berendt, their son, Zaki, and his friend, Ellie Goldman."

Sydney greeted them and sat down. Turning to Ellie, she asked, "Is your father Yuval, the Director of Intelligence?"

"Yes, he is," Ellie beamed proudly, and primped in her lacy pastel dress. Zaki, looking uncomfortable in a dark suit and bright flowered tie, gazed admiringly at Ellie.

Traditional Jewish folk dances and contemporary music filled the room as waiters brought steaming plates of international cuisine to the table, along with bottles of Golen Heights wine. Small talk focused on shashlik and kebab, stuffed vine leaves, pickled vegetables, and a platter of rainbow pasta with marinara sauce. Roland filled her glass with a Chardonnay.

"Have you gotten any word about Alexander?" the rabbi asked.

"No, just that we've been told he's safe for now," Winkowski said.

"Have the police had any luck in finding the kidnappers?" Benjamin continued.

At the last word, the ears of the others seemed to perk up.

Victoria lowered her soup spoon, and pulled back the long sleeves of her sheer silk gown with scooped neckline. "Kidnappers?"

"What kidnappers?" Moishe asked. He wore his ill-fitting black suit and grey striped tie with aplomb.

Sydney looked at Winkowski with raised eyebrows.

"It's all right. They're friends of Bill Jarvis and can be trusted," Winkowski said.

"Alexander was kidnapped at the Siloam Pool site," Sydney said quietly.

"The dig you're at now, Roland?" Victoria's voice rose.

"The same site where the professor was found dead?" Robert asked.

They all looked incredulously at Sydney and Winkowski. "The same site, and the police are still investigating Dr. Jarvis's death," he said.

"Did anyone see anything, or hear anything?" Ferah asked.

"It was late in the evening when everyone was gone. Yuval Goldman," Winkowski glanced at Ellie, "and his deputies have been sifting through the dirt and debris where he fell. It's all very traumatic for the students and for us."

Sydney looked down at the table. "Bill Jarvis was my mentor in grad school, and a dear friend. It's a huge loss. No one could take his place."

Winkowski put his arm around her shoulder. "No, of course not. Not even me."

"Did the kidnappers demand money for his release?" Robert asked.

Sydney gave a brief account of what had happened since she arrived.

"You were kidnapped?" Victoria asked, with a sidelong glance at Ferah.

Sydney hadn't realized the toll these recent ordeals had inflicted on her until she faced the indignant reactions at the table. Struggling with the difficulty in dealing with their curiosity, she looked helplessly at Winkowski.

Right on cue, he took Sydney's hand. "Would you like to dance?" he asked cavalierly.

Relieved, she rose quickly and led him to the floor. "Thanks for rescuing me." I guess he's not so bad, she thought.

He wound an arm around her, moving easily to the music. "They pummeled you with too many questions. You deserve a break."

Sydney appreciated his attempts, especially his smooth dance style that made it easy to follow him. She gazed at the other dancers, enjoying the music, the effects of the wine, and her body in perfect sync with this man she had felt uneasy about. He had a Middle Eastern air about him, with a faint sweet scent of desert spice. His grip was neither too tight nor loose, yet she seemed to float effortlessly with him.

At the next spin, she suddenly twisted her head at what she thought she saw. *Am I hallucinating again?* A spiffed up Marco in a black tuxedo with pink studded shirt and black bow tie! His hair was spiked as usual, with flecks of color at the peaks. She blinked at his blond partner. The student from the dig! The one who flirted unsuccessfully with Carter. What did Carter call her? Gena. Marco dancing with a student from the dig!

Sydney kept turning her head to the unlikely couple as Winkowski led her around the floor. Marco tore his eyes from his beautiful partner and met Sydney's gaze. His expression changed from adoring infatuation to anger. He abruptly stopped and led Gena off the floor.

"Anything wrong?" Winkowski asked.

"That's Gena! One of our students. Dancing with Herod's son."

"Where?" He looked around. "I don't see her."

The band stopped playing and the dancers cleared the floor. They returned to the table. Sydney was grateful she avoided explaining her horrible ordeal at the hands of the looters, and then Herod and his son, deciding not to discuss any more of her terrible nightmare. She looked around but Marco and Gena were gone.

The bandleader introduced the Chair of the Board of Directors of the AAI who strode to the microphone. His portly form fit snugly in his white jacket and black pants. "Your generosity this evening is most appreciated by the Antiquities Association of Israel and the Intelligence Division of the Police Department. Now, I would like to introduce the newest member of the Board of Directors. Mr. and Mrs. Wilhelm Werner are passionate fund raisers for the AAI." He turned and offered his hand. "Mr. Werner."

Sydney sat with her back to the stage, indifferent to the speeches, uncaring of the sympathetic eyes which she noticed occasionally glanced her way, and kept scanning the room hoping to see Carter. She sipped her wine and distractedly sampled the richly varied cuisine. When the waiter cleared the table and set out the dessert platters, she spooned the layered honey-soaked pastry stuffed with ground nuts and fruit onto a plate.

When Mr. Werner began to speak, Sydney alerted on his voice, her head jerked up and she quickly turned to the stage. "Omigod! It can't be!"

The whole table turned to look at her. "What can't be?" Victoria asked.

"It's Herod!"

Chapter 47

Distinguished in his black tux and bowtie with front pleated white shirt and diamond studs, Herod looked every bit the wealthy benefactor who would save the AAI. "The crime of looting is growing faster than any other business in the country," he began. "Our history is being systematically eradicated by well-organized criminals dedicated to the illegal antiquities market. They have flourished over the years in a climate of indifference by the public and complicity by the authorities, the very ones who should protect our most precious artifacts."

Sydney sat with her mouth open at the words coming from the man she knew as Herod. The biggest looter in Israel was talking about the illegal antiquities market, and the need to crack down on artifacts leaving the country!

"This is the guy who kidnapped you?" Robert whispered.

"The one who wanted you to translate the hieroglyphs?" Ferah asked.

"The same," Sydney said through her teeth.

Victoria looked around. "Where's Yuval? He should be here."

"I think I know what to do," Sydney said.

Herod sipped from his wine glass. "The only obstacle to stopping this illegal trade is to believe nothing can be done. Too many people think the poor will always be poor, so they will sell what they dig up to any buyer with money. They believe the rich will always be rich and will buy two thousand, three thousand-year old objects before someone else does."

She couldn't stand it any more. Sydney leaped to her feet and stood facing him. She proclaimed in a loud voice, "Is that what you believe, Herod?"

He lifted his head, eyes searching for the voice. The whole audience turned as one to see who was speaking. "Herod?" "Who's Herod?" "Who is this? Sit down!" echoed across each table and around the ballroom.

When his eyes narrowed on Sydney, he motioned to two men at the side of the stage.

"No, that is not what I believe," he answered calmly.

Her hands balled into fists as she felt a locomotive rumbling through her body. "Then your words ring hollow, *Mr. Werner*. You are no more a protector of antiquities than those poor looters you speak about," she said loudly, wanting the whole room to hear. "Your home is filled with looted antiquities, not only from Israel, but Egypt, Britain, Turkey and Peru."

He took a step back from the podium as if he had been slapped across the face. Sydney saw Lily seated at the dais, next to Marco and Gena. Lily's hands reached her face to muffle a cry. The room erupted in protests aimed at Sydney, from mild protestations that this was an honorable, generous benefactor of the Artifacts Association of Israel to vehement anger that she didn't know what she was talking about and should just sit down and shut up.

Sydney looked around the room and addressed the audience in a loud voice. "I know this for a fact. I've seen his home. I know what he has."

More outbursts from the audience, which was clearly supportive of Mr. Werner and wanted her out of the room.

Sydney saw Tomas and two of the thieves who had stolen the wall making their way through the tables.

Winkowski shouted to everyone at the table, "Come on! We've got to get out of here."

They quickly rose and headed for the doors, which were blocked by the ushers and waiters. Moishe and Robert forcefully pushed them aside and opened the doors, hurrying everyone out through the lobby and to the parking lot. On the way, Benjamin formulated a plan. He instructed Ferah and Moishe to drive off in their Suzuki, while the rest returned to their cars and drove toward the Old City, with Tomas and the others right behind.

Sydney rode with the Benjamin and Lana. Victoria and Robert went in the opposite direction, with the thieves following them. Roland took his own car.

Benjamin entered the Dung Gate into the market area of the Jewish Quarter and parked. They quickly made their way to the family shop, and dashed through the door.

Dim lighting helped to hide the young man sitting behind the cash register tallying a computer-printed sheet. Sydney remembered him from her earlier visit.

"Dad, weren't you going to the benefit?" The young man rose. "Mother ... and Dr. Grace."

"Don't ask questions, Reuben," his father said with a gasp, moving as fast as he could on his cane. "Quickly, we have to get into the tunnel. Where's your brother?"

"In the back. What's going on?"

"We're being followed. We need to get her into some rabbi clothes." They all went through the shop into the back room where they had met with the rabbi yesterday.

"What? I could never pass as a rabbi." She nodded at Joseph, the younger son who served them tea yesterday, who was straightening up the cluttered room.

"It'll work," Lana said, reaching for a black hat. "Here, let's fix your hair so it fits in the hat."

Joseph came to help his father. "Get my coat on the rack," the Rabbi ordered his son. "Here, Sydney, put this on." He handed her the coat.

Lana took it. "She won't fit in this," and grabbed another jacket. Sydney put it on.

Benjamin started shouting orders. "Joseph, get those black pants over there. And take off those heels. Lana, give her your shoes."

Sydney and Lana both shed their shoes, as Sydney pulled on the black jeans, stuffing her ball gown down into the pants, Lana helping adjust the gown in front. She stepped into Lana's flats which were nearly her own size.

"This is never going to work." She looked into a small mirror hanging on the wall. "I don't look anything like a rabbi."

"It's dark and we'll be in a tunnel and you'll be just another holy man at the prayer wall. Get the rug up, Joseph."

They all followed Joseph to the back wall hung with various colored rugs. He moved one aside and Sydney saw a smaller room behind it with a desk and two chairs. Joseph lifted a rug on the floor to reveal a large round ring. He pulled on the ring. It opened onto steps leading down.

Sydney turned to see Victoria and Robert dash into the shop. "Quickly," Lana told them, "sit down and I'll start the kettle. They'll be here any minute."

"Follow me, Sydney," Benjamin said. "You go first, Joseph. You know what to do, Reuben."

They were down the steps in no time and Reuben closed the trap door behind them. Joseph switched on his flashlight. The rabbi gave a light to Sydney and clicked his light on. The tunnel was narrow and dank, just high enough for

Sydney to keep her hat on. It scraped the ceiling on the first curve and she ducked her head to keep it from falling off.

She broke into a cold sweat and told herself not to think about how tight her surroundings were but to keep walking. It didn't work. The python slithered right behind her.

"How far are we going?" she asked anxiously.

"Not far. Just to the Wailing Wall," Benjamin said.

"I thought the Western Wall Tunnel came up at the Via Dolorosa in the Muslim Quarter?"

"It does. This is another one. Part of the tunnel system under the Temple Mount and Old City."

"I've heard there was another tunnel. How did you know it was here?"

"My grandfather used the tunnel to smuggle in food and supplies when the Jordanians held the Old City. Now we use it to check up on the Palestinians at the Temple Mount. There are many tunnels—known only to us."

They walked quickly through the tunnel, for which Sydney was grateful. She felt her neck tighten as the python got closer. She turned around and shone the light behind her. Then quickened her pace.

Suddenly the lights went out in front of her. She switched hers off. "What's the matter?"

"Light up ahead," Joseph said. They stopped walking.

"Oh, no." She felt the python approaching. "Who is it?"

"Can't tell," he whispered.

"Should we go back?"

"No, it's probably nothing. This tunnel hooks up to another tunnel under the Temple Mount that goes to the Western Wall. It can be toured by archeologists and others with permission from the AAI. We block off the tunnel to the shop. That's what Joseph saw—light coming from the slits in the door," Benjamin said casually.

She wasn't reassured. The python was on her ankle before she could try to control it. This was no place to panic. The air was thick with a musty odor which seemed to be carried down through the centuries into a time of repeated conflict in the Old City. Sydney tried to focus on the privilege of walking on an original street possibly walked by Jesus himself on his way to the temple.

"The light's out." Joseph opened the door that barred the tunnel. They turned on the flashlights and walked through the door. Sydney closed it, willing the python to remain behind the door.

It didn't.

"Not far now," Benjamin said.

The air was stale and Sydney wanted out of the tunnel. The python remained behind her but she walked quickly, telling herself she was not afraid, she could handle it, and that they were almost there.

"We're walking on a street built by Herod," Benjamin said. "Not *your* Herod, but Herod the Great over two thousand years ago."

"He's not *my* Herod. He's a thief, liar, and a *damned* hypocrite! Benjamin, you wouldn't *believe* the artifacts I saw in that place. I wish Yuval would arrest him as soon as possible and throw him in prison for the rest of his life."

"You may get your wish."

Before she could respond, Joseph said, "We're here. Wait here while I take a look."

She saw him disappear into the darkness. Joseph came back and motioned them forward. She knew the panic was subsiding as the python dissolved behind her. They squeezed through the wood-slatted barrier and climbed a few of the lower broken cement steps leading to the dimly-lit Western Wall Plaza.

Benjamin motioned her to remain on the first step. Sydney gulped the air as one who comes up from deep water with bursting lungs and takes that first big breath into the mouth. She adjusted her black jacket and tucked the unruly tresses back under her hat, leaning against a modern abutment adjacent to the holy wall.

Benjamin stood several steps in front of her. "I don't think we're offending anyone, Sydney. I'm not Ultra-Orthodox, but I am respectful of our traditions, and this is definitely one of our traditions."

"What? Crawling out of a tunnel?"

"No, saving a life."

"Come on!" Joseph urged. "No time for chit chat. We've got to get to the Dung Gate."

They turned off their lights and climbed the dark upper steps to emerge into the men's side of the Wailing Wall Plaza. A screen running from the wall to the upper plaza separated the men's and women's sides, both sparsely occupied at this hour of the evening.

Sydney kept her head down as they walked through the bowing supplicants and tourists who recited religious verses. Some looked up from their prayer books at what must have looked to them like a clean-shaven young rabbinical student who, thought Sydney, must have been easily recognized for her estrogen-laden presence in their midst.

At the top of the plaza Sydney looked down at the Wailing Wall and wondered why the men's side was twice the size of the women's area. Must be a Jewish thing, she thought, and one of the things that served to keep women from the rabbinate. She adjusted her hat and tried to keep her beaded coral gown hidden under the black jacket.

They wound their way through the small groups gathered on the upper plaza. Young people smiling at each other and sharing a cigarette. Older people on their way home. Tourists, after placing their slips of papers with prayers into any crack they could find, left the wall that was part of the retaining wall of the Temple Mount built by Herod the Great in the first century BC.

At the taxi stand near the gate they saw the black Suzuki Aerio waiting. Sydney recognized Ferah and Moishe through the windshield. Zaki opened the back door and stepped out to help Sydney into the back seat. She waved to Benjamin and Joseph as the car turned and drove out of the Dung Gate.

Sydney sat back in the seat and smiled at Ellie who seemed surprised by her strange garb. She exhaled deeply, relieved to be out of the tunnel, out of the plaza, and away from Herod.

She turned to look out the back window. As the car sped onto Maale Ha-Shalom Road, the familiar sense of dread once again descended on her.

Chapter 48

Victoria and Robert sat at the teak table in the storage room. Lana had brewed herb tea and served it in small porcelain cups with plates of pastries. They heard footsteps charge into the shop and voices shouting.

"Where are they?" A loud voice boomed.

Victoria knew Reuben was alone in the front of the shop, watching over the large selection of Jewish religious articles, fine art, ancient household objects and coins from archeological sites.

She heard him say, "Who?"

The footsteps closed in on the hanging rugs and the one in front of the storage room was rudely jerked aside. The two thieves burst into the room followed by Reuben.

"Where are they?" demanded the leader, a short dark-haired man with unshaven stubble.

Victoria recognized them as Herod's minions who chased them out of the Sheraton. They still wore their black dress suits.

Lana nonchalantly sipped her tea. "Who?"

"You know goddamn well who!" He yelled. "Where is she?"

"I have no idea who you mean," she said, biting into a prune Danish.

"The translator and your husband! Where are they?" he yelled.

"My husband went home. I don't know who or what the translator is," Lana said.

The leader's companion came up to the table. "You better tell him," he said to Robert. "He has a terrible temper."

"This lady invited us back to her shop for some refreshments. We don't know where the others are," Robert said as he set his cup down.

"I warn you," the leader said moving toward the table, pulling his pistol out of his pocket, "you better tell us or we'll tear your shop to pieces. And you." He circled the table, aiming the gun at each of them.

His threatening tone sent a chill up Victoria's spine. "Maybe you should look elsewhere," she said to him evenly. "There's no one here but us."

He hovered over the table. With his gun hand he swept the teapot, cups, and plates off the table. Shattered porcelain scattered everywhere. Victoria and Lana screamed. Robert and Reuben jumped on him before he could raise his gun hand. A scuffle ensued. Reuben stepped back, as the leader's hand rose and Reuben's leg came up, kicking the arm forcefully. The leader screamed in pain, dropping the weapon.

Lana leapt on the back of the other thief. She threw her arm around his neck while Reuben pummeled him and he fell to the floor. Victoria and Robert jumped on the leader. Reuben then took out the second intruder, spinning around with a roundhouse karate kick to the side of his head. The thief fell to the floor.

"Come on!" the leader shouted to his companion. He shoved Victoria back and wrenched free of Robert, running toward the front of the shop.

"Dmitri!" The fallen thief yelled, but he didn't have a chance as the men jumped on him. Robert secured him in a stranglehold while Reuben tied his hands behind his back.

"Everyone okay?" Robert asked, as he rubbed his knuckles.

"Whew!" Victoria said, straightening her evening gown. "They play rough!" She examined her dress for needed repairs.

They stepped over the broken porcelain and picked up the overturned chairs.

Victoria sat down, pushing her hair back from her face. "Lana, you surprised me, jumping on him that way."

"I surprised myself!"

"Mother, are you all right?" Reuben took her hands and sat her down.

"I'm relieved that's over! And very glad all those karate lessons we paid for were put to good use. Did you see him knock that guy out with one kick?" She asked proudly.

"Quite a feat." Robert smiled at Reuben.

"I'll know who to call when I need protection." Victoria said.

"Bruce Lee of the Jewish Quarter! That's what we'll call you now." Lana smiled at her son.

"Well, this Bruce Lee needs to clean up in here and call the police. As of now, this one is out of business. One less looter in the country. Father will be pleased."

Chapter 49

On the ride south Sydney related her harrowing kidnapping and escape from Herod to Ferah and Moishe. She sat with Zaki and Ellie, who huddled together in the back seat. "I know where he lives, so he'll be looking for me again. That, and because I have the Code." She glanced anxiously at the whispering adolescents, who looked up in interest.

Moishe checked his mirror as he drove through waning traffic. "You're safe now. And we haven't been followed. It's okay to talk in front of them—they know not to say anything to anyone, don't you?" He glared at Zaki in the mirror.

"We know," Zaki said, frowning at his father.

"I have to decipher the rest of the translation. There seems to be a time limit encoded in it, which means we've got to find the temple before he does." Sydney thought about the ramifications *after* she figured it all out, and that Herod would not hesitate to kill her and Alexander for the Code.

The church steeples and mosque minarets came into view against the night sky, announcing their arrival in Bethlehem. Sydney looked out at the rolling hillsides, shrouded in darkness and punctuated with a few twinkles of light. According to Christian tradition, shepherds kept watch over their flocks on the night of Jesus' birth.

"Rachel's tomb can no longer be seen as we enter Bethlehem," Ferah pointed in the direction of the site that legend says held the wife of Jacob, who bore two of his twelve sons.

"Wasn't the white dome a landmark in this area?" Sydney asked.

"Yes. The security wall hides the tomb now, but keeps it safe. Pilgrims of all three faiths still come. Some wind a red thread seven times around the tomb while praying for good health and fertility. Then they give away pieces of the thread as talismans to cure ill health and infertility."

Not far from the Old City, the ride to Bethlehem afforded Ferah the opportunity to tell Sydney about The Fox, the savior of ancient Israeli history. The museum heist had been thwarted by the superb efforts of Yuval Goldman and The Fox.

"Maybe we should get The Fox involved in your hieroglyphic wall theft, Sydney. Now that you know where it is," Moishe said.

"Who is this Fox? And where do I find him?"

"You don't," Ferah said. "The Fox finds you."

"I hope The Fox finds me before Herod does." Sydney noted they were on Manger Street, a wide boulevard winding its way into the town. Tourist shops lined the street, displaying various religious objects and finely carved olive wood manger scenes produced by local craftsmen.

"Some Christians still live in Bethlehem, but they're in the minority. This is the central plaza, Manger Square, and over there is the Church of the Nativity," Ferah said. "Since the Palestinians have taken control of the city, they've tried to implement economic plans for growth, which means bringing back the tourists."

"Has it worked?" Sydney leaned into the window.

"Depends on the time of year and whether road security lets them in." Moishe slowed the car as they passed the Biblical site. "Violence breeds violence. We Palestinians are learning to control our own destiny. *If* we want to."

He turned onto a dark, quiet street similar to any middle-class neighborhood in the Midwestern United States. Except one house had a Palestinian flag painted on the side. Another had Arabic writing on it. And another had goats and chickens in the yard.

Moishe slowed and turned into the driveway of a modest whitewashed house, surrounded by a six foot wire fence. Floodlights lit up the front yard, illuminating the shrubs and bushes. Two mongrel dogs barked and ran toward them, jumping on the fence. Moishe pulled the car into the free-standing garage. They exited the car and entered the house via the back door.

Sydney stepped into a large kitchen. Ferah led her to the living room where she turned on the lights. Moishe closed the back door, leaving the barking dogs on the porch. He returned with a large bag of kibble. The barking stopped.

"Please make yourself comfortable, Sydney. I'll make some tea." Ferah took off her jacket and went to the kitchen.

Sydney realized the deception of the external home—inside, the rooms she could see were quite large. The furnishings had colorful Palestinian weavings draped on them, the floors covered with plush rugs. In the corner of the living room sat a Japanese television with DVD. She immediately felt at home.

Sydney sat down on the sofa and took off the shoes Lana had lent her. Laying the hat on the coffee table, she shook out her hair, leaned back on the plush Arabian rug that covered the back of the sofa and exhaled deeply, a sense of safety wafting over her. A picture of Carter floated through her mind. Where could he be? Was he safe?

Moishe sat in the biggest chair in the room. "Our daughter is at a friend's tonight. You know how ten-year-olds are—they love slumber parties."

"They'll probably be up all night." Sydney said distractedly, looking around the room, an amalgam of Jewish and Palestinian objects that represented the Berendt household.

Zaki led Ellie to his sister's room. "You'll sleep in here tonight." The two had been listening intently to the grownups' conversation the whole ride.

Moishe smiled and waved his hand around the room. "We're raising our children to understand both cultures. Ferah is half-Jewish and half-Palestinian. She's adamant about their respecting the history and religion of their dual nationalities."

Ferah brought a tray filled with cups, a teapot, and a plate of pastries, setting it on the glass-top wood coffee table. "All this fighting is nothing more than a family squabble. After all, the Jews and Arabs had the same beginning, with Abraham, Sarah, and Hagar." She sat next to Sydney and handed her a cup of tea in a bone china teacup with matching saucer, similar to the one she had at Lily's table. It seemed so long ago, but was only that morning.

"Mom, we want to show you something." Zaki and Ellie stood in the doorway. He held a small object, which he handed his mother.

Her eyes grew large and her mouth dropped. "Look, Moishe, the very same ceramic opium pot we bought today. Khalid said they were all over Jerusalem. Where did you get it?"

"In the Christian Quarter. On David Street where the shops are. Ellie and I decided to do our paper on the antiquities black market in Israel. This will be the first piece we write about, because we know it was from an illegal dig." He took it from Ferah and handed it to his father.

"How do you know it's from an illegal dig?" Moishe asked.

"Because Ellie and I were there when the merchant got the delivery from someone in the north who said they were found near Megiddo. We know there are no digs at Megiddo right now, so they *had* to be dug up by looters."

Ferah smiled at her son. "Very astute, Zaki. Good thinking to put two and two together. You and Ellie are a good team."

"May I see it?" Sydney asked.

Moishe handed her the pot.

Zaki said, "We think it's a drug pot that held opium for medicinal purposes."

Sydney turned it upside down. "A poppy pod! How clever they were. Even little carved knife cuts so the opium base could ooze out for harvesting. The Egyptians didn't smoke it. They *ate* it! Eased the pain of childbirth."

"See, Moishe, I told you. She's an expert at these things."

"Not only that, but these little pots were found in an eighteenth dynasty grave in Egypt. Archeologists go back and forth speculating whether the drug trade was for medicinal purposes or recreational use." Sydney handed Ferah the pot.

"Definitely medicinal." Ferah handed the pot to Zaki. "Time for bed." He took the pot and guided Ellie to her room. "A few years ago in Beit Shemesh a tomb from the Roman period was excavated, and they found the skeleton of a fourteen-year-old girl who died in childbirth. A burnt black substance was on her stomach. At first they thought it was incense, but after analysis, it was found to be a mixture of hashish, dried seeds, fruit and reeds! Other glass jars with the same substance were found surrounding the skeleton, which she probably inhaled to ease delivery. Hashish increases the force and frequency of contractions and was used until the nineteenth century."

"I wonder if it helped her delivery," Moishe mused.

"It didn't. Studies showed she bled to death. But she left a rare legacy. It was the first time archeologists had ever found evidence of drugs used for healing. If the hashish hadn't been burned, it would have decayed quickly. The chemists were able to analyze it because it was carbonized and preserved."

Antsy, Sydney rose and went to the living room window. "I'm always amazed at new findings of ancient wisdom." She peeked out through the curtains.

"You expecting someone?" Moishe asked.

"Yes, and there they are. A car with two men across the street. They must have followed us!"

Chapter 50

Carter sat on the floor in the back of a truck with his hands cuffed in front of him. He realized too late he had walked into an ambush. The caller, who he assumed was Roland, had asked him to come to the excavation site immediately. He thought something urgent came up, either with one of the students or possibly with Herod regarding Alexander.

When he left the hotel to walk to his car, he felt a hard object against his back. A voice told him to get in the back of the truck, which sat near the entrance to the hotel. Then he'd been handcuffed by a gruff man with a salt and pepper mustache, wearing a Greek fisherman's hat. He refused to answer any of his questions and quickly went through Carter's pockets, taking his cell phone and nothing else.

Dazed and confused, Carter felt the truck roll down the street. He looked around and, in the dim light, saw chain saws, crowbars, lines of rope and grappling hooks, black canvas duffle bags, tool chests, large dollies, green cushioned storage blankets, and folded canvas tote chairs.

He reached for one of the canvas totes, unfolded it with his cuffed hands, placed it against the side of the truck, and sat down. Where he was being taken? Would he ever see his brother and Sydney again?

"She got away!" Herod shouted. "For the second time!" He sat at the dais in the Sheraton ballroom, deserted except by service staff clearing the tables. He shifted the cell phone to his left ear so he could more easily raise his snifter of

Courvoisier to his lips. "I was too kind—that was my mistake. She took advantage of my kindness."

"She won't get far—the tail's on her," the caller said, his voice sympathetic.

Herod wasn't assured. "I didn't get the translation. She gave me some cockamamie story about the pharaoh in Megiddo proclaiming his victory and leaving a record of his conquests."

"Did she say where he was, besides Megiddo?"

"Just that he was also in Urushalem and may have camped there, but she hadn't gotten that far. Why?"

"The trade routes between Egypt and Lebanon ran parallel to the sea and also to the Dead Sea area," mused the voice on the phone.

Herod's impatience was at its limit. "So what? I've got to get this translated. That other wall pointed to the writing on this wall, so it must be important."

"Can you read any of it?"

"No! Well, a few words here and there. I've got to get the translator back. I sent my men to follow them from the ballroom. Marco's such a dunce—he jumped in his car too—told his mother to make sure his girlfriend got home."

"He's still a boy."

"Yeah, yeah, I know. And I see myself at his age and how I desperately wanted my father's approval."

The caller was silent.

Herod sighed. "I doubt that Marco receives any more than I got, but I can't be sure. I spoil the boy. More than my father ..." His voice trailed off. He was the father to his son as his father was to him. He knew the truth of his relationship with his son. Still, he longed to be the kind of father he never had. But for some reason, he was unable to show his son love, except through gifts—anything that could be bought.

Herod remembered his father's first acquisition. It had been after his tenth birthday party when his father called him to his study and handed him a gift. He ripped open the paper and opened the small box.

"A gold coin. I'm rich!"

"It's Roman, very rare, an antique, with Julius Caesar on the obverse and the ax and fasces on the reverse representing the authority of Rome. I just made a big sale of my computer invention. Look at this—the first of many valuable artifacts." His father fondled the heavy object on his desk. "An authentic marble bust of Caesar found in Rome at an excavation near the Forum. Not another one like it in the world. A one-of-a-kind priceless piece."

Herod had no idea what a priceless piece meant, and had barely heard of Julius Caesar. But he did know the value of gold. He loved his coin, and carried it in his pocket from that day on.

The family moved to the estate in Haifa after his father sold his share of the DOS computer drive system. That invention allowed Herod's father to retire so he could indulge his favorite pastime of accumulating priceless antiquities. Though German, his father wanted to live by the Mediterranean for its climate and vineyards. His Jewish mother was pleased to remain in her native land and settled into a luxurious lifestyle.

Herod inherited not only the vast collection, but his father's belief that whatever he could retrieve from archeological digs he rescued for posterity. He could do no less than his parent, and planned to do much more.

"What? Did you say something?" Herod asked the caller.

"Marco is just displaying the irresponsibility of youth," the voice repeated.

"I'll call you later when I know exactly where the temple is," he said and clicked off.

Herod knew he had nearly surpassed his father, something Marco could never do. Herod could pick and choose the artifacts he wanted—Egyptian, Israeli, Persian, Turkish, Iraqi—and whatever he didn't want, he would sell to the highest bidder. No shortage there. He had organized the biggest antiquities ring in the Middle East. His tentacles were reaching out to Lebanon and Jordan. He made new connections daily due to the emergence of the terrorist network.

The sale of looted antiquities fueled the current insurgency in Iraq. The global network of stolen artifacts paralleled the sale of weapons. He knew the insurgency in Afghanistan was funded by drugs.

His network was aided by the perfect hiding place. The loot could remain in a numbered account, taken out years later and sold. He was emboldened by the Swiss banks and privacy laws that prohibited Interpol or any investigative agency from looking into the accounts. He now stood poised to take over the whole of the antiquities market in Israel.

Only one thing stood in his way—the American translator.

Chapter 51

"We know there's a car out there." Ferah peered out the window. "They're The Fox's men. Sent to make sure no one followed us. There's also a car in the back."

"Whew," Sydney said with a sigh. "Okay, now I feel better." Except that she still didn't know Carter's whereabouts. "Can I use your phone?"

Ferah showed her to the phone in the kitchen. Sydney called Carter's cell again. No response. She returned to the living room and settled onto the sofa.

"Can you tell us about the Code? You said you had the translation, but does it tell you anything?" Ferah refilled the cups with hot steaming cranberry tea and handed them to Sydney and Moishe.

Ferah and Moishe eagerly awaited the possibility of hearing something that might well be a valuable archeological discovery.

Sydney took a sip, relishing the tartness, and sat back on the couch. She decided she could trust these friends of Benjamin and The Fox, whoever he was, since he was keeping her safe. Retrieving the sheet from her pocket, she read the Code aloud:

One comes who sprinkles liquid gold across the land
At a time of complete darkness of Ra
Near the road of the king
Where desert flowers bloom in a garden
Sothis calls forth again the Shemsu Hor
Following beams from the eye of Ra
Across the ancient lake of salt

Awakening nine faces of the stone
She paused and looked up for their reactions. Ferah and Moishe sat stark still, mouths agape as they listened to the rhymes expectantly. Sydney continued reading:
Lighting up the Temple of the Code
Double seals protect the lock
And open but to double keys
A portal to the cosmic sea
Where magic statues hidden long
Await the Shemsu's last return
Thoth a mighty birth awakes
and sings the truth to reach the stars."
Sydney folded the sheet.
"That's the Code?" Moishe looked deflated. "It doesn't make sense."
"That's the translation. Now I have to decode it. We just have to figure out what they meant. The verse that came before has the cartouche of King Thutmose III and his proclamation of power in this land." Sydney sipped her tea.
"What kind of proclamation?" Ferah offered her the pastry plate.
Sydney reached in her pocket for another crumpled sheet and began to read:
"Ra in Heaven gave me his force and strength of the Two Lands,
Who fashioned me as a falcon of gold
I am his son who built great cities and conquered many.
The image of birth from the god Thoth
Who brought the Code in the beginning as a guide for the end.
It is written on the wall of the tomb of King Unas."
"Why would it be in the tomb of King Unas?" Moishe polished off an apple pastry from the tray of goodies Ferah

had set out. He went to the window and peered out, then returned to his chair seemingly satisfied with what he saw.

"The Code is part of the Pyramid Texts in his tomb. Unas copied the Texts from more ancient texts. And other pharaohs have copied from Unas. The Book of the Dead was taken from the Texts. But they're not funeral incantations, which most archeologists believe. In all my research for my book on the Texts, I've never seen anything like this. The last line is:

Which are used by the priests to see ahead in time."

Ferah's eyes opened wide. "They were used for prophecy?"

"Apparently. We know the five priests associated with the tomb of Unas were all known as prophets. This Code could put a whole new meaning on the Pyramid Texts—that they were not just for the dead Pharaoh, but guidelines for the living—*if* I can decipher it." Sydney laid the papers on the coffee table which held the refreshments.

Moishe picked up one of the sheets and read the verses, shaking his head. "So many wall writings have no meaning."

Ferah grabbed the paper, scowling at him, and handed it to Sydney. "Maybe not to you, but she translated it off the wall. That's the first step. Now she has to decode it."

"I've got the first verse and part of the second." Sydney picked up a strawberry tart and bit into it. "*One comes who sprinkles liquid gold across the land.* We know the Egyptians were advanced astrologers living in the Nile Valley, surrounded by desert. But the area around the Dead Sea had been a desert for centuries and nothing is so valuable as water—liquid gold. One comes, which means a change in the astrological signs that happens every two thousand years, more or less. The Age of Pisces, the sign of the double fish, just ended. The Age of Aquarius began at the millennium and its sign is the water bearer who pours out water, or cosmic energy, onto the land. So we're in the right time frame."

"Okay, but we're already several years into it." Moishe said.

Ferah rose, went to the window and looked out, then went to the kitchen. She returned and nodded to Sydney then sat next to her.

"That's just part of it," Sydney said, taking another bite of the tart. "*The complete darkness of Ra* could mean an eclipse of the sun, or when the sun is dark—the dead of night when Ra is gone. The next line, *near the road of the king,* could be the main road that ran parallel to the Mediterranean. Another one ran next to the Dead Sea. Since the Code was found in Jerusalem, I think it's more likely to be the Dead Sea road."

"*Where desert flowers bloom in a garden,*" Ferah read, leaning over Sydney's arm. "There are lots of places in Israel where flowers bloom."

"They do now, but not in those days." Sydney said. "This was a harsh land. I've thought about this line and the only thing I come up with is in the Dead Sea area, where there's running water, greenery, and blooming flowers—the oasis of En Gedi."

"Of course." Ferah nodded. "It's beautiful out there."

Sydney finished her tart and sipped her tea. "The next line is trickier. *Sothis calls forth again the Shemsu Hor.*"

"Sothis?" Ferah asked.

"Shemsu what?" Moishe leaned forward.

"Sothis was the early form of Isis—she came from Sirius, which was called Sothis. That's as far as I've gotten. The proclamation clearly states the Code was brought in the beginning to be a guide for the end. Some Christian prophecies claim we're in the end times now. And Hopi legends talk of a great purification of the planet starting around the year 2012."

"You think the Code is about the end times?" Ferah cleared the table and carried the tray to the kitchen.

"I think it's about a window of opportunity when these Shemsu can open the temple. Herod would love to have even this much, since it tells where the temple is located. I presume the rest tells *how* to find it and *when* the window is open."

Zaki came into the room. "We think we *know* when it will open!"

"What?" asked Ferah.

Ellie held a sheet of paper. "We heard Dr. Grace reading the Code and what she's decoded so far."

Sydney nodded. *"At a time of complete darkness of Ra."*

"The next eclipse is *tomorrow* morning!" Ellie said excitedly. "At ten thirty-four, to be exact. A total eclipse of the sun."

"Of course!" Ferah slapped her forehead with the palm of her hand. "I completely forgot about it."

"Tomorrow morning? Are you sure?" Sydney asked Zaki, taking the sheet from Ellie.

"Positive." He and Ellie nodded. "We googled the Computer Calculated Scientific Ephemeris."

"Solar eclipses are usually all over the news days ahead. Why didn't I hear about it?" Sydney checked the figures.

"Probably because you've been too busy trying to stay alive," Ferah said.

Sydney nodded, handing the paper to Ellie. "How far is the preserve?"

"At this time of night, a little over an hour," Ferah said.

Even with her eyelids drooping, Sydney's excitement increased. "This confirms the Code! There *is* a window of opportunity. These Shemsu, whoever they are, are meant to be at En Gedi tomorrow morning when the sun comes up. We're not only racing ahead of Herod, but now we're in a race against time!"

Sydney desperately needed to decipher the rest of the verse by the morning. She realized her brain was on overload and she couldn't remember the last time she slept. Only that the last two days had raced across her horizon like the Indy 500.

Chapter 52

Carter held her hand as they jumped over a piece of seaweed, scattering a group of gulls that fluttered, squawking, into the sky. The white sand cushioned their soles with the softness of vanilla foam. Carter's golden body was lean and fit, tufts of curly chest hair glistening with sun and sand, his face moist with sweat and sea water.

The warmth of the sun burnished her skin, tanned in all the places her bright yellow and fuchsia hibiscus bikini left free. She had no idea where they were or how they got there, and didn't care. The sense of freedom that bonded with the hint of an unknown future led her on.

Alone on the shore, they slowed into a fast walk, two laughing beachcombers surveying their domain, protecting their private enchantment, until the vision merged with reality, propelling them into a land beyond dreams.

The light turquoise water lapped provocatively at their knees, when he stopped suddenly and took her in his arms. He kissed her passionately. She wrapped her leg around his knee and pulled him closer, his hand sliding across her rising landscape.

They drank each other with open mouths until the light distilled their magic into ruby wine. No fruity, anemic sips from this lusty font. Rather, endless gulps of crimson alight with passion's flame coated their lips.

As the foamy white water caressed their ankles, they splashed into it with the boundless enthusiasm of their early morning lovemaking. Flowing sensuously into the daylight where bindings were buried under each footstep.

The warm breeze embraced them in its chords of splendor. The rustling of palm trees echoed their music into the sea. Solar rays painted themselves onto glistened pores outlined in reflected sparkles from the sea.

Lips still engaged, their bodies swayed and lost balance, falling into the lapping waves. Holding onto each other and laughing, Carter rolled her over and pressed her into the sand as ebbing water flowed over them.

Hungry for his mouth, she kissed him again, lusting for the next surging wave to wash over them. As it did, he whispered, "I'll find you, I promise, I'll find you."

She awoke to find a Glock 10mm pistol pointed at her head.

Chapter 53

After cleaning up the kitchen, Ferah sat at the table reading the Code. The crumpled sheet had fallen out of Sydney's hand when she slumped back into the sofa. Let her sleep for a while, Ferah thought. She's probably exhausted. Moishe stretched out on his recliner, his hands behind his head.

Ferah realized Sydney had not only translated the Code but had deciphered much of it—the pharaoh who left the writing, the location of the temple, and now with the quick work of her son and Ellie, the time of the eclipse. It was getting late, or rather early and they would have to leave for the En Gedi preserve soon. She had checked the car in front of the house a few minutes ago. She knew they were alert by the cigarette smoke wafting from the windows.

Suddenly the dogs started barking. Ferah jumped up and turned on the back porch light. The bodyguard's car sat at the rear of the garage, within sight of the kitchen window and porch. But it was empty.

Before she could run to the living room, she heard the front door burst open. By the time she reached Moishe and Sydney, one of the thieves she had seen at the banquet had a pistol pointed at Sydney's head.

Where are the bodyguards? Ferah thought. Moishe was on his feet, but held at bay by the other thief from the banquet, who turned his pistol toward Ferah and motioned her to sit down. Sydney was taken by the gunmen out the back door, past the barking dogs.

Moishe jumped up and ran to the car in front of the house. Ferah ran to Zaki's room, checking on him and Ellie. Then she crept to the kitchen and looked out. A car sped off into the night.

Moishe returned to the house. "Both bodyguards are unconscious."

"The one in back probably is too," Ferah said, pacing and anxiously wringing her hands. "What do we do?"

Moishe stepped out the back door to calm the barking dogs. "Herod wants the whole translation and that's why he sent those men to take her. He's going to force her to tell him the rest!"

Ferah picked up the phone. "I'm calling Victoria. They should still be at Benjamin's shop."

She dialed the number and told Victoria what had happened. Victoria recounted the attack at the shop by the armed thieves, how they all fought back, and had captured one of them.

"Now that he has Sydney again, when Herod sees the translation, he'll be headed for the Dead Sea, which is mentioned in the Code. Sydney thought the Code referred to a window of time when the temple would be opened." Ferah turned to Zaki and Ellie, who had just come into the living room. "Get dressed!

"Why?" Victoria said.

"Vicki, there's to be an eclipse of the sun tomorrow morning. Apparently, something is going to happen on the Dead Sea at sunrise that will lead to the temple. We've got to be there before Sydney tells Herod!"

Chapter 54

The white Saab careened around corners as it sped through Bethlehem on its way out of the city. As she was thrown from one side to the other, Sydney surreptitiously tried the door handles. Locked. She knew at this speed, jumping out would be dangerous. But she had no choice. She clicked the unlock button. Still locked.

It was late, the streets deserted and dark except for a few streetlights. The driver sped through all the stop signs he could.

Her mind raced. She recognized they were on the road back to Jerusalem, probably returning to the Sheraton. Herod might be able to figure out a few isolated words of the Code, particularly lake of salt. The placement of the king's cartouche would tip him to the importance of the wall's center. One cartouche began the segment and another ended it. Even if she figured out the rest of the poem, she could not tell Herod, but how could she not and stay alive?

She was brought back to the moment and slid off the seat onto the floor when the driver took a curve on two wheels.

We know the Egyptians plotted the stars. A total eclipse was considered of great importance by ancient cultures and many indigenous people today. Herod could figure this out with the help of an astrologer or simply looking at a calendar.

The next lines were more complicated.

Sothis calls forth again the Shemsu Hor

Isis calls again to the Followers of Horus, her son, or possibly in this case, Pharaoh, symbolized as Horus. Could this mean Pharaoh Thutmose III, since it's his cartouche on the wall? Was Isis calling the people of Thutmose, in Egypt then and reincarnated now?

It all seemed to be pointing to a temple at En Gedi. She knew ruins had been found there, but nothing Egyptian. It had to be buried. But why would King Thutmose build a temple in the middle of nowhere? The Code was creating more questions even before she had decoded the entire poem.

That was all she could remember. She reached in her pocket for the slip of paper. It wasn't there. Frantic the kidnappers might have found it, she searched through all her pockets. Empty. She recalled reading it to Ferah and Moishe just before she drifted off to sleep, and dreamed of a beach, and Carter.

The car looped around Jerusalem headed out of the city. So they weren't headed to the Sheraton after all. *Now* where was she going?

Her answer came soon enough. They were only a few miles north of the city center when the driver turned at the sign marked Atarot Airport. *No one will know where I am. Carter won't know where I am. Will I ever see him again?*

The small airport looked deserted. A few lights glowed in the building and she saw someone inside the tower. A Lear jet sat at the end of the runway, revving up. The car pulled around the airport buildings and squealed to a stop by the plane. One of Herod's men opened the back door and dragged her out. She wrenched her hand away.

"You don't have to drag me. I can walk!" she snarled.

"Don't get smart with me!" He roughly shoved her toward the plane and followed her up the stairs to the open door.

She stepped through and looked into the cockpit. Herod sat at the controls. Another man sat in the co-pilot seat.

"Dr. Grace," Herod smiled at her, "so nice of you to come flying with me."

"Where are we going, *Mr. Werner?*" she asked.

He frowned at her in contempt. "I decoded the verses far enough to know there's something at the Dead Sea. Something King Thutmose buried there, or something he found that's still there. The computer is in the cabin. You will decipher the rest before we touch down at the lake of salt."

"And if I refuse?"

"I don't think you will." He motioned to Tomas. "We wouldn't want anyone to get hurt, especially *him!*" He pointed behind her.

Sydney turned around and couldn't believe her eyes.

"Alexander!"

Chapter 55

Sydney and Alexander fell into each others' arms. They stood in the entryway of the aircraft, entwined in a long embrace of relief. "We didn't know if you were alive or dead," Sydney whispered in his ear.

"Very much alive," Alexander said, standing back to look at her. He wore jeans and a plaid shirt, tan work boots and a safari hat.

He was just as she remembered him—and so much like Carter when he smiled. "A little more grey in the mustache." She grinned at him. His dark hair remained the same.

Herod stuck his head out of the cockpit. "Everyone sit down. We're taking off."

Tomas stepped to one side as Sydney took Alexander's hand. The custom blue and brown interior reminded Sydney of a posh hotel room—plush oriental rugs, chocolate leather love seats, and seating areas of light blue leather chairs that swiveled to face walnut tables. Tomas motioned to a table holding a computer. They sat opposite each other and buckled up as the plane taxied down the runway.

Tomas sat close by holding his pistol. "No funny business!"

They swiveled to face forward as the plane gained speed down the runway and lifted off the ground.

"He told me to call him the Collector, and I saw why. He's got a whole museum at his disposal," Alexander said

"I saw it too. Unbelievable." Sydney briefed him on her experiences since she had arrived in Israel.

"None of this makes any sense," Alexander said. "I don't even know why I was kidnapped. The last thing I remember was that Carter left for the airport to pick you up. He wanted you over here to be with him."

"What do you mean?"

"Didn't he tell you?"

"Tell me what?"

"Sure, we needed someone to translate the wall, but he was so lonesome for you that he called you. He knew that was the only way to get you here. That you wouldn't pass up an opportunity to read hieroglyphs on an Egyptian wall in Israel. I told him to wait 'til summer when you'd have more time, but he couldn't wait. He knew you'd be on spring break."

This was a shock. *Why didn't Carter say anything?* Maybe this was why he was acting so different. "No, he didn't tell me. Just that they needed the hieroglyphs translated. When we found the colored wall, that put a different spin on it."

"What colored wall? The ones we found were faded."

When they were airborne, Sydney turned toward the monitor and clicked on the Code.

"Alexander, you should see it," she said excitedly. "Like new, colors brilliant as if they were painted yesterday. The wall you saw continued down below the floor of the pool. But before I could get to it, Herod's gang stole it."

Tomas stood over them. "Get to work, Dr. Grace, you don't have much time."

Sydney nodded. "Back to the Code. I've got the first verse and most of the second."

"What Code?"

She told Alexander about the spiral glyphs. He took paper from the printer and wrote it down.

She began to read. *"Sothis calls forth again the Shemsu Hor.* Isis was also known by her constellation name, Sothis, because she came from Sirius. Shemsu Hor means Followers of Horus. Her son was Horus. Over the millennia he came to represent the Pharaoh in all the dynasties. If the followers, or ancient Egyptians at the time of Thutmose III are reincarnated at this time, the line says they'll hear the call of Isis." Sydney sat back.

"This is all pretty amazing," Alexander said.

"Very interesting." Tomas had shoulder-holstered his pistol and sat next to Alexander with folded arms.

"In my research, I remember something about these Shemsu Hor being a lineage of semi-divine, pre-dynastic beings the ancient Egyptians believed ruled for thousands of years before the first dynasty." Sydney would have to find a way to mislead Herod.

"Semi-divine. You mean like gods?" Tomas looked out the window into blackness.

She had to watch what she said. "The dynastic Egyptians believed they were the ones who built the pyramids and Sphinx. Apparently they reincarnated during the time of Thutmose, at least that's what he's telling us." And she could easily mislead Herod by not mentioning the impending eclipse, which he may know about, but not connected to the Code.

"So they would go back at least five thousand BC." Alexander said.

"Tomas, do you have anything to drink?" Sydney asked, to get him out of the way.

Tomas glared suspiciously at them, and then slowly rose. "I'll check."

She motioned to Alexander to speak low.

"What's the next line?" Alexander whispered.

"Following beams from the eye of Ra"

"The sun's ray beams out?" He quickly wrote it down. Tomas had seen him write earlier, but didn't remove the paper.

"Across the ancient lake of salt. Herod decoded this himself, that's why we're on our way to the Dead Sea. It could mean the sun's normal twelve hour progression in the sky, or it could mean something else."

"What else?"

"The Egyptians studied astrology and astronomy. We know that from their writings and the tomb paintings of stellar scenes, mainly the Pyramid Texts in the Temple of Unas." She turned toward the galley in the back of the plane, and knew she had to talk fast. She kept her voice low. "At the Temple of Dendera, there's a zodiac on the ceiling, a map of the sky and the constellations divided into thirty-six sections. The Egyptians used these to tell time at night. When the section appeared above the horizon they could mark that point and know the hour."

"So they could plot the cycles of the sun and planets?" Alexander scribbled it all down.

"Not only the cycles of the planets but they understood *precession,* a way of tracking the sun through the signs of the zodiac at the vernal and autumnal equinox," she said quickly. "The sun cycles one degree every seventy-two years, or 2160 years to complete each section of the zodiac. The Age of Pisces was completed a few years ago and Aquarius began another 2160 year cycle. It's the next line that puzzles me."

"Awakening nine faces of the stone, " Alexander read.

Tomas peered around the galley door, a towel in his hand.

Alexander nodded at him. "What stone has nine faces, or facets?" He whispered. "It would have to be a cut stone, like a diamond." He saw Tomas return to the galley.

"Or a stone a diamond could cut," Sydney said, "like a ruby or even limestone or marble. What stone needs to be awakened? A diamond is awakened from carbon, and other precious stones from corundum, like rubies and sapphires."

Tomas appeared from the galley carrying a tray with two cups. He stared at them distrustfully and headed toward the cockpit.

"This is the biggest puzzle," she said in a normal tone. "There are miles and miles of shoreline and the only clue we have is the King's Road. Tomas," she asked when he returned, "do you have any maps of this area?"

"I'll look." He went to the galley, returning with cups of hot steaming coffee he placed on the table. Sydney picked up the cup and sampled a rich French roast brew. He glanced at the monitor, and then turned toward the back of the plane.

"Lighting up the Temple of the Code," Alexander said softly, leaning in to Sydney. "This temple will be lit up when the sun shines on it. That must mean it's above ground. But there are no Egyptian temples anywhere near the Dead Sea."

"That can be seen."

"You mean it's underground?" Alexander whispered. "It's a big area down there, both on the Israeli and the Jordanian sides. And a lot of it has been built up over the last three thousand years."

Her eyes darted around the plane. "The Canaanites were defeated by Thutmose at Megiddo, and subject to Egyptian rule until the Philistines invaded. This *Temple of the Code* must have had some significance. Why build a temple here instead of at home?" She could devise no way to come up with a plan. They would have to wait until they landed.

Tomas returned with a cup and sat down. "No maps."

Alexander saw Sydney's finger drop down several lines. He looked at the screen, but said nothing.

"As Thoth a mighty birth awakes," she read. "Thoth was the ibis-headed god who brought wisdom and writing to the Egyptians. Those two gifts alone were mighty births. But what is he going to *awake?*" She had deliberately skipped over several lines.

Alexander nodded that he got the message. "After he awakes whatever it is he's going to awake, or *whoever* he awakes, he *sings the truth to reach the stars.* That's a pretty big voice to reach the stars."

Sydney looked out the window at the black sky slowly turning purple.

The cockpit door opened and Herod walked back from the cockpit. "Do you have it?"

"Most of it," she said, "but we don't know the *exact* location, just that it's near the Dead Sea."

"You better tell me before I lose my patience," Herod growled, as he stood over her in a menacing manner.

She had to come up with something fast, and it had to be realistic. "My best guess would be north of Masada. Of course, the whole coastline was different thirty-five hundred years ago, and the Dead Sea has receded at least forty feet in the past century, so your guess is as good as mine," Sydney said.

"I'm setting down," he said as he walked back to the cockpit.

She looked out the window. The lake was a dark gray mass with clumps of white salt scattered around the surface. The plane started banking over the water toward a deserted spot near the shoreline. But that was not where the plane was headed. Herod was dropping altitude quickly, lining up over the water.

Sydney realized his desperation matched her own. "Omigod. He's crazy! He's going to land *on* the Dead Sea!"

Chapter 56

"They must be taking her to En Gedi," said Ferah, buckled into the passenger seat, reading the Code.

Moishe drove north to Jerusalem, then east toward the Dead Sea. At this hour of the early day, a few cars were already on the road toward the city.

Ferah fingered her cell. "When I talked to Victoria before we left, she said Robert would remain at the school and she would wait for Benjamin to get back from the Wailing Wall through the tunnel. They would meet us at the intersection of Highway 1 and the 90 South. They should be there about the time we are."

Ellie and Zaki sat in the back seat, whispering as usual. "Could we see the Code again?"

Ferah handed it back to Zaki. "You're right, Ellie. The line *Sothis calls forth again the Shemsu Hor* means that Isis isn't calling them for the first time—she's calling them *again* to come back to her."

"The two deities mentioned in the Code—Isis and Thoth," Ellie mused. "The Goddess of Magic and the God of Wisdom. This Code is telling us we have to use *both* to find the temple."

Ferah turned around. "Both deities?"

"*Both gifts—magic and wisdom,*" Ellie said.

"Well I'll be damned," mumbled Moishe.

Ferah smiled at her husband.

"Maybe those are the *double seals that protect the lock!*" Zaki exclaimed.

"*And open but to double keys.* Maybe they're the double keys!" Ellie said.

"How are we going to find them when we get there?" Zaki asked. "First the Code says at the time of a total eclipse. Then it says the beams from the eye of Ra awaken a stone that lights up the temple. It's contradicting itself."

"Yeah, I noticed that too." Ellie looked out the window. "As long as we're there by dawn, we can find the stone. But what if the stone's *inside* the temple. Lights it up from inside? Then how do we see it?"

Ferah and Zaki looked at the freckle-faced girl with the pink beret holding her light hair in place. Neither had considered this point. Silence descended over the occupants of the car as it sped down the dark highway on its rendezvous with Ra.

Chapter 57

The plane thudded noisily along, mimicking a stone skipping across the water's surface. Sydney held onto the computer as it slid across the table. Tomas sat next to Alexander, holding the arms of his chair.

"Those salt clumps are as big as a Jeep Cherokee," Alexander said above the noise. "He'll be lucky if he doesn't hit one."

Sydney glanced at the screen. No! She could not work for Herod! Her eyes slid to Alexander, looking for an answer, trying to communicate their need for an escape. But she felt a tug of the opportunity of a lifetime, finding a lost buried temple. Sweet Malarkey! She had no choice but to forge ahead.

Sydney looked out the window at a deep purple sky shrouding gray water unused to hosting vehicle landings. "This plane isn't a sea plane. Why did he land on the water?"

The plane swerved quickly to the left to avoid a salt clump, tossing the passengers against the fuselage wall. Tomas took the brunt of it and rubbed his head.

Sydney stabilized the notebook, stalling for time. She'd keep Herod guessing as long as she could. "We know the king's highway runs parallel to the Dead Sea. Bloom in a garden. Desert flowers. Where are there desert flowers? A garden. The only oasis on the Western side of the lake."

"Alexander," she said excitedly, "where is there a garden in the desert?"

"En Gedi!" they both said together.

Tomas yelled to Herod, "It's En Gedi."

"You sure?"

"Yes!" Sydney and Alexander said together.

"It *has* to be. The only place in the desert that would remind the Egyptians of home. Streams, waterfalls, tropical plants and desert vegetation. A natural health spa! People came to this lake for thousands of years to smear the mud on their bodies and soak in the water. The Egyptians built their temples along the Nile. This spot would appeal to them as the same kind of location. A healing respite in an alien land to remind them of the Nile."

"Good work, Syd!" Alexander said.

"We haven't found it yet, but I'm sure this is where the Code is leading us." She smiled at the possibility. Her senses immediately perked up in anticipation of following the rest of the verses. What a discovery! If only it were true! She could hardly contain herself against the potential of a major find. That it was at the point of a gun was regrettable. But she would do nothing to harm Alexander or herself.

The plane decelerated, bumping and swerving along the water until it slowed to a stop. "Tomas," Herod yelled. "Get the raft."

Tomas immediately got up and went aft.

Herod jumped out of his seat as soon as he cut the engine. "Best place to land a plane. Impossible to sink! Everything floats in this water. Everyone into the raft. Tomas, get the bags. Should be room enough for four with the gear."

"There's five of us," Tomas said.

"The pilot's staying aboard. He'll bring the plane to shore when we find the temple."

Sydney and Alexander unbuckled their belts. As she closed the notebook, ready to pick it up, Herod saw her and said, "Leave it. Get going."

Tomas carried olive green rucksacks and bulky canvas bags to the door then went back for the deflated raft and oars. He opened the cabin door, clicked on his light, placed the bags outside, and stepped out onto the wing. Next, he pulled the plug on the raft and threw it out, holding onto the line, which he tied to a loop outside the door. The raft began to inflate.

Sydney and Alexander approached the door.

"Get those bags," Tomas ordered from the wing. He stepped into the raft, now fully inflated. Alexander picked up a light and climbed onto the wing. He tossed the bags to Tomas, who caught them and stowed the gear under the seats. Then he lowered the oars. He turned to take Sydney's hand.

"Don't splash around in this water," Herod yelled to them, as he gathered the laptop and accessories into a bag. "You don't want it in your eyes. Burns like hell. And if you do get the water in your eyes, don't rub them, just keep them closed and your own tears will wash it out."

Tomas gave the water a suspicious look.

As Sydney stepped out the door onto the wing, she saw the loop which held the line. Without thinking, she quickly untied the line, grabbed Alexander's hand and stepped into the raft. Losing her balance on purpose, she fell into Tomas, who let out a grunt. They both tumbled to the bottom of the raft and Sydney grabbed the pistol out of his pants where it was tucked. Alexander jumped into the raft and pushed off from the plane.

She aimed at Tomas. "Get back and start rowing. Hurry!"

He did as he was told, as Alexander took another oar. She clicked off both lights, then aimed at Herod, who had appeared at the cabin door.

"You idiot!" yelled Herod. He ducked back into the plane.

"Faster! Before he starts shooting," she yelled. Too late. Herod returned to the open door and aimed a rifle at them.

Sydney pointed the revolver at him. "I'll shoot," she shouted. They were pulling away from the plane, using the pre-dawn darkness for cover.

A shot rang past the raft. Herod stepped back into the plane just as Sydney fired. She hoped she missed him. She was not prepared to kill anyone.

"Get down!" Alexander told Tomas, as they rowed rapidly toward shore.

Herod's rifle appeared in the doorway and fired again. That one ripped through the raft as Sydney exchanged fire. She suddenly felt prepared to kill him.

Unable to see the damage, they could hear the hissing air. "Over here," Alexander said.

She felt around and discovered the leak on the side and jammed her hand against it. "Give me a rag to plug this hole," she said.

"Get something out of those bags," Alexander told Tomas.

Sydney heard them fumbling for the bags. Escaping air forced her hand up. "Never mind, keep rowing." She reached into her pants, holding the barrel of the pistol away from her. She didn't want to lay it down for fear she might not find it again in the dark. Pulling up her gown, she hurriedly ripped off a piece, stuffed it into the hole, and slowed the escaping air. But not enough. The raft rapidly began to shrink.

"Hurry! We're sinking fast." How far? She wondered.

Nearly to the shoreline, another shot zinged past their heads. He would have hit one of them in the daylight. They couldn't see land but she knew they were close by the sound of water lapping on the shore.

She felt a bump that told her they'd hit the shoreline. Alexander grabbed the line and tied Tomas' hands in front of him. Sydney grabbed the piece of fabric out of the hole, causing it to resume the hiss. She shoved it into Tomas' mouth.

"Syd, untie the other end of the line," Alexander said softly.

She felt her way around the raft until she found the knot, fumbled with it until it loosened, then handed the line to Alexander. He shouldered a bag.

"Pick up the gear." Alexander held the line attached to the hands of the man who just a few minutes ago was his captor, and climbed out onto a sandy shore, with Sydney close to him.

Tomas awkwardly picked up two of the bags and followed Alexander into the darkness. Another shot skimmed the surface of the water.

"Keep down!" Sydney whispered, as a shot thudded into the ground behind them. She headed inland, while Alexander pulled Tomas. Her eyes became accustomed to the dark, her feet stumbling toward En Gedi. But she dared not turn on a light.

"I can barely make out the plane," Alexander whispered.

The Code was a jumbled mess inside her head. It all ran together and she could not get a fix on anything after the stone with nine faces. "Isis calls the Followers of Horus—the pre-dynastic rulers of Egypt," she whispered, trying to sort out her thoughts.

"What?" Alexander asked.

She looked out over the black lake, considering the meaning behind the words. "If the priests who came with

Thutmose believed they were the reincarnation of these Shemsu Hor, and if they *did* have the ability to prophesy, they believed they would reincarnate at a time in the future and leave clues to themselves."

"You mean they left themselves clues in pre-dynastic times to find at the time of Thutmose?" Alexander shifted the rucksack onto his back.

She looked behind to be certain Tomas was far enough from them not to overhear. "That's what it looks like. If they *were* here with Thutmose, and it looks like they were, they left the Code. Whatever they found enabled him to defeat the whole of Canaan and become a great warrior-king. It was a time of expansion for Egypt and they gained much wealth during his reign."

"And the Code was left during that time for *another* future time," Alexander speculated. He scanned the lake. "That means *we're* the Shemsu Hor."

Could it be? She thought. "I don't know. It just means we've *found* the Code *meant* for the Shemsu Hor. There may be more in these clues that only a reincarnated Shemsu would recognize or be able to figure out. A true Shemsu, I would guess, would have *memory* that we may not have. What's called *far memory*, the ability to recall past lives."

The ground changed into asphalt. They had reached the preserve parking lot. Alexander found the men's rest rooms, sat Tomas down in a stall and tied the rope to the stall post. He removed the fabric, stuffed toilet tissue in his mouth, and tied the fabric around his mouth. "We should be long gone by the time Herod finds him."

They left the men's room, hefted the bags, jumped over the turnstiles at the entrance, and found the path to the preserve. "Do you think we're far enough to take a chance with a light?" Sydney asked, stubbing her toe on a large rock.

"Not yet. We can keep to these markers on the trail."

The crisp air and sweet fragrance from the various preserve trees and plants brought an invigorating pleasure to Sydney's whole being and cleared her mind for the task ahead. Now the Code clicked into focus.

"The beams from the rising sun will point across the lake. The sun slowly cycles through the signs of the zodiac, which the Egyptians used to tell time. When the sun first rises, note the time. It may have something to do with the time at the vernal equinox."

"Okay."

"The beam awakens the nine faces of the stone." Sydney stopped and looked at the lake. "It could be buried under the sand of the *lake*, rather than the land," she said excitedly. "The sun will somehow cause it to rise."

"Which would be the only way to get it out of the sand, since we couldn't dive for it."

It was quiet and deserted, except for the sound of a rock sliding off a cliff. Sydney looked up and saw the outline of an ibex, a wild goat with large backward-curved horns that lives on the cliffs.

"And this stone lights up the Temple of the Code. *Double seals protect the lock and open but to double keys.* I have no idea what that means. They didn't use locks—they used granite to plug the entrances to tombs. That sealed them."

"Thoth was ibis-headed, wasn't he?" Alexander stumbled over a shrub in the rocks.

"He took the form of an ibis, a large bird like a heron, with a long slender down-curved beak. *Thoth a mighty birth awakes.* He must have another gift or birth for the Shemsu.

She watched the ibex watching them and stopped to set the bag down. *"And Thoth will sing the truth to reach the stars."*

"Or the Shemsu will sing the truth," he ventured.

"That's a possibility." She looked out to the other side of the lake where the sun would rise. The deep blue on the horizon faded to a lighter shade which she knew heralded the dawn.

"Thoth awakens a mighty birth," she said. "Something the Shemsu wanted to give to enlighten civilization whcn it is ready to receive this wisdom. One of those stages was the age of Thutmose III. *This* could be another time in the development of humans, *if* we're ready."

"To find the Shemsu?" Alexander asked.

"No." Sydney looked toward the horizon, "to receive enlightenment."

Chapter 58

The horizon shone with a deep pink glow as the Sky Goddess, Nut, gave birth to the Sun God, Ra, one of the enduring myths of the ancient Egyptians. Sydney and Alexander watched the delicate blush on the horizon heralding the sun. They had reached the bottom of the cliffs. Suddenly the ground began to shake and the lake churned from the force. They saw the plane in the distance rock back and forth in the waves.

"What's happening?" Alexander asked.

"It's time! The window is opening!" She felt a rush of excitement. "It's the message in the Code. We have to find the place of the eye of Ra!"

The shaking earth rolled under them. The sun peeked over the horizon. A rumble echoed from beneath the water. The first ray from the sun slowly crawled across the lake.

Sydney shouted to Alexander, "Get the time!"

They struggled to stay on their feet, got knocked down, and gamely tried to stand again on the shaking ground.

The plane rocked heavily in the surf, one wing dipping into the lake, then the other wing. The water heaved under it, a powerful surge that awakened the ancient stone from the sands of its slumber. The plane was no match for the rebirth of the behemoth, which arose from the depths of its bed like a huge fish.

"My God, look at that!" Alexander yelled.

They gazed in amazement at the sight of the plane, which was skewered on a pointed object rising from the water. The entity pushed itself through the plane until the point stuck out the top of the fuselage.

"The stone's a crystal! A nine-sided crystal!" Sydney shouted through the rumble.

The sight of the plane impaled on the gigantic crystal seemed to increase the quake, as they tried to stand their ground and gape at the extraordinary sight. Not a small plane, it dangled in the air with no more effort than a child's toy, the crystal determining its height and motion. They backed up involuntarily when the water roared and churned into waves, splashing onto the shore.

The stone and the plane kept rising as the sun's beam shone across the water through the nine facets and cast a ray in their direction. They watched the sunbeam slowly crawl to the cliffs. The huge point with the plane stuck on it rotated and cycled clockwise, colored light shining out from all nine sides, despite its appendage.

Sydney managed to reach the huge limestone cliffs in the semi-darkness on the Western side of the lake. The light moved up the cliff face in the Nahal David nature reserve. Before Alexander could reach her, she hung onto a tree and noted landmarks and other prominent burnt umber reflections left by the sun, now sitting on the horizon, carving a swath of orange glow through the deep crevasse encompassing part of the preserve.

Mesmerized by the refraction of light emitted by the crystal, she watched the rainbow climb, slowly setting down on a specific cliff face. The crystal stopped its cycle when the sun rose higher. The eye of Ra was lighting upon its chosen site, a gleaming point that seemed to stop in mid-turn. Then just as suddenly, the light reflected off the stone, but no more beams shone through the facets.

"That's it!" Sydney shouted through the rumble. She searched the cliff face for a way to find the spot, hoping the last thirty-five hundred years had not worn away the means to reach it.

They watched the crystal slowly sink back into the water, taking the plane with it. In the churning, gurgling water, the plane bobbed on the huge point, its tail sinking first, the nose pointed toward Ra in a final salute. The ground stopped shaking and the rumble ceased.

Sydney gazed at the swirling water that swallowed the jet, wondering if Herod and the pilot made it out.

"Come on. We can take the hiking trail. It probably goes all the way to the top."

"It does—there're waterfalls up there." He picked up the gear.

She was positive this was the right place. The refracted light from the facet landed in Nahal David, David's stream. Dark shadows and morning light now interspersed along the whole north side.

"Some ruins of a Chalcolithic temple are up there." Alexander pointed. "That was really something—the crystal skewered the plane like it was a toy. I didn't see if they got out."

"Don't worry about them. They won't sink. They can *float* to shore."

They passed cliffs that soared into the orange-red dawn. In the shadows lay green vegetation. After several minutes on the trail, Sydney heard the rumble of the waterfall. She reached the pool, a lush oasis in stark contrast to the raw umber and tan desert.

"What was the time?" she asked Alexander.

"Seven ten. What significance does the time have?"

"I don't know exactly right now, but I may later." She looked at the sun, shielding her eyes, and then scanned the sky. "We've got to find the temple before the eclipse!"

Chapter 59
7:15 AM

Sydney stood at the edge of a rock shelf, catching her breath, and looked out at the lake. She knew the ancient Egyptians practiced magic in all its many forms. The nature of initiation was based on the practical training of its principles. But she had never heard anything about a giant crystal. Or the process by which it could suddenly emerge out of water, thrusting itself into the plane.

Alexander sat against a tamarisk tree filled with masses of minute flowers. "I don't believe I saw what I just saw. That thing destroyed the plane!"

"Another mystery on top of all the other ones I've encountered in the past few days." *I don't know what to believe any more.* "Herod's landing was right over the stone mentioned in the Code. How ironic is that?" She slung a bag over her shoulder and started up the path.

Alexander got up and hefted the bags. "How could it have risen like that?"

"And who put it there?" Sydney suddenly felt small in the face of so many historical mysteries. She longed to solve some of these archeological puzzles and knew there was more to the ancient Egyptian culture, even here in Israel, than acknowledged by her peers.

She had always thought it strange that Egyptologists could not explain the true purpose of the pyramids. Nor the Book of the Dead, taken from the Pyramid Texts, in the context of initiatory rites and their connection to the pyramids.

Alexander looked back to see if anyone followed. The path was clear.

"A crystal that size must've had a lot of power. I wonder how they could have harnessed it. Must've been on some kind of cosmic timer. That means the temple itself may also be on a timing device." She gazed up at the cliffs. "The refraction from the facets came up over there to the north where it stopped. The burnt umber shadows are close to the spot where the eye of Ra points across the sea of salt and lights up the temple."

They kept climbing, looking back at the trail. Too early for the hikers, but the preserve guards would be coming on duty any time and would undoubtedly check for any damage from the quake. The roar of the waterfall filled the air before they came to it. Many side paths led to other ruins, according to the hiking signs, including a Byzantine irrigation system

They reached the fall that plunged into a stunning blue pool. "It's beautiful here." Sydney wished she had a hat for protection from the sun. "So much green in the middle of the desert. No wonder this oasis had settlements going back thousands of years."

"According to the Old Testament, David hid here when King Saul was trying to kill him," puffed Alexander, climbing over a rock. "Over there's Lover's Cave. Hikers strip and swim in the pool."

A flash of movement caught Sydney's eye. A desert fox ran into the cave and disappeared. On a hunch, she turned east to follow it. Huge boulders formed the cave. She shined her light into the darkness. A pool of crystal-clear spring water sparkled in the light.

Alexander came up behind her. "Lovers' Cave. The stream empties into the pool. It goes underground and then comes up again by the waterfall."

Sydney looked around for the desert fox. It was nowhere in the cave. But it didn't get out the way it came in. There must have been another exit.

"How big is this cave?"

"I've heard it extends several hundred feet back beyond the pool. The old myths tell of David hiding in there from Saul's army. He supposedly found a tunnel which led to another part of the preserve and was always able to evade the king's men."

"Is the tunnel still there?"

"They've searched the cave many times, but no tunnel's ever been found."

That bit of information intrigued her. "I'd like to see where this tunnel was supposed to be."

"You go ahead. I want to see if we're being followed. I'm sure they got off the plane."

She walked around the pool on the narrow ledge that circled to the back. Boulders surrounded the area, cutting off the path. Sydney noticed a dark spot next to a large stone. A hole in the wall! So that's how the desert fox got out! She got down on her knees and shined the light into the hole. If they searched for a tunnel many times, why didn't they ever find this hole? She thought. Maybe the earthquake dislodged some of the boulders.

Dark and cramped. Which was worse? An enclosed space. Musty air. Ahead, the unknown. Or behind her, a megalomaniac who would kill them both with no hesitation.

Herod or the python?

She didn't hesitate for a moment, rolled away the large stones, crawled to the wall, shone the light into the hole, and scrambled in.

Chapter 60

Sydney entered a large chamber with naturally formed pillars standing as sentinels. She stood up, brushed herself off, and moved the light around the rough-hewn walls. At least they appeared rough at first glance. The python crawled closer. Then something brushed against her cheek. She waved the light around her, seeking the source of whatever touched her. She saw nothing. Heard nothing.

From afar she thought she heard a muffled thud and looked back to the hole. Was it Alexander? Or the desert fox? The silence echoed against her ears. The chamber had a dank musty odor. Then she smelled something else. Fresh air! There was air coming in from somewhere, but she saw no holes except the one she came through.

Her shoulders arched in response to the closeness and she swept the chamber with light to keep the python at bay. She rubbed her neck and throat to reassure herself she was still there, still in command.

"This must be David's tunnel!" she said aloud.

The desert fox was not in the chamber, but it had to have a means of escape—just like David, who was renowned for the cunning of a desert fox. And water. He had to have water to hide for many days. So there must have been a way to conceal the hole in the wall of Lover's Cave.

She remembered the geology of these cliffs, composed of the same limestone that formed the Qumran caves a few miles north. The monastic community of the Essenes hid their precious Scrolls in those caves to keep them hidden from enemies. They lived in the area for over a hundred years until the destruction of their community and the city of Jerusalem by the Romans.

The Scrolls were forgotten until the middle of the 20th century when a Bedouin goatherd stumbled on the earthen jars in one of the caves. The heat and dry air of the desert had preserved the scrolls for two thousand years. The Dead Sea Scrolls were still being studied by academicians worldwide.

What else do these cliffs contain? Approaching the wall, she blew on the dust, wishing for the cosmetic brush she used for delicate jobs. Then backed up to avoid the powder flying in her face. Blowing on the next layer, she wet a finger and drew it downward.

Awed by the sight before her, she realized the wall wasn't rough-hewn at all. It was carved! And covered with at least a millennium of dust. She could hardly believe her eyes. Hieroglyphs! Raised hieroglyphs carved and painted onto the wall. Vivid colors came alive when she wet the carvings. Her excitement swelled as she read the first glyph. "Great house—the carver's designation for Pharaoh," she said aloud.

She attempted to wet her finger, but her mouth was suddenly dry. *Come on.* She tried to coax cooperation from her tongue. *The find of my career depends on spit.*

Could she chance going back to the pool? She blew on the wall again, coughing as the dust flew, clogging her throat and nose. Life-sized paintings of the goddess, Isis, and her son, Horus, become apparent. Managing a drop of moisture, she rubbed a section. The jagged water sign, the glyph for n, and other glyphs used in royal insignias. "The wish formula! This is it!"

She nearly jumped around the chamber in celebration. Looking around at no one in particular, she said breathlessly, "The Temple of the Code!"

Chapter 61

After she brushed away part of the wall with another scrap of her gown, she could read the hieroglyphs. They seemed to be speaking to the Shemsu Hor, who Isis/Sothis would call forth, according to the Code. She stood back to get a better perspective, but instead received a surprise.

The hieroglyphs were moving! They were rearranging themselves over the entire wall, changing the text as she first saw it, becoming something totally different. She looked around to see if anything else had repositioned in the chamber. Nothing. When she turned back, the glyphs were still in motion. She blinked, and blinked again, to get her eyes in focus. The colors swirled faster in all directions, changing so quickly that they became a blur on the wall, a hieroglyphic impressionist painting.

"What's happening?" she said aloud.

"Shemsu wrote the text to be read by the Shemsu. It has recognized you as a Shemsu, and is arranging the correct order of the writing," said a melodious feminine voice.

A chill ran up Sydney's neck. No one else was in the chamber.

"Who speaks?"

Out of the corner of her eye, the painting of Isis moved. Sydney watched as the figure turned from its side angle at which it was painted to the front, facing her.

The goddess looked straight at her. "I do, and I also spoke to you in the cave."

Sydney dropped her flashlight.

"My story is recorded in the stones and stream of the Cave of the Matriarchs. From the beginning of time on this planet it has carried the history of the past into the present. As you have discovered in the Code, the time approaches for our history to again be known."

Sydney picked up her light and shined it on the painting. The eyes of the goddess squinted. She lowered the light.

"It was my eyes that lovingly gazed upon you from the alabaster statue."

Sydney felt a chill, as a fleeting thought scurried across her mind that she was hallucinating again. Her reason should have agreed, but she was either in denial or too shocked at the notion the hallucinations were real. How could this be happening once more? Or was she merely wishing the goddess into existence to validate the Code?

"No. I am real." As if to prove she could not only read thoughts, but also was real, the goddess stepped barefoot from the wall onto the floor of the chamber. The powdery dust circled around her legs and hung in the air.

She wore the horn-shaped crown with sun disc upon which sat the cobra. Draped around her neck and shoulders lay the gemmed collar of royalty. Her ankle-length garment had colors that were intricately drawn in small designs of water-shaped patterns within which were small six-petaled flowers in white with blue centers. As displayed in all her paintings, the bodice of her gown strapped at the shoulders, under the collar, exposing her breasts.

Sydney stepped back, not believing her eyes, yet somehow enthralled by this extraordinary sight. The goddess of her life's work now stood before her. The magic of Isis was legendary in Egypt, the basis for their entire religious system. Isis magically rejoined all the parts of the god,

Osiris, after he had been dismembered by Set. Her son, Horus, was born of their union.

"Daughter of Isis," the goddess said while pointing to the hieroglyphs, "As you journey on the path of your destiny, you open the window of your soul."

Sydney walked over to read the glyphs, still arranging themselves in permanent order. She was baffled, and touched the wall to assure herself she was not imagining motion picture hieroglyphs.

Sydney read aloud from the section that had stopped moving, *"The hands of your cosmic timer return full circle to your chosen way. These words were written 3500 years ago—by you."*

Chapter 62
7:25 AM

A chill flashed through Sydney's spine as she gazed at the words, not believing her translation or her eyes. The hieroglyphs had stopped their movement, as the goddess motioned to the top right of the wall. Sydney began reading:

On the Orders of Pharaoh Thutmose III,
Year 1 of his Reign,
Recorded by Nhasul, Scribe and Army Officer,
In the Great Temple of Karnak

That name, thought Sydney, the one she saw on the papyrus slate of the boy in the temple of Karnak—the boy whose life she saved.

Take Megiddo and you take a thousand cities!

We, the Shemsu Hor, rode with the King at the head of his army. On the 21st day, the feast of the new moon sacred to Amon-Ra, His Majesty led the attack in a chariot of electrum. Every chief of every country joined together to do us battle. They sent their barbarian hordes out the gates, and then sealed them shut. Their wretched armies could not prevail against us and abandoned their horses and chariots of gold and silver.

When the chiefs looked over the wall at the ground covered with their fallen troops, the victorious army gathering the hands of living prisoners, they craved breath for their nostrils, and immediately surrendered to the most favored of the gods.

In tribute they brought gifts of silver, lapis, grain, wine, ivory, chariots, and slaves clad only in gold, standing on the sands as far as the eye could see. All perfect specimens, they stood at dawn as the first beams from the eye of Ra glistened on their golden shackles lighting up the land.

With this victory, and two more, we claimed allegiance from all the vile chiefs. The King built a fort at the gateway along the coast highway, and then headed to the lake, where our soldiers were given leave to soak in the healing waters.

The Shemsu were ordered to open the hidden temple to revive the ancient rituals and provide the King with means to subdue future enemies. We entered the temple and found the holy of holies containing the shrine of the god. We broke the seals and opened the doors of heaven. We gazed on the face of the god. To touch the golden statues of Thoth and Isis, as we had in other times, brought health and long life to the Shemsu.

The King took pleasure at the birth of his reign. The egg of Thoth became his emblem of power. With it, he enriched the temples and monuments and brought back the spoils of many battles. The Most Favored stretched the borders of the empire further than any of his ancestors. He became the mightiest warrior Egypt ever produced. His conquests were recorded in the lands of his victories. The egg remained with the King all his days. At his death, he commanded the egg be returned to the temple of Thoth.

The Shemsu left new writings for our return at a time in the future when the great goddess, Isis, would again reveal her magic and bring us long life. We set the guardian in place and sealed the temple. It awaits 3500 years to be reopened.

We went up to the city of Urushalem where we left a Code for our return to the temple—a Code understood only by a Shemsu.

Chapter 63

So in thrall at the words before her, Sydney stood in a hypnotic trance, neither seeing nor hearing anything. She read the name of the scribe again, which brought back the image of the boy lying helpless on the sand as the vicious crocodile sped toward its prey. And how she had somehow remembered early curses in the ancient tongue that stopped what most likely would have been quick death. Was it possible that she had traveled through time to save his life, *her life,* so he could grow to be influential in the reign of a great warrior-king?

Behind her, a step. Then a pistol cocked. She turned to see Herod aiming a Kobra .45 semiautomatic at her head. Alexander stood beside him holding a canvas bag, and then the pilot emerged from the hole.

Sydney looked back to the spot where the goddess had stood. She saw footprints in the soft dirt. Back on the wall, Isis stood sideways in the pose Sydney first saw. Did the goddess really come down and talk to her? More significantly, did she write those words 3500 years ago? *Was I, am I, Nhasul?*

"Alex …" Sydney could tell he felt contrite.

"I'm all right. They were closer than we thought," he said.

Herod motioned to Sydney with his pistol. "Read it!"

Her panic began again. She couldn't take any chances with this madman! She had to stay focused! She would not jeopardize Alexander's safety or her own. No sign of Tomas. He must still be trussed in the toilet.

Her thoughts raced. The pilot could be armed. Calculating her chances of escape seemed nil. Counting on reinforcements was likely, but when? Ferah and Moishe could be on their way with The Fox's men. For the moment, they were probably on their own.

She pointed, trying to stall so she could think of something. She decided to give a lesson. "The cartouche of Thutmose III," she mumbled, clearing her throat. She took a deep breath to settle herself. "The rectangular glyph with an opening on the bottom meant 'house' and the small rod-shape glyph on the bottom meant 'great.' They were used together as the common designation 'great house,' one way to write 'Pharaoh.' The 'wish formula' consisted of the letters '*nh wd3 snb.* '"

So far, so good, she thought. Herod seemed attentive.

"And the baby chick stood for male. 3 symbolized the guttural sound in the throat, like *hah!* S3 would sound like *sah!* So the glyph for S was an upside-down elongated U, the glyph for the sound of a bird, the glyph for B a half-leg, the jagged water sign we now call Aquarius represented the glyph for N. That part meant *be healthy."*

No one moved. Herod's interest in anything Egyptian, especially this particular Egyptian artifact, became apparent. He touched the glyphs with his free hand, as if reading with his fingertips, the gun hand distracted. Sydney glanced at Alexander, who also noticed

She continued reading. "The whole 'wish formula' reads 'His majesty, May he live, be prosperous, be healthy.' Usually they shortened it to three glyphs."

She pointed to them. "The King is bragging about his battle. He's returning to Egypt with 340 prisoners, over 2,200 horses, over 900 enemy chariots, 200 bows and 24,000 livestock. This temple commemorates his conquest of Megiddo."

"There's got to be more here." Herod was becoming irritated by her lesson. "The Code doesn't say anything about livestock. Where's the temple?" he yelled.

"This leads to it," Sydney said evenly.

Herod turned to the pilot. "Knock on the walls! Find the opening!"

The pilot picked up a hammer from the rucksack Alexander had carried in, and smashed the priceless hieroglyphs. Sydney watched in horror as the carvings crumbled to the ground.

"Not there, you idiot," Herod thundered. "Bang on the floor."

The pilot stopped, knelt down, put his ear to the ground, and softly hammered. He backed up, went sideways, listening for a hollow sound.

"No!" Sydney said, "The Egyptians were perfectionists when it came to their temples and tombs. Everything meant something. There's an easy way and a hard way to enter them. Unless you have the key, you enter the hard way. *With* the key, you enter the easy way. We may not have time to chop through. We'll use the key."

"Where's the key?" Herod asked.

Sydney brushed off another section of the wall. "Look at these hieroglyphs. Do you see anything different about them?"

They all looked dumbfounded.

"Here, the cartouche of the King, Thutmose again, which connects to the colored wall in Jerusalem. The account of his military campaign in the land of the Canaanite-Phoenicians and his victory at Megiddo. This same account is at his Hall of Records at Karnak."

"So what?" Herod grew impatient.

"The difference between these hieroglyphs and the ones at Karnak is this." She pointed to an ibis-headed figure in royal headdress and leopard collar preceding the cartouche. "Here's the key. Just like the Code tells us. Thoth." She pressed it.

A loud scraping sound echoed off the walls. The pilot dashed to the entry hole. Sydney looked at him with amusement and shook her head. "It's just the door opening."

The pilot sheepishly went to the open door and shone a light. Steps leading downward. "You go first."

Herod grabbed the light, pocketing his gun. "Get the gear. You, too," he motioned to Alexander. They picked up the bags and followed. Herod shoved Sydney in front.

She took a light from the bag and stepped through the door. Herod walked behind her. She desperately tried not to panic. Keeping the python away was easier when mentally challenged by the hieroglyphs, but it was still wrapped around her knees. She clicked the light. The steps were covered with eons of sand and dirt.

Nine steps. At the bottom, she said, "Wall ahead."

It was about four feet high and three feet long, with more carved hieroglyphs whose once bright colors were now covered with dust. She blew off the top layer and brushed off the rest. Particles of dust danced in the glow of the lights.

"What does it say?" Herod glared at her.

"The king is extolling his virtues to the gods. 'I conducted the Great Procession, following the god in his steps.' The festival of Osiris. He must have done the festival here instead of Abydos. It just continues on." She searched the wall for the key and found it. "The cartouche again and Thoth."

She pressed the hieroglyph. Nothing happened.

Herod took out his pistol and pointed it at her.

Alexander moved closer to Sydney.

She pressed again. Still nothing. "It must be another glyph."

She shined her flashlight at the wall, brushing off more of the dust. "The Code says Sothis, and there she is—Isis."

She pressed the glyph.

A loud scraping sound and one section of the wall swiveled to reveal a narrow opening. A rush of stale air swept by her as the light chased centuries of darkness from the space. She shivered involuntarily. Heightened senses led her through a half-door that seemed like a birth canal. Three millennia of silence and awe enveloped her like a shroud.

She realized her heart was calling out to the Shemsu to lead her to the truth, whatever it may be.

'It is the Source.' A voice said. She heard it in her head.

What is the Source? She thought.

'Find the Star.'

The Source and the Star are one?

The answer appeared before her in the light. She brushed off the dust. The glyphs for *nfr* which meant *good.*

She pressed the glyphs. Another wall swung open.

"Three walls, three keys, three openings," Sydney said.

But the Code said *double seals protect the lock and open but to double keys. Is the Code wrong or are we in the wrong spot?*

They stepped through the half-door and straightened up. Sydney saw a large chamber whose walls were black. No writing anywhere. On a pedestal stood a life-size black statue with the head of an animal, maybe a ram or goat, she couldn't tell, with horns raised straight up and cut off on top. A striped royal headdress rested on its muscled shoulders. It wore a short kilt with a sash around the waist. One arm was at its side, the other held a gold staff.

"It's Set," Sydney whispered. "God of Chaos."

She stood in front of the shiny, black, dustless statue, mesmerized by the power that seemed to emanate from it.

"Set had no fixed animal associated with him in the pantheon," she said quietly. "This looks like a combination of animals."

"Who was he?" The pilot whispered.

"He was the brother of Osiris, the first king of Egypt. And brother of Isis, the wife of Osiris."

"The king married his sister?" The pilot stood by the statue.

"They did in those days. Set was jealous his brother had the throne *and* Isis, so he devised a plan. He killed Osiris, cut him up, and scattered the fourteen pieces along the banks of the Nile. Isis was heartbroken and went looking for the pieces. She found them and with her magic, put him back together. She brought him back to life long enough to mate with him. Osiris then became Lord of Death and Rebirth. Their son, Horus, would inherit the throne. But Set wanted to kill Horus and take the throne. They battled before the other gods and goddesses, who each had their favorite."

"Not before the people?" The pilot asked.

"No. This was strictly a divine affair. The gods and goddesses would determine the next king. Horus finally won. From then on Horus became the God of Kingship. Set became the God of Infertility and Chaos."

"How did Horus beat him?" Alexander asked.

"There's only one way. After several battles, Horus beat Set when he figured out his own weaknesses. Horus proved to the gods and goddesses he was wiser than Set."

Herod moved to the statue. *"I'll* beat Set and I'll do it with his own weapon." He lifted the gold staff out of the hand of the statue.

Suddenly the eyes lit and filled the chamber with an eerie red glow. They stepped back as a palpable red mist settled on them. Herod dropped the staff.

Sydney felt a sense of dread and a chill ran up her spine. The python circled around her thighs and she felt the urge to run. She broke out in an icy sweat as she stared at the eyes. They bored through her with the ferocity of pulsing flames. A strange heaviness, the weight of thousands of years, descended over her, crushing her spirit. She looked away from the eyes. But they drew her back.

She felt an otherworldly presence, something forcing itself on her. Pressing into her, demanding control of her body. Her soul! She cried out for help, but no sound came from her lips. She felt herself growing weak, surrendering to its will. Unable to resist, to defend herself.

Herod drew his Kobra and pointed it at the others. "You aren't going to steal my statue! Get away! It's mine!" He circled the chamber with gun held at arm's length, pointing at everyone, even the statue. "I won't leave without it! No one can stop me!"

Alexander ducked as Herod's pistol swept the chamber.

Sydney sank to the ground, too weak to stand. The evil presence surrounded her, gaining strength in her debility, its power increasing as her will, sapped, left her defenseless. She watched Alexander moving toward her in slow motion. *He's walking like he's in water.*

The pilot started to scream and violently brushed himself off. "Snakes! Vipers! I know they're here! They're demons! All of them! Get 'em off me! Get 'em off! I gotta get out of here." He ran to one side and put his back to the wall with arms flat against it, trembling.

Sydney closed her eyes as she felt the weight crush her body. The python fell to the ground as the force continued its attack. *Shemsu, Goddess Isis?* She could not form a coherent thought, nor remember the names of any other deities. This was the time to pray, if she only knew how, and could recall to whom to pray. Her mind was outside itself, under the control of this evil thing that had taken the minds of them all.

Suddenly Alexander sank to the floor. "I can't die here!" he shouted. "If I'm trapped in this place, I'll never finish my work!"

Sydney heard him from far away, an echo in a mountainous depression that she was unable to grasp.

"My books will go unpublished! My discoveries will go unfound! I'll die unknown!" Alexander ran to the doorway. "I can't be a failure. I've got to get out of here!"

Sydney saw through the red fog—Herod pointing his pistol at her. "You'll die first!" he shouted. "After you tell me how to get into the temple!"

Dimly, she saw evil reflected in his eyes and looked away. He pointed the gun at the pilot, who screamed at him, "Get that snake away from me!" He ran out of the chamber.

As Sydney sat in abject horror, she realized the evil presence within her had the power to subdue the python. The solution to how she could finally rid herself of the overwhelming panic existed as a pressure within her being. For the first time in her life she sat in an enclosed space, free of the constricting presence of the python! Free of the fear it engendered and the vulnerability it brought. If she kept the evil alive, if she allowed it to control her, she would no longer be afraid of going underground into the darkness.

Her mind truly considered the possibility of allowing permanent residency to this repulsive evil. No, her mind did not think at all. Her fear wanted the python released. Could she negotiate with malevolence? Her mind would not, but her fear could.

The heaviness shifted. The red eyes drew her back. The possibility of life without the python enticed her into the snare. She would like that! The python appeared at inopportune times, restricting her archeological discoveries. She could be free of her fear of the dark, free of fear in enclosed spaces, free of panic. And able to explore new tombs and underground temples with ease.

Was she ready to bargain with evil?

Chapter 64
7:27 AM

Carter rubbed his eyes in the bright sunlight when the rear doors of the truck opened.

Dmitri climbed in. "Take those bags," he motioned to Carter as soon as the cuffs were off.

Carter stood up, threw the bags off the truck and gingerly stepped down. He rubbed his wrists, red from the cuffs, and stretched his back.

Orange flares glowed brightly in the blue sky as they shot up off the vermillion cliff face. Dmitri looked up at the vivid trails falling back to earth. He slammed the front door of the truck, which was parked in the preserve lot. The silver Porsche Boxter pulled in beside him.

"Up there," he said to Marco as he exited the car. When another flare went off, he said, "Let's go."

Hefting the canvas rucksacks, Carter followed Dmitri up the path, Marco close behind him. Herod must be here already, Carter thought, watching the flares, and preparing himself to meet the megalomaniac who kidnapped Sydney and Alexander. He had left Sydney hours ago. She would be worried when he didn't show up, but at least she would be safe at the hotel. He longed to see her. If he cooperated, maybe Herod would release Alexander.

Carter gazed at the burnt umber cliffs, then out at the blue lake of salt. He read the instruction sign alongside the trail for all hikers into the Nahal David preserve, cautioning them to stay on the paths. The Dead Sea and the garden in the desert—the place of the Code. Those flares must be marking the temple.

They trudged up the path, still too early for hikers, but not for the sure-footed ibexes, the wild goats that leapt from crag to crag in the early morning shadows. They passed the stream that gurgled down the cliffs, and heard the rumble of the waterfall in the distance.

Carter heard a shout from above. Someone appeared on a cliff ahead waving a white bandana. Dmitri waved back. The bags weighed down on Carter's shoulders as he maneuvered the rough ground, slowly climbing the trail. They finally reached the point on the path where Dmitri shouted at the one holding the bandana.

This last bit of the climb had exhausted Carter, who sank to the ground with his load.

"Carter!"

He looked up, saw his brother running toward him. "Alex!" He rose and embraced him. "Thankfully, you're alive." Getting close to his ear, Carter whispered, "We weren't sure what Herod would do if Sydney didn't give him the translation."

Dmitri reached the opening to Lover's Cave. He made a show of facing Alexander and Carter, and pulling his pistol. Then sat down on a flat boulder next to the other man, who offered him water.

Alexander looked over at Dmitri and Marco. "They got you too?" he said softly. "Sydney told me you were missing. She only gave him part of the translation." They both sat on the ground next to a large tamarisk tree. They were far enough from their captors to speak freely if they kept their voices low.

"They set me up with a phone call. I thought it was Roland. I've been handcuffed in a truck all night. At least Sydney got away from him and is safe."

Alexander shook his head. "She's not safe. She's here."

"What? How'd that happen?"

"Long story. She's in there," Alexander pointed to the cave, "with *him*."

"Well," Carter said getting up, "let's go get her."

Dmitri saw him and quickly stood up, pointing the weapon at Carter.

"Wait a minute," Alexander pulled Carter back down. "There are a few things you have to know."

Alexander told his brother everything that happened, including deciphering the Code and keeping it from Herod, the earthquake and the huge crystal, finding the cave, Herod and the pilot following them, and the chamber of Set.

At the same time, the pilot was animatedly telling Dmitri and Marco a shorter version.

Alexander lowered his head and played with the dirt at his feet. "There's something else. Something I'm not very proud of." He hesitated. "The Egyptians put some kind of mystical spell in the statue of Set and it creates fear in anyone who looks into the eyes. I thought I was going to die. And had to get out of there. So did he," Alexander shuddered and pointed at the pilot. "It made me weak, like I couldn't fight it." He shook his head. "I ran out on Syd. I'm so ashamed."

Carter touched his brother's arm. "It must've been horrible so don't blame yourself. But we've got to find Syd."

Dmitri came toward them. "Let's go. Take the bags."

"Do you have your strength back?" Carter asked Alexander.

He nodded.

They walked toward the entrance to Lover's Cave. The pilot kept his distance from the entrance. "I tell you there's a curse in that chamber! Don't go in—it will make you crazy! It made Herod so crazy he tried to kill me!"

Chapter 65
7:45 AM

"Wake up! If you don't, you'll go mad," a voice said.

Did the statue speak? From where she sat on the floor, Sydney could see the red eyes glaring down at her, a heaviness surrounded her. She heard laughing. Only she and Herod remained in the chamber, the others had run without looking back. Herod sat on the floor opposite her, not laughing, his eyes blank, the gun still pointing aimlessly in all directions. She looked up at the statue. The glowing eyes bore down at her, laughing.

"Get out fast!" It was the voice of the statue. *"The Egyptians put a curse in this statue that causes everyone's fears to be magnified—a force that emanates from the eyes. Don't look at the eyes."*

Sydney looked away, crawled opposite Herod, and then struggled to her feet. Of all the weird things that had happened to her in the last few days, this was the craziest. Another voice. Not prone to take others' advice, why listen to this one? Yet she knew the voices had led her to the Code and the temple.

And this voice had an urgency which she felt deep in her bones. She had to trust the magic of the initiation process— which had become her own instinctual trust in herself.

With Herod immobilized, she had her chance, if she could only walk. If I get out of here, I might run into the pilot, and be taken prisoner again, she thought. There's got to be another way out.

Shielding her eyes, she circled the statue, trying to find a point on the wall behind it. She lowered her hands bracing herself against the wall, still breathing heavily. The weight on her body shifted.

She stood behind the statue. No one was meant to get as far as where she stood in back of the statue. Without the voice, neither would she. If ancient thieves did break in, they wouldn't get further than this chamber, unless they had a guiding voice. Or they simply destroyed the statue, if the thought even entered their minds. If they got out to tell the story, one more legend developed about the Egyptians, their magic and their cursed temples.

Taking a few deep breaths, a sense of gratitude returned at being back in her body. The physical pressure had lifted, as she realized the necessity of coming as close to a willing acceptance of evil she had ever experienced. Or was it evil?

Set, himself, had demanded her to recognize her inner demon and the burdensome influence it had exerted upon her. She had chosen the path away from fear. Definitely the more difficult choice in Set's chamber.

She felt a sense of pride—another stage of initiation completed.

She knew now she could withstand the power of Set, the guardian of the temple. The King must have set the statue in place when he returned to Egypt.

Why leave such a powerful guardian?

Chapter 66

Still avoiding the statue's eyes, she searched for another key, the one she knew had to be there as part of the guardian's chamber. She looked back at Herod, who sat listlessly against the pedestal, his limp hand holding the pistol. The other keys were at about the same point on the walls. Thinking like an Egyptian, and if they kept to the engineers' plans, this one should be about halfway down. And there it was—a slight protrusion in the wall.

She pressed it. Nothing happened.

She placed her hand flat against the wall. It was smooth. And jet black for a reason. Anything on it could be cleverly disguised, and most importantly—no shadows. Even the most minute bump, carving or painting dissolved into the walls. The temple builders took no chances with irregularities.

She went to the opposite wall. A red glow permeated the chamber. Two red laser beams from the eyes of Set pierced the wall. She felt a small indentation, below the point of the gaze. She pressed. Nothing happened.

Undaunted, Sydney stared at the wall. Thinking like an Egyptian was tough. Maybe she needed to *feel* like one. She remembered the myth—in one of their battles, Set put out the eye of Horus. Later, his mother, Isis, magically restored it. In the following centuries his eye was used by the people as a protective amulet.

She reached into her ragged gown and pulled a pendant over her head. It had the deep blue emblem of an eye. She had worn it since her first trip to Egypt, a gift from Bill who told her the Eye of Horus symbolized healing and strength.

"Let's see if the Eye can magically restore my way out of this chamber," she whispered, placing the pendant against the wall where the red beams were projected by the eyes of the statue.

Her hands shook and the pendant fell to the ground. She steadied herself by placing her hands on the black wall, which appeared to respond to her touch, and actually quivered against her palms. She gasped at the tingle in her hands, looked around at the glyphs materializing out of the wall as if responding to a *fast forward* command.

Awestruck at the phenomenon of the wall seeming to transform into a living thing, moving beneath her hands, she watched hieroglyphs form onto the wall, emerging out of the blackness into the light. She pulled her hands away. The hieroglyphs appeared to be imprinted onto her palms and fingers, moving in the light with a vast inner glow that recognized the glyphs of the god, Set. The writing settled into place on the wall. Sydney stepped back and read the hieroglyphs in amazement—a story unknown since ancient times.

After the death of Osiris, the throne passed to his younger brother, Set, who ruled for many years. His staff of power had a huge crystal at the top. Horus stole the crystal, which he thought would make him wiser in the eyes of the other gods. Because Horus was not ready to rule, he could not see into the crystal ball. He aimed his fury at Set, accusing his uncle of putting out his eye. Horus believed magic resided in the crystal rather than himself.

The words of Set echoed across the land and were heard by Horus. *I am your truth. Look upon me to know your folly.*

Sydney realized the ancient story of Horus triumphant over Set in their battles was not true. Horus didn't beat Set. He beat himself. When Set finally offered Horus clarity of vision into his own recklessness, Horus humbly accepted the offer, and realized his irresponsible behavior prevented his evolution, not Set. With this insight, his wisdom grew.

Sydney now empathized with Set. He had taught the Egyptians the nature of truth, choosing in his magnanimous effort the role of vilified god down through the ages, proving evil only existed if fear held sway. He had accepted the Godhead of Chaos as a supreme gift to his people.

She bowed to the statue in honor of his true essence. Then picked up the pendant. Suddenly the chamber lit up with a gleaming white light. Astounded, she watched as the wall seemed to dissolve.

Chapter 67
7:58 AM

Sydney fumbled with the pendant and stared into the space where the wall stood just seconds before. Seated on a black granite pedestal, the life-size ibis-headed statue gleamed in the swirling white mist. The long black beak curved downward from the blue-painted head. His blue and gold-striped royal headdress supported the Thoth crown—sun disc within the crescent moon. The knee-length formal linen kilt swept upward in the back, the front folded over the inner garment. A white sash emerged from the left side of the kilt at the waist over his right shoulder. Draped around his neck and chest the royal lapis, turquoise, carnelian and gold collar.

Thick gold bracelets embedded with the same stones circled his upper arms. His left hand held a gold staff, while the right hand rested casually on his right thigh, palm up, holding an egg-shaped object. The swirling mist gave the statue an otherworldly appearance.

Slowly stepping through the doorway, Sydney approached the statue. Thoth. He gifted the Egyptians with writing and wisdom. Gazing up, she felt a distinct vibration surrounding the pedestal that she had never before experienced. Or had she? Was there something familiar about it?

She heard a scuff behind her. Turning, she saw Herod swaying in the doorway, one hand shielding his eyes. Hefting the staff of Set, he squinted into the chamber and approached the pedestal. Sydney saw the lust in his eyes and knew he wanted the staff of Thoth.

He reached for it, but it didn't budge. "They got it in there," he grunted. "Has to be a way to get it out." He set the staff of Set against the pedestal and pulled with both hands.

Sydney turned to him. "You might want to think about it. His eyes look just as intense as Set's."

Herod stopped, looking up at the eyes. They were black ovals of onyx set into creamy white glass.

"You could trigger the same thing, or something worse."

Herod seemed to consider the possibility. He looked at the right hand. "What's in his hand?"

Sydney shrugged. "Nothing of importance." She knew the creation myths told of Thoth coming from the stars. He brought with him a cosmic egg that stirred creation. He placed the egg on a mound of earth called the Isle of Flame. The egg cracked, hatching the sun, which rose up into the sky. The sun was a potent life force. With the waters of the Nile, it brought the people thousands of years of successful harvests, and a highly advanced civilization.

Herod looked at the goose-egg sized milky white object. He removed the egg from the statue's hand and held it in his palm. Sydney stepped back from the statue, expecting something drastic to happen.

Herod smiled at his conquest.

The egg on his palm slowly turned from milky white to a cloudy shade of dark gray-green. He looked up into the statue's eyes.

Sydney watched him suddenly come under the control of the statue, in a different way than he had with Set. Unlike most birds with eyes on the sides, this bird's eyes looked straight ahead, like human eyes. Herod held the staff of Set in one hand, the egg in the other.

Sydney turned back to the statue, thinking she saw a quiver in the hand that had held the egg. Then a light appeared in the empty hand, swirling around the body, down to the feet and up to the solar and lunar crown. Suddenly the statue came to life!

They both stepped back, watching in awe and disbelief as the statue raised his empty hand and lowered his head to look at what was no longer there. He rose to his feet, the ibis eyes gazing at her with love and kindness. She felt they were reading her soul. The long beak seemed to smile. Then he glared at Herod, who wilted under the harsh gaze and quickly returned the egg to the empty hand, sinking to the floor, seemingly unable to stand.

Sydney recognized a connection that reached into the depths of her being. When the statue stepped down off the pedestal, she knew she was being summoned into a dimension of reality both unknown, and at the same time very familiar.

The statue strolled toward the wall. Sydney didn't hesitate. She followed Thoth as they walked through the wall!

Chapter 68
8:10 AM

The chamber was empty!

Carter, Alexander, Marco and Dmitri entered the chamber of Set.

"Same statue we saw before. Except now it seems even more threatening," Alexander said, lowering his head and staying close to the entrance.

The eerie red glow seemed to penetrate the black walls, causing them to expand then contract in a hellish breath.

"Where are they?" Carter shone his light into every corner, carefully shielding his eyes.

Alexander looked around. "I don't know. Everything's the same—except the gold staff is gone." He averted his eyes.

Marco looked into the eyes of Set.

Dmitri turned to him. "Stop that! Didn't you hear the pilot? The eyes are cursed—you will be too if you don't turn away."

Too late. Marco blinked and recoiled in terror. "It's a demon! Get it out of here." He waved his light back and forth. "Don't let 'em get me—they're evil. Get away from me," he screamed.

Carter avoided the eyes. He kept his head down, looking away from the statue. Feeling a malevolent presence, he fought an overwhelming urge to bolt the chamber.

Dmitri tried to calm Marco without any success. He started swinging wildly at something he seemed to feel was attacking him. "Get it away! It's evil," he screamed.

"It's not real! Look away from the eyes," Dmitri implored him, hunched over as he turned away from the statue, then began cursing and shouting. "It's the dark! And the closeness. There's no air! I can't breathe."

Alexander stood near the entrance, his back to the statue. "I can't stay in here. I'm not good enough. I'll never be as well-known as my parents."

Marco ran out of the chamber, followed closely by Dmitri.

Carter crept backwards, a fiendish heaviness enveloping him, barely hearing his brother's wails. "It's mocking me! Without looking at the eyes, I know it is. The statue knows I'll die an early death. I'll die without ever having lived." He shivered and sank to one knee, his arms over his face. He only knew his own overpowering fear and knew he must get out.

"Wake up! If you don't, you'll go mad," a voice said. "Set brings all fears to light. Anyone who enters is forced to confront themselves, unless they flee."

From where he sat on the floor, Carter imagined he had heard a voice. But was it his imagination? He struggled to heed the words of the voice and crawled to the back of the statue, swinging his light at the flat black wall. Shoving the light into his pocket, he shielded his eyes from the red mist and began touching the wall. On his knees, he felt himself clawing the wall for life. Searching for... what?

He struggled to stand while he scratched his way up, hand over hand, finger over finger—feeling like a rock climber on a sheer cliff face without a rope. He knew logically there was no cliff, no drop. Never in his life had he been faced with the dire decision to fight for his very existence as he did now.

Why had he given in to the fear of dying early? He didn't know where or when the terror took him over, but it had kept him from truly living—and fueled his craving to cram as much adventure and sex into each day, destroying his relationship with the only woman he had ever truly loved.

A part of his mind urged him to flee the chamber. He would be safe if he left, but the terror would remain, keeping him enslaved in its control. Another part urged him on, compelling him to call out his power to brawl and fight for his right to exist without fear.

In his deluded state, he became the mountaineer that heaved himself off the ground and began ascending, actually scraping the wall with his clawed hands, his legs exerting against gravity. His foot slipped, but he regained his hand hold in what he thought was a slight indentation. He was in the dark, alone, muscles straining to elevate his body onto a safe landing. But there was no landing above him, only the place where the ceiling met the wall. And yet he knew the drop was thousands of feet into a rocky crevasse.

He willed his inner warrior to face the enemy—himself, and slay the fear. He had no choice. He *had* to make the top.

Chapter 69
8:10 AM

Sydney knew they were in the Temple of the Code. But where? It felt unreal. As if she had walked into another dimension—outside physical reality. Yet *very* real. More real than physical reality. It had a spatial quality, a dream world with vast reaches into the beyond. But this was no dream. She felt her body. Quite solid. Yet she had walked through a wall!

After Thoth removed his ibis headdress, he sat cross-legged on the floor of the circular temple. Both old and young, male and female, human and god, he radiated power, a vaguely familiar warm glow that filled her with a sense of well-being. The mysterious voice she had heard since Santa Barbara. They sat in a circular chamber ringed with columns.

"The planet is in the process of a dimensional shift. You experienced that shift—from the third dimension to the fourth—and back to the third." His voice emitted warmth.

Sydney sat before him. "I walked through the wall into another dimension?"

"The Egyptians would have said you were merely expressing religion, experiencing the increase in your own vibrational rate where compassion and love are the normal modes of being." He smiled.

"I've read that they could do magic by praying to their many gods and goddesses."

"To the Egyptians—magic *is* religion, and is used in many ways."

Sydney looked around the chamber in which they sat. Herod was not there. He must still have been back in the chamber with the empty pedestal.

Thoth straightened his blue and gold nemes headdress. After the ibis head came off, he had a distinctly human face—piercing blue-green eyes, aquiline nose, thin lips, and pronounced chin. "Magic was the foundation of their entire religious system."

"You mean magic, like Isis putting Osiris back together?" Sydney asked.

"Isis taught the people how to do what *she* could do. She became the first to use magic in a ritualistic way. For example, sit a moment. You will feel the magic of the Egyptians." He closed his eyes.

In a moment Sydney realized she felt something she had never experienced before. An equanimity of emotions—a profound sense of peace within herself and the world. A sense of unity with this being before her, whether he was a god, a man, a slave, or a king. And the sense of acceptance of herself merged into a wave that engulfed her, whether she was a woman, a queen, a slave, or a goddess.

She opened her eyes. *It was Thoth that led me to the colored wall and the Code of the King.*

"I must prepare you for the ritual you will perform during the darkness of the face of Ra. It is the same as that which Isis herself brought to the Shemsu Hor, Followers of Horus, the pre-dynastic leaders who taught the first pharaohs."

He waved his hand in the space between them to show the construction of the temple centuries before Thutmose III left his cartouche. She gasped at the beautiful landscape— palm trees, deep blue lake surrounded by large settlements of peaceful people. Built by the Shemsu, the forecourt was bathed in sunlight, gleaming in blue reflected off the water of the clear lake, circled by lush green vegetation. Inner chambers were set into the sandstone cliffs that rose over two thousand feet into the sky.

Around the circular chamber rose twelve columns in gleaming white limestone, topped with lotuses, scenes of gods and goddesses carved in raised reliefs, and painted in brilliant colors. The walls glowed with raised glyphs of bright blue and gold, the Pyramid Texts and Book of the Dead. She marveled at the craftsmanship that produced such exquisite glyphs.

Thoth kept his hand palm up, moving the characters on the pillars. "Many people today are attracted to ancient Egypt. As each becomes accustomed to the quickened vibrations in the world, they can ease into higher spiritual dimensions. This takes courage and responsibility because it removes them from the teachings of their traditional religious beliefs."

Sydney sat enthralled with the wisdom of the ancients, and the voice of Thoth. She had faced the first challenge of initiation into the priesthood. As Set magnified her fears in the chamber, so the initiates were faced with the full horror of looking into the mirror and seeing their truths. Their task was to overcome the fear, to pass on to the next level.

She felt the same rhythm as the heartbeat of the stone in the cave, as a golden glow filled the chamber.

"Modern archeologists deny what is before their eyes, that the Egyptians were far more awakened than they can imagine, and that these are not funeral texts," Thoth said. "There are those who feel the heartbeat of the planet as you do. You are conductors of this energy, attuned to the cosmic beat, reorienting the chaotic particle fields surrounding the planet.

"The electromagnetic field has become quite unstable. This also occurred thousands of years ago, causing Gaia to purify herself. The Shemsu helped steady the planet by attuning their bodies to the harmonic frequencies. I taught them 'As Above, So Below,' as the first lesson. Creating harmony in the physical creates balance in the outer. Those who resonate to the cosmic heartbeat have ascended to the fourth dimension still in the physical body. The Egyptians were familiar with this state."

Questions rattled around in Sydney's head. The main one: *Why me?*

Chapter 70
8:15 AM

Alexander thought he was going insane. He had never felt such fear. Tears rolled down his cheeks without any awareness of crying. He could not remember the last time he cried. Nor feeling such an overriding sensation of malevolency.

His shame at abandoning Sydney felt like a knife in his heart. He sank to his knees and toppled over sideways, aware of the penetrating eyes surrounding him. He felt himself descending into self-doubt about himself and his work whenever someone mentioned his parents.

Renowned for their discovery in Cyprus of the first Late Bronze Age tomb which contained bronze swords, gold and silver jewelry, and ivory boxes, they also found the first pictorial-style kraters, large jars used for mixing water and wine. His father was recognized for his discovery of a krater with a stylized elongated horse and chariot painted on one side, two rearing horses on the other. These beautifully decorated jars were also found in northern Israel. Believing he did not measure up to those two giants left him shrunken into oblivion.

"Wake up before you go mad!" Alexander thought he heard a voice. He jerked his eyes from the statue at the same time he realized he could not let himself diminish further. He roused himself enough to search his memory for his father's face, especially how he looked when conveying the great things he expected from his eldest son. Alexander rarely

disappointed his father, nor could he allow himself to diminish the responsibility that came with his own name.

Dimly, his father appeared before him holding the krater, and handed it to him as his legacy. He took it with the supreme joy of stepping outside the shadow of the giant, into his own light.

Through the red mist he saw his brother clawing the wall. Protecting his eyes, he crawled toward Carter at the wall behind the statue.

Carter turned to his brother. "Come on! I'm almost at the top. Take my hand."

Alexander looked up at the black wall. "What top?" He thought his brother had already gone mad, but took his hand anyway.

"We're almost out of here!" Carter stretched out his other hand toward the top of the cliff he could not see. He was blind to everything around him, except his brother who held his other hand. "Get a foot hold! Find a notch!" Without a rope he could make no mistakes. Without a rope he was living life truly on the edge.

Straining to reach the top, Carter saw the face of his mother urging him on. He had always longed for his father's approval, even though he had lagged far behind his elder brother in the academic realm. His mother accepted him unconditionally, even when naughty as a child and when, as a college student, he partied into the night and missed exams the next day. He knew she somehow understood his reckless assertion of independence as a show of his own being, which ran counter to those of his brother.

The fact that she was a professional in the same field he had chosen and loved him despite his failings brought him a measure of emotional security. But did nothing for his later relationships with women, who could not put up with his high maintenance, or his expectations of entitlement.

He grasped his mother's hand and fell onto the top ledge of rock, at the same time pushing on the wall and tumbling into the chamber of Thoth.

Alexander fell on top of his brother and rolled off. They both sat up, squinting in the light. Carter could see nothing, nor where the light came from.

A sardonic voice reverberated off the walls. "Just in time, boys. I was running out of air."

Carter reached in his pocket for his flashlight and shone it into the chamber. They gasped at the totally unexpected sight before them.

Holding a gold staff and flashlight in one hand, pointing a .45 semi-automatic at them with the other hand, and sitting on top of a royal pedestal—Herod.

Chapter 71
8:15 AM

Moishe pulled the car into the preserve lot—empty except for a truck parked near the entrance. "Did Victoria say why they were delayed?"

"Just that Benjamin hadn't made it back. And they couldn't locate Yuval Goldman. She'll call when they leave and we can direct them." Ferah exited the car and looked at the Dead Sea. A plane floated on the water, bobbing in the salty foam. "If that's how they brought Sydney, why would he land out there?"

"Look at it, Mom," Zaki pointed. "It's filled with water from that big hole in the top."

"That's strange." Moishe shielded his eyes from the sun. "What could have made a hole that size through the top of a plane?"

Ferah shook her head, puzzled.

"It could if something went through the bottom and came out the top," Ellie said. "Like a stone."

Everyone turned to her. "Do you think that's what caused it?" asked Ferah.

Ellie nodded. "According to the Code, the stone awakes. We thought it was in the temple, but this shows it could have been in the lake."

Moishe looked around the lot. "How do we know where to go?"

"If the stone was there, under the plane, assuming the plane hasn't moved too much, then Ra would shine over there." Ellie pointed. "Or the stone pointed in that direction."

Zaki looked around. "It's quiet. Maybe we can hear where they are."

"Listen up, you two," Ferah said to her son and Ellie. "These are dangerous people. With guns. I want you both to stay out of sight, in the car. No sneaking around. No arguments."

"We want to see the eclipse. We won't get in the way," Zaki pleaded.

"Listen to your mother! Stay here and watch for Victoria and the others," Moishe said.

"You can see the eclipse from here." Ferah placed both hands on his shoulders. "You, too, Ellie. Do you understand?" She held him close, took his face in her hands and kissed him.

They both nodded.

Ferah followed Moishe to the preserve entrance, her sense of unease increasing with every step.

Chapter 72
8:22 AM

In his delirious state of fear, Alexander had trusted his brother to get him out of the chamber of horror. Breaking through the wall became the psychological catharsis he so desperately needed. His internal questioning of his professional status was itself being questioned. Their father had appeared and gifted him with his archeological legacy. Alexander accepted the krater with a profound sense of gratitude. Honored by his father's gesture, he felt a new awareness, a stamp of validation that had long eluded him.

Herod quickly jumped off the pedestal and stood over Carter and Alexander, who lay in a heap on the floor. Alexander rolled off the top of his brother, where he had fallen, and looked up into the barrel of Herod's pistol.

"She told you how to read the Code!" Herod scowled at him. "Where's the temple?"

Alexander helped his brother up. "We're in it."

"You got through that wall. You can get through another one," Herod said, pointing to the opposite side.

"Where's Sydney?" Carter asked.

Herod glared at him and turned back to Alexander. "She got this far on the Code! What's the rest?"

Alexander knew he had to stall for time. If Sydney found a way out, he thought, why hadn't Herod followed? If she did, that meant there was another chamber that had a means of entry. He pointed to the pedestal. "Was a statue there?"

Herod hesitated, averting his eyes.

JERI CASTRONOVA

So a statue sat on the pedestal, thought Alexander. But where is it?

"Forget about a statue!" Herod pointed the pistol at Carter, moving him backward toward the Set chamber. Herod shined his light into an empty room, except for the predominant red mist. "Bunch of cowards! Go and get them. And bring the bags!"

Carter bent to get through the opening to the Set chamber, shielding his eyes as he hastened through it. He remembered climbing a cliff, taking his brother's hand and reaching out to his mother. When he reached the top he found himself in the Thoth chamber. How did that happen?

He recalled doing nothing to the wall, except overcoming his fear of falling into an early grave by his recklessness in trying to prove himself. He had dangled precipitously to a life he thought would be short-lived, and survived a moment of absolute terror. He knew now he wanted that life more than anything—prolonged and filled with heart-felt events.

He remembered Sydney telling him about certain temples that contained chambers the Egyptians believed could only be opened by a shift in consciousness. And that the Egyptian religious system originated on the assumption that each person had their own individual experiences that drew them closer to their god, or truth. With each experience they were able to climb the ladder to heaven.

He desperately needed to find Sydney. She had to be in there somewhere. He flashed on her small St. Jude medal she showed him after he picked her up in Yardenet. It had somehow given her comfort during her kidnapping ordeal.

For the first time in his life, Carter reached outside himself and asked the little medal of hopeless causes to return Sydney to him.

Chapter 73
8:23 AM

Sydney raised her head to ask a question but Thoth was gone. She sat on the floor of the circular temple holding the egg. It was a bright milky white. She watched it change to a marble blue-white swirl.

Suddenly a flash of blue-white light emitted from the egg and filled the temple. The smooth walls that were midnight black seconds ago flared to bright blue and dazzling gold.

Awed, Sydney lifted her hand and gazed at the egg, an iridescent gold flame that projected sapphire and white light into a star-shaped pattern. The star rotated onto the walls, now seen in all their beauty, covered with bright gold hieroglyphs on dark turquoise. Why had she not seen them before?

She rose and walked to the wall to examine the writing. She recognized it—The Pyramid Texts! The oldest writings on religion ever discovered. Found inside a pyramid at Saqqara, they were believed to have been written around 3200 BC. Everyone knew of the Dead Sea Scrolls, but the Pyramid Texts had been largely ignored by archeologists and were still unknown by many Egyptians.

These exquisitely carved hieroglyphs had the familiar cartouche of the king and read left to right with his proclamation.

'I, Thutmose, and the Shemsu Hor, consecrate this temple to commemorate my victory at Megiddo.

We awaken the words of Thoth into our hearts. We anchor this intent into our black land to prosper many thousands of years.

The Code of the King is written to be read in a place to be found. The Code awaits the return of the Shemsu Hor.

A Window of Time will open to the Shemsu after the rising of the stone from the Lake of Salt. While darkness covers the face of Ra.

The temple opens to those of right blood. All others are turned away by magic, according to the wand of Isis.

The Shemsu who read this wall awaken the words of Thoth.

The sacred rites will be remembered by the Shemsu to anchor the cosmic egg of Thoth.

As Isis reassembled Osiris, the diverse lands are unified again for the continuation of all races.

Sydney reread the words, scarcely believing her own eyes. *We are the Shemsu Hor.*

According to the wall, a window of opportunity had already opened, allowing the Shemsu to perform the magical ritual that anchors the old wisdom and awakens Shemsu in other parts of the world.

Sydney considered the huge responsibility if they were truly the Shemsu. It meant they were here with Thutmose to birth a new awakening in his land of conquest. If that were the case, it could only mean this land was next in line to come into existence as a new power in the world. Did Thoth himself choose the land of Canaan for the home of the Hebrews?

Chapter 74
8:35 AM

Carter crawled from the hole leading to Lover's Cave, and walked the path around the pool. Sunlight poured into the entrance to the cave. He shielded his eyes so they could become accustomed to the light.

Marco, Dmitri and the pilot were sitting outside on large flat rocks. Dmitri rose when he saw Carter emerge from the cave.

"You're wanted inside," Carter thumbed as he walked outside.

"Not me," the pilot shook his head. "He doesn't pay me enough."

Marco stood up. "I can do it."

"Just don't look at the eyes." Dmitri adjusted the shoulder holster carrying the Ruger. He quickly drew it out, pointed down at the path, and shouted. "Hold it!"

Carter turned to see a man and woman climbing the path, their hands in the air.

"What the Hell is this? A tourist destination?" Dmitri shouted.

Marco nodded at him. "Exactly what it is. And more will be coming when the preserve opens. Get 'em out of sight."

"Khalid!" the woman shouted at the pilot.

Khalid went toward the couple. "Ferah and Moishe, we meet again." he grinned. "You nearly met Herod the day you bought the two artifacts. He drove up to see the site I told you about—the grave of the Solomon priests. I didn't show you the spot, but I showed him. And he was very interested. We've already started a crew out there."

Ferah slapped him hard across the face. "You son-of-a-bitch Palestinian *fool*. Don't you know you're selling out your own history? Your ancestors lived here too."

Before she could go on, Dmitri grabbed her and shoved her to the ground. Moishe jumped at him, knocking Dmitri off balance, causing the gun to slip from his hand. He grabbed it just as Moishe got on top of him, fist ready.

Khalid rubbed his face and glared at Ferah. Moishe stepped away from Dmitri.

Carter pulled Ferah to her feet. "Who're you?" she asked. When he told her, Ferah made a point of drawing him close to loudly thank him, then quickly whispered, "We have the Code," and backed off.

She turned to Moishe. "I should've known he was on to the priests' graves. He was just leading us on to keep us coming back."

"We'll dig up everything in those graves before the archeologists at Sebastiya know we're in the area," Khalid said with a triumphant smirk. "I'll fly some of it out to our most impatient buyers. Herod will get the rest into the Swiss accounts."

Dmitri motioned everyone into the cave. Khalid folded his arms stubbornly and returned to the flat stone.

"You go first," Dmitri told Marco. "I'll kill anyone that does anything out of line."

Chapter 75
8:51 AM

The egg burned brightly in Sydney's hand, blue and gold starlight filling the chamber. Thoth had instructed her to revive the Shemsu wisdom by activating the magic of Isis. She needed other Shemsu. She looked for an opening, but saw nothing on any wall, even the one she walked through. I've got to get back to the Thoth chamber, she thought. But how?

A familiar voice said, *Use the egg.*

She recognized the voice, but had no idea how Thoth wanted the egg used. When she moved her hand toward the wall, the light gleamed brighter.

Suddenly the center of the wall swiveled in, revealing the chamber of Thoth with the empty pedestal. Herod sat on the floor with his back against the pedestal. He stared with open mouth at the wall which moved in front of him, the bright light directed at him, alarm crossing his face as if he had been stricken. Sydney walked through the light, enjoying his discomfort.

Alexander, who had been pressing every glyph on the wall, dashed to Sydney. "Are you all right?"

"I'm fine," Sydney was overwhelmed to see him.

Alexander stared past the open wall. "Looks like you found the temple."

Herod rose, walked through the wall that had swiveled open. "The Temple of the Code!" He gazed in awe at the magnificent columns and painted walls.

Sydney wrapped her hand around the egg, an obvious power object that could have long-term ramifications in the wrong hands. What else could it do besides open walls? She wondered. Did Thutmose use it to conquer this land and bring treasure back to Egypt? If so, the egg may prove to be the wild card in the Code, especially if this temple were similar to every other Egyptian temple. There was always a Holy of Holies.

Moving into the glittering chamber brought stunned silence. The twelve columns surrounding the circular chamber had painted carvings of gods and goddesses in resplendent royal garb accompanied by golden staffs, kingly thrones, leopards, baboons, herons and crocodiles.

Sydney felt a sense of familiarity with the temple, that she was showing off the chamber, which just happened to be decorated with beloved family members.

Chapter 76
8:59 AM

"Dad!" Marco dashed into the temple, abruptly stopping in the center when he realized the opulence that surrounded him. "She cracked the Code!" He looked ardently at Sydney.

"You should've stayed outside," Herod said. "You're in the way."

Marco shrugged, pointing at Dmitri, who followed Carter, Ferah and Moishe through the entrance. "He told me to come."

After a few obscenities directed at Dmitri about his decision to bring them all into the chamber, Herod ordered them to sit with backs against the wall.

"Syd!" Carter nearly bounded over to her, but Dmitri stopped him with his pistol against Carter's neck.

"I'm all right." Sydney said to him, relieved that he was alive.

Carter sat down next to Ferah.

Herod turned to Sydney. "Now—you will tell me where the pharaoh's treasure is!" His face twisted into ravenous greed.

She shivered at his menacing demeanor, taking care not to provoke him further and looked around the chamber. "What treasure?"

"The treasure of the Code!" he growled.

Unruffled, she said, "This isn't a tomb. It's a temple. The treasure's all around you. This is the encrypted Code." She shone her light onto the gleaming gold hieroglyphs. "The Pyramid Texts, a guide through the underworld, into birth, death and resurrection. Not for the king, but anyone trained for initiation. The columns show the primary gods and goddesses, who played a major part in the rituals of Isis."

Herod aimed his pistol at Alexander's head. "You will tell me where the treasure is by the count of three or I'll shoot him. One…"

"Wait!" Alexander hollered. "I know where it is."

"Don't tell him!" Sydney said.

"How do you know?" Herod said.

"She told me on the plane." Alexander said.

Herod lowered his gun, and then aimed at Sydney's head. "Don't tell him anything!" she shouted.

While everyone's attention was on Herod, Carter moved away from the wall, edging in Sydney's direction.

"Two!" Herod bellowed.

"Wait!" Ferah cried out at the same time she rose off the floor.

Moishe tried to grab her. "Don't!"

Ferah moved toward to Sydney. "She told you the gold is on the walls."

"Stay where you are!" Herod shouted, aiming at Sydney. "Three!"

Ferah threw herself in front of Sydney as the shot was fired, the loud retort reverberating off the columns and walls.

"No! Ferah, No!" Moishe wailed, as he flung himself to her.

Ferah fell backwards into Sydney, both tumbling to the ground. Moishe nearly broke their fall, as Ferah landed on top of Sydney, bleeding from the chest. Carter ran to them, positioning his hand over the wound to stop the bleeding. Ferah looked down to where the blood was spurting, opened her mouth to speak, but no words came out. Carter gently moved her slightly as Sydney slipped from under her.

"Ferah!" Sydney leaned over her. "Oh, my God."

Alexander knelt down. Moishe held his wife's head, which dropped to the side. Her arms fell and her body went limp.

Herod held his gun, smoke trails emerging from the barrel. He gaped at the mortally wounded woman and slowly lowered the pistol. Everyone stood silent.

"Oh, no, not Ferah," Sydney cried. It stunned her that a woman she felt so close to lay dead. The woman who seemed larger than life, and willing to risk so much to protect the precious artifacts of her land.

Herod turned his back and looked up at a column. Marco and Dmitri stared coldly at the dead woman. Dmitri callously stepped over her as he moved to Herod.

Moishe kept rocking Ferah, humming softly in her ear, tears running down his face. He closed her eyes. "She'll sleep now, won't you, my sweetheart?"

Sydney and Carter were still on the floor. Carter wiped the splattered blood mixed with tears off her face with his hand.

From the columns, the gods looked down and grieved. The goddesses wept.

Carter held Sydney as she buried her face in his chest. "She deliberately stepped in front of me. Why? It should've been me."

Carter shook his head and held her closer.

Moishe stopped rocking. "She took so many risks. I tried to stop her, but she wouldn't listen. She had to somehow stop the looting."

Herod perked up at this. "Was she The Fox?"

Through tear-stained eyes, Moishe glowered at him, and said calmly, "Even if she was The Fox, the work will go on." "Not me," Sydney murmured. "I can't go on. It doesn't matter any more."

Chapter 77
9:20 AM

"Goddamn!" Herod glared at the woman on the floor.

"You shot the wrong one," Dmitri said, "but it doesn't matter. *She's* the one you ought to eliminate." He pointed at Sydney. "We don't need her any more."

"He's right, Dad," Marco took his father's arm.

Herod paused as if considering whether he could make sense of the remainder of the Code. "The translator has served her purpose." His stony face looked fiercely at Sydney.

"We've got enough of the Code to find the treasure," Marco said. "The Egyptians always had gold."

"If she *was* The Fox, it's made my life a lot easier." Herod looked down at Ferah. "Get her out," he motioned to Dmitri.

Moishe put his arms out to block Dmitri. "Get away! I'll take her out myself."

Alexander helped as Moishe gently lifted her. Herod motioned with his pistol for Alexander to move back. Moishe carried her through the doorway back to the Thoth chamber. Herod motioned Dmitri to follow them.

"This is the last time I'll ask." Herod said to Sydney. "Where's the treasure?"

Sydney's wet eyes stayed closed. She was worn down and exhausted, unable to respond to him or even to stand. It didn't matter anymore. Ferah had taken the bullet for her. There was no way she could continue.

She had thought the Code was important. That it would lead to new knowledge about the Egyptians and the Pyramid Texts. Her book would be validated and she would write a new book that she'd present at professional conferences. Maybe the new findings would sway her traditional colleagues. Maybe not.

Things change in the blink of a star. What was once a gift to the world was smashed with the death of a loved one. Sydney realized her deep affection for Ferah. A gentle, caring soul with integrity and honesty who risked her own freedom to carry looted artifacts back across the Green Line, risking not only her life, but her family's safety.

Ferah risked the wrath of the Supreme Muslim Counsel of the Temple Mount, the Waqf, when her group, Palestinians for the Preservation of Temple Mount, challenged them. Demanded they account for everything taken out of the Dome of the Rock excavations, allowing the Antiquities Association access to the mounds of sifted debris. Even the government backed down from the demands of the Waqf.

"I'll destroy the hieroglyphs if you don't tell me!" Herod started firing into the walls. Gold and turquoise shattered into minute pieces as they exploded off the wall and fell to the ground. Sydney covered her ears, and couldn't look at the destruction she knew he caused.

Herod emptied his clip, ejected it, and inserted another.

Carter held her closer. "She can't help you," he said to Herod.

"Then I'll pick you off one by one, starting with him." He aimed at Alexander.

Sydney heard the voices from a distance, as if they were in a deep valley echoing off high cliffs. She wondered if she was still alive, or if her extreme guilt had forced her out to join Ferah. That would be welcome—to just leave when you are no longer effective. Why prolong it? She thought.

Unfortunately, she remained in her body, pulled against the current, as if swimming south in the Nile as it flowed north. And could not make the banks of either side, so engulfed in a swirling morass of pity, fear, guilt, and remorse. Where was Taweret, the hippopotamus goddess who would lift her up on her mighty back, swim through the undertow to a sandy shore, and deposit her into the warmth of Ra, who would sooth her grief and eliminate the pain?

It didn't matter that the Shemsu wrote the Code and returned to fulfill their own prophecy. Even if she were a Shemsu, how could she do what Thoth asked? The world wasn't ready for enlightenment. The world didn't deserve his wisdom. Not with murderers like Herod who loot, kidnap and kill innocent people. If Thoth wanted the Shemsu to perform the same anchoring as before, why didn't he stop Herod?

"Carter, please take me home," she murmured.

He brushed the tears away. "Are you sure?"

"I want to go back to Santa Barbara."

Chapter 78
9:35 AM

Exhausted and emotionally depleted, Sydney curved against Carter in a fetal position. When Moishe carried Ferah out of the chamber, a part of her went with them. Sydney felt as if she had died in the chamber with her friend. Nothing mattered any more.

She always thought as a scientist with a logical mind she could handle anything, even death—her own or another's. But *this* she could not manage. For the first time in her life, she was passionless, empty. Not even dead. At least death brought relief.

Alexander stood before Herod. *"A portal to the cosmic sea*—must mean this chamber is the doorway to death. The cosmos represented the pharaoh's journey to the gods."

Herod held his pistol up. "What portal? Where did he take off from?"

"It's not *real!* It's metaphorical. The pharaoh's *ka* or spirit rose up and flew out of the chamber, probably through a small opening somewhere," Alexander said.

Herod grit his teeth and aimed at Alexander. "This is not a *tomb*. It's a *temple*. The translator said it's in the Code. No pharaoh's *ta* or *ka* is going to fly anywhere."

Alexander shrugged. "It also said *only double keys can open the double seals.*"

Herod clenched his other hand into a fist, unclenched it and placed it on top of the gun, aiming at the wall. "This key can open anything."

"Wait!" shouted Alexander. "The answers may be on the walls. You could have destroyed some already."

Marco stood against a column with arms folded. "Dad, what about the C4?"

Herod took his hand from on top of the pistol, slowly turning to his son. "Get it. And the rope!"

Caught in a morass of guilt and grief, Sydney sank deeper into the oblivion of unreality. She saw a sea of sand surrounding her with a wall of dust that clogged her nostrils, cutting off any effort to breathe. It didn't matter. She fell backwards into the black earth, lying spread-eagled. A grounded sand angel in the throes of a dark pit, denied death. Relief came with the bitter sense of abdication of all past and present reality.

She opened her eyes, but the world was vacant. Her eyes held no recognition, no incredulity toward what they appeared to gape at.

Looking as immaculate in his tuxedo as when the evening began, Roland entered the temple. He held a rope in his gloved hand, a pistol in the other. Marco followed him carrying a white glob.

"Roland!" Alexander said. "How did you..." His question trailed off.

"Roland? What the Hell's going on?" Carter shouted, looking at Roland's gun pointed at him.

Roland smirked. "Bill always said I had a nose for new discoveries. I knew the hieroglyphs under the pool might lead to another room with more valuable glyphs. But I couldn't have imagined there would be a Code on the colored wall."

"You're with *him?*" Carter pointed to Herod.

"Been with him since the dig started," Roland said.

"How do you think we got there so fast?" Herod smiled sardonically. "Enough of this."

Roland glanced at Sydney. "And after Dmitri and his men lifted the wall, we were glad she was here to translate."

Sydney felt her blood flowing again, heating up in the volcanic words she just heard. Not only the words, but the voice and something else way in the back of her mind. She tried to bring it up, but it felt unformed, out of reach. Yet connected to this voice, and very recent. It nagged at her from behind, an annoying prod that stirred her ire and ... That was it!—from behind. The whiff of something distinct when she had been attacked in the cave—sweetness from the desert. His raspy voice threatened her to quit the translation. She had blocked the odor as she had repressed the whole experience.

Then at the benefit she had heard the voice, not raspy, but the same tenor, and smelled the same trace of sweet desert spice—similar to myrrh or spikenard—when she danced with Roland. She never made the connection until right now, with the same scent drifting through the temple. *He attacked me in the cave and knocked me unconscious.*

Boosting herself on Carter's shoulder, she struggled to her feet. "What do you know about Bill Jarvis's death?"

Stunned by this sudden re-emergence, Carter and Alexander lit up.

"Poor Bill," Roland said derisively, pointing his pistol at Sydney. "He figured out I wanted more than mere professional recognition in scientific journals. I wanted the treasures still waiting to be discovered. The only way to do it was to hook up with a kind of professional—the kind with resources and global outlets."

"You killed Bill! And attacked me!" Sydney forgot he was holding a gun. Carter jumped up and held her back.

"I knew we were on to something when we found the tunnel under the pool. That either the Canaanites or Egyptians could have buried valuables." Roland turned to Herod. "Little did we know how valuable. I told Bill the spirit ancestors didn't like archeologists poking around their sacred grounds. He wasn't the least bit superstitious, and sadly, he poked anyway. He simply got too close to the edge of the Cave of the Matriarchs."

Herod nodded. "We knew The Fox would hear about it soon enough, so we were ready."

"After Sydney arrived, we didn't want her to get too close. We had to do something to keep her away from the wall for a while." Roland feigned a hood over his head.

Sydney felt her energy rush back into circulation, her head clearing, her focus returning.

"I figured it wouldn't scare you off, but it did buy us some time," Roland said, pocketing his gun. "With Alexander kidnapped, we had control." He moved to Alexander, turned him around, and tied his hands behind his back.

"You killed an innocent man to get at an unknown treasure, one that might not have been there?" Now she knew why she was repulsed by Roland—his reptilian nature revealed itself in full force, despite his fashionable GQ appearance.

"Roland noticed the cartouche and the text in the middle, which turned out to be the Code." Herod motioned Marco to tie Sydney's hands first with the yellow nylon rope, then Carter's, holding their arms while he sat them down against the wall.

"That's why you kidnapped Sydney," Carter said.

"Tell me one thing," Sydney turned to Marco. "Did Gena have anything to do with this?"

Carter and Alexander stared at her in surprise, then at Marco.

"My personal life is none of your business. I happen to enjoy the company of beautiful archeologists," Marco leered at Sydney.

"Set the C-4," Herod motioned to Roland, who took the white rubbery glob from Marco.

"You can't set explosives off in here—you'll bring down the whole temple," Alexander said, as Marco lowered him to the floor.

"So what? I want the artifacts!" Herod exclaimed.

Smirking at Carter, then Sydney, Roland began kneading the high velocity military plastic explosive. He stretched the white rubbery mass into two long strands, which he stuck on the wall. Sydney watched as he retrieved a small explosive from the bag with a cord attached to it.

"A blasting cap," murmured Alexander.

"What does that do?" she asked, not relishing the answer.

"Transmits the charge and sets off the explosives," Alexander said.

"Ready." Roland nodded to Herod. They headed for the doorway.

"You can't leave us in here—we'll be killed!" shouted Carter.

Herod turned and said, "That's the idea."

Chapter 79
9:50 AM

Sydney and her companions sat against the pillars with hands tied behind them. Alexander and Carter worked furiously at their ropes. She didn't believe Herod would destroy the chamber.

She looked up to the column of Thoth, down-curved beak in profile, his hands holding the royal record of deeds and misdeeds. The brilliant blue and gold nemes headdress and neck and shoulder collar of gems and lapis stones blazed in the dim light. His eyes focused on the near pillar, which drew Sydney's gaze to Isis, the Eye of Horus on her crown.

Physically and mentally exhausted, she tried to recall the Code, but only jumbles of words entangled with hieroglyphs emerged. How did she wind up in this situation? Three days ago she was a university professor—secure in her classroom, safe in the confines of campus life, looking forward to time off. Spring break in Santa Barbara meant walks on Butterfly Beach, lunches on Stearns Wharf, and shopping on State Street.

A few minutes ago she didn't care if the chamber blew up. Finding out that Roland killed her former lover and friend shocked her. Why did he confess? Was he bragging that he had killed his mentor? That his own protégée took Bill's life, after Bill gave him the opportunity to work at the site in Jerusalem? Her feelings of revulsion and betrayal engulfed her in powerful waves. Fuming at her inability to escape her bindings and to demand justice for Bill and Ferah, she sat helpless.

Yesterday the only thing that mattered was the Code, a major discovery—the find of her life. With each hieroglyph decoded, she moved closer to the King's temple and the treasure of Thoth—whatever it was. She had risked her life, Alexander's life, and Carter's love to fulfill her destiny as a Shemsu.

Was it all worth it? Did the sacrifice of Ferah mean anything? She felt a stir in her heart, the same beat of the stone in the cave, and suddenly the swelling of the sound reverberated off the walls and into her deepest soul. Her life's work was compromised by the death of a woman she hadn't known long, yet knew intimately. Their passions ran parallel, their fruits ripened with the glow of righting inequity and injustice of their causes. They played the same game on different courts, sometimes breaking the rules to gain a higher ground.

Why had she not realized this before? Her perception of herself as a ground-breaking Egyptologist aroused the continuing search for improbabilities, fueled by the indignation of those she most desired to accept her work. Rough edges and blatant denials of her need for approval by traditional colleagues filled her with a sense of unreality.

Bill had warned her, others knew—the author of a book on alternative Egyptology would be an outcast by mainstream archeologists. Her professional challenge of walking in both worlds caused rifts with colleagues and the unexpected pain of awareness that she was not taken seriously. The double-sided ax cut deep into her self-esteem.

Ferah's death brought the death of something else—a loud, proud, arrogant part of herself that wrestled daily with its opposite—a fear of succeeding in an unknown field. It could no longer survive within her, or within the purview of integrity so prevalent in Ferah herself. Enough that Sydney trod on new ground; the lack of support and constant challenges she shouldered had taken their toll, and she felt weakened further by the psychic splinters of going against the grain.

The Code recalled a past when she had been something better, nobler, striving to revive the original message of the God of Wisdom. Her fate as a Shemsu now revealed, Thoth spoke to her as an equal, as one without human fears or doubts, whose own multi-dimensional realm was as real as her physical senses. He had led her through *a portal to the cosmic sea* into the world of the deities.

She had no time to grieve for the death of arrogance or pride. She must embrace the integrity brought back to life by Ferah's death.

She chose to sacrifice for a greater cause which would allow her family and the Shemsu to carry on the work she began—her free will choice.

Why couldn't we do it while she lived?

If she lived, many would not join her cause. Now that she is gone, they will embrace her work. Just as you will also continue, knowing the greater purpose that is being fulfilled.

She looked up at the pillar. The eyes of Thoth were gazing at her and she realized the purpose of the Shemsu. She felt the heartbeat of the stone and knew she was attuned to its cosmic rhythm. She couldn't quit. She had to continue for Ferah and Bill.

Suddenly Sydney understood. She remembered sitting on the stone in the cave, becoming one with the Great Earth Mother, and how she had been reborn by the experience. Hot tears filled her eyes as the scientist died in order to give birth to the Shemsu.

Chapter 80
9:55 AM

The two deities on the pillars seemed to flash into brilliant colors. "Isis and Thoth," Sydney mumbled. "The two keys mentioned in the Code."

"What keys? I can't think about the Code right now." Alexander shifted so Carter could get at his rope. "I'm trying to find a way out of here."

"But it's the same thing. The Code is *telling* us how to get out."

Carter stopped working at Alexander's rope. "It is?"

Sydney nodded. *"Double seals protect the lock and open but to double keys.* I'm not sure what the double seals are, but I think I know what the double keys are."

"What are they?" Carter asked.

"We have to use Thoth and Isis—wisdom and magic." Thoth had instructed her to do the magic that Isis performed in the ritual of the Shemsu. But what was it? She couldn't remember and besides, how could she do anything tied up?

The Code is your initiation—use the magic to release yourself.

She looked up at the pillar. Thoth gazed straight at her. Trying to overcome fatigue, remorse and anger at this latest situation, Sydney laboriously shifted her mind into high gear. How could magic cut the rope?

She struggled with the knots until her wrists felt bruised from rope burns and her shoulders, stretched backwards, ached. Frustrated that she could not think, her anger at Herod, the loss of Bill, a gnawing remorse for Ferah, and grief at the death of part of herself, all merged into one instinctual force.

She recalled the essence of shamanism. When a sick or wounded member of the tribe came for healing, the shaman called forth the spirits to aid in the process, as the adepts or priests of Egypt called on their magic. They learned in their initiation process to focus their intent on what they wanted to achieve. It sounded so simple, but must have been very powerful to enable the Egyptian civilization to endure longer than any other.

Her gut instinct was to pull against the rope, but she remembered shamanic teachings that stated the secret to power is *not* to force. Rather, *embrace* the opposite. She realized Thoth was encouraging her not to think but to act— to bring the opposing forces of her fatigued anger and grief together to create magic. Sydney felt her hands behind her and embraced the rope, honoring its function of binding her hands.

The rope was tight. The more she focused, the more the rope began to soften. Did it move? Did her wrists loosen slightly?

Suddenly, the rope itself shifted. It definitely moved around her wrists—slithering under and over the knot until she sat up straight to hold her arms away from her body. Her skin was caressed by the smooth motion, until the rope was no more.

When she realized why, her senses congealed into a single synergistic force. Tiny droplets appeared on her forehead. It was no longer a rope around her wrists, but had become a thing alive, uncoiling itself from its tightly wrapped cell—and slithering around one hand into the other.

She knew she must allow this, and not show fear. It would sense fear as an imbalance of her being and would not make the complete transformation. Could she maintain her focus while it changed from rope to snake?

Feeling doubt in herself, that the python had returned, the movement stopped. The rope was binding her again. Balance. Focus. She must be a shaman. She must not show fear. She knew she had to maintain concentration that would allow the snake to return. How? What does a shaman do to facilitate transformation?

Stay out of the head and *in* the heart. Don't think—*Feel!*

She must trust herself, but mainly she must trust the snake. Unbind the fear and welcome the snake with love.

I must become one with the snake.

Chapter 81
10:15 AM

As it unwrapped itself from her wrists, Sydney turned to see the snake was the same length and circumference of the rope. She moved both wrists apart when it completely loosened, stretching out full on the floor and quickly slithered away. She watched it glide gracefully out of the chamber.

Eyes wide, mouths agape, Carter and Alexander sat in awe of what they'd witnessed, unable to speak.

She hurriedly untied Carter. "How did you do that?" he asked, as he moved to untie Alexander.

Still overcome by the enormity of an experience she didn't fully understand, Sydney wiped her eyes and looked in the direction of the snake. She silently thanked the reptile for her freedom and for the trust it had allowed her to express.

"We're Shemsu. I remembered the old ways—magic and wisdom." Sydney tried to slow her breathing and settle herself. She felt way out of her league, yet familiarity with the shamanic process brought even greater belief in the truth of her experiences.

Alexander stood and massaged his wrists. "You look different, Syd."

"I *am* different, and beginning to be aware of everything that's happened in the past few days. Understand it, but unable to put any of it into words."

Carter nodded. "There's no way to verbalize it, but I somehow realize it's possible, transforming a rope into a snake."

Alexander looked around. "Why haven't they blown the chamber?"

"Maybe it was a ruse, to make Sydney talk." Carter examined his untied rope.

Alexander checked the C4 in the wall. "*This* is no ruse." He deactivated the charge line. "I think I know where it is."

Sydney reached in her pocket, pulled out the egg, and held it up. "All Egyptian temples had a Holy of Holies which housed the god. I'd be willing to bet this one does too. They've all been lined up. The chamber of Set, the chamber of Thoth, the circular temple. The Holy Sanctuary must be on the other side of that wall."

She pointed the egg at the wall. It sparked and shone with a blue light that filled the chamber. A small doorway swiveled and grated against the floor. Involuntarily, they all backed up. Carter shined his flashlight into a small room. Hieroglyphs covered the black walls. Sydney stooped to enter, while the brothers followed.

She held the egg so the door swiveled shut after them and shone her light around the floor and walls. Thin, musty air assailed her nostrils. Very little dust remained on the floor after thirty-five hundred years. Strange, thought Sydney, that no insect, bat dropping, or other evidence of life was anywhere in the room. Though tightly sealed, they were able to breathe.

A solid black basalt cube about three Feet Square covered in vertical hieroglyphs filled the center of the room. Atop it sat a closed black cabinet of the god. In every temple the sanctuary was dedicated to a particular god or goddess. The statue was housed in the stone shrine. He or she would be removed daily, washed, dressed, fed, worshiped and put back in the shrine. In this way the occupants and visitors of the temple received the deity's favor.

Sydney examined the double doors of the shrine. "Here are the *double seals*. The cartouche of the king. To break a cartouche guaranteed the fate of whoever broke it—the source of legends that temples had curses built into them. No one wanted to tempt fate by tampering with the seal of a pharaoh."

"Except the tomb robbers, who didn't believe in curses," Carter said.

"Neither do we. We're the Shemsu. We're supposed to open these locks." Sydney broke the seals.

Everyone seemed to hold their breath.

Had she been the last Shemsu to seal the cabinet? And the first to break the seals after 3500 years? Sydney slowly parted the doors. Minute specks of white dust floated into the air. Her eyes widened. The gleam of gold shone brightly in the lights.

"The solid gold statue of Thoth!" Sydney said. "It *is* real! I thought the stories were fairy tales. Part of the old Egyptian mythology." About a foot high, it was a miniature version of the life-size statue with whom Sydney walked through the wall. It wore a delicately carved nemes headdress of lapis and gold.

She touched the gleaming gold and enameled hieroglyphs on the kilt, smooth under her finger—as precise as if burned by a laser. The solar crown symbolized the sun god in the form of a winged scarab, its claws gripping lotuses and symbols representing eternal protection. On the upswept wings a lunar barque supported the sacred cobras on each side of the Eye of Horus. "It's the healing pectoral worn by the king." Sydney could barely breathe.

"Look at it! Beautiful!" Carter whispered. "It's inlaid with precious gems, carnelian, lapis, turquoise and onyx."

Alexander said softly. "Nothing like it has ever been found—anywhere!"

Sydney looked around the cabinet. "It's not here."

"What?" Carter said.

"The statue of Isis. It was in the Code, the part I left out. Why is it not here?"

"That was in the Code?" Alexander paused. "So that's why your finger skipped down several lines on the plane. You were keeping those lines from Herod."

"What do the hieroglyphs say?" Carter asked.

Sydney's fingertips moved slowly across the glyphs, as if absorbing the meaning through her skin. "The legend says Thoth created Earth with sound. This statue is supposed to increase the oscillation in the human body in the same way. Simply being in its presence produces a higher state of energy."

Alexander nodded. "I do feel a sense of calm."

"I feel it, too," Carter said. "Amazing. I've never felt anything like this."

"I don't feel tired any more," Sydney said. "Thoth said the Egyptians could create an atmosphere of what higher dimensions *feel* like—a sense of unity. And that this statue was supposedly a crucible for alchemical transformations in stone and metals, turning rock into alabaster, lead into gold."

"How?" Alexander asked.

"Wouldn't Herod love to know," Carter said.

"It must be in the same way this egg works, and how the rope changed into a snake. Through some kind of heart connection. In fact, the egg may be just a power prop. The real power lies elsewhere."

"Where?" Alexander asked breathlessly.

Sydney looked at the statue. "The alchemical transformation may take place in another crucible—the human heart."

Chapter 82
10:30 AM

Sydney slowly translated the hieroglyphs on the left door. *"The power within is revived by the Keys of Ra,"*

Carter held open the doors of the black basalt shrine. "What keys of Ra?"

"Another code?" Alexander asked.

"No, I don't think so. This has to do with the original Code. It's telling us..." She remembered the Code. "Quick! What time is it?"

Alexander looked at his watch. "Ten thirty."

"Almost time for the eclipse!" Carter said. "And we can't go outside—not with that lot out there."

"We're supposed to do the rebirthing of the Shemsu." Sydney looked around the room, wondering how they would carry out Thoth's instructions. "Let's see what else is on the door. *The portal opens to the cosmic sea of Ra. The Keys of Ra anoint the Eyes of Horus.*"

"Oh, no. We don't have time for *another* code," Carter said with a groan.

Sydney jerked the pendant over her head. "*This* Eye of Horus must have something to do with opening the portal. The Egyptians called the sky the cosmic sea." She looked up at the ceiling. It was filled with blue stars on a white background. "*There's* the portal, but how do we open it?" She had a sudden thought.

Pulling the egg out of her pocket, she held it in her palm, and aimed the egg at the solar disc in the crown of the statue.

A flash of light exploded straight up from the crown to the ceiling.

Suddenly a heavy scraping sound filled the room.

"What's that?" Alexander shouted.

"Look!" Carter pointed to the ceiling. "It's opening!"

The eclipse was about to start.

Begin the words as Isis began her magic. Sydney cleared her mind, hoping the memory of what Thoth had shown her would return. She felt three-and-a-half millennia compacted into a moment of time.

"We are the Shemsu Hor. We return to bring the old wisdom back to the world." Sydney recalled the history Thoth imparted. "As Isis re-membered Osiris, we re-member ourselves and our true names." The statue glowed with a dazzling light emanating from the winged scarab on the crown. The light swirled, creating an energy vortex whose sound whirred in the small chamber.

Carter's face lit up from the brilliant light.

"It's a circular force," Sydney said. "We're building power for the ceremony."

They watched as a star of gold light twirled into the vortex. A spiral thrust itself down into the earth.

She took a breath, feeling very humbled to have been singled out for such an auspicious event. "We have entered the Duat, the Egyptian realm of the underworld where we came face-to-face with Set. We looked into the mirror and faced our demons. We overcame our fears to pass into the chamber of Thoth to ascend to the realm of illumination— the fifth dimension. These walls tell the process of Birth, Death, and Resurrection which, if we choose, can be ours." Sydney raised her arms, and in the immensity of the moment, stepped into the role of priestess.

They looked up to the ceiling, which had disappeared, leaving a starry sky. Blocked by the moon, an eclipsed Ra awaited the golden glow heading toward it.

The spiral climbed into the blue sky toward Ra. In astonishment, they watched the curved light penetrate the darkened sun and continue out into the galaxy on its journey to the stars and the Great Central Sun.

She felt the heartbeat of the cosmos fill her body, thumping in rhythm as it reverberated in the chamber. She recognized it as the beat in the cave, when she sat on the stone and the great Earth Goddess, Gaia, spoke of her history.

In awe, Sydney hesitated, lowered her arms, then felt the words flow through her. "The golden spiral connects the core of the earth with the Great Central Sun of the entire universe, which has awaited the message of Isis and Thoth since the last anchoring time thirty-five hundred years ago, when Pharaoh Thutmose opened the temple. The earth has quickened again to achieve a state of consciousness allowing humanity to ascend into the higher dimensions. As in ancient Egypt, some may choose these higher vibrations, some will not. It is a choice for all."

Carter and Alexander gazed at Sydney, then each other, as they seemed to puzzle over her sudden knowledge of an ancient ritual.

She felt lifted into another realm, and had to remember to breathe so she wouldn't become overwhelmed with emotion. "Thoth teaches that the cosmic heartbeat changes the DNA in those who are sensitive to it. We are called to awaken Shemsu to their true mission in all parts of the world. Thoth says this is what the Shemsu have awaited—a time of earth's death and rebirth, what the prophecies call 'the end times.' The Shemsu have reincarnated many times when the earth has passed through similar changes. This time it's a *major* transformation. We're preparing to ascend into the fifth dimension, a state of reality based on love and compassion."

They stared up at the eclipse, their logical brains challenged to accept a new paradigm of reality. The Egyptian's reverence for Ra became a tangible blue-black that filled the chamber. She held her hands up and felt an orgasmic sparkle in her body.

Connection to the spirit realm brought tears to Sydney's eyes. An essence of her being had just awakened from a long sleep, and she recalled a forgotten name just out of conscious reach, a lost dream behind the veil. She sensed Thoth wave his hand before her to remove the veil.

The spiral circled the sun for the last time. Ra's face slowly emerged from the darkness, peeking out in a new birth of understanding.

"The eclipse is over. *Ra anoints the Eye of Horus* on the other door." Sydney said, feeling that she, too, had just been anointed.

They watched as the sun shone into the chamber directly onto the solar disc.

Alexander seemed to revel in the event he just experienced, his demeanor accepting, even worshipful.

The spiral gradually dropped back to the statue. The whirring sound was still, the energy vortex quiet and the ceiling returned to the chamber. Carter gazed at the golden statue with a far-away expression. His face seemed younger, more innocent.

"Thoth said when we're ready to graduate, our prayers are being awaited by cosmic beings. Then they can help us evolve to the higher dimensions," Sydney said, enjoying the sense of well-being, the feeling of being reborn into a state of spiritual rejuvenation totally outside the realm of language.

"Amazing," Carter said diffidently. "We *are* the Shemsu."

Chapter 83
10:50 AM

Sydney held the gold statue of Thoth. "The mysterious healing statue of Egyptian lore," she said breathlessly. "Historians thought they were only a myth."

"They?" Carter asked.

"The other one was a statue of Isis. Must still be in a temple somewhere." She handed the statue to Carter. "According to Thoth, he teaches inter-dimensional travel throughout the universe—like a visiting professor. He said we can all travel via thought to his home in the Pleiades, to Isis in Sirius, and to Osiris in Orion."

She leaned in to the solar disk on his crown. "I didn't see these hieroglyphs before."

"What do they say?" Carter asked.

"I am Thoth of the Shemsu. I offer my healing to all females who touch my crown."

"Why just females?" Carter asked.

"How do we get out of here without Herod taking the statue?" Alexander asked.

Carter nodded. "They have the guns. Maybe we can bargain with them."

Sydney shook her head. "And risk someone getting hurt?"

"We can't just hand it over," Carter said.

Sydney held the egg toward the entry. "Thoth has said the statue is to be taken out so people can see it and use it. Activating the statue activates the Shemsu and vice-versa.

We *have* to get it out of here." The door swiveled open.
"We'll just have to take our chances."

Herod, Roland and Marco were leaning against the
pillars in the circular temple. They looked up in shock at
what appeared to be three intruders emerging out of a hidden
doorway.

The first to regain his composure, Herod shouted,
"Where the Hell've you been?"

"And how did you get in there?" Roland asked.

Marco saw the statue held by Carter. "Look at that!"

Roland dashed to the statue, the gleam in his eyes
greater than that from the statue. "There's more! I know
there's more!"

Herod moved quickly to Roland's side. "I'll take that!"
He sneered at Roland, as he grabbed the statue from Carter.
"Gold! I knew it! Where's the rest of the royal stash?" he
asked Sydney.

Roland ran into the sanctuary and examined the shrine.
"There's nothing in here!"

"This was all we found," Sydney said.

Herod entered the small room. "What's this place?" His
voice echoed off the walls.

"The Holy of Holies," Sydney said. "The place of the
god."

Herod looked around. "Where's the god?"

"*This* is the god." Sydney pointed at the statue.

Herod pulled his pistol, and then touched the
hieroglyphs. "Beautiful! What does it say?"

"I haven't translated it yet." Sydney desperately needed
a plan.

Herod raised the gun. "In that case, you will all be
guests at my estate."

Roland shook his head. "You can't do that! It's too dangerous taking them back there." He pointed to Sydney. "She could've told someone already."

"Shut up! I know what I'm doing." Herod waved the pistol at Roland.

"I don't think you do! We can dispose of them here and now!" Roland pulled his gun from his tux pocket.

"Not until she tells me where the rest of the treasure is," Herod snarled.

"I'm telling you we don't need her any more! I know these temples!" Roland shouted. "There may be a chamber off the sanctuary. And I'll find it one way or another!"

Herod turned to Marco, handing him the statue. "Get a blanket. Wrap the statue and let's get out of here."

Enraged, Roland began placing explosives in one of the walls. He picked up a hammer and began banging on the turquoise hieroglyphs, searching for prospective hidden rooms. Sydney watched helplessly as blue and gold flakes fell to the floor.

Herod kept his gun on Carter and Alexander, and faced Roland. "Get that out of there, you idiot! You're not going to blow the temple. It's too valuable."

Marco went to the wall and pulled out the explosives.

"Get away from that wall!" Roland shouted at him, grabbing him roughly and pushing him to the ground. The statue fell out of Marco's hands and rolled to one side.

"Leave him alone!" Herod yelled.

Roland raised the pistol. Marco was on one knee and lunged for the gun. Roland turned, shoved Marco away from his gun hand, causing him to fall backwards.

Herod dashed to his son's defense.

"Get back!" Roland shouted at Herod.

Suddenly, past, present, and future congealed into a single gunshot that thundered off the temple walls. Stunned, Sydney watched as Herod fell to the ground.

Chapter 84
11:11 AM

"Dad!" Marco bent over his father.

Roland lowered his gun and backed up, pulling his foot from underneath Herod. Unmasking his contempt and loathing, he glared at the man on the ground and moved slowly to the chamber entry.

Marco braced himself against the wall as he cradled his father's head in his lap. Herod looked down at his chest. Blood gushed from the wound.

Unable to move her feet, Sydney could only look down at her tormentor, mortally wounded. She scooped up the blanket and threw it to Marco. Carter knelt down beside Herod.

"Dad! Hold on!" Marco pressed the blanket onto the wound, trying to stop the bleeding.

Herod looked up at his son. His eyes misted, he began coughing as he tried to speak. "So much of your life I lost... years spent in the senseless search for my own father..." He labored to breathe. "...to exceed my father in what he did best... doesn't matter anymore."

"Dad! Don't die!" Marco grasped his father's hand, his eyes wild with fear.

Sydney saw tears in Herod's eyes. They held something else she had not seen before. He reached up and touched the face of his son, as if for the first time, and stroked his hair.

"I love you," Herod whispered, his arm falling limply to his side. "... I never said it to you, Eleazar... because I couldn't. From the time you were a boy... I was too busy."

He coughed again, spitting up blood. Carter wiped his mouth with the blanket.

Marco's jaw dropped, his eyes blinked at the sound of the name his parents christened him, that no one spoke anymore. He had a puzzled expression, mixed with pride.

Herod held his son's hand. His weakened voice strained to get out the words. "I just bought you ... things and let you be... let your mother raise you. As long as you ... stayed out of trouble ... all I cared about. She did ... good job with you and your sister ... never told her, but she did..."

Marco choked back tears. "You can't die—not now!"

Herod's voice broke, and Sydney saw a tear trickle down his cheek. "... too late to be the father *I* never had ... don't be like me ... chasing after *things*. My son, be who *you* want to be... do what *you* want to do..."

Marco stroked his father's hair, wiped the tears from his cheeks, and tenderly kissed his forehead.

Herod looked into Marco's eyes and smiled. "I'm a happy man ..." he gasped. "... I've found my son ..."

"Dad," Marco choked, "I love you."

Herod expelled a long breath, his last.

Marco sobbed. "I've lost my father."

Chapter 85
11:15 AM

Out of the corner of her eye, Sydney saw Roland head for the temple entry carrying the statue. His expression reflected disdain for the group huddled around the man he had just shot and killed. She turned toward him. He abruptly stopped, slowly walking backward into the circular chamber, his hands raised in the air, the pistol wrapped loosely around his right thumb. Puzzled by his strange action, Sydney then saw the reason for his retreat back to the temple.

Victoria entered the chamber pointing a gun at Roland. Carter and Alexander stared at this unknown woman.

"I've been waiting for this moment a long time. Hand it over," Victoria said.

Roland arrogantly gave her the pistol. She motioned for the statue. He glared at her with extreme loathing and passed it to her.

Sydney, surprised at the sight of Victoria, felt very relieved that Roland had given up his weapon. "Victoria! How did you find us?"

"Ferah and Moishe told us the Code pointed to En Gedi." She motioned Roland to the floor. "We were delayed waiting for Yuval and Benjamin. When none of you answered your phones, we figured something was up. Yuval had a couple of deputies follow us. We saw Zaki and Ellie in the lot—they pointed to where the flares had been set off. That's quite a rough climb—took longer than we thought." Victoria looked at Marco, still holding his father. "Too bad he's dead—we won't get to prosecute him and his gang."

"You've got this one," Sydney motioned to Roland, "for murder, two counts, and the assault on me. And another one trussed up in the men's bathroom at the preserve entrance."

"Good work, Sydney. You've done well." Victoria glanced quickly at Sydney, then glowered at Roland.

"Wait a minute," Carter moved to Sydney's side, "who's this?"

"Allow me to introduce myself," Victoria began.

"No, allow *me*." Yuval Goldman stepped into the chamber behind her. "Everyone, meet The Fox."

"What?" Roland shouted. "You're The Fox? Can't be."

Victoria faced him with a huge smile. "I'm The Fox and you're under arrest."

"We've been waiting for you to tip your hand and knew it wouldn't take long." Yuval pulled his cuffs from his back pocket. "The Fox had an inkling you were in on the museum heist, but didn't have enough evidence to arrest you. Not until Jarvis was killed and Carter mentioned a mole at the excavation site."

"So that's how Herod's Hoods were at the colored wall a few hours after we discovered it," Carter said.

"Turn around." Yuval said to Roland, who obsequiously placed his hands behind his back while Yuval cuffed him. "We thought the mole was Tovar for a while or one of the students. Even after Roland brought me in to investigate Bill's death, we didn't suspect him." He saw the body of Herod on the floor. "A shame we couldn't get the mastermind over there. His band has been terrorizing all the archeological digs in the country."

Now that Roland was cuffed, Victoria lowered her pistol. "We disarmed the one out front, Khalid. He told us everything in exchange for leniency. I know him from Ferah's dealings with him. We thought he was deranged when he said not to look at the eyes of the statue, so we hurried through. But what we saw next ..." she shook her head, "my dear friend ... dead ... Moishe told us what happened. Tragic. Simply heartbreaking."

Sydney went to Victoria. They embraced in a sad moment of mourning for their friend.

"Moishe said he heard another shot and thought it might be one of you," Yuval said. "I had one of my men call the coroner and an ambulance."

The deputies came in, saw one cuffed prisoner and a body on the floor. Yuval turned Roland over to them and helped Marco carry the body of his father.

Sydney, Victoria, Alexander and Carter followed them out. Moishe sat by Ferah's body in the chamber of Thoth.

"She was the best of us all," Victoria said.

Moishe nodded. "It was the way she would want to go—protecting valuable artifacts. It was her life's work."

"We'll all carry on for her—what she started," Sydney said.

Yuval came in to help Moishe carried the body of Ferah out of the chamber.

Sydney returned to the circular temple and sank into the Thoth column with exhaustion, a wave of relief flooding over her. Carter sat at the next pillar, Alexander and Victoria opposite them.

"We did it!" Sydney sighed, holding the golden statue. "We not only found the Shemsu mother lode, we broke the biggest black market ring in Israel! With Herod gone, Roland, Dmitri, and Tomas in tow, they should sing like banshees."

"Don't forget Khalid, the pilot who was able to get a lot of the loot out of the country," Victoria said. "The Fox lives, and with the help of Ferah's group, the Palestinians for the

Preservation of Temple Mount, we'll continue her work to keep the artifacts of Israel in Israel. I hope we can return to the spot where Khalid found the priests' graves from the Temple of Solomon. Ferah thought that was an important place to dig. Khalid may get a lighter sentence if he shows us the spot."

"So you're The Fox." Sydney smiled at Victoria. "Like I always said—never underestimate a teacher!"

"I can't believe Roland," Carter said. "His manner seemed insensitive at times, but Bill swore he was an asset on major digs,"

"He was so grieved at Bill's death. What an actor." Alexander shook his head.

"There was something about him I didn't trust, but never knew what. I didn't know him that well, but he always seemed like a snake, coiled and ready to strike." Sydney shuddered.

"What an awesome event!" Victoria looked up at Thoth on the column, then the statue. Alexander nodded at Sydney. "If you hadn't figured out the Code, none of this would have happened."

"The whole thing is a miracle—a word not normally in my vocabulary, but the only one to describe what's happened," Sydney paused "I wonder why Thoth chose me?"

"Why not? You're the Egyptologist," Carter said.

"It's more than that, something else." She shook her head. "I don't understand it all, but guess I'm not supposed to, not yet."

Chapter 86
11:25 AM

Victoria rose and headed for the temple door. "Moishe needs me. And I want to be with him and Zaki."

Alexander followed her. "I'll go with you," he turned to Sydney and Carter. "You two coming?"

"In a while," Sydney said. After watching them leave, she pulled out her Eye of Horus pendant. "I can't go yet. There's still something unfinished. Waiting for us." She fingered the pendant, looking up at the figure of Thoth, whose column she leaned against.

"Something undone here in the temple?" Carter sat against a pillar with his legs outstretched.

Sydney flashed on her vision of Thutmose's army camped near the Dead Sea, and the stone rising into its place. "I saw the temple being built! There's another chamber here!"

Carter gawked at her. "You saw ... what?"

"And there's something else that keeps nagging at me. The last two lines—*Thoth a mighty birth awakes and sings the truth to reach the stars.* He hasn't awakened anything and hasn't sung anything."

"He awakened us to who we are—the Shemsu Hor," Carter said.

Sydney shook her head. "I don't think that's what it means. Those last lines—they're telling us something, but it's just out of reach."

They looked at each other with the unspoken question— what have we missed?

360

Sydney paced from pillar to pillar. "What if … What if, besides the window of opportunity when the beams of Ra awakened the stone, what if *we* have a window of opportunity—a time-coded inner clock, or DNA-encoded cosmic timer, that tells us it's time to shift into a higher dimension of consciousness. Be who we really are?"

"We're the Shemsu. Now we know who we are."

Sydney felt Thoth's vibration racing through her veins. The sense of excitement filled her again, the completion of the Code in sight. "What if the Shemsu all have the same DNA-encoded timing that clicks on at the same time, whenever they all reincarnate together, like during the time of Thutmose? The windows all open together?"

"So our DNA is kicking in and we're in the window of opportunity?"

"We're in our cosmic time-code *now*. And the Isis chamber is ready to open." Sydney looked for the glyphs that would lead them through the window, but none stood out.

She paced the temple. "Wait a minute!" She stopped. "I had it figured wrong. Omigod, the genius of the Code! It's brilliant! It isn't about *Thoth singing to the stars,* but *us. We sing to the stars!* The Egyptian creation myth says Thoth birthed the earth through *sound. He sang it into existence!* That's what we have to do. We sing!"

Carter gaped at her. "What do we sing?"

"Everyone has a sound, a tone, a chant, a vibration— that's what we'll sing. Thoth said the Shemsu sang this temple into existence. All we have to do is find our true sound."

"How do we do that?" he asked doubtfully, holding the statue of Thoth.

"We all know it; we just have to rediscover it. The Egyptians chanted whenever they created, knowing sound creates vibration, a powerful force. They used that vibration in their temples for healing, and in the tombs and everything else they produced." She sat against the pillar and felt the exhilaration of an explorer who uncovers a lost pyramid in the middle of the jungle.

He leaned forward. "So it's *our* truth we sing."

Sydney nodded. "Right. Singing brings our truth into existence and it's heard beyond the stars! The Egyptians were very deliberate and precise in everything. We have to do what they did." She sat up straight with her back against the pillar in lotus position, then began chanting.

Carter cleared his throat and self-consciously hummed a deep tone that began to slowly align with Sydney, each voice becoming stronger and more stable, sensing the vibrations bouncing off the pillars and walls. The tones seemed to find their own level and blended together in melodic fervor.

Sydney remembered when she would stand with her back against a tree as a child, absorbing the energy, feeling a union with the tree.

The sound increased. The pillars seemed to sing with the voices. Suddenly the turquoise and gold wall began to swivel until finally the wall completely rotated and stopped to reveal an opening.

She motioned to lower the chant gradually and then end. She stood and walked to the open wall, gazing into another chamber at the brilliant walls of the gods.

Chapter 87
11:45 AM

"These don't look Egyptian, but they don't look like anything else, either." Sydney gasped in stunned disbelief. "These must be the only paintings of the deities actually painted by them, not by those who worshipped them. The figures are raised, painted, and outlined in gold. Everything is trimmed in gold, even their nails and eyelids."

She stared at the huge pyramid-shaped room. Wide steps on four sides led to white walls with paintings of the gods and goddesses in strange costumes—modern Egyptian design—long flowing pants, translucent capes, enameled gold jewelry, and headdresses with feathers, ribbons and bird shapes.

Sydney had never seen these poses. They were not tomb paintings. Rather, renderings of deities at play, dancing, cavorting in blue pools, participating in athletic games, playing musical instruments, on horseback, painting pictures on walls, and several erotic scenes. Sydney realized they were painting *themselves* on the walls.

The paintings on the lower levels were larger, diminishing in size as they reached the pointed top. Strange that Thutmose didn't glorify himself somewhere amid the deities. But then, he was no god.

"What are these?" Carter walked around two oval tables of solid gold. He stooped to look underneath. "There's no legs. They're suspended in mid-air." He brushed his hand under the table.

Sydney walked around the tables. Then she saw it. On a round three-legged silver table stood a gold statue of Isis. She wore the solar disk crown between the outstretched horns. Her right arm extended from the body with the palm up, her perpetual blessing to the people. "The golden Isis!" Sydney reached out to touch her. "The legend is complete."

"Beautiful," Carter whispered, rubbing the glyphs with his fingertips. "What does it say?"

Sydney leaned in to the solar disk, which held the hieroglyphs. *"I am Isis of the Shemsu whose bloodline is carried into eternity. My hand offers healing to all males."*

"This one for males and Thoth for females." Carter said, placing the statue of Thoth next to Isis.

"To heal the male-female split in the world," Sydney said breathlessly. "They were ritual objects used in ceremonies. The Shemsu knew they would hit a timeline when they returned—when they would complete what they began in Egypt.

"Omigod!" Carter stood by one of the tables. "There's writing on the table! Something's writing by itself!"

Sydney turned to the table. In beautiful script her name was being written on the table—*"Sydney Grace."* Below her name the script continued. *When Ra is high the pyramid seals. Be swift.*

"How can that be?"

"Your name is on this table, *"Carter Carlini."*

"How *did* they know? Whoever *they* is?"

Sydney stood by the golden Isis. "We're back, that's how they knew. In fact, as Thoth told us, *we* built this temple. *We* knew we'd be back. These are *our* tables, and we programmed them to engrave our names to appear at the moment in time when we were here. We encoded our DNA with a cosmic wake-up call for this moment in earth's history."

His intake of breath paralleled her awe at the enormity of her words—as if a cosmic computer had everything on hard drive and simply awaited their appearance to hit 'enter.'

"This is beyond human understanding," he said.

Sydney turned to the table on which Isis stood and read the hieroglyphs.

"The statues were used in the beginning and at each return of the Shemsu. To touch the statues brings relief to those who suffer. In the healing image they are made whole."

Sydney stood at the table, absorbing the realization of the powerful objects they had discovered, and the cosmic timetable that had recorded their future deeds at the same moment of their actions in the present time. It defied logic.

She lay on her table and Carter did the same.

"I never knew gold was soft—it's like lying on a water bed," he said.

"It is. How can that be?" She moved as if the table molded itself to her body.

They lay with their heads pointed to the statues. Sydney felt the presence of Thoth without seeing him. A sudden whirring began at the statues, a spiral of gold light swirled, first from Isis, then in the opposite direction from Thoth, rising to the top of the pyramid, taking the top stone with it on its way to the sky.

"It's turned into a double spiral!"

Sydney gazed at the awesome, mysterious sight, eyes filled with joy, spirit soaring with the spirals, her hand reaching for Carter who lay on the next table. He had undergone some kind of transformation about which she knew nothing. She saw him for the first time, his big heart wide open, awaiting her. She entered with an open palm, carrying the seeds of spirit into the spiral they entered together. His eyes held the promise of a pharaoh who united the two lands of the heart.

As one, the Shemsu felt the band of rainbow light weave a luminous connection around the pyramid that circled the planet. No separation, doubt, or mistrust could exist within this wondrous band. They had stepped together into a new universe.

Sydney began to intone her sound as Carter joined in, the harmonies reverberating off the walls and floor. The amazing rainbow deepened, synthesizing the colors into melodic chords, melding with the voices into the glowing spirals.

Angelic tones vibrated their bodies into a sensation of floating on the majestic colors of the spectrum, a glistening fire of light forming into a ball of creation, exploding into a shimmering glow that birthed the sun and moon in a glorious dawn of rejuvenation. The Cave of the Matriarchs brought creation into existence, the way Thoth's egg birthed the sun.

Sydney recalled the message of Gaia in the cave, her heart beating in rhythm with the stone that culminated with her deeply moving experience of birth. She had come a long way on a journey that began with the voice in her classroom

The Code had led her to a promise of the past—the resonance of her truth—the sound that reaches out to touch the stars.

Chapter 88
12:00 PM

The melodic vibration danced in the air of the pyramid. The beauty of the sound enveloped her in its embrace, at the same time it tugged on the fringes of her consciousness. She slowly sat up and re-read the lines below her name.

"When Ra is high! Carter, what time is it?"

He looked at his watch. "Noon, why?" he said lazily.

"The window's about to close! When it does, the inner chamber will seal! We've got to get out."

They bounded from the tables.

A low whirring seemed to emit from the floor. "What's that?" Carter grabbed the statue of Isis.

"The inner chamber opened with sound. It will close with sound. Come on. Quick!"

Sydney took the Thoth statue and looked around the pyramidal chamber. The rumble that heralded the closing of the window matched the roar at the opening of the window at the Dead Sea. She hoped it would not be accompanied by another earthquake.

Chapter 89

They emerged outside the entrance to Lover's Cave, shielding their eyes, not from the wrath of Set this time, but the brightness of Ra. Pristine air and the warmth of the sun embraced their skin. The statues of Thoth and Isis were securely wrapped in a spare blanket from one of the chambers, the egg still in Sydney's pocket.

"Ah, fresh air." She took a deep breath, glad to be in the sunlight, and then gave Alexander, Victoria and Yuval a recap of the Isis chamber.

Alexander put his arm around Sydney. "I always knew when you wrapped your mind around something it would come out with a big red bow."

She smiled. "My good friend, Jess, told me once, you don't always find what you start out for. And you sometimes find what you least expect."

She watched a solemn Moishe and Zaki accompany the emergency team as they wheeled the stretcher carrying the body of Ferah down the rugged path. Ellie walked beside Zaki on the trail.

Yuval's guards covered the cliffs, parking lots, and hiking trails. "They'll be here day and night. We'll have the gates up by tomorrow to secure the cave. No one will be able to get in. It won't take long for news to get out about the discovery of an Egyptian temple out here."

They watched hikers along the trail, some wanting access to Lover's Cave; the guard's denying them entrance.

Sydney knew when the window closed, the inner pyramid returned to its cosmic timer, sealed until the time

Isis determined if and when the Shemsu were again needed. She felt suddenly protective of the temple and the statues, determined to have a voice in their future.

Weariness etched on their faces, a collective glow also emanated from each of them as they started on the path down to the parking area. They had survived!

Sydney felt a sense of elation carrying the blanket that held the deities. "We'll arrange with the AAI for the statues to be exhibited at museums in different cities. With one stipulation—that they'll be available to anyone who wants to touch them." She chuckled. "What a shock it will be to the museums' staff—a gold display that can actually be touched! That's never happened before. They'll be traumatized at first, until they realize the purpose of these pieces."

"I assume the Israel Museum will be first, and then the Cairo Museum. Who are the other lucky ones?" Carter asked.

"I think the British Museum for all the work they've done both in Israel and Egypt. And the Metropolitan Museum in New York," Sydney said, stepping over a large rock on the trail. "You're kidding. The biggest rogue museum in the States? Why should they get them?" Alexander asked.

"It's the biggest museum in the biggest city. And they won't be able to resist. Of course, they'll be horrified at the condition of acceptance—that they can't charge admission! Or charge to touch the healing statues. The hordes that come from all over the country to their museum will be enough for them to appreciate the exhibit. The AAI will have to put a limited time for each museum, maybe three or four months. Then the exhibit can travel to many cities."

"Great idea!" Victoria hung onto Alexander on the sloping gravel path. "The Antiquities Association of Israel can decide how to exhibit the temple. An *in situ* site would be a major tourist attraction."

They reached the lot, which had filled with tourist buses and cars.

Yuval had a deputy accompany Marco and the wrapped body of his father. Another helped Moishe, Zaki and Ellie lift the body of Ferah into the ambulance.

Victoria rode with the deputy. Sydney, Carter and Alexander sat in Yuval's car as he pulled out of the parking lot.

When they reached Highway 90, Yuval slowed to watch the activity at the edge of the Dead Sea, where Sydney imagined the deputies, puzzled at the hole in the top of the fuselage, were pulling Herod's plane out of the water.

Alexander looked at Carter, who was gazing at Sydney. "We've got to get back to the dig."

"No, I don't think so." Sydney took Carter's hand, his face beaming. "Can you drop us at the Hyatt Regency Resort down at the southern end of the Dead Sea?" she asked Yuval. "Carter and I have a lot of catching up to do."

Epilogue

One Year Later

Los Angeles Times. Sunday, March 25.
Ancient Egyptian Mystery.

After a successful run at the Metropolitan Museum of Art in New York City where thousands visited and touched the magical Egyptian statues of Isis and Thoth, the exhibit will open at the County Museum of Art in Los Angeles.

In order to accommodate all requests, the Board of Directors will allow hospitals, clinics and doctors to bring their patients the week before the exhibit opens. All visitors must reserve their time-coded access tickets in advance, similar to the King Tut exhibit entry.

According to the Met, many women touched the statue of Thoth and many men the statue of Isis for a variety of chronic and acute illnesses. Some people reported 100% cures, with others claiming partial cures.

Medical doctors are at a loss to explain how or why simply touching a slab of gold could cause these miraculous healings. Nevertheless, these golden statues will travel from city to city on a regular basis.

Another Ancient Egyptian mystery remains a mystery.

Bibliography

Atwood, Roger (2004). *Stealing History: Tomb Raiders, Smugglers, and the Looting of the Ancient World.* St. Martin's Press: New York.

Bauval, Robert & Gilbert, Adrian (1994). *The Orion Mystery: Unlocking the Secrets of the Pyramids.* Three Rivers Press: New York.

Cahill, Jane. Jerusalem in David and Solomon's Time. *Biblical Archaeology Review,* Nov/Dec 2004.

Clow, Barbara Hand (2001). *Catastrophobia: The Truth Behind Earth Changes in the Coming Age of Light.* Bear & Company: Vermont.

Davies, W.V. (1987). *Egyptian Hieroglyphs.* University of California Press/British Museum: Great Britain.

Eyewitness Travel Guide: *Jerusalem & The Holy Land* (2002). DK Publishing: London.

Fodor's Israel (2001). Random House: New York.

Hancock, Graham & Bauval, Robert (1996). *The Message of the Sphinx: A Quest for the Hidden Legacy of Mankind.* Three Rivers Press: New York.

Keyser, Jason. Israel Center of Ancient Drug Trade. *The Jerusalem Post.* Aug. 9, 2002.

Lamy, Lucie (1981). *Egyptian Mysteries: New Light on Ancient Spiritual Knowledge.* Crossroad: New York.

Malkowski, Edward F. (2006). *Before the Pharaohs.* Bear & Company: Rochester, Vermont.

Naydler, Jeremy (2005). *Shamanic Wisdom in the Pyramid Texts: The Mystical Tradition of Ancient Egypt.* Inner Traditions: Vermont.

Oakes, Lorna & Gahlin, Lucia (2003). *Ancient Egypt.* Barnes & Noble Books: New York.

Rossini, Stephane (1989). *Egyptian Hieroglyphics: How to Read and Write Them.* Dover: New York.

Scham, Sandra. The Lost Goddess of Israel. *Archaeology,* Mar/April 2005.

Sellers, J.B. (1992). *The Death of Gods in Ancient Egypt.* Penguin Books: London.

Shanks, Hershel. The Siloam Pool: Where Jesus Cured the Blind Man. *Biblical Archaeology Review,* Sept/Oct 2005.

Shanks, Hershel. Sifting the Temple Mount Dump. *Biblical Archaeology Review,* July/Aug 2005.

Shanks, Hershel. Update: Finds or Fakes? Israel Museum Declines BAR's Offer to Purchase Forged Pomegranate. *Biblical Archaeology Review,* May/June 2005.

Spencer, Neal (2003). *The British Museum Book of Egyptian Hieroglyphs.* Barnes & Noble: New York.

Winer, Stuart. Mount Destruction. *The Jerusalem Post,* Feb. 1, 2002.

**Watch for Book 2 of the Thrilling Supernatural Trilogy
Master of the Edge**

QUEST FOR THE EMERALD TABLETS:

THE SECRET OF ALCHEMIST GOLD

The fabled Tablets of Thoth, lost for centuries,
claim ancient knowledge for transmuting lead into gold.
Dr. Sydney Grace begins a new adventure
into the mysterious land of Egypt
Where a whisper of hidden lore flows endlessly on the Nile,
known only by a shadowy native shaman
and evil black magicians.
Timeline memories and the Goddess of Magic, Isis,
link her to the pre-dynastic Shemsu Hor and
the secrets that lay within the Great Pyramid.

LaVergne, TN USA
18 August 2009
155121LV00002B/2/P